VICTORY?

by

Rufus Marlowe

Sheltus & Picard

First publication September, 1992
Copyright © 1992 by Sheltus & Picard, Inc.

Canadian Cataloguing in Publication Data:

Marlowe, Rufus 1929–
    Victory?
Fiction

ISBN 0-9696296–0–5

PS8576.A7418V43 1992   C813' .54   C92–090391–6
PR9199.3.M37V43 1992

Cover design by Arpel Grafics Inc.
Printed in Canada by Cowansville Printing
Bound by Multi Reliure S.F. inc.

Sheltus & Picard, Inc.
P O Box1321, Bedford, Quebec, Canada, J0J 1A0

Dedication

When I was in high school, half a dozen of us conducted an experiment in chemistry. We poured various chemicals and acids into a retort "to see what would happen". Each of us in turn chose the next chemical additive. Nobody considered what the "experiment" might do to the school or to us. The retort grew hot; then it exploded.

The Canadian constitutional process is being conducted today on the same basis. Politicians don't ask if an offer being put forward is good for Canada or for Canadians, it's "well, if Alberta (or Quebec or Ontario) doesn't like that, they can add this." A constitutional explosion may be more serious than the one I experienced in that old lab.

This book is dedicated to the people of Canada who will suffer if any of the "reasonable" proposals, in combination, self-destruct.

It is also dedicated to Canada's soldiers, militia and regular, who under their "unlimited contract" will have to pay for a failed experiment. In particular, it is dedicated to the people of the Eastern Townships of Quebec. who have been conducting a successful experiment in living together in friendship and as neighbours for two hundred years.

This is a work of fiction. It is intended to warn the leaders who are experimenting with the country temporarily entrusted to their care that they run the risk of destroying one of the best nations on earth.

Rufus Marlowe

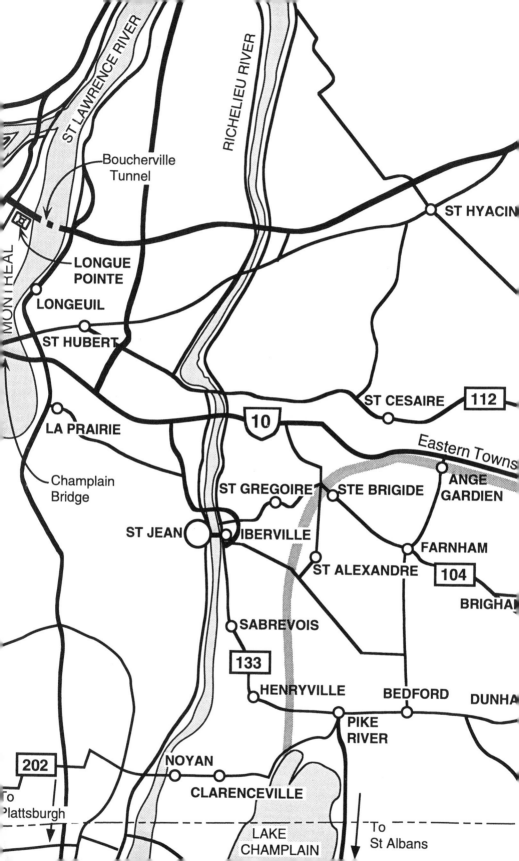

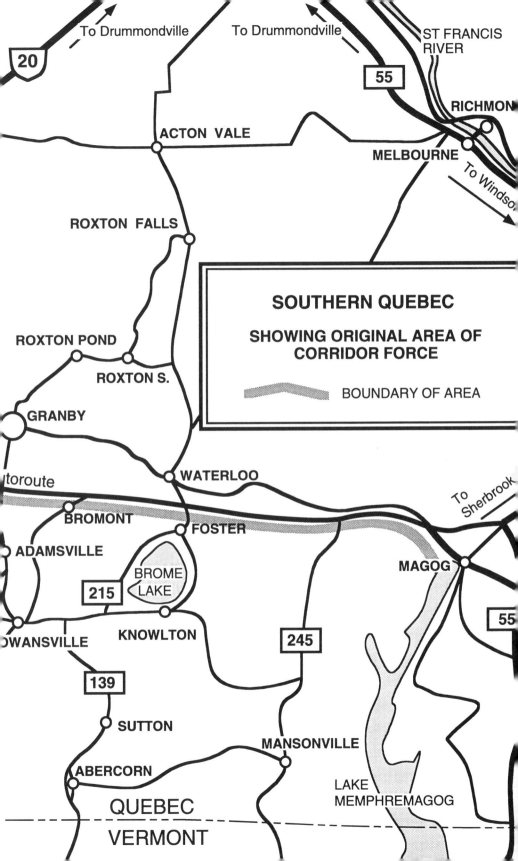

A number of military readers of this book, especially those who are serving or have served at Canadian Forces Headquarters in Ottawa will object to the attack made on our unified military system in this book. As members of the CAF they have no choice but to defend the present system. The anti-unification position here is not my opinion alone. It has been confirmed by many active officers, several of them of general officer rank, during private interviews. Perhaps the most damning and concise indictment of the system that is Canada's final hope in case of anarchy or war was made by Lieutenant-General S.C. Waters, a former Chief of Defence Staff and until his death Canada's only elected senator. Here is an excerpt from a letter he wrote to me in 1985:

"I am satisfied that the 'grand experiment' has failed in most important respects, the most significant of which to the Army are in the areas of Leadership, Training Standards, Operational Effectiveness and Logistical Capability. **I contend that unification would crumble under the pressures of mobilization and war.** And if Armed Forces cannot mobilize and prepare for war, what good are they?"

CHAPTER ONE

The Barn

The old general sat in the largest of the bunker's four offices. He wanted a smoke, but the minimal ventilation of the underground command post of his Quebec liberation army did not permit it. His long-time aide came in with a sheaf of files.

"Here are the Brigade nominal rolls, mon général." The general grunted non-committally, and the aide smiled at the pseudo-tyrant forty years his senior. The general hated paperwork, and his scowl deepened as more folders joined those on his desk.

"Location and readiness reports of each brigade," the aide went on remorselessly. "Recruiting. Equipment status. Everything is reported as ready—for once."

"Because after four such exercises we have corrected our mistakes. The real thing is less manageable." The general (a Korean war veteran) was the only man in the secret army who knew what happened when armies fought across a land. He had insisted on revolution without war. They would fight, a little, but Quebec could not win a war. As he looked up from the files, he stared at the six by four foot-flag on the opposite wall. To the centre of the familiar blue and white fleur de lis of Quebec he had added a flaming sword, blade pointing upwards, the standard of his Armée de la Libération de Québec. "Let's go outside, Jacques. I need a cigar."

They went through the Operations Room and up the ladder into the barn. The general meticulously returned the sentry's salute and stepped between the sagging front doors into the cool October air. "It is early, but I hear it will snow soon," the aide offered as he lit the general's second cigar of the day. "And soon we march."

The cigar began to draw well. The general leaned against the sun-warmed boards. "But not tonight, mon cher Jacques. Be patient. This is but a rehearsal that stands down on Sunday—our last rehearsal, I hope. Next weekend is when it will actually happen. We can hold Canada's military equipment in Montreal for another week. But what we do depends, as always, on Canada.

"They offer power sharing. We demand real power. They offer better terms—and demand a land corridor to link Ontario and New Brunswick if we separate. Prime Minister Cyr responds by dropping two demands and suggests a narrower corridor in return for guarantees of northern sovereignty. The reaction by the opposition, the media and radicals to this trial balloon dooms it from the start, and in a panic, M Cyr now desperately looks for alternatives. Canada's reply to his compromise offer that will be made on Monday will not assist his endeavours.

"Tonight M Cyr will ask his party for authority to declare independence, to be ratified by a referendum. He will promise to use the power only to pressure Ottawa.

"If he gets it, the street demonstrations that follow the Canadian reply to his offer will 'force' him to demand independence within a loose Canadian federation—to be negotiated. Canada will refuse to negotiate because if they agree to discuss even partial independence, the precedent will allow the international community, particularly France, to support our claim for independence later. By next week, Cyr will be desperate.

"The separatists will then join his nationalists to defeat him and declare independence. M Bouget will take over and Quebec will be free."

He stabbed with his cigar like a sword. "That is when we march, Jacques. That is why our Army of Quebec Liberation was formed three years ago and why we conduct exercises."

"But General," Jacques protested. "By such indecision, M Cyr risks losing the honour of being the first president of an independent Quebec."

"Yes, but he is not a bold man. Tonight, if he does not get the new authority, he may accept Ottawa's demands, including the corridor. If that looks likely, his nationalists will depose him at once, and if so we may have to strike this weekend." He winced as he spoke. How easily the evocative words came: strike, march. Each day he reminded himself that it would be others, the youth of Quebec, who would strike, march—and die.

"The Canadians are fools!" Jacques spat the words out. "Surrender the South Shore? I would die first!"

The general spoke sharply. "Tais-toi, Jacques! This is not how a soldier speaks. Our mandate is to create a new Quebec, not to destroy Canada. If they want a reasonable corridor, we will talk, not march. We need the industrial part of the South Shore but not all." He waved the cigar warningly. "You never get all. However, the Canadians have said 'no force' so often that everyone believes it now—everyone but me."

He prodded the aide admonishingly on the chest. "The English are a strange race, Jacques. They hide their fire. Too many québecois discount that." He shrugged. "However, we serve. If Canada refuses our just demands we will seize power to show that we are serious, then politicians will work out the final details—and borders—of our land, which, as soldiers, we will accept."

He tapped the two-inch cylinder of ash from his cigar and ground it into the earth with his heel. "To join the United Nations, we must have full control of our territory. If Canada disputes our claim, we will teach them prudence and there will be more talk. Once Canada accepts our independence, after we grant them a much smaller corridor than they demand, soldiering will become dull again."

"What can Canada do? Almost all of their equipment is here in Quebec. They must agree to our demands."

"Perhaps," the general said slowly. "The Americans favour a united Canada—but they must stay neutral or we are lost. If they side with Canada we can be frozen out of the UN, and Canada will be tempted to fight. If they do, it is the end, Jacques. We cannot win such a war."

"We have allocated only two brigades to control the corridor we propose to let them have eventually. Is it enough?"

The general shrugged and spat. The cigar was getting stronger. "Even more we must protect the land we do not plan to give them. Anyway, who can stop us?" He dug a trench with his heel and buried the cigar. His staff called the area the Graveyard.

"Come, Jacques. To work. The Mobile Command[1] plan needs fine-tuning, and we must find ways to issue equipment faster. Three days' delay is unacceptable."

"A suggestion, mon général. If our people start loading the trains with equipment to be 'returned' to Canadian bases, most of the stores will be ready to ship when we need them." The general nodded and Jacques went on. "There is also a red-flagged envelope from Intelligence for you."

"I expected it—a new list of those to arrest. I told them what to do with the previous one. Why cannot people who aspire to work in Intelligence understand that an army of slightly more than five thousand men is unable to seize a whole country and arrest almost two thousand potential troublemakers at the same time?"

British Airways Flight 601 (Heathrow to Mirabel) was late as it began to let down northwest of Montreal. In the first-class galley a flight attendant was stowing coffee cups in a rack when her co-worker returned to get a mini-bottle of rye.

"Great. I have to clean up while you grab the only two passengers worth a second look. I will remind you, Liz Marsh, company seniority does not give you first dibs on the passenger list."

"I hate Liz and this may be love," Betty stuck out her tongue, "or sex." Her hips sketched a vestigial bump and grind. The slender thirty-year-old brunette had the kind of legs that explain frequent revivals of mini-skirts. Her slightly olive complexion contrasted with nordic high cheek bones and cool grey eyes.

"Love? Sex? Wow! But hey, how come neither of them gave you more than the usual three looks at boarding time?"

"I briefed him well. I wasn't sure that I could: a, get this week off; b, get Sue Masterman to give me her flight; and c, find someone to take my place back on the Monday sked. It came together and I told him it was on—once we got to Canada."

"What's on?" Betty's friend asked suspiciously, then laughed. "What the hell. It's time you cranked up the genes again. Three years is long enough to hide."

---

[1] The headquarters for Canadian land forces, also called FMC

Betty's husband had been an officer in the Rifle Brigade. Three years ago he had been posted to Ireland. The IRA had taken exactly two days to shoot him down on a Belfast street.

"Which one is it? Surely not the squat, bandy-legged Sloerill. The slim elegance of Mr Forbes would do you proud, though. I bet he even looks good before he shaves."

"You've got a dirty mind and he isn't squat or bandy-legged."

"Forbes isn't—it *is* Sloerill. What's the attraction?"

"He's a writer," Betty said a touch defensively.

"Dear girl, there are millions of those in the world. Most are broke, alcoholic or both—wait. That Sloerill?"

"Yes," Betty said firmly. "I started reading his stuff after . . . anyway, I met him in July when his publisher—that's Mr Forbes—threw a party. I conned a ticket from my boss, detached my quarry from an impossibly super-structured upper-clawss bitch who wanted him as a bedroom trophy, and the rest, as they say, is none of your business."

"In my experience, men with hands and shoulders like his prefer impossible superstructures. You aren't flat-chested, I admit—but your bosom is well within the limits of physical laws. How'd you separate him from the bitch?"

Betty giggled. "I used Sue's trick to check potential partners for strange appetites. I suggested that her ladyship liked kinky sex, hinting at bondage, and voilà, he was mine!"

"What if he'd liked it and gone hotfooting after Lady Whatnot?"

"At least I'd have been well rid of him, and according to rumour, I wasn't all that far wrong."

"I'd be more interested in checking out those shoulders. On the other hand, the face takes a bit of getting used to. The words 'frog-like' spring easily to mind when one is searching for a revealing adjective."

"They do not!" Betty protested. "You've never seen him smile. I know the shoulders are not built into the suit. I leave his hands to your imagination—and that's all I know," she insisted, a bit miffed at her friend's knowing look. "As a matter of fact, this trip is to decide if I want to find out more. At least he's convinced me that he wants to know more. Anyway," she shook her hair back and picked up a tray, "he's my frog prince and I'd better not keep him waiting."

"If he's a frog prince and you know about his shoulders, how come he still looks like a frog?"

"Because he turns back into one if I don't kiss him a lot, and this has been a long flight." Betty winked and slipped out of the galley.

The objects of the analysis were in the near-empty first-class cabin. Sloerill's friend deserved the admiration of Betty's co-worker. An athletic body, unfairly handsome face and expensively understated Gieves tailoring always drew admiring glances from women. His single status, British Guards officer polish and position as head of a long-established publishing house provided Peter Forbes with a rich social life. He had faults and exposed one of them when he took out a silver cigarette case. The man beside him frowned and he put it away with a sigh.

His anti-smoking friend, currently the hottest writer in the house of Forbes, MacIllraith and Cotton, was waiting for his rye. George Sloerill was stocky and thick-shouldered with straight thin lips, a strong twice-broken nose and lank brown hair brushed straight back. He usually maintained an impassive expression. The tanned, all-weather face could have belonged to one of his fictional mercenary soldiers, and his hands and face were marked with the tiny scars that men of action accumulate.

The impassiveness was a carefully contrived facade. Most people found it hard to reconcile the humour and understanding revealed in his books with the aloof, dispassionate man they met. Peter Forbes (and very few others) knew why the facade was maintained. Sloerill had once nearly killed a boy in what had been a normal teen-age fight until his temper exploded into a monstrous rage.

As a result of that and other incidents he had hidden an outgoing personality behind a mental gate, caged with a temper that had to be controlled. After twenty years of practice he could relax with friends, but he still shut out strangers.

"Ah, your bird's returnin'," Peter drawled in his best Oxford tone. "Amazin' it took this long. She's been hovering over us—you anyway—like a flea stalkin' a Persian cat."

George stirred uneasily as if he'd been caught in an improper act. "You may not remember, but she was at the *Africanus* party in July."

"I don't," Peter said firmly, "And I'm amazed that you do. Until you vanished—a bit fast even for a 'name' author, as I did mention—I doubt if your beady eyes rose more than an inch from Lady Matterhorn's invitin'ly displayed bosom all night."

"It was Lady Hamerfield—pronounced Hemfeld—and stick with British understatement. Besides, she wasn't that big." A grin flickered on his face, but before he could go on a tray was being held out to him.

"Here you are, Mr Sloerill. Canadian rye, straight up."

"Thank you, Miss Marsh." He hesitated over the formality. "I'm sure you hear this a lot," he said softly, one eye on the other passengers, the other on Forbes who was frankly eavesdropping, "but could you meet me once you're off duty?"

Peter noted that his friend's personality was open and relaxed. It was obvious that these two knew one another and that they both enjoyed playing out their 'make a pass at an airline hostess' game.

"I am sure the company has a rule—somewhere—forbidding it, sir," Betty replied, voice prim, grey eyes smiling.

"Surely unremembered rules are rules seldom obeyed," George countered. "However, I'd hate to make the company unhappy. Walking home from this altitude can have serious effects on one's expectations."

"It can, sir. Is there anything else I can do for you, within—" The No Smoking/Fasten Seat Belts sign came on to end the by-play. "I hope, as a gentleman, you'll not molest me in the upstairs bar while I unwind from another stressful landing?"

"I really don't mind," Peter complained as Betty moved away, "but I did try to get you into a better circle of society. Now I discover you've established some grubby relationship with an air hostess. Is this life imitating a character in one of your books?"

"What I discovered, thanks to Betty, is that some women in your better circle are more at home in a pentagram—especially the 'pent' part. As a result, Betty and I took off to try a bit of white magic and get better acquainted.

"In fact, we aren't as well acquainted as I'd like. Still, she's agreed to come to Canada so we can explore the idea of going a bit—a lot further than we have so far."

"Assignations, yet. Is this dingy sylvan retreat of yours in the Eastern Townships, whatever they are, sufficiently large for three?"

"It is," George said, "but we aren't playing house. She'll stay with friends in Montreal and come out Monday. You," he said firmly, "are chaperone."

"I absolutely refuse." Peter sniffed. "How long will your dalliance at the bar delay us?"

"Time appreciation." George checked his watch. "An hour of dalliance will enable you to collect my rental car and learn that Canadians hew to the right-hand side of the road. We'll leave at four. An hour into Montreal. Then off to the Double Hook book store for a bit of autographing to demonstrate how popular colonial writers are at home."

Forbes looked out the window past his friend as the aircraft creaked and rumbled towards a landing. "Considering printing costs, your advance and freight for *Africanus,* I'll be happy to break even on the damned thing in the outposts of Empire. Tell me, do you really think that in the reported turmoil below people are actually reading?"

"Turmoil? Oh, the political thing." Sloerill squirmed more deeply into his seat, smoothing his hair back with short hard fingers. "Sheer stupidity. Etienne Messier will fill us in tomorrow." He took half his drink in one gulp. "After careering around with an absentee publisher who involves me with kinky women and suggests impossible book ideas, I really miss Etienne."

"I'm not absentee, only idle. MacIllraith and Cotton have been dead for years, and since Sir Barney Sandford runs the shop far better than I ever could, I'm free to go round findin' things for him to publish and make me even richer. It's all right." He lifted a minatory hand. "I only suggested you base your next opus on an Argy plan to recover the Falklands. Easy job, nubile Latins crawling into your suite to meet the famous author—forget it. I'll do it myself. Before Father joined the Great Publishing House Up There, I was known for my cogent, even trenchant military staff papers. You and John Masters got started that way, why can't I?"

"Be my guest," George challenged grumpily. "And I notice you didn't respond to my kinky-woman charge."

"I ignored it. I but brought you to the circle and am not to blame if one member was somewhat flawed. The new book?" Forbes probed.

"In the Falklands, the thin red line yomped through shot and Argentinian shell. Too organized. I like my people to have more freedom."

An extra edge to the normally grating voice caught Peter's ear. "Is that why you quit the Canadian army? According to the stuff we put on dust jackets you were in the top ten at Staff College, commanded a regiment at thirty-one, did the usual UN chores and got a fast-track posting to Ottawa. The rest is silence. The first I knew that you'd bolted was when you showed up on my doorstep, a manuscript in your eager hand and a silly civilian smile plastered all over your face. What happened?"

"You made a mint on the book," George reminded him. "And it wasn't a silly smile, it was nervous. I wasn't sure you owned a publishing house or that the supercilious British Guards officer I'd met in Cyprus would even read the damned thing—in fact, from what I'd heard of Guards officers, I wasn't sure you could read."

"Sir Barney does grumby work like reading. Stop evading. And don't think I haven't noticed the sly digs you take at Canadian soldiers. I'd love to meet the original of that pompous UNIFORCE ass in *Africanus*. Every time I bring the subject up, you snarl and walk away. Got you trapped for once."

Sloerill gave in. "All right. Canada had a military until Paul Hellyer got visions of Prime Ministership and unified the armed forces to prove how tough he was. It has a Chief of Defence Staff because having no defence policy he got confused when three service chiefs gave conflicting advice. He put everyone into green suits, tied military ranks to the civil service, gutted the regimental system and fired everyone who fought him."

"That was in '67-'68, George. Were you even in the military then?"

"I went to military college in '72. They said unification would help our careers. That's all it helped. My father was a career officer, but that was a compliment then. Now too many officers think the military exists only to promote them. Jobs for the boys. Everyone shifts into a new job every one point nine years and promptly institutes a new system, trying to look good. Mistakes are 'corrected' by the next career man. They think a 'manager' can manage anything. The business sector left a trail of bankruptcies around the world on that theory. Since the military hasn't got profit as a bottom line, its failures will stay hidden until a war comes along."

"It sounds like a right mess," Forbes encouraged.

George shook his head, his eyes pained. "Today's slogan is 'cover your ass.' The few good men still around—Fred Scott, Babe Trinker, Marcel Laporte—they're blind. Nobody has the guts to say Canada doesn't have armed forces, only a few lightly armed civil servants!" His fist pounded the chair arm once. "I quit when I made colonel and found that problems I'd 'solved' as a major were still around because the real solution was incompatible with unification. Change the record, Peter. I'm still not rational about it."

"All right, try this. Most newspapers that don't boost circulation with pictures of semi-naked women say that Quebec is about to separate from Canada. You live in Quebec. What do you do if it happens?"

"It won't," George grunted. "Our so-called federal government finally found enough guts to demand a corridor between Ontario and New Brunswick along the U.S. border. The Cree up north want the right to separate from Quebec if Quebec separates from Canada. I can't promise a vacation from politics, only from rebellion."

"But if this chap Cyr rejects a corridor, can't he pull the plug on Canada?"

"No. The federalists in his party will stop him, men like my riding MNA,[2] and he can't go the unilateral declaration of independence route. The UN hates that—remember how often you and I went a-peacekeeping in places that tried UDI? Cyr hasn't the guts, and the political reality is that if our belatedly fearless Prime Minister loses his Quebec MP's, he's out. The bottom line is that a corridor makes independence too pricey for Quebec. There'll be lots of noise but nothing will change."

"But if Quebec does go UDI? Politicians often do some remarkably silly things despite the reality—again as we both have discovered."

"Quebec can't do that without an army to back up a declaration."

"From what you say, Canada doesn't have an army to stop them."

"Only a few soldiers know that, and a hell of a lot fewer have the guts to tell—ah, I think we've arrived."

The jet stopped near the terminal. Moments later there was a bump as a passenger transporter fastened its entry port over the first class exit door. Sloerill and Forbes waited until the other passengers had left.

"Why must you be last off?" Peter asked as they collected their hand luggage. "I mean apart from the chance it gives you to whisper an obscene suggestion into our hostess's pink ear."

---

[2] Member of the National Assembly, the Quebec legislature

George flushed slightly. "I leave things like that to you. No, this way, as soon as you get to the transporter the whole thing moves off and you don't have to sit around waiting for people who can't get their luggage organized."

The general slid a folder towards his aide. "Tonight, Jacques, just in case, this list goes to brigade commanders. There are 823 people to be detained Saturday. Units tasked for St Hubert airport and Mobile Command HQ must learn new rules of engagement. We must avoid bloodshed at almost any cost. Remind them that all men temporarily assigned to these tasks must return to their regular brigades once the targets are secured."

As he spoke, the general skimmed the list. "No, no." He shook his head. "Take Armand Chantilly off. Arrest him on Sunday."

Jacques looked dubious. "He is said to be particularly dangerous to our cause, mon général."

"We must seize airports, borders, power stations, the James Bay dams, bridges, and the National Assembly, and arrest the people on this list. Chantilly can wait."

He cut off Jacques' protest. "He commands the militia artillery, but think. Their commanders confer daily. Arrest Chantilly and we must arrest them all. We can't."

Jacques made a notation. "I suppose it doesn't matter," he conceded. "The militia cannot act without orders from Ottawa, and we have infiltrated them so well that we would know about any orders to intervene as soon as they did—sooner."

The general nodded. "We hope so, but even if we are wrong, without ammunition what can they do? Have you done your homework, Jacques?" he teased. "What is the potential opposition?"

"In Montreal, fourteen units, 2412 men. Of these, 714 are ours. There are 1698 against us—but many are recruits. They may have nine hundred trained men to—" Jacques broke off as a message was handed to the general, who frowned. "Bad news?" he asked.

"Yes, and not a matter of shuffling lists. The Canadian Grenadier Guards are in Camp Farnham this weekend. This is the kind of thing we must always be ready for, Jacques. That area was not involved in this exercise."

"But units were ordered not to train this month!"

"A mistake was made." The general shrugged. "And not the last. Get used to this. Something will always go wrong, no matter how we prepare." He thought for a moment. "Use Colonel Bertrand. He and his officers can visit the camp, then tell us how they would have handled the situation. On the other hand, if things go wrong for Cyr tonight, he will actually have to do the job. He's a hothead, so make it very clear that he must not move until independence is declared. He is not to use excessive force. He will observe all legal niceties."

"He would have only seventy-three men left after he augments the Mobile Command attack force," Jacques reminded him. "The Guards have nearly three hundred."

"But without ammunition. It's an exercise, Jacques." The general smiled bleakly. "Even so, we must plan how to stop them. The two detached militia companies out there are small, but the Guards could make them an effective force that would be hard to deal with in a fight."

"In view of your order to arrest militia commanders Sunday, are there any special instructions for their Colonel—" Jacques checked a folder, "Colonel Victor Bosch?"

"No. He seldom goes into the field. We should probably let him escape anyway."

"His rating is high competent, mon général."

"Tchah! High competent at paper war. High competent at sucking up to superiors. His tongue is black with bootpolish. Having the Guards in Farnham five years ago would have been serious. Bertrand can handle them now." He dismissed Bosch with a wave.

"The best men are Armand Chantilly of the Artillery and Pierre St Pierre of les Fusiliers Mont-Royal. Jan Berkowitz of the Black Watch is also good. The rest are on our side, leaning our way or useless—again?" A red-flagged message had landed on his desk and he tore it open, "Merde!"

Jacques waited without speaking. When the general swore, silence was called for.

"At a news conference this noon, the American consul in Montreal in response to a question by a reporter from Le Devoir stated, unfortunately in passable French, that his government fully supports Canadian unity. He saw fit to add that they would not look favourably upon unilateral action."

The general sighed. "A riot has begun. Riots complicate life. They frighten timid nationalists. Cyr will win his vote. We have waited for two hundred years to be free. Another week will not kill us."

He picked up a file. "Once independence is declared next week, our people in Sherbrooke and the Gaspé must receive their heavy equipment quickly, especially tanks and guns. We take over the Longue Pointe depot as the declaration is made. As you say, the camp staff will have loaded the trains with winter clothing, weapons, ammunition, armour and artillery. We will finish the work and send the trains out on Sunday."

Some passenger baggage was late in arriving on the carousel. When Peter Forbes came through the gate, Sloerill was waiting impatiently.

"What were you smuggling?" he demanded. "Here are the papers. Pick up the car. I'm off to meet Betty," he started for the stairs, "and I don't want to see you for—"

"Where are you going? The exit is over here," a voice announced behind them.

George turned. "Etienne! Etienne Messier! What are you doing out here?"

"Providing transportation. You have probably rented a four-cylinder mini that would fall apart if struck by a hard wind."

George was almost bouncing in delight. "Peter, my oldest, best friend and car snob, Etienne Messier. Etienne, my publisher, Peter Forbes, late British army, late through customs."

The two men shook hands, a little warily at first, then with warmth. Peter saw a tall slender man, with thinning black hair and long-fingered expressive hands, wearing a perfectly tailored suit but with the tanned face of a man who spent a lot of time outdoors. The dark eyes were wide-spaced, interested and friendly.

A young man in a dark suit, a replica of his father except for shoulder-length hair, came up to them. Messier introduced his son to Peter but it was obvious that the boy hero-worshipped Sloerill.

"Robert is driving, George. Take the bags, my boy. Play the part you have assigned yourself." Etienne shrugged. "George taught the boy to drive and now he must show off his skill to his mentor. I suspect he bribed my chauffeur to be sick today."

The boy grinned at Forbes. "The examiner said that I had made the best driver test he had ever seen."

His father pulled his hair fondly. "Of course, you're my son." He turned to Peter, his face a mask of exaggerated resignation. "One tries to bring up one's young with proper values, and I must confess, Robert is not too bad except for one flaw. He dotes on this military écrivain who contributes nothing to our gross national product."

"Etienne, you contribute enough for both of us. I hope your empire is going well?"

Messier shrugged again. "As well as can be expected given gallic flightiness and the newly socialist horde in Ontario who insist on supporting unions. Enough of commerce, we can talk of more interesting things when we're in the car."

George turned away. "Not yet, Etienne. I have something to attend to first. Peter will explain. I'll be back soon."

Etienne stared as his friend half-ran up the stairs. Peter smiled. "He's meeting an acquaintance, female, lovely, employee of Brit Air, an avid reader of his books I hope, and soon to be a guest. From the way he looks at her, we may be in for a bit of a wait."

"Ah." Messier smiled. "I am glad to hear George is—or should I say, may be serious? Your English air must have extraordinary properties. His reputation to date is that of a man who dallies and leaves."

There was a short comfortable pause before Messier continued. "So you're the man who prints George's military tales. I wish he would be more literary. I cannot see why books about fictional wars are so popular."

"People enjoy escapism, M Messier. The real world is so . . . real."

"Please, you must call me Etienne. You are far enough from London that none of your friends need know." He touched Peter lightly on the elbow. "I understand what you say, but is he trying to make mercenaries popular?"

"George's soldiers don't commit atrocities. They fight each other— like the Italian condottieri of the thirteenth and fourteenth centuries and the Swiss and German lansquenet that came after them. It wasn't until we invented national armies that war became total."

"Are you saying that modern war is worse than, say, the old wars of Europe? I doubt if the civilians in their path would agree."

"Armies no longer live off the land but their weapons are worse."

"And they ensure that nobody can live off the land."

"George told me that you have businesses in Ontario and Quebec?" Peter asked to change the subject.

Messier smiled deprecatingly. "Ah, I am the first Messier to take up commerce. My ancestors were priests and lawyers. A hard-headed Scot married into our family in 1753. Her genes finally surfaced."

"Extremely successfully, I gather."

"A matter of luck. I found myself the owner of a textile plant that I had invested in. My accountant urged me to retain it as a tax write-off. That worked so well that I purchased a plastics company in Sarnia. Now, thanks to this recession, that loophole may be useful again. I suppose that England has similar tax write-offs?"

"Happily, yes. Too often our books fail to sell as well as my editors predict," Peter replied, shifting to fluent Parisian French.

"Wonderful!" Messier exclaimed. "I must teach you the local version of that exquisite tongue while you are here. Anyway, to end a dull tale, there was a plastics boom which gave my accountant an ulcer. Have you and George been friends for long? I know your name, of course."

"We met in Cyprus a dozen years ago on UN peacekeeping duty and kept in touch. By the time he began writing I'd left the army and taken over Father's publishing business and—hullo. Lothario returns. What's the matter, George? Have a fight?"

"She'll come on Monday, but the bar television was carrying a story on a riot. What do you know about that, Etienne? Is it serious?"

"It depends on which side you are on. The American consul made what some consider an unfortunate speech at noon. The more radical members of our society were not amused."

"I thought things were settling down. In your last letter you called it the calm before the comic opera."

"It seemed like a good phrase a month ago. At the moment, if you hold stock in a plate glass company, dividends will be in order. A radio station has been occupied, and one of the most atrociously written manifestos in revolutionary history was broadcast. I fear the danger to the French language lies not in North American English but in our schools. Shall we go? It would be a pity for Robert to get a ticket on such a big day."

Messier's car, a perfectly kept twenty-year-old grey Bentley, was parked on the ramp as they emerged. Robert opened and closed doors with a flourish, then eased the car into the traffic flow and headed towards the autoroute.

Peter looked appraisingly around. "They were right about this at home, you know," he observed. "We'd have to sacrifice an entire county to build this airport."

"Size is the North American curse," Messier answered drily. "Have you heard about the Englishman who spent the sea crossing to New York extolling the navigational virtues of the ancient mariners? He then travelled by train to California. After four days and nights he turned to his companion and said, 'How could they miss the bloody place?' "

After a dutiful chuckle, George leaned forward. "What's going on, Etienne? The British and European papers are full of doom and gloom. How are things at home?"

"Tranquil. If Quebec separates we are in the land reserved for a Canadian corridor. Even the wilder locals are calm because their jobs are in the corridor even if their hearts are in free Quebec."

"And Cyr?"

"His party is federalist, by a slim majority. He has radicals, of course, they're everywhere now, but the polls are too unclear for him to risk a decision. Life will go on."

"You sound awfully sure, Etienne. In Europe it sounds as if he's backed himself into a corner that even an eel couldn't slide out of."

"Ah, M Cyr gives lessons to eels. Besides—what was the line in the PBS Civil War documentary that described Quebec to perfection? Yes. 'The South is too small for a republic and too large for an insane asylum.' It applies here. We make fiery speeches, but when it comes to cutting Canada's apron strings and risking American displeasure, we shrug and walk away to claim a moral victory."

Bored with politics, Robert looked back. "Now that Papa is no longer mayor of Cowansville, we may have time to ride while you are here. He bought me a horse. It's at Bromont. Also, you must come to the school and talk to our hockey team."

"Tend to your driving," Messier said sharply. "Robert extends the invitation as the assistant coach. I confess I was not surprised when shortly after his appointment I began to receive hints about assisting the assistant coach. If you stay until the ice is put in, we might give a sedate demonstration of how the defence is properly played. And if you stay long enough, we can do some ice fishing."

The man the ALQ considered to be too dangerous to arrest sat in the study of his two-storey house at the south end of Outremont, near the University of Montreal, high above busy Côte St Catherine on a rocky outcropping of the mountain.

Armand Chantilly sat relaxed, his large head and iron-grey hair resting on the high back of his chair. His right hand lay on the neat desk, fingers inches from the phone. He showed no impatience; his fingers were still. He waited.

"For the last time, will you come?" His wife stood in the doorway, a small, intense woman with a model's body, elegantly dressed for travel. Behind her stood two leather suitcases mottled with stickers from a hundred airports.

Chantilly's eyes shifted but he didn't move. "No," he said in English because his wife hated to hear that language in the house. "I will stay, Adèle, as I have said."

"Fou!" she snapped. "Come to Quebec City with me."

Chantilly sighed softly. "Adèle, we made our choices years ago. I am federalist, you are separatist. You know something will happen soon. You are high enough in the party even to have planned it."

"If so, you have not shown much interest in finding out what I may have planned. Not once have you asked why I am going."

"Would you tell? And if you did, what if I tried to prevent it?" Chantilly asked calmly.

"I will come to you Monday or Tuesday." Adèle turned towards the front door. The awkward phrase was constructed subconsciously out of her knowledge that her husband's name was number 271 on an ALQ arrest list. Adèle knew that if he thought he had a chance, he would use his regiment of Gunners to resist separation. She had insisted on early detention for him to avoid the possibility that he would act foolishly and be killed.

The phone rang. "Hello, Chantilly here—a moment please." The call was from Major Dupras. Armand looked steadily at his wife, waiting.

Adèle returned the stare for a moment, then with a tiny shrug went down the hall with her bags. She had tried at least, more than many would have approved.

When he saw his wife approach the waiting cab, her luggage on the walk for the driver to collect, Armand picked up the phone. "Denis. Say nothing sensitive now—is this sensitive?" His battery commander spoke briefly. "Come to my place tonight. Bring the A List people. We will discuss it then."

He hung up and opened a desk drawer. A tiny eye in a black box winked green at him: the line was not bugged. He punched out a series of numbers beginning with the Ottawa area code, a private line into the Prime Minister's office. The phone rang once.

"Lawrence? Armand here. It is happening. Adèle has gone and my sources are worried. Is the Prime Minister still saying 'no force'?"

He listened briefly. "He's a fool. Tell him I said not to say it again. It will be less embarrassing when he has to flip-flop. Besides, it encourages the radicals. I have supported that man for fifteen years. He can't count the money I've raised for him. We French-Canadian federalists will not be discarded. If he changes his tune about force, call me."

The man in Ottawa asked a question. "Are you all fools? Hold Montreal? Of course not. If I began now I might find a thousand men by Monday. If there is a coup, our one chance is to seize and hold land along the American border—part of the corridor—and that will only work if we get help quickly and the Americans are friendly."

Chantilly listened again briefly. "No. I have to go now, there are other calls, but hear me. Tell the great man that weaklings like Cyr often do unexpectedly stupid things." He hung up and sat back to wait, calmly, patiently, his mind probing and turning pieces of the political puzzle over and over to see all the ways that they might fit together.

Seventy-five kilometres east of Montreal on the outskirts of Cowansville a large two hundred-year-old stone house stood surrounded by almost equally old maples. George, Etienne and Robert were catching up on news and gossip in the living room while Peter Forbes prowled. Deep windows let in the late afternoon sun. Trees blocked his view of the road, but to the northwest he saw an open field and low hills.

The sun made the fifteen-inch natural red pine floorboards gleam where their pit-sawn irregularities were not hidden by braided rugs. The walls were covered in militaria: a sword, commission scroll, cap badges and pictures. An eight by ten photo showed George on the bridge of a destroyer, binoculars slung round his neck, the four wide gold bars of a colonel gleaming on the shoulders of his greatcoat.

"I say," Peter interrupted the flow of talk, "you look positively dashing as a naval hero, George. What made you decide on the infantry?"

"I considered the navy," George said reflectively, "but a combination of my literary bent and rather thin legs decided me against it."

"Thin legs? Literary bent? You've lost me there, I'm afraid."

Messier grinned in delight and sank deeper into his chair. "You have imported a foil, George."

"Not at all, Etienne. It's quite simple, Peter. I have thin legs relative to my size. In the intimate society of a ship that would be known within minutes of my going aboard, and I'd have spent my military career known as Thighless Mariner."

There was a hush. Robert snickered. Etienne regarded him sternly. "Come. This is no place for a well reared boy." He stood up, glaring at George, who was grinning like a happy gargoyle.

"If you promise not to repeat that, you are invited by Andrée and me to dinner tonight. Your fridge contains only the lingering aroma of a chicken, the body of which I caused to be removed last week. Promise, George? Andrée is delicate and needs time to adjust to your humour."

Sloerill promised, and they went to the door. "I confess that the man I sent to decontaminate your fridge managed, somehow, to damage your TV. It is in the shop and can be collected tomorrow. Now, I will mention this later, but I'm riding at Bromont in the morning if we do not get that early snow Vermont TV spoke of last night. I hope you will join me. I think I have a horse that will interest you. Do you ride, Peter?"

"I manage to stay on most of the time. Is it jumping or what you call trail riding?"

"Robert has a dressage lesson. He dreams of Olympic glory. We might ride through the hills while I show off our countryside and pass on any stories Andrée will not let me tell tonight. Six for six-thirty? It doesn't leave you much time to wash up, but I'll send the car."

They agreed, and Messier left with his reluctant son, who wanted to stay and talk.

"The lad's a bit set on you, isn't he?" Peter asked when they'd gone.

"Well, we're almost neighbours, and despite what he says, Etienne works damn hard at his business. I had a Montreal posting while Robert was at an impressionable age. I lent him books—including *Silas Marner*. We rode and fished and I told him military lies. That sort of thing."

They returned to the living room from the big maplewood front door. "Your room's second on the left upstairs. Bathroom at the end of the hall, towels and things in the bureau. If you need anything, yell."

"Aren't you coming up?" Peter stopped on the second step.

"Soon. There's a friend at Mobile Command I want to call. Even on a Friday, with a serious riot on they won't have gone home. Fred Scott will know what's happening."

"I've heard you mention him. Full colonel, isn't he?"

"Ought to be a general. We were on staff course together and got our battalions the same week." He dialed a number.

"Why does Messier drive a Bentley?"

"He says a Caddy's too vulgar and he has too much money for a Chev." George flapped his hand at Peter as the phone was answered.

"Mobile Command."

"Colonel Scott, please."

CHAPTER TWO

First Blood

Herb Kerner sat for a moment at the wheel of his five-year-old Ford pickup outside an apartment building on Nuns' Island. For the first time in months the back of the truck was clear, and he was home hours early. The riot had frightened his boss enough to spike the various jobs on tap and close the shop for the weekend.

He walked slowly towards the apartment wondering how to persuade his wife to leave the city without alarming her too much. Gloria was pregnant with their first child. "Not very pregnant," she liked to say; in the third month she didn't really show. However, with a riot on, he wanted them in a safe place.

Gloria was sitting on the floor of the small living room. Two open suitcases on the sofa were surrounded by piles of clothes.

"Are we going somewhere?" Herb asked before kissing her. Then he saw the look in her eyes. "What it is it, honey? What happened?"

"Herb?" her voice quavered slightly. "I want to go to Mother's. I'm scared."

"Of what?" he scoffed, his fear forgotten in a desire to reassure her.

"Remember Simone Ménard, the girl I shared with before we got married?" Herb nodded. Simone had taken Gloria in when she moved to Montreal from the Eastern Townships, showed her how to dress and corrected her French. They still saw each other every week.

"She phoned. She said to go away for a week—home—the States—anywhere."

"She's got her nerve. Did she say why?"

"She usually tells me everything but not today. She just said she loved us. Why are you home early?"

He told her and they sat together on the floor for a few minutes, thinking. At last he looked up. "OK, we go, and let's face it, we may not be back. Where to?"

"Abercorn," Gloria said firmly. "Mother's plumbing needs you. What can we take? I want the bedroom suite, Herb."

"We'll make a list," her husband said resignedly.

Cyr's party held eighty-nine of one hundred and twenty-five seats in the National Assembly, but not firmly. Forty-three members believed that Quebec needed more power but within Canada. Thirty-six demanded near-sovereign powers as the price of loyalty. Cyr's position rested on his control of ten waverers. To take a pro-nationalist stand, he needed them all.

He told his caucus that the Canadian government was split between hard-liners and appeasers who needed threats in order to grant concessions. One man with contacts in Ottawa stood up to claim that if Quebec took a strong stand the Canadian hard-liners would win. The debate became bitter. "If you split the party," Cyr warned, "we will lose the referendum, the election, everything. Canada's offer on Monday will grant us some power, but not enough. I only want the authority to declare political but not economic independence to provide that threat. This is perfectly reasonable. We *have* the moral right to do this. The Prime Minister won some of the concessions we need to stay in Canada. With this ultimatum, he will offer more. I do not intend to use the power but I must be seen to have it."

After so many changes of political direction the federalists didn't believe him. The motion that should have passed forty-six to forty-three was defeated forty-nine to forty as six of the ten waverers, panicked by the riot (and tempted by federal offers), reneged on their promised support.

Furious at the defeat, the nationalists claimed that the vote meant capitulation to Ottawa and (with no warning to Cyr) demanded an emergency debate in the National Assembly on Saturday morning. That won converts, and their motion passed sixty-nine to twenty.

When the meeting broke up, Cyr sent his strongest federalist minister to tell the media that Quebec, even now, would offer Canada one more chance. He remained behind to re-establish control over those who had forced a debate that the federalists would control. For an hour he reasoned, argued and even begged for their understanding and support. The thirty-eight who had stayed listened impassively.

Finally Cyr's Transport Minister stood up. "You do not have our confidence, Prime Minister. You would sell us out for even an extra hour of indecision and we dare not give you time to betray us. We demand that you listen to us—and others—who as real québecois and québecoises will determine the future of our nation." She turned to a colleague. "Open the doors, Bernard."

Cyr's stomach churned as twenty-eight members of the separatist party trooped in. Powerless to stop them, he listened in horror as Quebec's future was decided. As if he were not there, it was agreed that while he would never risk separation, as premier he had more international authority than the separatist leader Lionel Bouget. He was given the choice of accepting greatness or of becoming an historical footnote, cast aside with the federalist chains that had too long bound Quebec.

Cyr made one attempt to delay the feared confrontation. "It can mean violence," he protested. "Canada will not allow a unilateral act. All the premiers have told me this."

His Minister of Finance cut him off. "Fight? The English are pampered, weak, divided, and their leader promises 'no force to hold Quebec'. They are afraid to lose our markets. Don't be a coward. Seize the moment!"

The reluctant Cyr let them hang the mantle of leadership on his shoulders and agreed (in writing) to declare Quebec's independence at 11:00 AM the next morning once the National Assembly, in closed session, approved the wording.

As Cyr signed, a government minister who had been diverting money to the secret army from his departmental funds called the bunker, causing near-panic. "Impossible!" he was told. He insisted, and by midnight teams were moving to seize citizens of special influence who would be "temporarily" held.

Brigade leaders worked through the night to assemble enough men to do their assigned jobs. The exercise had required only a thirty percent turn-out. The changed schedule increased the pressure, and almost at once parts of the plan began to break down.

An ALQ major at Bell Telephone cut off service to Quebec City at 6:00 AM before joining the Gaspé brigade. At 7:00 AM an irate former employee arrived at the office and confronted the supervisor indignantly because she had been unable to call an ambulance for her sick husband.

According to the worksheet the cut had been to allow line repairs, but as no work was scheduled the supervisor restored service. The woman made her call. When she tried to leave she was arrested as an unauthorized person by the ALQ security team that had arrived as part of the plan to take over Quebec's communication networks, but it was ninety minutes before the ALQ learned that some telephones were working. In that time word of the arrests spread. As the timetable slipped further behind, some commanders decided to start their operations ahead of schedule in order to catch up.

At 8:45 AM Saturday, Armand Chantilly woke up, still in his chair. He had spent most of the night talking to his officers and men. His throat was sore and his eyelids seemed to have sand under the lids. He looked around to see what had wakened him.

He heard a sharp rap on the glass door leading to the garden. He was reaching for his 9mm pistol when he recognized the visitor: Pierre St Pierre, Colonel of les Fusiliers Mont-Royal. He let him in.

"Well, Pierre?"

"I may be foolish, my friend." St Pierre ran his fingers through his tousled reddish hair, and draped his coat over a chair. "But my sales manager called this morning. He wanted me to come to the office tomorrow. Sunday! And he didn't ask, he *told* me. He is separatist. I do not trust him."

"Where is your family?"

"Visiting friends in Winnipeg. Where is Adèle?"

Chantilly shrugged. "In Quebec City. Something is up. I feel it. Adèle, like your sales manager, seems—arrogant is as good a word as any we might use."

"Have you heard that the Mounties and CSIS [1] believe that there is a secret military organization here in Quebec—an army, in fact?"

---

[1] Canadian Security & Intelligence Service

"No, I hadn't. How do they know?"

"CSIS began picking up coded signals a year ago. The government was afraid of bad publicity if they found a terrorist cell and ordered them to back off. My friends in Ottawa are damned scared, Armand."

"So are mine. I was afraid it would come to this. Cyr is a weak fool who tries to look strong to prove he is not weak. He does not understand people. Worse, he does not understand the English. He believes they will give Quebec all it wants and will not listen to contrary advice. To me, that makes him the most dangerous man in Canada. God knows what will happen at that special National Assembly meeting he called for today."

The men regarded each other silently. Both were influential and powerful. When they spoke, others listened, but for the first time in years, they felt unsure. The sphere of their influence had shrunk to this house and the militia soldiers they commanded. Their political contacts, business power and personal wealth were now useless.

"I told the Prime Minister's office that I will not be bound by a 'no force' policy," Chantilly said quietly. "My officers agreed last night. If Cyr attempts a coup there will be resistance somewhere, and we must support it—however we can, Toupée."

His friend's wiry red hair usually looked more like a wig than natural hair. The nickname had been invented by his men who combined the two P's of his name into a bilingual pun.

"I agree. How many of your Gunners will follow you to a fight?"

"All my officers are loyal and over a hundred men, plus the sixty-eight in Cowansville under Major Bush. That battery is my fall-back position if things get too hot here."

"Who else is on our side?" St Pierre asked as he considered their slim resources. "Which units are in and which units are out?"

"The Guards are out," Chantilly growled.

St Pierre looked surprised. "Why? They're an English-speaking regiment. They're the second largest—ah. Colonel Bosch? I had thought to call their training officer, Major Markos."

"He's good," Chantilly agreed. "A bit young, but good. No, I called Bosch last night. My training plans were cancelled. His men are in Camp Farnham. He was not. He hates field training because he can't watch everyone. How well do you know Colonel Berkowitz of the Black Watch?"

"We spoke yesterday. He too is ready to take action. He claims to have about three hundred men ready to go."

"That's four hundred, infantry-artillery." Chantilly wrote the figures into a notebook.

"What about the Van Doos?" St Pierre asked

Chantilly shook his head. "Jean-Luc's a federalist but he's in Europe. His training officer, Henri Levesque, is he sound?"

"I think so, but if we can find more than a hundred men between the fourth and sixth battalions I will be amazed."

"Le Régiment de Maisonneuve? I've been phoning for three days but their colonel never returns my calls."

"Same here," St Pierre agreed. "Write them off."

"One of my officers, Major Dupras, was on Staff Course with their Major Pepin. He swears he's a federalist."

"We'll see. Any use calling the RMR?"

Chantilly shook his head. The armoury of the Royal Montreal Regiment had been looted and burned Friday night. The colonel and most of his officers were in hospital, and the police had arrested over fifty men for using "excessive force" to defend their building.

"They have men in Knowlton, but they're too far away to help. As you see, there isn't much, Pierre." Chantilly consulted his notes. "Without the Guards, I count perhaps five hundred. Add another hundred from the Engineers, Medical and Service Battalions. What about your Fus M-R?"

St Pierre looked pained. "On Tuesday, I suggested we train today. Less than half of my four hundred signed up. The rest—" he shrugged. "Busy—sick—away—busy—busy. If there is a secret army, I fear that I have trained many of them."

"We all have. There are also the Royal Canadian Hussars in my armoury. They have over a hundred men."

"With that CO?" St Pierre asked dubiously.

"You're right, he will not move without written orders from Mobile Command. His men, however, might be persuaded."

Chantilly looked at his figures and winced. "Eight to nine hundred men, with almost no ammunition. How safe are we, Pierre?"

St Pierre smiled tiredly. "I am here. I saw a pistol in your desk. You answer your own question, Armand."

"Some Gunners are coming here. This is my headquarters for now. Start calling your men. Use the basement phone, it's another line. Have them gather in the homes of officers or sergeants and wait. Tell them not to wear uniform but to bring their kit."

St Pierre started out. Chantilly called him back to show him the small box in the drawer. "There's one downstairs too. If the light is green, there's no bug—probably. Red means a tap." He sighed. "This will be a long day, my friend."

Colonel Bertrand arrived in Camp Farnham at 0930 and arrested the commissionaire on the gate. He went forward until he could see the Guards milling in front of the drill hall. Waving his men into a ditch, he checked his watch. The declaration of independence was not due until eleven. By then the Guards would be scattered into a dozen training areas. They were issuing ammunition now. It looked confused. Typical English.

"Where can we wait, mon colonel?" a young officer asked nervously. "We are exposed here. Shall we move back to the main gate?"

Bertrand shook his head. "No. We attack now. Do you want to chase three hundred men through the bush? They have radios. One mistake and they will all be warned, and they might reach the live ammunition stores. Hit them now, together."

"But sir, it is not legal. The orders are only to attack after 1100. Besides, with so many, if they resist we may have to kill some of them."

"That is my problem. My orders give some flexibility in case of emergencies. This is an emergency. If we shoot a few, so what? It is their fault for being here against orders. Besides, anyone who fights is a militant. If they die, they cannot oppose us later. Their bodies will warn the fools in Ontario of the price of opposing us. An order," Bertrand snapped as the young man opened his mouth to protest further.

"Take your men to the right, to the river. Lieutenant Bolduc will follow me to the south end of the parking lot. When I demand the Guards' surrender, you appear from the trees and fire a few shots. They will see they are trapped and give up. If any resist, that is not our fault."

The young officer led his men away, too slowly for Bertrand's liking, but since he didn't dare shout he had to let it go. Once the thirty men entered the trees, Bertrand waved Bolduc's platoon forward. They moved down the road, half of them on each side, rifles at the ready, the men frightened but determined. None had ever fired a shot in anger.

When they came within two hundred yards of the huge grey drill hall, twenty Guardsmen came around the corner, deployed into line and began to advance, rifles at the ready. A sergeant followed them, shouting at anyone who did not maintain proper spacing or held his weapon sloppily. They saw the ALQ platoon and stopped.

The sergeant was late on his training schedule because some fool officer had first issued live ammunition, not the blank for exercises. It had taken twenty minutes to hand it in. Now he saw a ready-made training aid and took advantage of it. "Hit the dirt. Enemy to the front!" he bellowed.

"Go back! Surrender!" Colonel Bertrand yelled. "Fire a warning!" he ordered his men, still in English, then repeated the command in French.

His men knelt and opened fire, shooting deliberately high.

"Range two hundred!" the sergeant called, pacing behind the sprawled Guardsmen. "At your target in front, single rounds, fire!"

Bertrand panicked. Were the English expecting him? Was this a trap? "Fire!" he screamed, pulling his pistol. "Kill them! Kill the English bastards!" He fired at the sergeant who was staring at his training aids, puzzled by their reaction. Colonel Bertrand's bullet caught him in the hip and he went down with a scream as his men ran.

The ALQ in the trees heard the shots and they too opened fire, hesitantly at first, aiming to warn. After all, their enemy was unarmed.

As Guardsmen began to fall under the fire from Bertrand's group, a Guards sergeant swung the rifle he'd been unloading and began to shoot back, tumbling three ALQ into the grass. Corporal Weitz seized another weapon and opened fire on the people in trees. In seconds, forty rifles were firing. The ALQ, badly outnumbered, sought cover as the Guardsmen grabbed their rifles and ammunition and ran for the drill hall.

Still standing in the road, Bertrand yelled in fear and fury as he emptied his pistol at a running squad of men. He missed every shot.

The stirrings that had alarmed Chantilly and St Pierre had not been felt at the big house in Cowansville by the time George and Peter Forbes, in shirts and riding breeches, finished breakfast. They both felt sluggish after a long evening of food and wine at Etienne Messier's.

George stretched and reached for his coffee mug. "I'm not sure my head and a saddle are compatible this morning, although my mouth feels like a stable. I may phone—" He looked out the window. "Thank God I don't have to, Etienne's here."

The back door opened and Messier entered, dressed for riding. "I am glad you are nearly ready. I came to offer a ride. Neither your Land Rover or that dreadful Opel has been driven lately, and both may rebel at being asked to perform without a major tuneup."

"After the hospitality last night, I have no intention of going anywhere without at least a gallon of coffee in me," Peter said firmly.

George saw that Etienne was tense. "Problems?"

Messier shrugged. "I must admit that all is not entirely well. Have you heard the news this morning?"

"No. My transistor batteries are flat, you stole my TV, and Peter and I are suffering from itchy teeth and drums in the head. What news?"

"Our dollar closed at seventy-two cents on Wall Street. The Bank of Canada is buying dollars. Cyr's party split last night. Some say he is now negotiating with the separatists. Some say he breakfasted with the Lieutenant Governor, others . . ." He shrugged. "Take your pick of rumours today, but I have decided to ignore anything not on the front page of the New York Times."

"Is the Montreal riot over?" Peter asked undiplomatically. "Lothario has a date with Miss Brit Air tonight. He spent an hour chatting her up before your driver arrived and I barely restrained him from calling when we got back—at three AM."

Messier looked pained. "George, you must not go to Montreal. There are new riots. The US Consulate was bombed early this morning. Another bomb exploded at the consul's home and injured his wife. Our once lethargic police are now very active. Andrée suggests that we invite your Betty to stay with us. I can send the car for her while we ride."

"I'll think about it," George muttered, his heavy jaw set, "but I'm damned if a mere riot will . . ." He paused and looked up sheepishly. "I mean, thanks, Etienne, but, ah, Betty was going to stay here and . . . "

Forbes decided to rescue his friend before he floundered. "I suppose if the rioting keeps up the government will send in troops to impose a proper respect for law and order?"

Thankfully, George picked up the bantering tone. "Actually they'll do it to prove they're in charge."

"And if the natives resist, send more troops. That's how we did it when *we* had an empire—it's how we *got* an empire. More coffee?"

Sloerill nodded. "Army shoots a few rioters, rioters shoot back, we call them terrorists, and we're off and running."

"Fascinating," Messier said dryly. "From a single riot you build a full-scale war. The military mind really must be examined by medical science now that we have electron microscopes. I suppose, Peter, you too have some experience along these lines?"

Forbes looked modest. "The usual bit in Ireland, tamer UN stuff— and someone actually shot at me with malicious intent in the Falklands. Still," he went on more seriously, "shooting terrorists is fine. Collecting civilian bodies while you squabble over an area isn't."

"I thought war was all computerized now," Etienne muttered.

"Never," George answered. "Humans make mistakes, not computers. The winner is the side whose humans make the fewest mistakes *with* computers. That's what makes war fascinating."

"Since I consider all war to be a mistake, I do not see how you can tell that a mistake has been made," Messier said testily.

"Careful," Peter warned. "Don't start George off on that subject."

"Military mistakes? How can anyone object? The words go together like pie and ice cream, wine and dinner, port and cigars."

"Military mistakes kill," George said quietly. "My last army job was a study of Viet Nam Land Ops. It got shredded. The official reason for my leaving was the rocket I got for writing a report our Americans friends wouldn't like."

"If you said that Viet Nam was a mistake, I agree, but haven't you always defended the American presence there?"

"They had the right to be there, they just did it all wrong."

"A lot of that was poor training. That leads to poor morale," Peter added. "Your chaps facing the Mohawks in 1990 showed how much blood good training and morale can save."

"Training's only a part. To fight well you need . . . motivation isn't quite right . . . there's more involved, you need . . ." George hesitated.

"A cause?" Messier suggested softly.

"Jesus, no. You can commit genocide under that threadbare flag. A soldier must meet the unspoken aims of the war as well as try to win. That takes leadership, from the top down to corporals. Mostly officers, though. If they're in front, not up in a helicopter, the men fight harder and better. In Nam, the officers served six months up front and six in the rear. Grunts had their ass in the grass the whole time.

"In addition, they left division-sized units in-country and rotated the men through as individuals. On any given day a third of your unit was green, a third was gung ho and a third was being careful because they were going home soon."

"Why should your people get upset?" Peter asked. "Don't you have roughly the same regimental system as ours?"

"Not any more. See that picture?" George growled, pointing to a framed photograph of a group of green-clad officers.

"They represent twelve units but you can't tell without a magnifying glass. Regimental system?" he went on, his eyes growing smoky with anger. "In the battalion I took to Cyprus, less than half the men had been with me six months. The rest were posted in before we went and when we got back, they were sent away again, to courses, Germany, different units— then I got posted. A manpower hole had occurred and the computer picked me to fill it. I hadn't had that ticket punched yet. It was a good career move, but it screwed up my battalion training plan."

"Why didn't your replacement carry it out?" Peter asked.

"Because then he wouldn't get credit for any improvement. CO's have about two years to make a mark. That means do things differently from your predecessor—and don't make waves."

"And of course you did?" Messier inquired, glancing at his watch.

"Small ones. My men wore combat everywhere on the base. I held formal parades, taught regimental history and insisted on men acting not as interchangeable cogs but as men of a special regiment. We did things our way, not the army way. When I left, we had the top re-enlistment rate, the best pass rate on courses and were winning the most competitions. With another year I could have—ah hell, I'm out, why babble about things nobody gives a damn about."

"Do your territorials, er, militia, have the same problem? Your dust jackets claim that you'd commanded the Canadian Grenadier Guards. As an ex-Guardsman of the British variety, I hope to visit." Forbes missed the anger that flared in Sloerill's eyes at the mention of the Guards.

Messier didn't. "George doesn't visit the Guards these days," he said gently, waving an admonishing finger.

Peter ignored him. "Come on. At times you're even more Guardee than I. How can you stay away?"

Messier tried an injection of severely pruned truth to divert the conversation from the dangerous line it had taken. "George does not approve of the man who now commands."

He failed. "Headquarters put in Victor Bosch when my successor was moved to Winnipeg by his company. Bosch stamped on traditions, called men 'privates' not 'Guardsmen', turned company commanders into paper pushers, asked men to spy on officers—whom he treated like dirt— cut back on field training and bragged about firing more officers for 'incompetence' than had quit in the previous ten years!" His voice rose sharply.

"George!" Messier gripped his arm, feeling its rigidity and noting the near-blank eyes that warned that an explosion was near. "As you said yourself, it does not matter now."

Sloerill resisted for a moment, then relaxed. "All right. Etienne. I'm OK."

Messier loosened his grip, reassured not by the words but by Sloerill's eyes. During a rage they became blank cast-iron shutters that hid all signs of reason.

Peter wanted to drop the subject he'd made a mistake in pursuing. "Well, being able now to consider the prospect of personal survival with relative equanimity, what say we accept Etienne's ride, George?"

"I recommend it," Messier added. "In addition to the comfort provided by a Bentley, Robert has packed a picnic that even he could not demolish alone—including two bottles of a '53 Bordeaux and a Sauternes for dessert. Do I tempt you?"

"Pomerol or St Emilion?" Peter asked suspiciously.

Messier smiled in delight. "I had hoped you would ask, considering the year. It is quite safe, the Bordeaux are Château Petrus and the Sauternes, a 1960 Château Caillou."

"Humm," Peter mused. "A Barsac and only deuxième cru, but it does have to survive a car ride. Come on, George. Stir your stumps."

"I would, but we seem to have company." From his seat near the kitchen window, George was watching four cars coming up the drive.

Messier rose with a sigh. "I am too late. This will not be a good day, I fear."

"Do you know what this is about, Etienne?"

"Oui, malheureusement. You are honoured by a delegation led by Sam Thackery. The Montrealais riots upset local businessmen, and they want you to lead a vigilance committee to save them from the separatists."

"Damned foolishness," George muttered. The men were getting out of the cars and heading for his back door. "I have writing to do."

"My Falklands book, I hope," Peter interjected. "I happen to have brought the background papers, just in case."

"Blow the Falklands. My new one will be set in Greece."

"It's been done," Peter grumbled. "Long ago. What's the plot?"

"Murder. Two friends on an Aegean cruise. One is poisoned and cut into bloody chunks to feed the sharks. Lots of gore and suspense."

"And what will this opus be called?" Messier played the straight man, even as he moved towards the front door to escape the delegation coming in the back.

"Why, Arsenic and Old Thrace!" George exulted. "Still want to come, Peter?"

Forbes slumped. "I don't want to go anywhere with you. Come, Etienne. Let's make this terrible man walk."

Messier shook his head. "George needs you. To Sam Thackery, people are audiences. He orates." He looked at George. "Turn them down. It is not needed. You know where I'll be. I expect you before lunch." As he slipped out, the back door opened and a dozen men crowded into the big kitchen.

Canadian Armed Forces Headquarters (officially NDHQ, irreverently among the military, Disneyland North) is in Ottawa, populated by generals, deputy ministers and bright young officers managing their way up the unified promotion ladder. The army's operational headquarters is FMC, known as Mobile Command. It is located in Quebec, south of Montreal. A four-storey warren of offices topped by communications antennas forms the actual HQ. Across the road is Base St Hubert with its hangars, repair facilities, canteens, and two air reserve squadrons. Military jets share the airfield with civilian aircraft.

On Friday, General Pittman, Chief of Defence Staff, had ordered Mobile Command staff to carry weapons and had placed a military police guard on the building. Ten men were on duty when the ALQ struck at 1102.

Five trucks, their drivers in Canadian uniform, parked by the main door. One backed towards the steps. When the tailgate fell to reveal two machine guns, the guards surrendered.

From the other trucks, a hundred men raced into the paneled lobby, grenades hanging from pocket loops, rifles ready. Ten dashed for the commander's office, but General Thomas had left for an emergency conference in Ottawa the night before.

At the airport, jeeps and trucks spread out across the airfield. The control tower was occupied, the hangars were opened, and a special ALQ team began moving out heavy equipment to block the runways.

They missed two Huey helicopters illegally parked behind a hangar. When the first shots were fired, the pilots abandoned their coffee, raced to their machines and took off.

Across the field by the flying school, Andrew Bryce, a twin-rotor Voyageur pilot, was talking to a friend as the attack started. He took off and flew over the field to see what was happening. The control tower brusquely told him to land. When he ignored the order, the ALQ opened fire.

Blood flowing from an arm wound, Captain Bryce banked away and headed north to warn incoming traffic as the Hueys headed for the US Air Force base in Plattsburg. Bryce quickly determined that Dorval, Mirabel and Cartierville were all under military control. Growing dizzy from loss of blood, he set his helicopter down on the sport field of the military base at Longue Pointe. The ALQ met him.

The arming of Mobile Command staff turned the takeover into a battle. Having weapons the soldiers used them, fighting in isolated groups, office by office. The ALQ tried to take prisoners, but when their commander died in a doorway demanding the surrender of six majors, a grenade became the standard announcement of the attackers' arrival. After an hour the only free area was the underground communications center where General Laporte's defence still held off the ALQ while the teletypes chattered to Ottawa.

*

George greeted his visitors by name as they came in. He knew them all. To his surprise his old friend Tom Bush was with them. Tom owned a real estate company and commanded the local artillery unit. He wouldn't support vigilantes.

In the living room, George turned on a delegation which showed its inner divisions simply by the way it positioned itself. Sam Thackery stood in front of six men. Tom Bush had moved to the back, far to one side. Five others stood slightly apart from Sam's militants, but not as far removed as Tom. "Well?" George challenged.

Thackery, a perky bantam rooster, threw out his chest. "Colonel Sloerill, we're concerned with the situation in Quebec. We distrust that bastard Cyr. He's a damned separatist. We're afraid the Montreal riots will spread, and we intend to—"

George cut him off. "For God's sake, Sam, it's too early for a political speech. As far as I'm concerned, anything you do will cause more trouble than you can handle."

Thackery had expected a better reception. "Come on, George," he began more reasonably. "You've been away. It's serious, whatever Etienne says." They'd seen the Bentley. "The American consul's home was bombed. His wife's in hospital. Phone service is lousy—and a lot of local separatists are missing. We need a local defence unit."

"You have one," George shot back. "How many Gunners in your battery, Tom?"

"Not them," Thackery interrupted. "Tom won't move without orders from Ottawa in triplicate. We don't have enough local cops, and we don't trust the Provincials. Nobody knows *who* to trust anymore." He looked genuinely lost and afraid.

"And your local defence force will all be English?"

"Why not? We aren't trying to separate," Sam shot back.

"We settled this area." Terry Williams, manager of an American-owned plastics factory, spoke up. "If we don't fight, who will?"

Thackery recovered his drive. "My family came here over two hundred years ago. My grandfather sold two farms to buy a mill. My grandfather and father built it up, and I'll be damned if I'll throw away the work of four generations!"

"You have a point, Sam, but it's buried under such honest bigotry that it's lost."

"Bigotry!" Thackery exploded. "You listen here, George. You've got no call to—"

Sloerill cut him off. "I gave you honest, Sam, don't push me. We may need to reinforce the police, but the mayor has to ask, not you."

"Ease off, Colonel." Williams tried diplomacy. "We cranked this up pretty fast. I know the mayor. He's no more a separatist than I am. He'll ask if you'll agree to run it."

"He'd better," someone growled. "We can't expect help from anybody else. The fucking feds'll sit on their asses reading reports while we go down the drain. Cyr will do anything the polls say won't irritate the radicals, and our weenie prime minister is babbling about 'no force'. The son-of-a-bitch comes down here, he'll see some force."

Sloerill didn't bother to identify the speaker. It was clear that to varying degrees, this opinion was held by everyone but Tom Bush, who still stood aside.

"Use your heads," George growled, seeming to grow several inches, dominating the room simply by being there. "Without Quebec the prime minister loses power, and without Canada's OK, Quebec can't join the UN. I'm not saying the next few weeks won't be exciting, but if you go off half-cocked they'll be more exciting than you want. Go home and don't get upset if some idiot spray-paints a separatist slogan on a wall."

As he moved to the door, pushing the delegation ahead of him like a tugboat, the phone rang. He gave Peter a look of appeal and saw the visitors off the front porch. When he got back, the delegation had gone but Tom Bush was waiting.

"I wasn't part of that, George." He smiled wanly. "Etienne asked me to come riding and I was walking over when Sam picked me up. Probably thought I'd have some influence on you."

"Walking? What's wrong with your car?"

"The wife went to see some hysterical relatives in Knowlton. They think we're all about to be murdered in our beds. Me, I'm waiting until after Cyr's emergency session before I panic. There's a speech at eleven—about now followed by a news conference."

"And my radio's dead. Come and meet my friend Peter Forbes."

George stopped to take Tom's arm. "And give me a SITREP[2] on your battery. Just between us, I'm not quite as sanguine as I let on. How are things?"

"Not bad. Thanks to the corridor idea, a few Montreal companies came this way instead of going to Ontario. As a matter of fact, some people *want* Quebec to separate to get more factories out here. Anyway, recruiting isn't bad. I got nine warm new bodies this summer and my total strength is sixty-eight. Thirty-four have been in two years or longer."

"That's good. Officers and Senior NCO's all right?"

"I've only two junior officers, both green. The sergeants' mess is better, three ex-regulars—one of them knew you in Cyprus. Sergeant Wilson?"

"Good man. Who's running the regiment in Montreal?"

"Colonel Chantilly, one of the best. He built two strong batteries there and whenever I need support, I get it. You should—"

"George?" Forbes came through the kitchen door. "The call's for you. Chap named Ashworth's in trouble in Farnham. Wants you. Now."

George plunged into his study, and Peter studied Tom Bush. He saw a man in his mid-fifties, not spectacular but one of the dedicated plodders, the ones who made the plans of more dynamic men work. A man to be relied upon. "Coffee in the kitchen," he invited. "Better have some. It looks like being a busy day."

"What's happening—apart from the usual political garbage?" Tom accepted a large mug of very hot, very black coffee.

"Not sure. Who's this Ashworth anyway?"

"The Guards QM. Good lad, George trained him. I suspect he's behind the Guards' getting permission to train this weekend."

"Is that a problem? Aren't units supposed to train?"

"Not this month. Fucking politicians. They stopped training due to the 'delicate political situation'." Tom's voice took on a simper and his hand flapped limply at Peter then slammed the table. "Some of us aren't convinced, and some units are training today—like mine, unofficially. The RMR in Knowlton is too."

"Ashworth?" Peter prodded gently. "A captain, I gather. Rather insistent, even for a Guardsman. 'This is an emergency,' he said. 'I don't

---

[2] Situation Report

care what Colonel Sloerill is doing, I must speak to him. Get him for me now.' He did add 'please' but it was most definitely an order, so I cranked up and did as instructed. Is he always like that?"

"No. John's one of those quietly efficient fellows who usually 'suggest' things. I know—he wants my machine guns."

"It didn't sound like that," Peter said dubiously.

"It is. I sneaked ten out of Farnham on the old boy net. Normally their training officer Major Markos would call, but they probably think John can make George lean on me. George and I started together in the Cowansville Battery—way back."

"I doubt it," Peter said slowly. "His voice was edgy—scared would be closer—and on top of that, I heard shots being fired."

"Shots?" Bush sat up straighter. "You mean blanks?"

"No, shots. I can assure you—" They heard boots coming downstairs two at a time. "But perhaps now all will be made clear."

Sloerill flung open the kitchen door. He was wearing combat uniform, and a dark blue beret bearing a small gold cloth grenade was pulled low on his forehead. He laid a double-barrelled shotgun on the table and began to fill his pockets with shells from a box in his hand.

"Tom? How many over-eighteen trained men can I have?"

"Considering what I know now, none. What's up?"

"At 0930 the Guards were attacked by men in uniform with military weapons. Ten dead, twenty-two wounded. Enemy casualties unknown. The Guards are in the drill hall under fire. John alerted Mobile Command, then called Bosch, who said to surrender. John wanted a second opinion."

"How are they holding the hordes at bay with blank ammo?" Peter asked, pulling on his riding boots.

"The 'blank' ammo they drew from Longue Pointe was live. As it was being recalled they got hit, returned fire, got into the drill hall and kitchen—and they're taking casualties. They need help." He looked directly at Tom Bush. "Those were my men. I have to go to them."

Tom looked pained. "I'll come and so will some others, George, but we can't take military weapons—no ammo for them."

George gave him a flat stare. "You have. How much did you squirrel away after your last range shoot?"

"About three hundred rounds," Tom admitted.

"Minor question?" Peter asked. "Why can't the Guards break themselves out? Too few of them?"

"They have about three hundred, but they aren't trained as you or I understand the term. They've never been shot at. The area around the drill hall's a killing ground." He took the phone in one hand, fishing an address book from his pocket with the other.

"Should have tried this before." He dialed a number. "Marcel Laporte was my boss in Ottawa when I quit. He's running communications at Mobile Command now—hello? Hello? Is General Laporte there?" George listened briefly. "It's Colonel Sloerill. The same thing happened at Farnham. Perhaps I can help. Get the general, major—now!"

There was a short pause. "Marcel? George. You've been attacked? Who by?" He listened intently, his brow furrowed.

"The Guards were hit earlier this morning. I have the CO of the Cowansville Gunners with me. Can you give authority to call out his men? Can you appoint me in command out here?"

The pause was brief. "Thanks, Marcel. Good luck. If you can hold on we'll try to help you once the Guards are loose." He hung up.

"Well?" Forbes and Bush demanded together.

"Mobile Command was attacked ten minutes ago. Marcel's organizing a defence of the underground communications centre. He'll hold out as long as he can."

"What are his chances?" Peter asked.

"Zero. He needs an infantry company and he's got armed clerks." George turned to Tom. "Canadian forces went on a ten-hour notice to move last night during the riot. Close enough for me, and Marcel's word makes it official. I'm in charge. How fast can you get your men together?"

"You always had shit-luck, George. We're training today. I'll have Battery Sergeant-Major Lessard call the laggards."

"Look at this first, Tom." George pulled a grease pencil from his pocket and began to sketch on the formica table top.

"The camp." He sketched a rough road diagram. "The Yamaska River's on the east." He drew a wavery line. "The TDM's [3] are here." He added an X. "Come in the gate northwest of them and drive to the sandpit

---

[3] Temporary Dump—Munitions

area. Send five men there as an advance party ASAP. We'll get the ammo for you and meet the main group here." He pointed to a bend in the river southeast of the ammo dump.

"Got it." Tom made notes on a pad. "Anything else?"

"Not now. I have to look around, but I think the best thing to do is go down-river into camp. There's cover, and here," his finger stabbed out, "the drill hall is less than two hundred metres from the embankment. The attackers have to be a bit thin there."

"Good enough. Shall I bring my machine guns?"

"Bring anything that shoots. How long before you can roll?"

"Half an hour to get organized and call the no-shows—I should be on my way inside of ninety minutes with at least forty men."

"Good enough. Remember, nobody under eighteen, and my five must be steady. It'll be rough." Bush nodded thoughtfully.

"I might as well tag along." Peter stood up. "Never can tell when an extra body will come in handy."

"You will not," George snapped. "You don't even have a work permit." He poked his friend in the ribs with a stubby finger. "You will call Betty, make my excuses and strongly suggest she ship out on the first plane going anywhere. Next, take a cab to the Bromont Equestrian Centre. Find Etienne. If the proverbial has hit the fan, we'll need him."

Bush looked up from the phone. "Just a sec. What do we need, George?"

"Personal weapons, ammo, flares, radios, spare batteries." He took a paper from his pocket. "This is the Guards' radio frequency. Send me two sets, one on that frequency and one on yours. If I come on the air it's bad news. If I need help I'll send the code word JACKRABBIT. If I say anything else, you're on your own."

As Tom turned back to the phone, George picked up the shotgun and opened the back door. "Remember, Peter, no heroics. Go to Bromont. Stay out of trouble. Forget to call Betty and I'll skin you." The door closed sharply behind him.

CHAPTER THREE

Camp Farnham

It took Sloerill half an hour to reach the camp. The slow-paced shooting he heard told him that the Guards were still holding out. On the drive the guilt he felt at dragging Tom and his men into a fight they weren't trained for nagged at him. It passed. Militiamen or regular, this was what they had sworn to do if necessary.

Sloerill parked his Land Rover by the sand pit in Farnham camp. He had considered hiding in the trees but decided against it. He didn't want to be shot if the nervous Gunners he was expecting saw someone lurking. As he waited, he added to his sketch of the camp.

"I should have asked for maps," he muttered. "If I don't get my head in gear, we're all in trouble."

He was 2000 metres north of the drill hall. The main gate had been guarded but not the gate on the west he'd used. The ammo dump was about 300 metres due south of him with a good covered approach.

He studied the crude map. A lot had been left out because he didn't remember every building. Now to christen the ground so he could direct men to specific features by radio without telling the enemy what they were.

The road to the ranges would be RIFLE ROAD; to the ammo dump, NORTH ROAD. The last building on it, the quartermaster's shed, was BUCKLE. The paved parade square, TARPIT. Of the line of barracks be-

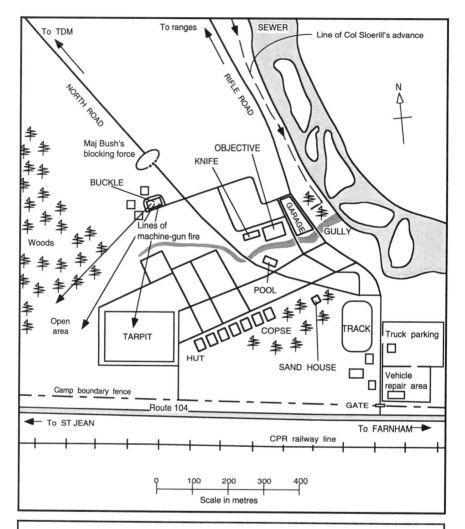

CAMP FARNHAM

Redrawn by Capt. J.M. Ashworth
From a Sketch by Col. G. Sloerill

(By Permission)

side the square, the metal one nearest TARPIT would be HUT. East of the barracks was a stand of trees and a building with sandbags around it—COPSE and SAND HOUSE. The main gate was GATE; there were enough others to confuse any listener.

The Guards were in the drill hall: OBJECTIVE. The mess hall behind it: KNIFE. The steep-sided creek beside the buildings: GULLY. The parking area: GARAGE. The Yamaska River: SEWER.

The Gunners would block NORTH ROAD at BUCKLE. The narrow area between OBJECTIVE and SEWER had to be a weak place in the enemy's cordon. The Guards could break out there.

He put down the pencil and waited for Tom's men, the loaded shotgun across his knees, thinking about the trapped Guardsmen.

The regiment had changed under Bosch. Now he only knew five or six of the junior officers. Bosch had driven away the majors he'd trained by accusations of incompetence and abuse.

Captains Dave Phillips, Pierre Coté, Al Potter and John Ashworth were still there. John had been his adjutant; his easygoing exterior concealed a ruthless streak that compelled him to get any work that he had been assigned done right and on time. Under Bosch he'd taken over the QM, turning that potential disaster area into a model of efficiency. John was the only one he'd maintained contact with.

Sloerill smiled as he remembered Regimental Sergeant-Major Grigson. Grigson had thrown him off the parade square of his own regiment in his first week of command. Sloerill had been watching a drill period and spoken twice to sergeants about their men. At the second incursion, Grigson's patience snapped. He'd marched up and saluted crisply. "Sir! One of us is redundant on this parade. Have I your permission to take up other duties—sir?" Sloerill had returned the salute and abandoned the field.

Grigson, a twenty-year veteran, was utterly dependable and solid. He bullied young sergeants into becoming self-starters, and the tiger skin he drew over an essentially pussy-cat nature ensured that nobody bothered him for trivial reasons. His attitude towards officers in general was one of reserve, tinged with respect for the few he thought worthy of it.

Sloerill's thoughts were interrupted when a car stopped behind the Land Rover and a man got out. Sergeant Wilson. He'd been sure the tough ex-regular Gunner would come. He went to meet him.

"Sergeant Wilson, that looks rather civilian." He pointed to the short hunting Marlin 30-30 the man carried.

"Good in the bush, sir," Wilson replied, saluting. He waved the other four up to him. "Major Bush sent this." He handed Sloerill a map, folded to show the camp area.

As the others came closer, Sloerill smiled. "We Guardsmen don't like saluting in the field. It shows the enemy who's worth shooting at."

Wilson introduced them. "Bombardiers White and Jackson, Gunners Tovey and Henderson, sir." Sloerill shook hands, studying them. Wilson was in his mid-thirties; White and Jackson, about twenty-two, the others were younger. The four carried standard military rifles.

As Sloerill outlined his plan, they nodded, knowing the camp better than he. He left Sergeant Wilson to review their sketchy infantry training and headed into the brush to see the ammunition dump he had to capture.

Twenty minutes later he returned and hunkered down. "Piece of cake," he assured them. "Chain-link fence and only five guards.

"Sergeant Wilson, Tovey and Henderson, take a position near the TDM gate and give covering fire while White and I go close." He turned to the tall Gunner. "Go up to the wire and if there's shooting, blast anything that moves. Got that?" White nodded, his face pale.

"Any idea who they are?" Wilson asked.

"Not a clue. They're in uniform and speaking French. That's all I know. If they surrender, fine. If they resist, shoot to kill. Got it? Aim between shoulder and hip and keep firing till the target goes down." The men nodded, tight-lipped, finally realizing that they might have to kill someone.

Sloerill went on quickly. "Be in position in five minutes. I'll demand their surrender when you're ready. Get moving and good luck."

Wilson left with his men. Sloerill gave them three minutes; then he and White advanced towards the cement block building. Four men were stacking grenades and rifle ammunition by the gate. With no grenade range in camp, there shouldn't be grenades here, but then boxes marked "blank" should not contain live rounds either.

He checked left. White was coming up to the fence carefully. He slid right to cover the door, willing the working men not to look his way. Would the young Gunners actually fire when ordered to? He had to trust Sergeant Wilson to make it happen.

Time. White was in position but his rifle was sticking through the wire. He could only shoot straight ahead. Sloerill cursed silently.

He checked the spare shells in his belt and stood. "Levez les mains!" he called sharply. The working men froze, their weapons against the wall a few metres from their hands.

Their leader saw a thick-bodied man in uniform crouched about outside the wire. A shotgun weaving slowly back and forth, covered the group. He made a small finger signal to the man inside the building.

"Forces Armées Canadiennes!" Sloerill snapped. "Hands up!" He gestured unmistakably with the shotgun.

A rifle cracked from the right and a man inside the door fell, fingers clutching a bloody face. The others dived for their weapons.

Sloerill killed the leader, the buckshot nearly decapitating the scrabbling man. He blew out the chest of another who was lifting an SMG, then dropped into the ditch to reload. White hadn't fired.

When he raised his head the last two enemy soldiers were dead, their bodies still jerking as the fire of Wilson's men tore into them.

"Cease fire! Cease fire, you assholes!" Wilson screamed. There was a single shot, then silence. Sloerill knelt, eyes scanning the area.

"Sergeant Wilson? All clear?"

"Yes, sir."

Sloerill moved forward slowly, eyes on the door of the building, stepping carefully over the torn bodies until he was sure that nobody was still alive inside. He waved Wilson forward.

"What next, sir?"

"I want two hundred rounds, two smoke grenades and two real grenades per man. If there's machine gun ammo, leave it here. I'm going on recce. If I'm not back by 1400, tell Major Bush he's in charge."

Sloerill pulled out his map. "Use my Land Rover to carry ammo to the assembly point here." He pointed to the river bend. "Send a guide to the gate we came in by. You and one man stay here. Now, in fifteen seconds it will be 1243. Any questions?"

Wilson set his watch. "I guess not, sir. Can we really pull this off?"

"Guarantee," Sloerill assured him. He checked the magazine of the submachine gun he'd appropriated. "Keep the men busy and speak to White. He froze. Tell him it's no big deal. Good luck. I know you won't let me down. Gunners never do." He slung the SMG over his right shoulder and slipped into the trees like an Indian.

Colonel Bertrand stiff-armed the door to the QM building open and stamped into the room. The three men inside jumped up in alarm.

"Merde!" he raged. "Why should such a simple thing be so difficult? If we do not finish by dark some of the Guards may escape. If our new plan does not work I will burn the drill hall and everyone in it!"

"Shall I notify headquarters that we are having . . . difficulties?" the radio operator asked, half reaching for his headset.

"Fool!" Bertrand screamed. "What can they do? We would only look incompetent. Ah!" His head snapped up as a truck arrived. "Perhaps things are happening at last."

A rumbling two-and-a-half-ton truck had pulled in. Two officers jumped out of the jeep leading it and came into the QM hut.

"Well?" Bertrand growled at them, ignoring their salute.

"We have a volunteer to drive the truck, mon colonel," the older man reported. "My sergeant says it will take two hours to build a bullet-proof shell around the cab."

Colonel Bertrand tried to control himself and failed. "Impossible! Do it faster. Two hours! Why so long?"

"The sandbags for the cab must be filled, and we must find chains to attach the railway ties. It takes time, colonel."

"Too much time. Tie them in place with ropes."

"If a bullet cuts the rope, the ties protecting the radiator and motor will fall and the truck will be stopped before it can ram the front door."

"Use tire chains then." The two officers nodded. "And protect only the side of the truck the Guards can shoot at as it approaches."

"Very well, colonel. What about the driver once the door is down and he is inside the building?"

"Our attack will be right behind him. The driver gets behind the sandbags and waits for rescue. See to it—now."

The older officer left. "Lieutenant Bolduc?" Bertrand's face softened as he looked at the other one, his daughter's fiancé. "Your attack follows the truck. I forbid you to take foolish chances. My Marie-Annette's wedding must not be delayed because you were rash. Tu comprends?"

"I must lead my men!" the young man protested.

"Of course. I merely say you need not be the first through the door. Be brave *and* careful. Now, get into position. Follow the truck closely and throw grenades from the door. Shoot anyone who does not surrender."

Herb and Gloria Kerner had stowed their furniture in the truck and headed for the Champlain Bridge, unaware of Premier Cyr's declaration of independence. They were amazed at the barely moving lines of cars heading south and the armed guards trying to control the traffic.

"What's going on?" Herb yelled at the soldier who had stopped an overloaded Honda to let him into line.

"You are leaving Free Quebec!" the young man yelled back. "To hell with you. Head for the United States by the most direct route."

Gloria leaned forward. "We have to get my mother in Abercorn. We have to go that way—she's old and alone!"

The soldier didn't know where Abercorn was, but his orders were to be reasonable if possible. The young man driving was of military age, but if they stopped every Anglo in that bracket the jails would overflow. "Take this pass." He gave Herb a stamped paper. "You can stay in Quebec tonight. After that we will arrest you."

Herb tried to thank him but the rising tide of honking behind them drew the soldier away, and they inched forward onto the bridge.

Two army trucks, four cars and a jeep bumped over the uneven field. As they moved into the trees along the river bank. Tom Bush slid out of the jeep and trotted towards Sloerill, his worried face relaxing slightly as he came up to him. "You've no idea how glad I am to see you, George. I have forty-three men, two officers and three signallers. With Sergeant Wilson's gang we have fifty-three. Not many for a real fight."

"Enough to start one," Sloerill said reassuringly, then peered suspiciously at a group of men. "As I thought. Peter conned you, didn't he?"

Bush nodded. "It was easy. I don't know beans about infantry and you might have been dead."

George beckoned. On his way over Forbes spoke to Battery Sergeant-Major Lessard and came on. Lessard began moving his men into a better defensive position. A few ran to the Land Rover for ammunition.

"Cab driver got lost," Peter offered laconically. "Betty sends regards and a lucid description of how the airport was taken over. Foreign airlines can fly out once passengers are cleared. She'll be airborne by now. I thought you might need me more than Etienne would."

"Well, as long as you're here, look at this." He showed them his sketch map of the camp and explained the nicknames. Tom and Peter wrote them down as he gave orders, one finger tracing the moves on the map.

"I want two platoons, one of thirty-two, that's mine, and one of seventeen, including Sergeant Green and crew for you, Tom. Use them to set up a roadblock at BUCKLE. Take the machine guns you brought.

"Peter, we divide the rest between us and follow SEWER, under cover of the river bank to a position opposite GARAGE. Move your group into GULLY and after my men take out the enemy force in the trees between GARAGE and SEWER, give covering fire for the Guards' breakout.

"The Guards and Gunners will then sweep west, clearing the camp to roughly the line HUT/BUCKLE. Then stop to let the machine guns go to work. Sergeant Wilson has the ammo."

"I don't think I can see a target from the QM, George."

"Put the guns on the roof. It's a map shoot without dial sights, but at that range it'll work. Once we push the enemy into the flat area past TARPIT you can hammer them.

"Now, issue two hundred rounds per man. They'll waste a lot because they're scared. Two grenades per man plus smoke grenades. The radios work?"

Bush shrugged. "They did in Cowansville. Six sets."

"Right. The Guards switch to our frequency once they break out. Peter, you're Call Sign 1. Tom, you're 2. I'll see how many platoons the Guards can put together but they should at least be Call Signs 3, 4, 5 and 6.

"Code words. When you capture BUCKLE, Tom, send WHOOPING CRANE as your success signal. Time check."

The men looked at their wristwatches. "In ten seconds it will be 1518 . . . in five . . . now. Any questions?"

Tom shook his head, studying his notes. Peter hadn't made any. "Report lines? Start lines? Casualties? Prisoners?" he asked softly.

"Forget it. It's KISS time. Casualties and POW's left on the line of advance. Time of attack, 1620, sooner if we can get it together. Do a fast map recce, then give your orders. I want to move out by 1530. Tom, any problems with that map shoot?"

"I never used machine guns as artillery before, but with a known gun position, measured ranges and ten guns I can plaster a big area for you."

"I knew you would. Your guns are Call Sign 8. I'll control their fire myself. Who are my signallers?"

"On our net, Gunner Laurin, a real good kid. Gunner Moore is on the Guards frequency. Can I go now? I have to work out this indirect shoot of yours and brief my men." Sloerill waved him away.

At 1535 Forbes and Sloerill led their Gunners down to the river bed and south towards the objective. At the halfway point, Sloerill called a halt and beckoned Gunner Moore forward. He took the radio handset. "Hello, One, fetch SUNRAY,[1] over."

"SUNRAY not available, SUNRAY MINOR here," came the reply. Sloerill recognized John Ashworth's voice.

"One, ETA figures seven-five minutes. On my signal, break out west."

The static-blurred voice repeated the order and went off the air.

Forbes cocked an eyebrow. "A bit of duplicity there?"

"We set it up by phone. Drop an hour from timings and reverse directions. God knows who's listening. Move it, we have fifteen minutes."

As they moved off, Gunner Laurin tapped his arm. "WHOOPING CRANE, sir." Tom Bush was in position.

They stopped again northeast of the parking area. Bullets cracked overhead, making the men crouch nervously. Sloerill climbed the river bank to peer out between two bushes, holding the position until several shots snapped over his head before sliding down again. He hadn't seen much, but the gesture had reassured the men that instant death wasn't lying in wait for the first man to show himself.

They moved on a hundred metres and halted. Forbes and Sloerill climbed the bank. Between them and the drill hall was a narrow road and a thin screen of trees. In the roadside ditch fifteen feet away, they saw the head and shoulders of a man lying prone and firing at the big grey building. A dozen other men seemed to be in the trees.

---

[1] Code designating the senior officer of a unit

They slid down again. "Peter, I'll take out this lot with my men. You get into GULLY and cover us." Forbes led his men around to the outlet of the gully and turned right into it, placing them individually, making sure each man had a grenade ready and his rifle was ready to fire.

"Tell the Guards to cease fire this side now," Sloerill told Moore. After the reply, he counted to five slowly, then blew his whistle sharply, hoping the sudden sound from behind them would startle the enemy into raising their heads, making themselves more vulnerable.

On the whistle, a ragged line of grenades flew over the road. Some, thrown too hard, bounced off tree branches. Another barely cleared the bank, rolled drunkenly across the road and exploded on the far edge. On the second whistle blast, smoke bombs flew more evenly than the unfamiliar explosives, going off with muffled pops. White smoke began to billow through the trees.

"Go!" Sloerill screamed. "Up and at 'em! Go! Go! Go!" He scrambled up the bank, looking for the man he'd seen before. He was dead, his body riddled with grenade fragments. A light breeze carried the smoke into the trees, masking his men.

Among the trees, everyone seemed to be shooting at everyone else. Men screamed and fired at shadows and crashed through the brush. Sloerill killed a running man with a short burst of three shots and swore. Everyone wore the same uniform. He should have given his men some sort of identifying mark. At least the Gunners knew one another.

One Gunner, confused by smoke, blundered into the open. Shots from the right caught him and he went down. As Sloerill looked, a ten-wheeler truck appeared, its front and sides protected with railroad ties. Behind it, twenty men jumped from a ditch and began to run forward.

Sloerill crouched and looked around for his radio operator. Laurin was there, now carrying two sets. "Guards," Sloerill snapped.

"Here, sir." Laurin held out a mike, his hand steady.

"One, clear main door area now, enemy about to ram."

"Roger, out," came the strained reply from Ashworth.

"Shoot those men!" Sloerill yelled at the Gunners crouched at the edge of the trees, still dazed by their victory. Obediently, they opened fire on the running enemy. The officer leading the attack went down and those following him faltered, unsure of where the fire was coming from.

From the gully, Forbes's men poured rifle fire into the truck as it lumbered forward. A Gunner half-rose and pegged a grenade into the cab like a catcher getting the throw to first. It exploded as the truck smashed into the twenty-by-fifteen sliding door. The flash and smoke of the blast were cut off as the door splintered and the now unguided truck lurched inside.

It was becoming a dogfight, Sloerill realized. Nearby, a young Gunner officer crouched with one of the regular force sergeants at his side. Both were looking his way.

"Shoot them!" he ordered, pointing at the enemy platoon, now retreating. "Watch your right flank—and cover me. I'm going in."

When the rifle fire thickened he sprinted for the drill shed across the open parking lot. A score of abandoned weapons and a dozen bodies lay tumbled among the ammunition boxes. Seven or eight more had died near the door. He recognized Guards cap badges as he plunged inside.

The place was in turmoil. The truck had gone the full length of the building and tipped onto its side when a wheel had tried to climb a stack of folding tables by the stage. Around the walls Guardsmen lay on the floor, firing through loopholes smashed out by fire axes. Smoke from the burning truck brought visibility down to a few yards.

"Sir?"

A stocky, fair-haired officer knelt beside him. The name came to him. "Wayne Jones? Got a platoon?" Jones nodded.

"Get them into the ravine half-right from the front door. Report to Major Forbes, civilian clothes. Do whatever he tells you."

"Right." Jones began collecting his men, calling them by name, every second word a curse. They assembled quickly. Sloerill spotted another face through the smoke.

"Sarn't Green! Over here."

"Sir?" A powerfully-built man crouched and dashed past the shattered doorway, a thin trickle of blood running down his right cheek from a minor head wound.

"Place a few good shots at the front door. Enemy, quarter-left, ten o'clock. If they attack again, stop them."

Green darted away, calling out names. Sloerill looked around to see who was in charge. "Captain Ashworth!" he yelled.

"You rang?"

Sloerill spun around, relieved. "What time to go for a shit. Jones is moving off, get the rest into the gully. Where's Major Markos?"

"Next door in the mess hall. He left Jim and Wayne's platoons here and took four others. Want to talk to him?"

"Tell him I'm coming. Get out and report to the only man in the gully who doesn't look scared. That's Major Forbes. Civilian clothes. Tell him I'll be back with Markos and crew. Where are your wounded?"

"Indoor range. It's the safest place. Take them with us?"

"God, no. Put out that truck fire and get into the gully."

Sloerill turned and almost collided with Gunner Laurin. "Can you reach Major Bush?"

"Yes, sir."

"Tell him OBJECTIVE taken and be ready to open machine gun fire on my command. Got that?"

"Yes, sir." Laurin began talking into his set. Sloerill looked around at what was happening. Green's men were firing short bursts from the doorway as the last of Jones's platoon sprinted out. More men, less organized, followed. As the first started out, two were hit and fell. The others froze. Sloerill ran forward but he wasn't needed. The platoon commander booted one man and slapped another, sending them staggering through the shattered door. The others followed.

"Keep 'em moving," Sloerill called to the slender officer who stood fully exposed, waving the platoon through with a rifle.

"Hi, Colonel, welcome to Farnham." Dark brown eyes and long lashes looked up at him from under a steel helmet fringed with loose strands of short golden hair.

"My God, Gail Buckley!"

"Why not? You need a good officer for this lot—run, you idiot! Recruits!" The last of her men ran past. "Can I go, sir? They can get pretty lost without somebody holding their hand."

Sloerill nodded dumbly. He had given Gail the job of platoon commander in the recruit company three years ago. Bosch had shifted her to a desk job, and Ashworth thought she was going to quit. He watched a small platoon go past led by a man he didn't know. The attack on the drill hall had failed, but bullets were tearing through the thin metal walls. A third platoon started forward.

"Hey, Jim!" Sloerill called to the young officer leading them. Lieutenant Fox turned, nearly falling over his feet. Another of the old gang.

"When you get outside, tell Major Forbes I said to secure the main gate. There were half a dozen enemy there when I went by."

"Main gate. Will do, sir." Fox ran to catch his platoon, snagging his sleeve on a splinter as he went past the shattered door.

Sloerill ran to the back of the hall, hearing the growing volume of fire from the gully. Nobody could attack them now. He stopped at the rear door. The mess hall and drill hall were six metres apart. He took a deep breath and dashed across the gap. The mess door opened and he dived in.

"Your name?"

Sloerill saw a slender, dark-complexioned officer crouched over him. A hairline moustache drew a fine stripe between the jutting nose and clenched lips. His pistol was aimed at Sloerill's head. "I'm Colonel Sloerill. Are your men up to some more fighting, Major?"

"We have fought all day!" Markos shot back hotly, then the coiled spring inside him seemed to relax as he sized up his new commander and felt the confidence he radiated. "Orders?"

"Jim Fox is clearing the main gate, the Gunners have the QM, the enemy's out there," Sloerill pointed northwest, "and a bit confused. Leave a guard here. Get your men into the gully and wait for orders. The plan, in general, is to form a line and drive the enemy west through camp towards TARPIT, the parade square."

"Good. That is open country, so we can hunt them down."

"You halt at TARPIT. Machine guns hunt beyond that point. We have to move fast. If it isn't over by dark, a lot of enemy will get away."

Markos flashed his white teeth in a shark-like grin. "No they won't." He turned to the platoon commanders assembled behind him, hunkered down between the big cooking stoves.

"Armstrong, leave two men here. Everyone else, move out in order of platoons. Inspect your men in the gully, check ammo and wait for orders. No noise. No hesitation. Soon we'll be killing those bastards who attacked us. We will do it in an orderly and Guards-like fashion. Move out: now."

The kitchen emptied quickly with little of the confusion Sloerill had seen at the drill hall. Markos obviously had a tight grip on his men. Too many faces were still missing, Sloerill thought as he followed Markos into the eight-foot ravine. Regimental Sergeant Major Grigson, Captains Coté, Potter and Phillips—no, Al Potter was among the dead by the door, his body half lying against the wall as if he'd gone to sleep.

Sloerill built a mental picture of the battle. Gunners and Guardsmen were stretched along the gully and the river, firing at an enemy pinned down across the parking lot. As each new Guards platoon arrived, the line spread north and south, curling around the outnumbered attackers.

In the gully, Forbes strolled among the men, encouraging, instructing, clearing rifle stoppages, indicating targets, helping the occasional wounded man to safety. The ALQ began to withdraw west, their only escape route. Peter's radio operator touched him on the shoulder.

"Orders Group, sir. In the gully by the drill hall."

Forbes looked around for an officer. The Guards lieutenant who seemed to be up to speed was with a signaller near by.

"Lieutenant Jones!"

"Yes, sir."

"I'm off to an O Group. You're in charge. Keep doing what we've been doing but try to do a bit more of it. Keep them pinned down till I find out what we intend to do next. Got it?"

"No fuckin' sweat, sir."

Sloerill gave his orders twenty minutes later. He divided the force into three groups. The larger two went to Peter Forbes and Leo Markos, and he sent a dozen more with Ashworth to reinforce the Gunners at the QM. There were few questions, and in a few minutes Sloerill was left alone.

"Sir?" Laurin reported, still carrying two radio sets. "The main gate is secure, but the platoon commander is hurt."

"Wounded?" Sloerill asked sharply. Laurin spoke into the radio.

"No, sir. He hurt his leg. The sergeant says he doesn't need help."

"That's good, I don't have any. Now, let's get up to SAND HOUSE and control this mob scene from there. Hello, who's this?"

Tom Bush was coming down the gully.

"We captured the big cheese in the QM," he reported with considerable glee. "I brought him along. John Ashworth knows more about this infantry stuff than I do, so I got out of his hair."

"Where's the prisoner now?"

"Coming, with two guards." Tom waved back along the gully. "They're not up to the sort of things Ashworth was talking about. Sergeant Wilson is setting up ten machine guns. He estimates the beaten zone will be about a hundred metres by six hundred. OK?"

"Great. Look, Tom, I won't talk to your prisoner now. Once we advance, lock him in an office, then check the wounded. Check bodies. A few may be alive. Check the dead for papers, anything to say who in hell these guys are. You and your men did well, Tom. Really well."

"We did, didn't we?" Tom was grinning hugely. "Call on the Guns any time." The smile faded. "Two of my men are dead, and I know of at least six wounded, George. I'll have to face their parents tomorrow."

"Blame me. I'll see their families too. Remember, you couldn't have saved them once they volunteered, nobody could." He thought of the crumpled bodies scattered around the camp, friends and enemies lying where they had fallen. Back in the gully, a wounded man sobbed in pain.

"Nobody could," he repeated softly, "unless we hadn't come, and we couldn't have stayed away, not really. When you take the shilling, it's a lifelong contract."

On Friday, after the US Consul in Montreal had made his inflammatory statement on Canadian unity, an ad hoc group had been called together by a CIA officer in the International Activities Division. After the bombing, a series of urgent phone calls early Saturday morning reconvened the group (with two additions) in Fort Meade, Maryland. Everyone came, sleepy but not surprised at the summons.

As Fort Meade belongs to the National Security Agency, the world's highest-tech spooks, the meeting was chaired by a third assistant director who felt under-utilized in the system. Robert Eldridge Thraight, a Virginian of impeccable background, limited espionage experience and romantic ideas about cloak and dagger work, felt lost in an organization that spied by intercepting microwaved phone calls.

"Well," he said briskly, "for the record, can we sign in?" He waved towards the ceiling microphones. "I'm being formal because I can see one face that was not on my list of invitees." He smiled. "It makes life awkward when a guard calls to ask if he can shoot the man accompanying an approved CIA visitor."

Lenny Bruce, a mid-level CIA officer making suitable progress up the cryptoanalysis career path, shrugged. Thanks to parental lack of foresight, he could never use his full name. "L. Bruce, The Company. It was felt that a UK representative would be useful at this time juncture as Canada still falls somewhat within its purview. I assure you that while he has all due clearances, officially he isn't even here."

"Before I was not here," the Brit said dryly, "I called the Firm. They offer support and in fact are, even as we speak, tugging at lines into DGSE[2] to see if the perfidious Gauls have aught to do with this contretemps." The speaker, one of the two real agents present, was vaguely rumpled and looked as if he could disappear into the background by simply shutting his eyes. "We'll inform our cousins if we get a nibble." The man from MI6 who was not present didn't give his name.

The IAD man who had started the process grunted "Sure you will," but without malice. "John Bleeknapp—two e's, two p's, also the Company, and the man who originally cranked up this meeting."

"Which you'd be chairing were this not our turf and thus our rules," Thraight assured him. "What says the Bureau?"

"Frazer, William, with a zee—in Frazer, not William. The Bureau enters a question mark. We're grateful as all shit that we got invited to a spook party, but we don't feel we really have an interest."

"Patience, Bill." The man to his right spoke in a rough whisper. Having his throat savaged by a Czech guard dog fifteen years before had ended Adam Henry's active career. He'd become a valued (if unpromotable) asset to DIA, the Defence Intelligence Agency co-ordinating Military Intelligence reports. He was present because his agency had access to National Reconnaissance Office satellite photography. "Your computers have my voice print, such as it is. They know who I am."

"Thank you, Adam, always security-minded." Thraight turned the tiny snub aside politely, while recording a demerit in his mental file. "If you'll allow, gentlemen, I'll begin, because our people have been keeping their ears to various electronic keyholes all night.

"Something's rotten in Quebec, and Premier Cyr may be involved up to his neck. There are mysterious movements and coded radio orders, and

---

[2] The French equivalent of the CIA: Direction Générale de la Sécurité Extérieure

some kind of declaration is due. Conventional wisdom insists that he will not declare full UDI, merely threaten to do so as a tactic to pressure Ottawa. Even then we think he'll fudge it unless the ALQ, that secret army group we mentioned in September's INTSUM,[3] has a good grip on his short hairs. As for the bombing, does anyone have anything new?"

Bruce shook his head but Bleeknapp nodded. "Our people say it's freelance radicals who get upset at English signs. They didn't like the consul's statement and decided to punish his 'insult' to Quebecers."

"Strange," MI 6 muttered. "The consul is known to be pro-Quebec. Odd envoy to a potential break-away province I'd have thought."

"We hoped he'd garner separatist trust and be an asset if it happened—I gather," the IAD man said. "It was worth a shot. He was to have received a rocket, now he may get a medal. When his wife died this morning, it warped the internal handling scenario, I assure you."

"Cyr surprises me," the DIA man rasped. "I thought going for a pee alone was about as risky as he liked life to be."

"According to a tame politician we rented recently, he had no choice. Lead valiantly or step aside. A hollow threat, actually." MI 6 steepled his fingers. "Whatever happens, they'll need an elected premier to impress the masses that everything's on the up and up. The Russian coup failed largely due to lack of respectability."

"Considering the importance—and despite the fact that I still see nothing for the Bureau—why no White House rep? Isn't the President interested?" Frazer-with-a-zee sat back with the air of a spectator.

"The President's Security Adviser is not here because even as late as last night his considered and weighty opinion was that nothing was going to happen," DIA informed them. "The only thing he said that I agreed with was, quote, 'Cyr doesn't have the balls to lead a coup and Bouget hasn't the credibility.' To put it a trifle more circumspectly, Cyr's a figurehead."

"He's a *cock*-head if he thinks he can pull off a coup," Bleeknapp growled, "or that he can stay in charge of it if he does try. Tell him to ask Gorby what-his-name about that. Did anyone try to—I don't know—alert the Canadian government that this was in the wind?—warn Cyr?—hire a skywriter to inscribe 'Not now, idiot!' over Montreal?"

---

[3] Intelligence Summary

"No, and the skywriting would have had to be in French," Thraight answered. "What we are interested in is any potential involvement of foreign powers in violation of the Monroe Doctrine. We should also start an assessment process on the military forces Quebec and Canada can put together in the event that things go wrong. Would our non-guest like to start?"

"Well, reference the Monroe Doctrine, which as an aside originally needed Royal Navy teeth to enforce, we are attempting to discern ripples on the diplomatic scene. The most likely player is France, and as I mentioned we are delicately approaching their intelligence people to see if their government is tossing rocks into Mare Diplomaticum."

"Are you that cosy with DGSE?" DIA asked suspiciously.

"No," MI 6 admitted, "but we have contacts in areas where our interests coincide. The main thrust of inquiry is through the Bundesnachrichtendienst.[4] They have excellent ties with the lads at the Swimming Pool.[5] Incidentally, the Other Mob," he referred to his sister service MI 5, "passed on a tidbit. Canadian Intelligence was warned off investigating things rotten in the state of Quebec about a year ago."

"That sounds too stupid even for a committee decision," the FBI opined. "Allan Pinkerton padded his reports but nobody told him to stay out of the South prior to the Civil War."

"A cabinet decision, I hear. The rationale being that if CSIS found anything sour the PM would have to *do* something, and since he claims Quebec's a secret hotbed of federalism, discovering a sedition plot would not look good. If nothing were found but the feds were caught not finding it, he'd be hammered in Canada for stupidity and in Quebec for 'interference in their internal affairs'. Under both scenarios, his popularity with an election due would hit the shit level. As a final point, the Firm mentioned arms shipments in the Atlantic. I'm waiting for amplification on that one."

"Thank you, non-guest," Thraight said. "Can DIA throw even a bit of light on the military situation?"

"Only a bit," Adam Henry admitted. "Our analysis—mostly based on NSA intercepts—," he nodded at Thraight, "is that Quebec can field four to six thousand reasonably trained men, but without heavy equipment

---

[4] German Secret Service
[5] Slang term for DGSE

except for the Canadian stuff in the province—which happens to be most of it. Considering the low-testosterone level of leadership there, it's considered safe from seizure. For Canada's sake it had better be. We refer to the Canadian *Armed* Forces only as a courtesy to an ally. Is this the time to ask a pertinent question?"

"Of course, that's why we're here," Thraight assured him.

"Then it's this—or these. One, what side are we on? Two, do we have a prime interest in preserving Canada the loyal ally and occasional pain in the ass? Three, do we have a prime interest in Quebec resources? Four, should we promote a brisk little fight before coming down on the side of Canada? The tilt here is due to the fact that our sagging defence industry needs major orders, and Quebec doesn't have a big enough army or enough money to help McDonnell Douglas."

"We'd like those answers too." Bleeknapp ticked off several notes on the same subject. "If the Company's involved, our department provides propaganda support, and knowing the *real* operational aims does prevent putting out stories that give away secrets we didn't know about."

"The thinking in NSA is that we should go with Canada, but this is not accepted at all levels. Some roosting hawks are waving the Manifest Destiny flag and a surprising number of people are saluting it. One unknown is the border states' reaction, particularly New England, which relies on Quebec electricity." Thraight looked invitingly at the FBI man. "What does the Bureau have to say on such things as voter attitudes in Vermont, New Hampshire, Maine and New York—to start?"

"The Director will be pleased you asked. I may have a surprise. The ecology lobby has more votes than the cheap power gang. On the other hand, the area's economic health is due to Canadian cross-border shopping. However, a build-up of U.S. forces along the border if we had to seal it off would make them even richer. There's also a growing irritation with Quebec unilingualism that pisses off Americans who used to vacation there. In fact, New Hampshire has a cause célèbre.

"Last spring a Quebec car hit a tree. Three people died. They had signed off organ donations in French on the front which the doctor couldn't read. The English version on the back which they did see was unsigned. One blood type matched last year's Miss Teen New Hampshire who's cute, gutsy, photogenic, and has leukemia. Whole towns are turning out to be blood-tested. The story got out, and Quebec drivers are not popular there. If we decide to support Canada—"

"Hold the thought, please," Thraight broke in, his eyes on a computer screen set into the table at his place. Everyone waited. He sighed. "So much for conventional wisdom. Cyr declared UDI, no fudge. A Canadian army headquarters in Montreal was overrun. Intercepts are of teletype transmissions. There may also be action in southern Quebec. I regret to announce that four US officers are missing, presumed dead."

Thraight looked up. "The ALQ have taken over almost everywhere. I think that since we are already convened, if somewhat prematurely, we constitute ourselves a quasi-permanent advisory body. As a first step." He looked up, "Stop tape, erase tape." He paused. "Now that we're alone, I suggest we massage some hard-copy minutes to show how on top of this we've been. Is there any objection to tucking ourselves under a National Foreign Intelligence Review Board wing? They have a budget surplus, and the Chairman's a reasonable man who knows his limitations."

There was no objection. "Good, now we'll also need a name."

"How about the Special Canadian Emergency Resource Working Group?" Bleeknapp suggested. "That could keep us together for years."

"Doesn't the acronym SCERWG hint at screw-ups?" Henry rasped. "Why not think big? A Special North American Emergency Resource Planning and Advisory Working Group. SNAERPAWG I think might give us a longer shelf life, if this revolt or revolution—we damn well better decide which it should be—behaves as we predict."

"Promising," Thraight admitted, "but 'Committee' has a more permanent ring than 'Working Group', and the word 'Action' is always useful. Northern Emergency Advisory Resource Planning Action Committee covers all bases. NEARPAC has a nice intimate ring. Agreed? Good. Now, forward planning-wise, let's call for coffee and get an INTSUM, in our name, to the National Security Adviser. Then we need an action plan, without which we'll get a 'thanks a heap, now go back to what you were doing' note. If we succeed, significant career advancement movement may well result from our labours. Managing this crisis will be a lot more rewarding than watching democracy grow in Tajikistan, I promise you."

CHAPTER FOUR

Firing Squad

The Prime Minister had felt confident in calling an "emergency" cabinet meeting Saturday morning. His contacts in Quebec had explained what the nationalists had tried to do on Friday night and how Quebec federalists had foiled them. The PM had also worked to prevent Cyr from getting the votes he needed to pass his secession threat. At least four nationalists were playing both sides of the fence, and their support had earned them Senate seats or any other lucrative appointment they desired.

He intended to use the threat of the vote's succeeding next time to coerce the cabinet into making two final concessions. Cyr wanted Ottawa to abandon the English-speaking Canadians in Quebec, and to state clearly that Canada would not support any attempt to separate a Cree "homeland" from the province. That would satisfy Cyr. The Justice Minister claimed that the Supreme Court would strike down any such agreement in about three years. By then, Quebec would have signed a new Constitution, and regardless of the next election his place in history would be secure as the Prime Minister who had snatched unity from the jaws of separatism and saved the country.

As for the separatists, he'd effectively neutralized them with the demand for a corridor in the case of separation. Their indignation and fury had ensured that their energies were devoted to fighting that proposal, not working out ways to defeat Cyr.

The meeting had been called for ten-thirty because he didn't want his ministers to watch Cyr's speech. It promised to be a vintage performance, firmly supporting both sides. His own staff would analyze and explain it. If Cyr went too far, the spin doctors could massage it. By the time they sat down at eleven-thirty, he'd managed to squeeze in almost an hour's worth of private stroking to ensure that the divisions he'd marked on his list still held and to find out who was having second thoughts about Cyr's commitment to federalism.

As his pollster had said last night, this was a crisis point. Growing opposition to "greedy" Quebec was forcing him slowly into toughening the federal position; but he'd finally persuaded Cyr that these concessions were the last. Another would cause an uproar in English Canada and send twenty-six MP's across the floor to vote against the government. Cyr faced the same dilemma. If Canada did not up the ante his government would split. Because nobody knew the deep game he and Cyr were playing, their public positions were often misinterpreted, even by political experts.

He brought the meeting to order. "Ladies and gentlemen, to work. With a bit of luck we'll be home for dinner. Will the acting clerk read the first order of business?" The absence of the Clerk of the Privy Council annoyed him. This meeting was important; Bastien should be here.

"The first item on the agenda," the clerk read, "is the refitting of military equipment in Montreal. There are summaries in your folders that explain how far the work has progressed. The first speaker is the Minister of National Defence, who is allocated ten minutes. The next interveners, with five minutes each, are: Interprovincial Affairs; Industry, Trade and Commerce; and Public Works. External Affairs will close."

"I suggest each of you make a brief summary to start," the Prime Minister suggested. "We'll digest the meat of your report before getting the details later. Alfred, you're up."

Alfred Banner, Minister of National Defence, was glad that he did not have to give all of his report at once. This was only his second cabinet meeting, and he was still unsure of his grasp of the military world.

"Basically, the work is almost complete. The total cost is in the thirty million ball park, but the work, General Pittman tells me, will extend the useful life of the equipment by three to five years. HMCS *Iroquois* is in dry dock now. *Athabaskan* will start her refit next week."

"Thank you, Alfred. You seem to have everything in hand, not bad given the time you've had the job. Trade & Commerce. What impact is the refit programme having on the Quebec economy?"

"Big," Harry Thorne grunted. "Without this deal there'd be nearly five thousand layoffs. Bunch of good federalists down there now."

"That's what we want, Harry. Can Interprovincial Affairs add anything?"

"I have applause from Quebec," Grace Dunbar said, shuffling her papers, "and complaints from other provinces. BC wants the second ship refit. So does Nova Scotia. The damage is containable."

"Good stuff. Yes, Bill?"

"My Public Works report isn't good, Prime Minister," Bill O'Hagan said gruffly. He'd been against the refit programme from the start and against giving anything to Quebec. He would have liked to take away many of the things already given. Unlike some, he had a safe seat and spoke his mind. "I'm stuck doing Grace's damage control. I've got a list of contracts we can use to calm key provinces down but I don't think it's enough. A lot of people are mad at what we've done already, and after the refit programme, I can't help two big English outfits in Quebec that do need help because it will only make the others madder."

"I'm sure you can find jobs for the unhappy crowd before the election. Now External isn't really involved in the refit programme, but I asked Joe to speak here because his report leads into our next order of business, the Cree in northern Quebec."

Joe Gates, Minister of External Affairs overflowed his chair as he sat forward ponderously. "The Cree have a great deal of support in Europe. Like the Baltic States, they can make a case for discrimination that Europeans can identify with. My ambassadors report that most countries will not recognize an independent Quebec until native claims are satisfied. That's the good news. The bad news is that the Cree want Canada to promise to defend them militarily in case Quebec separates."

"Something's coming, Joe," the Prime Minister said cautiously. "OK, now let's hear the good news about military equipment. What does it look like, Alfred?"

Banner wanted to say it looked like a boondoggle. So much equipment was in Montreal that most training had stopped. He'd been told that almost half the weapons didn't need refit and that in addition a new order of combat uniforms, boots and parkas was sitting in Longue Pointe instead of being distributed. He didn't know much about the military but he knew when people were mad, and his soldiers were angry.

"The Leopard tank update will be finished by the end of next week, the tanks will be shipped back to units soon after. Same for the artillery. The APC [1] programme's behind, but the militia will get their armoured cars back in two weeks. The sale of the old Centurion tanks we re-engined will pay for most of the army refit, I'm happy to say—" He fell silent as a messenger came in with a note for the Prime Minister.

"Sorry, Alfred. Do you know why General Vinet wants to see you? He's outside now. Isn't he retired?"

"General Pittman replaced him as CDS [2] last week. Shall I go out?"

"No. The fucking army can't interrupt cabinet meetings. He can damn well wait. The Russians are down for the count so it can't be war—unless the Americans have invaded us." The sally drew a chuckle. "Tell him the Minister will be free in about half an hour."

The messenger left and Banner sorted through his papers to find his place. As he opened his mouth to speak, the door opened again and an impressive man in civilian clothes marched in. General Charles Vinet was a lanky, square-shouldered six-foot three and, despite his fifty-five years, he could still wear the uniform he'd been issued as a cadet at RMC. He had been the first infantryman in years to head the Canadian Armed Forces, and during his tenure he had fought for new equipment for the regulars and for the militia, mostly to no avail. He'd expanded the militia, and against opposition from the bureaucrats (and his successor) given the reserves priority in the allocation of any new equipment.

The Prime Minster turned in his chair, face red, his famous temper on the verge of exploding. "Get the hell out of here, general. This is Canada, not Russia. The damned military doesn't burst in without leave whenever they want. Get out!"

Vinet suppressed a smile. Telling how he'd taken this bastard apart in front of his cabinet would keep him in dinner invitations for a year.

---

[1] Armoured Personnel Carriers
[2] Chief of Defence Staff

"General Pittman ordered me to come," he began formally. "He considers this an army matter, and as an airman he lacks the expertise to answer your detailed questions about the outbreak of civil war." That got their attention.

"What civil war?" the Minister of External Affairs demanded. "I have no reports of any new trouble spots in the world."

"This trouble spot is Quebec," Vinet replied coldly. "At eleven ten this morning the province declared independence. Premier Cyr is still on TV explaining the announcement."

"Impossible!" the Prime Minister shouted. "I spoke to him last night. He wants to keep Quebec in Canada. He'd never declare independence without telling me first. Never!"

"I have a videotape of his announcement, sir." Vinet held up a black plastic oblong. "He claims the protracted and fruitless negotiations with Ottawa are humiliating to Quebec and that he will henceforth only deal with Canada equal to equal."

The Prime Minister saw that the men and women around the cabinet table were in shock. "He may have done it to head off the separatists, but he doesn't mean it. He'll find a way out. He's a federalist but he has to keep the separatists in his party on line—balance the forces. Give a bit, take a bit."

"He sure as hell has separatists, he picked 'em!" O'Hagen shouted. "He signed their goddam nomination papers and put them in his cabinet. This proves that he's a fucking separatist. I say he's always been one!"

Vinet cut off the Prime Minister's reply. "General Pittman said to inform you that Mobile Command is under attack and cannot hold out. The attack came, for your information, ma'am," he looked at Justice Minister Karen Ormsby, "eight minutes *before* the declaration of independence. There is also a signal indicating military action in the Eastern Townships. We have no further information on that at this time."

Knowing he had their full attention, General Vinet continued the verbal whipping. These people had cut his regular forces, handed them international peacekeeping duties, the Gulf war and the Oka confrontation, but refused to spend the money the military needed to do those jobs.

"Quebec has seized her borders and all major airports. Most phone links are out, and we can't access overseas cable lines. General Pittman says that in his opinion there now exists a state of civil war. He wants permission to move the Airborne Regiment to Ottawa."

"Jesus!" Alfred Banner had recovered enough to realize that all Canada's heavy equipment was in Montreal. "The tanks, general?" he almost begged. "Did we save any?"

"No, sir," Vinet said flatly. "General Pittman called Longue Pointe during Cyr's speech. An officer answered who claimed to represent l'Armée de la Libération de Québec."

"At least the equipment isn't serviceable," Joe Gates said as he recovered his wits. "We've just heard a report—"

"Don't trust that report, sir. The equipment may be fully operational. Also, sir, thirty percent of French-speaking NDHQ officers either do not respond or refuse to come in. The same is true of civilian employees. When I left a team was looking for evidence of sabotage, especially to computer programmes. The Canadian Forces are naked, sir."

"You can't be naked," the PM protested weakly. "We have eighty thousand men."

"We haven't." Vinet shot him down ruthlessly. "For land ops, the Air and Sea Elements are useless. The army consists of a weak brigade group in Europe and two small battalions on peacekeeping duties. In Canada we have one battalion of RCR,[3] two Patricia[4] battalions and the Airborne. Armoured and artillery units can act as infantry if necessary. In three days we can assemble a force of some fifteen hundred to two thousand fighting men."

"Surely that's wrong?" Banner protested. "According to those figures each battalion and the Airborne would only have about two hundred men each. I don't believe it."

"I did not include the Van Doos. We cannot consider them reliable at this stage. The base commander told General Pittman that—"

"You say the Van Doos are not loyal?" the Prime Minister's Quebec lieutenant broke in furiously. "They have fought for Canada. To say this is to insult every French Canadian who ever served. I protest, general. In the name of all Quebecers, I protest!"

---

[3] The Royal Canadian Regiment
[4] Princess Patricia's Canadian Light Infantry (PPCLI)

Vinet looked pained. "I'm sorry, sir. These are my people too. The Van Doos aren't all disloyal, but until we know how many will serve Canada and how many the new state of Quebec, we simply can't count on them. That is essentially what General Levesque, the base commander at Valcartier, told me just now."

"Well, shit." O'Hagan sat back, blowing out his cheeks. "It finally happened. Good, say I. We may have a small army but it's a hell of a lot better than the one that bunch of traitors across the river has. Put the troops in even if we don't have all the bells and whistles—the way we did at Oka and to the FLQ in 1970. Once we shoot a few traitors, the rest will switch sides fast enough."

Five Quebec cabinet ministers leapt to their feet, faces scarlet, hurling abuse, shouting in a furious exhibition of bilingual rage. General Vinet silenced them without raising his voice.

"If ordered into Quebec now, General Pittman will resign. So will any senior officer. Without heavy equipment it would be a slaughter of our men, not theirs."

"You say the army will mutiny if I order them to end this rebellion?" the Prime Minister demanded, releasing his anger to prevent fear from taking over.

"No sir, I am saying that no professional officer will commit troops to an unknown battlefield. If we are defeated, it will be the end. The military is your last resort. Lose that and you've lost everything." Vinet looked around the table. Twenty-four of the nation's most important leaders sat in defeated silence.

"Play for time," he went on, almost gently, seeing their shock. "We can defend Ottawa. Quebec doesn't have unlimited forces either. We need time to call out the militia under the Total Force Plan. With two weeks to integrate them into regular units, we can fight."

"But we have no tanks," Banner almost wailed. "It will take months to replace them." He heard the Minister of Finance mutter "and millions of dollars."

"Not necessarily," Vinet corrected the minister. "British and Germans do their tank training in Alberta. Their tanks are more modern than ours. We may be able to borrow them. But crews need time to get used to the new equipment. It's not like changing cars."

*

The Prime Minister dismissed Vinet after almost two hours of questioning. Then the battle started in his riven cabinet. Of the twenty-four, eight were now with O'Hagen the anti-Quebec hawk. Ten were in the peace-at-any-price camp, and six were aligned between the extremes like fence posts in a field, separate from the others yet bound together by the wire of cabinet solidarity. Unfortunately for the peace group, the Prime Minister, formerly the principal dove, was now a hawk.

He wouldn't let Quebec go. World opinion would support Canada. On the other hand, the legal situation was so delicate that even a phone call to that bastard Cyr could constitute sufficient recognition of the coup as to question the legitimacy of all Quebec MP's. If they couldn't vote (especially those with ridings in the proposed corridor area), his majority was gone and so was the government.

It would take a while for that mundane bit of political reality to sink into the confused and shocked minds around the table. He let them fight, his mind busy. A split would destroy his government's last shred of credibility. War would give him a chance to survive. Once the people around the table worked off their anger, he'd adjourn until Sunday. That would give him time to go after the waverers—and touch base with the opposition. They had to be prevented from acting precipitously.

Vinet was too cautious. Defeat had to be avoided, but as leader of the country, like Lincoln in 1864, he needed a victory. He also needed a General Grant. Cyr lacked the ruthlessness to make a coup work. After one sharp reverse, one that even he couldn't rationalize into a victory, he'd panic and cave in.

What was that idiot Attorney General saying about lack of information? The fool was responsible for the Canadian Security and Intelligence Service. Why hadn't CSIS warned him of the coup? Sure, they'd been told to stay out of Quebec, but didn't they know the difference between orders and political necessity? Paul was a wimp who'd have been replaced sooner or later. After today it would be sooner.

"We must negotiate!" a Quebec minister exclaimed. "We must talk to Cyr. We cannot have civil war. It is—unthinkable!" The Prime Minister noted another minister who had to go. Unthinkable? Somebody sure as hell had thought of it.

*

In Camp Farnham the firing sputtered out just before six PM. The sun was disappearing behind a bank of sullen-looking clouds as Guardsmen and Gunners went to take charge of their surly prisoners. The ALQ, trapped in the open, had been cut down by the invisible machine guns firing from a quarter of a mile away, covering the whole area with a web of deadly bullets.

It had been a vicious fight with little quarter asked or given. The ALQ, determined not to be the first Quebec unit to be defeated, had fought for every building. Remembering their first terror under fire, the Guardsmen had attacked like inexpert pit bulls, driving their attackers by sheer numbers into the killing area of the former parade square and sports area.

Now the ALQ, leaderless since Bertrand's capture, stood sullenly in small groups, hands behind their heads. Suddenly free of fear and elated by victory, Guardsmen prodded and shoved the dejected band into a make-shift jail, the fenced camp swimming pool.

With his signaller Laurin, Sloerill had run the battle from the front porch of the building he'd named SAND HOUSE. When the shooting stopped he sent more orders. "Call Sign 1, guard prisoners and set up road blocks at every gate. Call Sign 2, sweep the camp to make sure nobody's hiding out on us."

"Can I help, sir?" Sloerill turned. Jim Fox was limping up the steps.

"You all right, Jim?" After wrenching his knee in a fall at the main gate, Jim had turned his platoon over to the sergeant.

"I'm fine, sir, I just can't run much."

"Report to Major Markos. Tell him I told you to grab ten men and patrol towards Mobile Command. If there's still fighting going on, phone, otherwise come back at once. Use civilian cars. God knows what's happening out there."

Fox saluted and limped off, leaving Sloerill sinking in a sea of questions. What was going on? Who had attacked them? How many more of them were there—and where? What would happen next? This attack could not be an isolated incident. Would local towns be the next target?

Tom Bush drove up in a jeep and trudged across to the littered six-foot folding table, nodding to Laurin at the radio. "George? The wounded need medical attention. Two men just died, and six more are critical cases."

"Warn the Cowansville hospital and send the wounded there with a dozen men and a good officer. Call Mayor Castonguay. Tell him what happened and warn him to expect an attack." Bush nodded, taking notes. "Your men can guard the town hall."

"Shouldn't I go myself?

"You've got a bigger job. Look at this." Sloerill pointed to his road map. He had drawn a rough oblong on it with a grease pencil taking in an area of about thirty square kilometres. The line ran from the north end of Lake Champlain to the autoroute, east past Knowlton and south, skirting the town of Magog, to Lake Memphremagog. [5]

"You're into real estate, this bit is yours."

"Mine?" Tom yelped. "What am I supposed to do with it?"

"Show the flag. Grab twenty of your best Gunners and add ten of Leo Markos's Guardsmen. Do a tour of the whole area. Hit the towns. Warn the cops. Pass the word. Your men know the area and people. Try to set up local defence units based on volunteer firemen and game wardens. Take lots of weapons—and, Tom? Tell them to be careful. I've no idea what they may run into."

He leaned against the wall, rubbing his tired eyes. "It's important to show that the Canadian Armed Forces are alive and well and that things are under control."

"Are they?" Bush challenged bluntly.

"No, but if we fake it long enough, it may happen. Two Gunners per jeep. The Guardsmen are there to start learning the territory. I want patrols moving by 1900. Set overlapping routes and establish RV's [6] where two or more patrols can meet. I want people to see lots of activity, not just one jeep and then nothing.

"Stir people up. Warn people not to fight against automatic weapons. Set ambushes, put people on rooftops with hunting rifles, trucks across the road with defenders in the trees. Same goes for your men. They're better armed, but they're not to get into fights they may not win."

"I shouldn't ask, but is there anything else?"

"Get your recruits here ASAP. If you find volunteers, send them

---

[5] See map at front of book
[6] Rendezvous

over. I assume that all militia units are now called out in Aid to the Civil Power, so we can recruit—but until I know more, I'd rather have the gung ho crowd looking after their home towns."

"Is that it?" Tom asked hopefully.

"Make sure your men get something to eat," Sloerill continued relentlessly. "John Ashworth will issue rations, stoves and parkas. It looks like an early winter. That's it. There'll be an Orders Group here later. You'll be notified."

Bush nodded and the two men walked towards the jeep. "Tom, I want Laurin. He's a marvel. When Moore got wounded, he just worked both sets as if nothing had happened. OK?"

Tom started the jeep. "Oh, sure. You only want the best signaller in Quebec. He won the trophy at Valcartier this summer. Thanks a whole heap." He drove off with a resigned wave of his hand.

Next Sloerill briefed his senior infantry officers inside SAND HOUSE. Peter sat on his right with Leo Markos at the far end of the table. Opposite Peter sat John Ashworth, acting QM, Adjutant, Ops Officer and Headquarters Company Commander. Sergeant-Major Grigson pulled up a chair on Sloerill's left, a bit aloof from the officers but part of the group. His place was traditional, "at the left hand of God" as he called it.

Sloerill told them what had been done and stated that in his opinion there had been a coup and they would have to consider themselves cut off from help for at least a week.

Leo Markos nodded enthusiastically. "Good. We can look after ourselves. The brass in Ottawa are the idiots who ordered us not to train this month. We'll probably be court-martialed for disobeying that order."

Sloerill smiled. "Not quite. Now then, slim down your companies to about eighty good men each in three small platoons. Everyone else who isn't in HQ or QM joins a training company."

"I've more than that," Markos protested. "So does Major Forbes."

"No you don't. Too many so-called trained men aren't, not in my book." He saw Peter nodding agreement. "Weed out the worst ones. Some you'll get back. The rest form the nucleus of a 3 Company once I find a commander for them."

"Captain Coté?" Markos asked doubtfully. "He's the only one left if Captain Phillips gets the recruits, which he should—in my opinion, sir."

Sloerill nodded. "I agree. Dave is an excellent at training officer, so I'll consider Coté first."

Three years ago Pierre Coté had been a social soldier who had only been kept on because he ran the best officers' mess in Montreal. He had to earn the right to command men.

"Next point. Peter, I want you to interrogate the prisoners now in the swimming pool." He looked at John Ashworth. "Where did you put Colonel Bertrand?"

"In a hut. He's a fanatic. I doubt if he'll tell us much."

"He has to," Sloerill said sharply. "I knew Bertrand and never suspected he was a separatist. He's probably the only man here with the information we need. He must talk." Sloerill leaned back. "All we know is that this bunch call themselves the ALQ. Once Peter finds out a bit more, we'll go after Bertrand."

Grigson cleared his throat. "Do you have a gem for us, sergeant-major?"

"I checked the guards on the hut where Colonel Bertrand is confined, sir. He asked about a Lieutenant Bolduc."

"There is a dead Bolduc," Ashworth confirmed from his list. "Initials P.R?"

"That's him," Grigson confirmed. "I think it's a family thing. I said I'd ask but I haven't had time."

"Keep it that way. Nobody speaks to him till I do. Let him stew." Sloerill became very serious. "Gentlemen, I assume Mobile Command is gone. I've no idea what will happen next or has already happened. They may have attacked Ottawa. Every radio station is urging people, in both languages, to be calm. They claim Quebec is now independent but with close ties to Canada. I may have to do something quite illegal. I'll take sole responsibility for it, but we need facts. If Peter can't get them, I'll try my method. John."

"Sir?"

"I want to promote Peter to Brigadier or Colonel, liaison officer to the British High Commission in Ottawa. That should shake Bertrand. Can you find badges? Good.

"Now, we have a terminology problem. If we are the good guys then the ALQ are the bad guys, usually called 'the enemy'."

"Aren't they?" Markos challenged. "When a bunch of bastards start shooting my men without warning, they sure as hell are the enemy."

"Yes, but remember, if this is a civil war, we'll all have to get back together later. The Americans took a hundred years to recover politically from theirs. I have too many friends on the French side to wait that long. At least 'enemy' is relatively neutral. We can refer to them as the ALQ, but whatever you say, they aren't 'frogs' or even 'the French'."

"Why not?" Markos demanded. "They are French."

"So are half our Guardsmen and most of Tom's Gunners. I won't stand for it. I'm sure the sergeant-major will have his own methods, but I promise you, the next man I hear say 'frog' will have a small jumping amphibian in view or I'll have his balls. Yes, John?"

"It's already in hand, sir. Battery Sergeant-Major, Lessard is it?" Sloerill nodded. "He nailed one of our men for a crack like that. After a noisy few minutes in both official languages, our boy was doing thirty push-ups, counting en français, then leading a cheer 'pour les québecois fidèles et loyaux!'"

"Good. Play it any way you want, but get it stopped. I recommend humour. It's always less abrasive and usually more effective."

"I have an idea on a totally different subject," Peter said thought-fully. "I saw a Guardsman with a video camera. If I tape my interrogation, the evidence can be useful, as we found out in Northern Ireland. If they admit to attacking without warning we may get some TV, 'clips' I think is the term, that will do their cause serious injury."

"Good. To your duties, gentlemen. John, get this place organized. Company Commanders back in one hour for a briefing after Peter's interrogation. Sarn't-major, a word with you now."

The officers rose and saluted. "By the way, gentlemen. I prefer all Guards officers to be on a first-name basis. Also, no saluting in the field or amongst ourselves. I know Colonel Bosch preferred more formality, but that is not the Guards way. Carry on."

As the others left, Grigson moved closer. "Sir?" he asked in a tone that clearly spoke of having a lot to do and wanting to get at it.

Sloerill knew that Grigson wouldn't last long. His hair had thinned and his waist thickened. For the moment, however, nobody could handle the nervous green sergeants better.

"This building has a sandbag wall around it," Sloerill said conversationally. "I'd like a new one, facing east, three bags thick, six metres long and two metres high. I may need it in about one hour, sergeant-major."

"Sir," Grigson replied dubiously. "We'll have to strip the house."

"Fine. I also want four stakes driven into the ground in front of it. The wall is a backstop for a firing squad."

"Sir!" Grigson's tone verged on mutiny.

Sloerill explained his plan. At last Grigson nodded reluctantly. "What shape are the men in, sergeant-major?"

"Tails up, sir. Excited. They keep remembering mistakes that should have killed them but didn't. It's hard to get them to work. They've won their first battle, though, and that helps morale."

"I hear not everyone contributed to the victory?"

"A few, sir. At least a dozen men didn't fire a shot. Three men were put on charge for not firing when ordered to. My NCO's will sort it out, sir."

"Meaning, 'officers keep out', eh?" Sloerill grinned. "All right, but from now on, when a man screws up, we don't put him on charge, he's in the book. He loses his name the way Guardsmen are supposed to."

"Right on, sir. Can I also revive the terms Sergeant and Corporal-in-waiting?"

"What in hell *have* you been calling duty personnel?"

Grigson gave the hint of a shrug. "The term Orderly Sergeant has crept in, sir."

Sloerill shook his head. "We have work to do. From what I saw today, the men are slack. Worse, they're idle. They obey orders but there's no snap. I don't want soldiers, sergeant-major, I want Guardsmen."

"You'll get them, sir."

"I know. By the way, how did this start? Where were the officers?"

"In the drill hall getting orders from Major Markos, sir. Drill Sergeant Coutts and I were collecting the live ammo that had been issued. We'd finished one group and sent them off when the ALQ came down the road. Someone yelled. It might have been a call to surrender but nobody heard it clearly. Then they opened fire. Coutts grabbed a rifle and let fly. Corporal Weitz joined in and so did a few others, particularly Guardsmen Tobias and Ferrier and Corporal Normand.

"The ALQ ran for cover and so did we. Major Markos had us cut loopholes in the wall with fire axes. After that we just kept shooting till you and the Gunners showed up."

Grigson went out and a few minutes later John Ashworth came in. "Excuse me, sir, we're setting up desks and maps in the next room, and we got the stove going. Would you like tea, and do you still take six spoons of sugar?"

"Of course, that's how I keep my sweet disposition." They exchanged grins. "By the way is Corporal Zukrowski still with us?"

"Yessir, he went with Jim Fox on recce."

"When he gets back, ask him if he'll volunteer to be my driver, batman, cook and general dogsbody."

"O-okay," Ashworth replied slowly and dubiously, "but I can find you a better one. Zuke's a great driver, but he's unmilitary. He's insubordinate. He's lousy with a radio, when he bothers to use one, and altogether, sir—"

"I know all that. He also has a minor criminal past and refuses senior NCO rank because it would require a security vetting. I've got Laurin for the radio, and if Zuke will come I want him to drive me."

"I'll tell him when he gets back."

"No, John, *ask* him. You assign drivers. The things I want call for a volunteer." He saw that Ashworth wasn't convinced.

"John, you and I will be working like twins. I haven't changed since you were my adjutant. When you think I'm wrong, tell me. You're in third year McGill, so if I can't convince you I'm right, how will a grade eight dropout react to my orders?"

"OK. I think the colonel should have the smartest, best trained soldier I can get."

"Fine. Now here's my side. Zuke's been in the regiment since before the Dead Sea reported sick. He's more of a Guardsman than most officers. He's probably the best scrounger in Canada, and he's a fighter. I like that. Finally, I'd rather be safe with him than dead with a better-looking man. In a fight I can rely on him to hold up his end."

"Colonels aren't supposed to get involved with fighting."

"This one will. John, our Guardsmen are a nice bunch of guys. I want fighters. Sixty ALQ gave them a hard time. I'm a pro, so's Peter Forbes. RSM Grigson's OK. Zuke, Leo Markos, Wayne Jones, you, Drill

Sergeant Coutts and Corporal Weitz have the right attitude. The rest are babies. We have to turn them into a highly disciplined team that can kill when necessary but who aren't afraid *not* to kill when they don't have to. As for Zuke, I want a man I can depend on from day one."

"OK, I'm convinced. Now, do you still want that tea?" Sloerill nodded and Ashworth left to find the sugar supply.

Under the old barn, the ALQ headquarters staff worked with feverish intensity, buoyed up by the magnitude of their success. Activity halted at 11:00 AM to hear President Cyr's speech to the nation. Unfortunately he had arrived at the studio ten minutes late and the announcement was delayed. After declaring independence he outlined the problems they faced. He rejected any meeting in Ottawa. As leader of a new nation, he had Quebec's pride to consider. Then he spoke to English Canada and, more important, to the United States.

"No one regrets more than I the loss of life today," he said, looking into the camera. "All Quebec joins with the American consul in mourning the loss of his wife. I assure our American friends that those responsible were not of the Quebec military and will be punished. The bombing may even have been done by English extremists to discredit us. As for military deaths, those too we regret, but the world must understand that Quebec's legitimate demands have been frustrated for over two hundred years.

"I assure Americans who rely on Quebec Hydro power that we will continue to supply you as before. Any interruption will be due to English terrorists in Quebec who, unwilling to accept the majority's will to be free, may attack our legitimate national forces or they may resort to sabotage. I am sure you will place the blame in the proper place. Like yours, our republic is dedicated to the principles of freedom and justice, and we look forward to close co-operation between our two nations. We hope that, as General Lafayette assisted you in your struggle to be free, modern Americans will be equally generous in coming to our aid as we free ourselves from our oppressors in English Canada.

"To Canada I say this. For too long we have been a thorn in your side, pressing upon you our legitimate demands which were contrary to your own needs. The thorn has been withdrawn. As is natural, some blood followed, but I assure you that our soldiers are under strict orders to prevent needless casualties. In a few places, some misguided Canadians resisted and regrettably they had to be overcome by force. My military commanders assure me that they used the minimum force necessary.

"I also wish to deny most emphatically that any military action took place before Quebec became independent. Do not believe these lies. Now that we have our rightful place in the world, we hold the warmest feelings for all Canadians, and I urge you not to let emotion destroy the many unbreakable bonds of trade that bind us together. You need Quebec milk and cheese, we want your beef. Reason and common sense dictate that you will continue to buy from us as we will buy from you. Your many investments in Quebec will be protected by the same rules that protect our own, and you will find us in the future, as in the past, good business partners. In fact, now that Quebec has achieved her independence, I look forward to negotiating economic union and political ties with our Canadian partners. All we ask is that Canadian military forces leave Quebec as a guarantee that Canada will negotiate in good faith.

"To the international community, I appeal for understanding. I forgive Canada the attacks so far, but their soldiers must now withdraw, and I invite the United Nations to supervise this. As I speak, Quebec is under the full political and military control of a legitimately elected government. We ask for the same support and recognition that you offered Ukraine. Like Ukraine, we will ask the people to ratify what has been done. However, this cannot take place with foreign soldiers on our soil. After recognition, I can meet UN representatives to discuss a cease-fire and, I hope, find peace between the great peoples of Canada and Quebec.

"For those with relatives in Quebec, I wish to assure you that they are safe. I have personally ordered our soldiers to permit anyone who wishes to leave our new Quebec to do so. Such departures will be facilitated to the best of our limited means.

"In conclusion, I urge all non-francophone Quebecers to remain. You are safe. You are respected. We need and want you to help us build a new nation. I also offer my hand in friendship to English Canada, and I look forward to working constructively with you to strengthen our financial bonds. Do not be deceived by those who claim that we threaten you in any way. We wish only to be left in peace to work with others in the international community to build a better world."

The general switched the set off glumly. The speech would anger English Canada. The claim of legality was shaky. The declaration of independence could date from when the Lieutenant-Governor signed it at 10:50, but that was too fine a point to be appreciated. He liked the appeal for all Quebecers to stay to build the new society, but as his reports showed, almost a third of those fleeing were French. He wished he could seal the borders until people calmed down.

A few moments later his aide came in with a new pile of reports, his face glowing with pride. "What now, Jacques?"

"There is success everywhere and only minor fighting. We hold every major city but Sherbrooke. Hull is ours, and its citizens helped block the bridges to Ottawa. There is no sign that Canada will attack us."

"They can't so soon," the general reminded the enthusiastic aide. "Next week is when we must expect that. Sherbrooke and the Ontario border are the key areas. Do the brigades there need more men?"

"Everyone demands more men," Jacques replied sourly. "They demand them hourly as if we had an inexhaustible supply."

"Take some from the base at Longue Pointe. The stores are secure, and the men loading the trains can guard them. What is wrong in Sherbrooke?"

"We captured the airport and all federal installations, general. Trouble began with sniping in the English suburb of Lennoxville. It spread to Sherbrooke. The report claims that some militiamen are taking part."

"We hold their armouries and weapons?" Jacques nodded. "Good. Send the spare men from Longue Pointe. What about the other brigades?"

"Of the six South Shore brigades, four are committed in Granby and Sherbrooke. The one in St Jean is occupied with the officer college and the recruit base. When do the regular forces from Camp Valcartier arrive?"

"Monday," the General grunted. "They have their own way of working, the Van Doos. Tomorrow they hold a parade to divide the regiment. Those loyal to Canada will go to New Brunswick, the rest are ours. I allow it because I have no choice. Are the supply trains loaded and ready?"

"We finish tonight, sir, but the men are exhausted. The Gaspé train will carry guns, twelve older tanks, twenty armoured cars, ammunition and stores for a thousand men. The Hull train is bigger and carries sixteen new tanks. Both will leave at 0800 tomorrow."

"Very well. Get a report from Bertrand. We need those men of his back where they are supposed to be."

It was early evening when Sloerill returned to his headquarters in SAND HOUSE. The new sandbag wall was finished. Laurin sat in a corner by the radio set with John Ashworth beside him, holding a sheaf of papers. Peter Forbes, looking the quintessential British officer, was at a table facing a solitary chair. Leo Markos was prowling the room.

"What did the prisoners tell you, Peter?"

Forbes opened his notebook. "I interrogated ten men. They are members of the MacKenzie Brigade. The other brigades they mentioned are Papineau, Levesque, Martyrs and Rose. Each brigade numbers between one hundred and one hundred and fifty men. Their brigade was under strength because forty-six of their best chaps had been detailed to take part in the Mobile Command attack. Now this is the interesting bit." He flipped over several pages of notes.

"They admit they attacked early. They don't give a damn, and since we shouldn't have been here in the first place, it's our fault. It's all on tape and will play beautifully on TV. In addition, they claim that the Canadian army can't help us because they have no equipment. Lots of smirks and nod-nod-wink-wink looks from them, but they won't explain what they mean. I hope Bertrand can expand on that point. In the main, that's it. They were down, but they're a cocky bunch now."

Regimental Sergeant-Major Grigson stepped inside and saluted. "Firing party ready, sir. Prisoners standing by. Spare firing party detailed."

Sloerill sighed. "I'd hoped not to have to do this. Ready, John?" Ashworth nodded. "Very well, sergeant-major. You may begin." Grigson left, and a moment later a volley of shots broke the early evening silence.

"Did any bullets penetrate the wall, sergeant?" the officer commanding the firing party asked.

"No, sir."

A moment later two grim-faced corporals came in, escorting a bound prisoner past the door guard and a clerk. It was Bertrand. His face was pale but defiant.

"George, I demand to be untied. I am a prisoner of war. I also demand to know the meaning of that charade outside." He spoke in French.

Sloerill replied formally, also in French. "In the legal opinion of Mobile Command you are terrorists, not prisoners of war."

"Mobile Command does not exist."

Forbes looked up from his papers. "Sit him down, escort," he said in English. "I am Brigadier Jeremy Peter St James Forbes, British Army attaché. I was at Mobile Command this morning, and I assure you that apart from too many useless casualties and a lot of bullet holes in walls, the headquarters is fully operational. General Thomas gave his orders after the attack was beaten off. I was asked to convey those orders to the troops out here, and I can tell you that local field commanders have been given a number of discretionary powers—such as those I am in the process of implementing now." He turned to Sloerill. "Sit down, colonel. I have a few questions for the prisoner and I may need your version of events."

"Merde to your questions. You have my name, rank and number. That is all you get from me." Bertrand turned back to Sloerill. "Surely you do not take orders from a Brit?"

"Théo, Brigadier Forbes is in command. Written orders from General Thomas. In this emergency, I'll do as I am told."

Bertrand stared at him silently. At the back of the room, Laurin's voice could be plainly heard as he spoke into the radio.

"End SITREP, roger so far?" The radio crackled an acknowledgement. "Message continues with list of dead terrorists. Acier, J.C. Allard, B. Baillargeon, J. L. Bertrand, F.X. Bertrand, R.L. Bertrand, T. " The emotionless voice droned on.

"What is this?" Bertrand cried wildly. "I am not dead. Allard is not dead. He was captured with me at the QM. Who is that list being sent to?"

"Mobile Command," Forbes drawled. "Rejoice, Mr Bertrand. The MacKenzie Brigade is on its way to becoming a Quebec legend, a band of misguided zealots who died to the last man in the rebellion."

Bertrand tried again. "I am a colonel in the ALQ. Tell him, George!"

"He knows that, Théo. I can't help unless you co-operate."

"What do you want to know about my brigade?" Bertrand asked, beginning to explore the possibility of a compromise.

"Why, nothing, old boy." Forbes opened his notebook. "I mean, at this point, those details are hardly relevant to the larger scheme of things, now, are they? What I want from you is the big picture—at least as much of it as they'd tell a little fish like you."

"Go to hell. Shoot me if you dare."

"I will," Forbes answered coldly, "but last." There was a noise outside. "Ah, finally ready. Are your Guardsmen quite up to this, colonel?"

Sloerill shrugged. "They're all volunteers who lost friends in the attack, and we have a spare squad standing by. They'll be all right, sir."

They heard men march past and halt. "Tie them to the stakes. Look lively there," Drill-Sergeant Coutts growled. "We don't have all night." After a short pause he spoke again. "Stand clear. Prisoners ready, sir."

A new voice began issuing orders. "Firing squad ready—present—at your targets in front—" A wild scream of terror raised the back hair of the listeners. "One round." The voice shook slightly. "Fire!" Ten rifles exploded in a ragged volley.

Bertrand shot out of his chair. "Murderers!" he screamed, then regained control. "It was a trick. You did not shoot my men. You would never dare!"

Wearily Forbes waved a hand. "Let the silly man see, Corporal Weitz." He turned to Sloerill. "We get the same hysterical reaction in Ireland. Terrorists are full of it when they're planting bombs to kill women and children. Show a bit of fight or catch one of them, and suddenly the Geneva Convention's a document carved in stone for their express protection."

The scene Bertrand saw was garishly lit by truck headlights. Four blindfolded blood-spattered bodies were being cut from the posts. Each fell bonelessly to the ground and was dragged off, leaving smears of blood on the gravel.

Before the dead men were out of sight, four more were brought forward, fighting savagely as they were bound in place. One fainted, two fought silently and the fourth, a teenager, gave up the struggle and began to plead for his life.

On Forbes's signal, Bertrand was hauled back to the chair as the officer outside began his sequence of orders again. "Area clear. Firing squad ready—present—"

"Vive la victoire!" a prisoner screamed. "Vive—"

"Fire!" The rifles cracked again more nearly in unison. Bertrand jumped, then sagged in his chair.

"Théo," Sloerill intervened. "Answer the brigadier's questions and I'll stop this."

"Delay it, you mean," Forbes retorted. "I will delay executions until we hear what he has to say. If it isn't enough, I'll encourage him further."

Sloerill gave him a steady look. "My men obey my orders, sir. I understand the operational necessity General Thomas spoke of, but if Théo talks and I am satisfied he's telling all he knows, I will order the executions stopped. We can fight about which one of us is right later in Montreal."

Outside, a third group of prisoners was readied and a moment later the officer began the dreadful litany again. As another volley rattled the windows, Bertrand shook as if the bullets were ripping into his own body.

"I require the following information," Forbes said, studying his notes. "How widespread is this revolt? What is the name of the man or men leading it? Where is your main supply depot? Will you attack Mobile Command again? Will you attack Ottawa? What forces are in Montreal? What forces do you have in this area? Start by giving me that, and the executions will stop—at least until we double-check your story against what the survivors of the Mobile Command attack told us."

He leaned back in his chair. "I lost three good friends today. Don't look to me for mercy. You might give some thought to this too: your men, far from seeing you as a hero, think you're in here spilling your guts while they're getting shot."

Bertrand lunged forward, but Corporal Weitz slammed him back into the chair. Outside, four new ALQ prisoners faced a row of ten Guardsmen unbelievingly. They heard the commands, saw the rifles rise and aim, then came the volley.

On the command "aim" four men rose above the sandbag wall behind them, holding short padded clubs. On the command "fire" they bludgeoned the captives as bullets tore into the sandbags between them. Four Guardsmen in blood-stained uniforms dashed forward to smear a mixture of water and ketchup against the chests and faces of the unconscious men. Eight others dragged the limp bodies away.

Inside, Bertrand tried to bargain. "I don't know anything about a new attack on Mobile Command," he begged. "We expected it to succeed. There are no foreign troops. We are setting ourselves free—I need time to think—God! Let me think! You ask me to betray my people—my nation—myself!"

"Your nation is Canada," Forbes said icily. "You've already betrayed yourself, and you're betraying your men by letting them be shot while you dither. Yes, sergeant?"

Sergeant Green saluted from the door. "Sir, you wanted to know when Bolduc was up? He's in this next batch."

Forbes nodded. "Thank you, sergeant. You know him, I believe?" he asked the trembling Bertrand in a bored tone.

"My daughter's fiancé," Bertrand whispered. "Not him. Not him, I beg you. He is barely twenty."

"Old enough to die." Forbes strolled to the window. Four dead ALQ were bound to the posts, Bolduc at the far end. Fine wires and ropes held them erect, and makeup, reluctantly applied by a female clerk, looked sufficiently lifelike in the headlights. Blindfolds concealed the dead eyes. Under each tunic was a condom containing the ketchup and water mix. The stark scene looked grimly realistic.

He gestured. "Let the prisoner have a last look then."

Bertrand joined him at the window. "Paul!" he cried in anguish.

Casually Forbes backhanded him across the nose. "I said you could look, old boy, not hold communion with him."

As Bertrand saw the rifles come up to the aim he began to tremble. "Non!" he shouted. "It is a trick. You do not dare let me watch murder."

"Fire!" As the rifles jerked and the corpses shuddered under the impact of the bullets, the four men's chests flowered with bloody spouts. As Bolduc and another man fell sideways, their bonds partly shot away, one Guardsman dropped his rifle and spun aside vomiting.

Sergeant-Major Grigson materialized in full voice. "Fall out that man! Sir! With your permission I will change over the squad. Old firing squad, right turn! Quick march! New firing squad, to your duties, at the double!" The officer belatedly nodded his permission.

Sloerill led the sobbing Bertrand away. "Listen, Théo. If you talk, you can save the rest. It may mean my head, but I will stop this if you tell us everything."

Gasping, Bertrand nodded. "Anything, George—anything—but to you, please? I cannot talk to this murderer."

Forbes shrugged. "You can talk to a bloody post so long as you talk to good effect." He turned from the window as if reluctant to see the carnage end. "Major Markos. Stand down the firing squad but have them ready to resume on my command. I suggest you start taking the new bodies we're accumulating and scatter them around camp so we can photograph them in the places where they gallantly 'fell'."

Sloerill looked up. "Leo. Scatter the bodies, but the executions will resume only on *my* command." He shot a challenging look at Forbes.

They glared at each other. "Very well, Colonel, but you'd best prepare very convincing excuses for your actions. General Thomas will hear them tomorrow." He moved away as Sloerill took his place. Behind Bertrand, a clerk prepared to take notes. Outside, Major Markos stood the men down and called a Guardsman forward from between the two trucks, a video camera in hand.

Inside the building, Sloerill asked his first question. "Let's start with things we already have a lot of information on and can check. Describe your main supply base."

Weeping, Bertrand began to explain what was going on at Longue Pointe.

CHAPTER FIVE

Stating the Problem

After Bertrand's interrogation, Sloerill had the ALQ officer returned to solitary confinement and, finally knowing what was happening, sat down to make his plans.

First he rewrote his orders to Tom Bush. They wouldn't show the flag, they'd plant it. He added fifty men to the thirty Tom already had. Instead of touring, the men would drop off in three- and four-man detachments in small towns, a dozen in the larger centres of Cowansville and Knowlton.

Then he called an Orders Group. At 2030, his six senior officers gathered around a slivery six-foot folding table, the kind ubiquitous in every military camp. The faded green plywood walls were scratched and dented, but a few maps and embryonic organization charts were starting to make the room look like a military headquarters.

John Ashworth, Peter Forbes and Leo Markos sat along one side as a sort of inner circle. Next to Tom Bush opposite them was Pierre Coté, social soldier and real estate salesman in civilian life. Captain Dave Phillips, a broad-shouldered man with an almost classic Greek profile who was in charge of recruits, sat at the end opposite Sloerill. RSM Grigson had been excused to start the process of sorting out his NCO's.

Beside Ashworth's chair stood a two-foot metal cylinder with a hinged door on the side. Officially a container for a full dress ceremonial bearskin cap, it usually held the officers' after-hours camp liquor supply. Drinks in hand, they waited for the briefing. As Sloerill cleared his throat preparatory to starting, there was a rap at the door.

"Come!" he called.

Grigson stepped inside. "Just as I thought," he said, looking at the glasses disapprovingly. "Come on, step lively." Six Guardsmen followed him into the room. "I took the liberty of organizing some food for you gentlemen. The men have eaten and I assumed you'd want dinner here, sir." He turned to the Guardsmen standing awkwardly, steaming trays in hand.

"Well? You aren't going to eat the bloody stuff yourselves, you idle individuals! Set the plates on the table for the officers." The men scurried to obey as he stood by the door, erect, pace stick under his left arm exactly parallel to the ground, fingertips precisely one inch from its end. "God, what a crew! I'll shake the cobwebs out out of your tiny brains tomorrow. YOU!" His voice rose to a scream as one nervous recruit dropped a knife.

"Don't put that disgusting object on the table! Get another! Why do you think I made you bring spares? I did because I knew what silly, idle men you were. You! You with the spastic hand! What's your name?"

"S-S-Sutherland, s-sir," the boy stammered.

"It was your name. You've lost it. It's in the book. What's your number?" The Guardsman gave it, rigid with fear. "*That's* your name till tomorrow." He turned to Captain Phillips. "Yours, I believe, sir. Morning orders. Idle while on mess detail!"

The officers suffered the roaring impassively as the play unfolded. Phillips nodded. "Very well, Sergeant-Major. 0730."

The plates had been placed on the table, the silverware in a clump to the left of each plate. "God!" Grigson eyed the table with distaste. "If the food weren't getting cold, you'd go through the whole drill again. WELL?" The word was a near-scream. "What kind of military formation is that?"

The huddled men scurried into a jagged line facing him. "Not this way! Face the officers!" They turned. "Never turn your back on officers until you're trained, you idle people! You never know what they'll do!" He opened the door with his right hand.

"My apologies, gentlemen. Things will have improved by breakfast time, I assure you." He saluted.

"Mess detail, right turn! Right wheel! Quick march!" The parade-ground voice echoed in the small room. The door closed and the detail marched away, harried by a relentless "lef-right-lef-right-lef" in impossibly quick time.

"Jesus!" Bush sighed. "Give me the guns." He probed his stew suspiciously. "I mean, that private isn't really under arrest, is he?"

"Of course he is," Phillips confirmed.

"The theory is," George added, "that men should be more afraid of their NCO's than of the enemy because their NCO's can get them any time. The enemy can only be unpleasant occasionally. Also, if a man can't take some yelling without getting confused, what happens when he's being shot at? It's only a play, Tom. The men know it."

"And," Peter added mildly, "if you lack a sense of humour, why'd you join up?"

"Can't people abuse the rules?" Bush asked.

"If I hear about it, they'll yearn for a return to flogging," Sloerill promised grimly.

"But what's the charge? All he did was drop a knife."

"Idle," George and Peter chorused. George continued.

"It covers anything not done to Guards' standards. It covers dropped knives, dirty rifles and sloppy thinking—idle thinking, usually expressed in such terms as 'Your feeble, idle mind, temporarily attached to a Guardsman's body, had better get itself in gear.' The hyperbole prevents it from becoming sheer abuse."

Sloerill looked around. "Now, before I charge myself with being idle while commanding this force, to business." He checked his notes.

"First, instruct your men that there were no real executions. Show them our video. An order will be published tomorrow stating it was done on my express order and will never, I say again, never be repeated.

"Next, the order banning phone calls to relatives in Montreal remains in effect until tomorrow morning. This is important."

George looked up from the notes that summarized the interrogation. He didn't need them. Every word forced out of Théophile Bertrand stood out in his mind like the testimony of a rape victim.

"The revolt is province-wide. Revolt, not revolution. The rebels are l'Armée de la Libération de Québec, the ALQ, and that's what we call them, right?" The assenting nods came, reluctantly from Leo Markos, firmly from Pierre Coté.

"There are ten Montreal brigades, nine without Bertrand's bunch. They control bridges, airports, armouries, the works. Five more took over Quebec City. Some members of the National Assembly and senior civil servants have been 'detained'. One lightly armed brigade is up north to guard the power stations. Five are in Hull. Gaspé has four. ALQ units in the latter two locations are full strength. They expect a counter-attack.

"Granby and Sherbrooke have two brigades each. The Granby bunch is well placed to give us trouble, but not immediately. The same for Sherbrooke.

"St Jean has a big separatist population, but that brigade has to take over the army's French-language recruit training centre and Collège Militaire Royale. Bertrand didn't know what was going on there. My guess is, a lot of confusion.

"Two independent brigades of a hundred men each are assigned to cover the area from St Jean to Sherbrooke. They have seven border points to cover, plus the towns. They'll be busy. Altogether, the ALQ may number five thousand, two hundred of whom are an immediate danger. Another thousand may be able to hit us within a week."

George let them digest that for a moment, then his hands went out on the table and his head came up. "I don't intend to wait, we'll hit first. We gave them a good rap today, and a few more will keep them nervous until we get properly organized. Since Bertrand did not report the disaster here, I think we have until late tomorrow before they send anyone after us specifically.

"In about half an hour, Major Bush will lead a force of eighty Gunners and Guardsmen against the two local ALQ brigades. He will build local defences based on three or four of our men, plus police, firemen, game wardens and anyone else that wants to take a hand. These men will only have sporting rifles and some limited radio communications. The force isn't large but—"

"What an idiot I am!" Bush's involuntary cry cut George off.

"What's wrong, Tom?"

"The Royal Montreal Regiment! They put a detached company in Knowlton last year. What an idiot I am to forget them!"

"How many men? What level of training?" Sloerill snapped.

"I guess seventy or eighty. The company commander's Lieutenant—no, Captain Rothman. NCO's come from Montreal to train the men. They have five local corporals and three ex-regular force people."

"Couldn't be better, Tom. You'll command the whole force. Warn Rothman, and leave his phone number with a clerk. I'll talk to him after I finish here. The more rifles we can put into the defence, the better.

"Now," he returned to his orders. "Roving ALQ brigades can't hold ground, so they may hit towns, shoot up any resistance and terrify the people into submission. Tom will put a crimp in that operation. While he does, we'll hit the ALQ where it hurts, in their supply system."

"Can it be worse than ours?" Markos grumbled. "Longue Pointe put live ammo into boxes marked 'blank'. That's pushing stupidity."

"No, carelessness," Sloerill corrected him. "The government sent most of our military equipment to Longue Pointe for refit or repair. As a result our tanks, APC's, artillery, mortars, plus most of our ammunition stocks are in the hands of the ALQ."

"Dear God, we're naked," Tom Bush whispered. "We can't fight."

"We can and we will, but it gets worse. Longue Pointe also has the winter equipment, tents, uniforms, et cetera, as well as radios, engineer and artillery stores."

"Treachery!" Leo Markos exploded.

"Yes. Once the plan was approved, ALQ people in the Canadian Forces and the civil service used the approval to collect everything they could get their hands on. This revolt was planned to take place while the equipment was in Montreal. Bertrand said the date was fixed for next week but was pushed up. You got live ammo because they couldn't control everything at Longue Pointe, and it slipped through the cracks."

"But how could it happen?" Dave Phillips protested. "Isn't there anybody in charge up there? Didn't anyone see what was happening?"

"Dave, with a centralized system like ours, a very few people in the right places can do almost anything. Nobody's in a job long enough to take responsibility, and lines of authority are so fuzzy that anyone can assume a problem belongs to somebody else."

"You must have a plan or you wouldn't be so discouraging." The comment came from a cheerful-looking Peter Forbes.

"Major Forbes is a spoilsport," George sighed. "I have a plan. But there's one more bit of news to announce first."

"If it's as bad the rest, can't it wait?" Ashworth suggested, picking up a bit of Peter's optimism.

"It's good. The ALQ are Canadian-trained and while they'll have our ideas on centralized control, they lack the manpower to make it work. Also, they could only sneak out small arms for the brigades. They couldn't get the good stuff until Cyr's declaration this morning."

"They must be issuing equipment right now."

"No. They'll wait to see where it's needed. They expect the main threat to come from the RCR and Canadian Airborne in Ontario, so most of the heavy stuff will go to that theatre. If we become a thorn in their side they may divert some of it here, but that will take time."

Sloerill stood up, hands on hips, his head back. "We can hole up or we can finish the work we began this morning." The gravelly voice reinforced the confidence of his words. Even Forbes, who had seen it before, was caught up in the demand for action.

"The things we need to fight with are in Longue Pointe. Most of it's on trains, ready to roll out. The ALQ have done our work for us. We need that equipment, and I propose to take it! What we can't take, we'll burn!"

His confidence and bold plan lifted the officers, cheering, to their feet. Pierre Coté grabbed a bottle of brandy and splashed some into each glass. "Longue Pointe!" he yelled. The toast was bottoms up.

Sloerill put his glass down and shook his head. "No more of those or we'll set fire to things by breathing on them. Sit down, gentlemen. We still have work to do."

A sharp rap on the door cut through the elation, spoiling the effect. John Ashworth took a message from a clerk and handed it to George.

Sloerill scanned it quickly. "It's begun. An ALQ patrol entered Cowansville a half hour ago. The Gunners we sent with the wounded killed one and chased six more out of town. Are you ready to roll, Tom?"

Bush stood up. "You won't need us for this Montreal thing?"

"If you have spare drivers, yes, but your job has priority. If you can hold the lid on until tomorrow night, we'll be able to help you for a change."

"OK." Bush pulled on his parka. "Forward the guns. See you mudfeet later. I'll call Rothman and then I'm off."

Sloerill returned his attention to the remaining officers. "Orders at 2300. This is a Warning Order. I need a hundred strong men, people who can work hard and fast. I want QM staff who know Longue Pointe. I want drivers and I want fighters. I will command. Majors Markos and Forbes will remain in Farnham. Here!" he snapped as both men protested.

"Peter, you aren't even official. If we fail, I want my two best officers here to run the defence." He spoke so forcefully that both men sat back, accepting the inevitable.

"Leo." His tone moderated. "I don't know the men well now. You and Grigson pick them. Maximum one ten, minimum ninety. While you do that, I'll try to organize a train to take us in."

"A train?" Phillips asked in surprise. "We have trucks here."

"And they're staying here. We're bringing stuff out, not in. Dave, tomorrow I want training to start at 0600. Tom's recruits are coming tonight, and there'll be RMR as well. We may need them soon, but I want to get as much training under their belts as possible before they're tossed into the meat grinder. Concentrate on discipline and shooting." He sat back.

"That's the plan. Make sure your men get sleep. After my orders they'll be rehearsing damned hard." He handed a rolled paper to Ashworth.

"I found this map of Longue Pointe. Go over it with your QM people. Add estimated distances between buildings and especially between the railway line and the two gates. Make at least six copies. Questions?"

Each man met his stare and shook his head. "Right, then. Scoot. John, you stay. I have an extra job for you." Ashworth sat down again.

"Sir, may I have a word after?" Pierre Coté was hesitating unhappily at the door. Sloerill nodded and he left.

"John, I may be trying for too much, but this might pay off. Can you find about ten fluently bilingual Guardsmen to go with you to St Jean?"

"That isn't many men to capture a large city with."

"No." George grinned. "But enough to raid CMR.[1] There must be over two hundred cadets there. The loyal ones will be locked up, but the ALQ can't spare hordes of men to act as guards. Spring them if you can and bring them here—particularly instructional staff. They're about the best in Canada and we need them.

---

[1] Collège Militaire Royale, the French-language officer training college,

"Next," Sloerill said and hesitated. "If that goes well, think about the recruit centre by the airport. It's possible the whole class there are ALQ squeezing the last bit of free training out of the Canadian system, but some instructors and men may be loyal. What do you think?"

"I'll talk to Jerry Cantin. He was at CMR before he joined us. Dead keen. He and I can pick the men we'll need. I'd better start protecting some before they're dragooned into this Montreal thing." He started out.

"Send Pierre in, will you—and phone this fellow Rothman's house to see if Tom reached him. If he didn't, fill him in and crank him up."

A few minutes later, a troubled Captain Coté came in. "Sit down, Pierre," George invited. "If it makes it any easier, I know you're more worried about this revolt than most. Lay it out and let's see what happens."

"It isn't the revolt, sir. I decided which side I was on a long time ago. What bothers me is that my fellow officers don't trust me. Leo took away my company and ignored me during the fight. Peter Forbes has my men now, and they look at me as if I were some kind of separatist. John's overworked, but I didn't even get the clerks. I may ask for a transfer into a French-language unit."

Sloerill had been thinking about Coté. The one ability he'd shown was running parties. At regimental affairs he was everywhere, mixing people into new groups, breaking up conflicts, tending bar, drinking steadily but never losing control. Could those talents be put to military use?

"You're going to Montreal with me," Sloerill replied carefully. "My second-in-command. How does that suit you?"

Coté's smile was stiff. "I volunteer, of course, but it doesn't explain why I'm unemployed while everyone is busier than a one-armed fiddler."

"To be blunt, Pierre, your reputation is that of a 'social soldier'. I've never seen you exercise leadership in the field. For that matter, I've never seen you try to get a field command." George poured two small brandies and handed one to Coté. "Your being passed over today was habit. Jerry Cantin wasn't passed over. He's French. He's twenty-two, a radical age, but he proved himself. You have to do the same."

"How can I when you don't trust me?"

"You'll have your chance tomorrow—and Pierre, I just want a job done. Keep things on the rails, relay my orders and handle emergencies.

That's how you'll impress me, not running around with a gun in each hand, shooting people."

"You think I wouldn't do it?" Coté challenged. "You sent the other officers charging off with guns in their hands."

"No I didn't. Tom, Peter and Leo will be too busy running things to shoot anyone. Officers lead, men shoot. Mostly, when officers shoot, they aren't leading." Sloerill sipped his brandy. "The war will be hard on English Quebecers. It'll be twice as hard on men like you. There's a tendency to try too hard. It happens in all civil wars. It may happen this time but *it will not happen in the Guards!* Is that clear?"

"Yes, sir, but trust—"

"The men will trust you when they see you're looking out for them, protecting them, leading them. *They* might trust you faster if you shoot a few ALQ, but I won't."

"But I don't have any men to protect or lead."

"You will. Tomorrow is a test of obedience, leadership, initiative and all that. Do well, and Three Company's yours."

Coté nodded his head slowly. "I tried hard when I joined up, but I always felt a bit left out. I guess I'll have to start trying again."

"You can start by giving Leo Markos a hand with the selection process. Watch what he does and learn. He's a good man."

"Yes, sir. I'll get right on it."

"That's the second time you've done that."

"Done what, sir?"

"Said 'yes, sir'. When Guardsmen get an order, they obey it. The 'yes' is superfluous. It's a regimental quiff that I want to see back."

"So what does a Guardsman say when I ask if he's feeling OK?"

"You can get a positive 'sir!' or he can hang a question mark on it as an invitation to delve deeper. A while ago, Grigson replied 'sir' to three statements or questions. The first told me to be quick because he had a lot to do. The second implied that what I wanted was possible but not very bright. The third was almost mutinous—but all he'd said was 'sir'."

Sloerill grinned. "It's the mark of a Guardsmen, some individualism in a mass world, part of the Guards image. Once they have the image, they'll buy the whole package and try to be better than anyone else because they're Guardsmen. That's what makes the difference. Understand?"

"I'd better, sir. I've sold unserviced river-front lots that flood every spring. This looks like a snap."

George leaned back in his chair, suddenly aware of the jet-lag that had been dragging at him all day. His interior clock said it was after midnight. "Another thing, Pierre. Whatever we do, we must never forget that after it's over, we all have to come back together again, English and French. That fake execution today was an aberration. It will hurt us after the war, and I regret it already even though we had to do it."

Coté smiled. "We'll make it if enough people in Canada think the way you do."

"Don't bet on it. There's a lot of anti-Quebec sentiment out there, and it's only been held back by a desire to keep the country together. Now— I don't know. We'll have to wait and see."

Coté left feeling better, and Sloerill began to make notes on his raid until John Ashworth came in, a mug of coffee in each hand.

"I had a pot brought over. Want some?" George nodded. "This one's the syrup, mine's mostly coffee."

Sloerill knew that after Peter Forbes and Leo Markos, Ashworth was his best officer. He should be given a command but he was too badly needed at headquarters. "I thought you were selecting people for the raid?"

"I did that. How are we doing?"

"It's coming together. My friend Etienne Messier told me the government reinstated the Farnham–Montreal commuter train. I have a couple of people trying to find a volunteer train crew willing to take one into Montreal tomorrow morning."

Ashworth leaned back in his chair. "Well, now that you've seen us in action, how do we rate?"

"Not high," Sloerill said bluntly. "The NCO's aren't bad, but I've only seen about eight officers I'd want to rely on, and one is Gail Buckley."

Ashworth flushed. "I'd put the number at twelve."

"Convince me. What I did as CO seems to be down the drain. The men have the basics, but they're slack. There's no pride. Who did that?"

Ashworth shook his head. "Colonel Bosch ripped up the command structure and began inviting ensigns and men in for a chat without telling their company commanders. Officer morale is way down. Tell people too many times that they're incompetent and they start believing it.

"Actually you're lucky," John went on. "Last year we didn't have a single major. When Leo Markos arrived from Toronto things began to look up. He told Bosch that unless the unit got back into the field, he'd not only quit, he'd spread enough shit around to screw him. Bosch was near the end of a one-year extension and wanted a replacement so he could be promoted to headquarters. Rock and a hard place, so he gave in."

Sloerill digested the information silently for a moment. "At least I know what I'm up against. Now, when I'm in Montreal, I'll invite other unit CO's to join us at Longue Pointe with as many men as they can scrape together. The camp may get a bit crowded, so QM better be ready for it.

"Also, tell junior officers that they're Guardsmen and soldiers in that order and they'd better shape up. This will be a Guards regiment again."

That stung Ashworth. "I think we are right now, sir."

"No, we aren't. A few hundred men with a common cap badge are no more a regiment than a man with five hundred acres of rock and fifty dry cows is a farmer. We need a regiment, John, and fast."

"Speaking of fast, will we get some help from Ottawa? The RCR are in Petawawa, and they have the Van Doos in Valcartier, not to mention the Airborne. Surely someone can give us a hand."

"Don't count on any of them. The RCR and the Airborne will protect Ottawa. The Van Doos will probably cease to exist. Their separatists will join the ALQ, the federalists will try to get out of Quebec and most of them will head for home and keep their head down. The same is true for the Gunners and tankers up there—poor bastards."

"We're on our own then?"

"If we work on that premise, any help that does arrive will be a pleasant surprise. Another question. What's your opinion of Dave Phillips?"

"Hardest worker in the regiment. Give him a job and he won't stop until he has every detail tied down tight. Not terribly regimental. Doesn't play mess games. Dislikes and ignores regimental quiffs."

"The work part is fine. Speak to him about the regimental part. His attitude isn't new. Either he changes it or I'll put him in an administrative job. That way it won't matter whether he's regimental or not."

"Don't we need everyone who can walk and chew gum at the same time? Right now I'd settle for somebody who can do even one of those relatively well."

"We have to train people before the Green Machine screws us up. Come on, John. If a hockey team is winning, everyone calls it 'team spirit' and cheers. Say 'regimental esprit', and people's eyes roll up and their minds go blank. Believe me, you don't have a hockey team or a regiment until you have spirit. The difference is, in an army men die if you fail."

Sloerill grinned suddenly. "You know, the phones work. I could pick one up right now and tell Ottawa what's happening. I won't, because I want them off my neck until we get organized.

"They'd take my raid, set up a task force to study the tactics and another to look at the legality. Next a computer would find that ten of our best men had never been in Maritime Command and post them away. Screw it. Once we're done, we'll tell the whole world. Until then NDHQ can sweat."

"It sounds as if we're fighting Ottawa, not the ALQ."

"We've enemies on both sides, John; but war may prove that unification is basically stupid. If we can show what real regiments can do, things may change."

"Won't they just pour in enough men to overwhelm our system?"

"Pour? They may drip, and we'll absorb them as they come in."

"I hope we can hang in long enough to absorb somebody. With you and Tom Bush taking the best men away from here, things will be a bit thin if the ALQ decide to get feisty."

"Leo and Peter can handle it. We'll beat anyone they send after us. They can't overwhelm us with numbers, and man for man we're better."

"Yes, well, looks like gung ho time. We *will* notify Ottawa at some point, won't we? I mean, we aren't planning to surprise them by taking the whole province back by ourselves?"

Sloerill laughed. "We'll call when I get back from Longue Pointe with all the shiny toys they lost." He put his beret squarely on his head and shaped the felt lovingly around the grenade cap badge.

"Orders at 2300, all officers, even if they aren't involved. Now, as the spray can said to the mosquito, I'm off."

Ashworth winced. "The Sergeant-Major complained that you hadn't make a bad joke all day, so things must be worse than you let on. This will make him feel better."

Grinning, Sloerill left to arrange his train.

CHAPTER SIX

Longue Pointe

A hundred and six men waited in five groups by the railway tracks near the camp. Behind them, faintly gleaming as the waning moon sank into the bank of clouds in the west, was a four-car train, windows cross-hatched with masking tape to prevent flying glass and blacked out with blankets. On the roof of the front and rear cars a four by six-foot wooden platform, hastily built by regimental handymen and stacked with sandbags, supported a 30-calibre machine gun.

The men waited for the officers, who were with Colonel Sloerill. Weapons slung, pockets bulging with grenades and spare magazines, they clinked softly as they shuffled mukluk-clad feet in the frozen grass. Each man wore a white nylon camouflage suit; American radio stations were calling for snow. Around their left upper arms they wore dark brassards of green-dyed sheeting as identifying marks.

"They ran my ass off for two hours. It's three AM. I'm cold and my feet hurt. How do I get out of this chicken-shit outfit?" a Guardsman complained to the world in general.

A short, hard-faced corporal, acne scars hidden under dark slashes of camouflage paint, rounded on the man sharply. "You get out when we carry you out, Wisebraugh," Corporal Weitz growled. Then he spotted a group of men approaching through the night. The leader's massive shoulders identified him as Colonel Sloerill.

"Dummy up, you re-tards, it's the colonel." The men fell silent. A figure by the front of the train, tramped forward to intercept. "Sir. One hundred and six men present. Train prepared. Civvy crews on board and ready—sir."

"Very well, sergeant-major." Sloerill turned to the six men behind him. "To your posts, gentlemen."

Pierre Coté stayed with Sloerill. Wayne Jones and Sam Armstrong went to their platoons, the raid's fighting men near the train engine on George's right. Jim Fox mingled with his drivers. Sergeant Green, the regular force NCO, hunkered down like an Indian with the men who would bring the trains out of Montreal. RQMS [1] Klybniaw Spitzak joined the cluster of storesmen, Gunners and Guardsmen on the left who knew where the stores in Longue Pointe were located.

Sloerill lifted his voice over the muffled sound of the idling engine. "Move in, I want to see you and I don't want to shout." The groups contracted as the lines curled inwards.

"Men, this may be the most important operation you'll ever be on. Yesterday was survival, and we taught the ALQ to respect Guardsmen and Gunners. Now we'll show them something else. We're the only ones who can do it, partly because of where we are, mostly because of *who* we are."

He paused for emphasis. "We will not allow the ALQ to steal every modern bit of equipment in Canada. Your taxes and mine paid for it, we'll get it back or burn it."

He paused again to keep the men with him. "We're going to surprise them. Roads into the city are guarded. Railway bridges aren't—the ALQ don't have the manpower—so we'll get in easily. We'll hit at dawn, and we'll be gone before they know what's happening. We aren't looking for a fight, but we'll give them a damned hard one if they insist."

Time to lighten the mood. "Even Guards and Gunners appreciate help sometimes, and we don't want to hog all the glory, do we?" The men smiled uncertainly. "Once the base is secure and the trains are moving, I'll invite other units to join our party. They'll be handy with the work, and with a bit of luck we can leave Montreal with four or five hundred more men than we went in with."

---

[1] Regimental Quartermaster Sergeant

That made them feel better. A hundred men weren't enough to take on a whole army. "In addition, Major Markos will have people start calling your parents, wives and girl friends about ten AM. They'll be invited to join us, and we will find accommodation for them, I promise."

The men's cheer was fiercely snarled down by the NCO's, but that and the half-hidden smiles told George that he'd removed a major worry.

"Now, you know your jobs and I know you'll do them. My headquarters will be where the main camp road crosses the tracks. Captain Coté is in charge there. Sar'nt Green's party will bring the trains out. Sergeant-Major Grigson is in overall command, so once they roll, they're ours— unless you think someone in the ALQ has the nerve to tell the sergeant-major he can't do something he's been ordered to do."

The sergeants joined in the laughter. "Right. Lieutenants Jones and Armstrong will secure the camp and gates with their men. Mr Jones on the north side, Mr Armstrong on the south."

Jones waved in acknowledgement. Armstrong, always the clown, bowed. "Have no fear when Three Platoon is near." His slightly nasal voice croaked slightly as he tried to force it below his usual tenor.

"With the base in our hands, RQMS Spitzak and crew will locate and load the stores we need and can take with us. They will also prepare the buildings for burning. We can't take everything we find but we won't leave much behind.

"Once Mr Fox finds some trucks, everyone will help load them up until they creak. That's the plan. Minimum fighting. This is a raid, not a war. Don't be afraid to ask questions or make suggestions on the way in. Finally, I'll remind you it took the Israelis a week to mount the raid on Entebbe. We're moving a lot faster."

He waved airily. "All right, get on board. Smoking allowed, snoring restricted, and don't worry, it *will* snow."

The men boarded swiftly. Some Guardsmen swarmed up the ladders to the roof to man the machine guns, pulling woollen masks down over their faces. Sloerill heard an oily clatter as guns were loaded and cocked and the soft clinking of ammunition belts being checked to ensure they would run freely.

"Sir. St Jean Commando reporting."

George ran a professional eye over Ashworth's men and nodded.

"Good. You're in the last car. Sam has the seating plan. We'll let you off in town. All organized?"

"Jerry Cantin thinks we'll get at least a hundred cadets, and most of them have cars. We'll drive back rather than wait for the train. Considering the situation, even officer cadets may be useful."

"*More* trouble?"

"In spades. Major Bush called. Small fights everywhere. His men are arriving about three minutes ahead of the ALQ. If the schedule changes, we'll have a rough night."

"Get back fast then. Form cadets into platoons with their instructors in charge of them. Load up and good luck, John."

"Same to you, sir." Ashworth's group moved off, leaving Sloerill alone with Sergeant-Major Grigson.

"What about the train horn, sar'nt-major? Engineers like to sound off at every opportunity."

Grigson looked impassively smug. "We clipped the terminals when we masked the lights, sir."

"Great minds think alike, sar'nt-major. Fortunately, so do yours and mine. After you." They mounted the steps into the lead cab.

"All ready, Mr. Harmon," George said to the engineer. "Let's highball—or whatever it is you railroad types do." The engineer automatically pressed his air horn as the train slid forward. The silence was broken only by his annoyed grunt and Grigson's chuckle.

The ALQ, prompted by an urgent political order, had tried to arrest Armand Chantilly Saturday night. All day such orders had been draining away desperately needed manpower, and the four men who could be spared for the job had no chance against the dozen Gunners who were guarding the house.

Chantilly realized he needed a new base. He chose the armoury that his Gunners shared with the Hussars on Côte des Neiges at the western edge of Mount Royal Park.

The armoury was guarded but he had keys. Once it was his again Chantilly went to his office, sat down at his familiar desk and began to issue orders. Call the men. Issue weapons. Load trucks. Limber up guns. In another office, Pierre St Pierre began to gather his Fusiliers. Captain Levesque called militia Van Doos; Majors Pepin and Dupras of the Régiment de Maisonneuve phoned their men. The Royal Montreal Regiment was leaderless, but someone reached a sergeant who promised to do what he could. The Black Watch were ready, and Colonel Berkowitz's Highlanders began arriving within half an hour of Chantilly's call. Their CO wasn't with them; he was raiding his armoury to save the regimental treasures.

Chantilly's intention had been to escape into Ontario. A patrol soon reported that every road to the south and west was guarded and blocked with traffic. As more and more men trickled into the armoury, many carrying hunting rifles, he tried to work out a new plan.

"What do you suggest, Pierre? We can't fight. We can't get away. But we have men here who trusted us to save them."

"We wait, mon ami," St Pierre replied. "Things may change at dawn. I am sure the ALQ are not ten feet tall. If necessary, the men can leave individually and join us later. But," his face twisted in a grimace, "I do not want to leave Quebec, Armand. I did not become a soldier to defend Ontario. It is my *home* these bastards are stealing from me."

After dropping Ashworth's men in St Jean, Sloerill's train had crept across a railway bridge into Montreal, hidden and muffled by thick flakes of the season's first snowstorm. The scratch CPR crew checked signals and opened switches, working their way to the western edge of Base Longue Pointe, where they stopped half an hour before sunrise.

Twenty-three men got off the train, and four of them began to patrol ahead. At the railroad gate they used bolt-cutters to cut the lock chain. Corporal Weitz moved forward, returned and pressed the talk switch on his radio twice, then twice again. The four clicks he broadcast would mean nothing to an uninformed listener.

To Sergeant Green it meant that he was needed. He led the other nineteen men to the gate and met the scouts.

"Guard post a hundred metres ahead. Only one guy, but he's awake," Weitz reported in a low voice.

Green spread his men out to watch for other guards and began to advance down the track, an SMG slung carelessly over his left shoulder. In his right hand, hidden behind his leg, he held a long hunting knife. He moved openly towards the guard post.

"Qui va là?" The low challenge slowed him, and he turned towards a figure standing beside a rough fort made of railway ties. "Bon," he approved. "Et maintenant, la cosigne."

According to Bertrand, the Sunday password was the challenge "je me souviens" to be answered by "un Québec libre". Green gripped his knife hard. As the colonel had said, passwords were easy to lie about.

The guard was at ease, calmed by Green's open, slow approach, but his rifle was still ready. "Je me souviens," he challenged properly.

Me too, Green thought. "Un Québec libre." To his relief, the man relaxed. Green pulled a thermos from his jacket pocket. "Café?" he asked, moving still closer.

"Ah, merci." The sentry propped his rifle against the improvised fort, reached out and hesitated. Green's face was unfamiliar. Too late.

The Sergeant pivoted, his right hand sweeping up to drive the heavy knife into the guard, slicing under the ribs and into the heart. The man grunted, collapsed across Green's shoulder and fell to the snow.

Cautiously Green looked behind the wall. The man had been alone.

"What now, Sarge?" Corporal Lavoie had arrived and was staring at the doubled-up dead ALQ soldier in the same uniform he wore.

Green waved three men forward to continue scouting down the track. His mouth tasted sour and he could still feel the grate of steel on bone as the blade went in.

"What do you mean, what's next?" he hissed savagely. "We find the train, saddle up and get the hell out of here as fast as we can. Get back to your section and—"

There was a rush of feet behind them and both men spun, weapons coming up. Green heard the click of Lavoie's safety catch.

"The train's just ahead," a breathless Guardsman reported excitedly as he dashed up to them.

Green's voice shook. "Robillard, you come running up like that again, you'll get shot. Get back on point." The man trotted off, startled and scared.

"Lavoie. Why was your weapon on safe? That can get you killed. When I said be ready to fight, I meant *ready,* not whenever you found your fuckin' safety catch. See me when we get back. Now move out."

The patrol advanced cautiously until they saw the train engines, and Green identified the sound he'd been hearing for several minutes: the diesels were running. He signalled that the trains had been found with two fast clicks on his radio, followed by three more.

As his men gathered around, he gave his orders. "Lynch, take your men left. Lavoie, between trains. Weitz and I and the rest go right. No shooting. There'll be guards. Go slow. Check everywhere, train cabs, under the wheels, open boxcars. Watch the roof line too. From now on, talk French. If you're challenged, remember the password. It works. Stay cool. Get close. Got it?" The men nodded. "Go."

They moved off, feet squeaking in the fresh snow, camouflage suits barely visible against the snow-plastered boxcar sides. Green stopped at the first tank.

The steel monster loomed nine feet above the flatcar, the long 105mm gun locked into a bracket over the engine. A 50-calibre machine gun, wrapped in canvas, drooped from a mount on the turret. Green nodded at Corporal Weitz.

"Byrd, Thomas, check 'em out," Weitz ordered in French. "Bang your rifle on the hull and I'll feed it to you."

The patrol continued past a string of eight tanks. Then came a boxcar with the door open and a light inside. Green sent two men past the door in a crouch, then looked in. Six ALQ were huddled around a stove and a coffee pot.

"Bon," he said sarcastically. "Aucune garde, aucune cosigne, mais beaucoup de café. Avez-vous froid, mes braves soldats d'été?"

The men lunged for weapons, then relaxed as the solitary figure in the door did not move.

"Sois raisonnable," one protested. "Il est cinq heures du matin. Il n'y a pas d'ennemi ici."

One man, keener than the others put his hand on a propped-up rifle. "Je me souviens?"

Green applauded softly. "Enfin! Bon. Un Québec libre." He smiled as the men relaxed. "Ou sont les autres?"

The man who had challenged, blinked. "Les autres? Nous sommes tous ici—ah—ah."

As the barrel of Green's SMG appeared in the door, two men

flanking him stepped into view, rifles ready. Green levered himself up and collected the ALQ weapons.

"Blake, Robillard, guard these clowns," Weitz ordered as Green jumped down. "No talk. They face the wall, kneeling on their hands. Anyone moves, belt 'em."

They continued down the line of boxcars to another line of four tanks and a string of APC's,[2] six more boxcars and, just before the caboose, four armoured cars. Corporals Lynch and Lavoie were waiting for them. "All clear?" Green asked and got two nods. "Did the other train have tanks and APC's too?"

"Yeah, Sarge."

"See if they're gassed and if they're carrying ammo." The corporals sent off four men as Green signalled that the trains were secure with three evenly spaced clicks.

"Lynch, you and Weitz put men on the train. Lavoie, stay with me. Anyone who knows machine guns, put them in a tank turret. Make sure you can move from one end of the train to the other. Go."

Green and Lavoie doubled back to the engines in time to see the civilian crews climb on board. Sloerill and Grigson were waiting.

"How many tanks, Sar'nt Green?" Sloerill demanded.

Green had forgotten to ask Lynch for a count of the other train, but he'd seen twelve and the other train was longer. "Thirty, thirty-two, sir."

Sloerill nodded. The figures sounded right. Canada had bought one hundred and thirty-eight German tanks in 1976. Forty-three were in Canada, but only about thirty-five were fighting tanks.

"Get rolling, sar'nt-major. I want you on the South Shore by full dawn. If you get trapped, destroy the armour. You have the demolitions?"

Grigson nodded. "No problem sir, this train's off the ALQ inventory as of now."

The train crews from Farnham climbed on board and the first train moved ten minutes later, creaking as the dead weight hit the engines. The crash of freight car couplings echoed like muted thunder despite the engineer's attempts to take up the slack gently.

"Wayne."

---

[2] Armoured Personnel Carriers

Jones trotted forward. "Sir?"

"You and Sam move now. The noise may alert people. Secure the gates, then check the barracks for ALQ. Look for prisoners. Somebody must have been loyal." As Jones sprinted off into the snow, Jim Fox came forward.

"Find the vehicle compound and get jeeps and trucks. Did you bring enough sugar to immobilize those we have to leave?" George asked over the sound of the train grunting and straining past them.

"Enough even for you, sir. A hundred two-kilo bags and a hundred kilos in reserve."

"Since we don't know how many trucks we can save, put a bag in each cab so all we'll have to do is pour it in the gas tank. Better start."

As Fox jogged away Pierre Coté arrived, started to salute, then remembered not to. "Our train's on the siding at the fence." The supply train was slowly picking up speed. Guardsmen in the tanks waved at those who were staying behind. Sloerill saw Corporal Weitz leap between two flat-cars, stagger, grab a tank tread for balance and toss a package up to the man in the turret.

The demolition kit was a grenade to be taped onto a shell, pin loosened with a cord tied to it. Five seconds after a soldier pulled the cord, the grenade would explode the shell, blowing the tank in Corporal Weitz's elegant phrase "to rat shit".

Laurin touched Sloerill's arm. "BINGO NORTH, sir."

The codeword signaled the capture of the main gate by Wayne Jones. "Anything else?" There were other codewords to indicate trouble, problems or casualties. Laurin shook his head.

The caboose of the first train creaked past, and the second was already moving on a track that joined the main line by the gate. Its engineer had taken up the slack between car couplings under cover of the first train's movements, so the process had not been heard. Dimly through the snow Sloerill saw men settling in behind the tank machine guns, uncovering and swinging them from side to side to ensure they were free to fire.

"BINGO SOUTH, sir."

"Good. Pierre, move our train up once the track's free. I haven't been here in years, and I want to look around. Once work starts, use your cell phone to start calling unit CO's. Try armouries to see who answers. Get on the radio if you need me, and remember the key word is speed. We pull out at 1000 hours, no matter what we're missing."

"All aboard, sir." Corporal Zukrowski skidded up in an open jeep. Laurin climbed in back, and Sloerill took the right-hand seat. "To the south gate, Zuke, then across to Hochelaga Street."

The jeep shot off, spraying snow and fishtailing slightly. "Hold it down. I hope most of the ALQ are still asleep. Don't wake 'em up." The jeep slowed to twenty kilometres per hour.

Sam Armstrong was holding six ALQ prisoners. George made a few suggestions for defence and left for the main gate. After crossing the tracks, they met a group of about fifty men walking up the road. The jeep stopped beside the head of the straggling column.

"Who are you?" Sloerill asked the nearest man, a major.

"Camp staff, sir. We were prisoners in the officers' mess until some men burst in and rescued us. A Guards lieutenant told us to head this way to meet a Colonel Sloerill. Is that you?" George nodded. "I am Major André Taschereau, sir."

Another officer pushed forward angrily. "That damned pip-squeak was giving orders like a goddam general. I want him arrested. The son of a bitch threatened to shoot me in the leg!"

Sloerill saw the four gold bars of a full colonel, his own rank, and a name tag "Bennet". "Base Commander?" he asked. The man nodded, but before he could speak again, Sloerill spoke again, his voice icy. "Lieutenant Jones told you that this was a rescue mission? He told you that we're here to recover equipment you let fall into rebel hands?"

Bennet had listened impatiently; now he exploded. "Nobody has authority to do anything!" he shouted. "So far as I know, you're no better than that gang that shot their way in yesterday. Now I'm going to go to my office and phone Ottawa."

Sloerill pulled his 9mm pistol and cocked it. "Since you object to threats by junior officers, Bennet, here's one from me. You're under open arrest. You will work under Captain Coté. If you resist or even go *near* a telephone I will shoot you, and not in the leg. Clear?"

Bennet paled as the bore of the pistol fastened unwaveringly on a point between his eyes. He looked up and met the flat stare of the man holding the weapon and for the first time realised that this officer meant exactly what he'd said. He would shoot without regret, levelling a barrier on the path he had decided to take.

"I was only following regulations!" he cried, his hands rising in front of his face as if to catch any bullet fired at him.

"Forget regulations, these are orders. We're at war. Do you understand that?"

Bennet licked his lips. "Yes, sir."

Sloerill's pistol disappeared in a single move. "Major Taschereau, you are in charge of these men—including Colonel Bennet. Captain Coté is just ahead. Report to him. I'll appreciate any help you can give us in locating stores we can carry off or burn. You can leave when we do. Are you with me?"

"All the way, sir." Sloerill returned his salute and swung into his already rolling jeep. The crowd of base personnel began to move again. looking a bit more disciplined, their morale lifted by clear orders and a look at the man who was giving them.

At the Hochelaga Street gate Wayne Jones met them, his normally serious face looking delighted. "All secure, sir. I took ten prisoners here, six in the officers' mess and twenty-two in that barrack over there. The bastards were asleep." Wayne pointed south. "There's also a chopper on the sports field—a Voyageur, no less, and the pilot's in the mess with about fifteen others. A few have minor wounds."

"Why aren't the unwounded with the base staff work party?"

"These are fighting troops sir, not like the paper pushers I sent to Coté. We've got Princess Pats on their way to Cyprus, and several Gunners and tank types just back from NATO."

"We can use them. Any idea how many ALQ are here?"

"About fifty, plus or minus a few. They had twice that many yesterday, but half of them got pulled out last night."

"OK, we have forty-four prisoners. There may be up to a dozen loose. Warn Pierre and stay alert. I'll go talk to the gang in the mess."

The gang were in the bar to the left of the front door when George arrived. He introduced himself and gave an abbreviated version of what was happening. They took the news with professional calm. Four were Infantry, two officers and two sergeants from the PPCLI. An Armoured Corps major and five corporals represented the Royal Canadian Dragoons, and a captain, a sergeant and three men were Gunners. A sergeant and a helicopter pilot, his arm in a sling, stood at the back of the group.

"Captain Porter?" Sloerill read the name from the tag all Canadian soldiers wore because officers were often not in a unit long enough to learn men's names or the men, theirs. "Are the Pats willing to join us?"

The young man grinned. "Hey, Cyprus just doesn't cut it compared to this, sir. Do we get neat little grenade cap badges like yours?"

"What's wrong with your own badge?"

"I only got it last week. I'm really RCR. I've been rebadged so often that I check the mirror every morning to make sure I have the right hat on. The Pats needed a captain in Cyprus, and my name came up."

"OK, report to Captain Coté by the tracks. He'll give you a job." He turned to the RCD's. [3] "Major René, report to Coté too. Tell him I told you to find armoured cars. We're going to need as many as we can get to protect the outbound convoys when we leave. Take the Gunners. They're always useful."

As the soldiers left, George turned to the helicopter pilot. "Will that bird out there fly?"

"Yessir." The pilot shifted his wounded arm. "Andrew Bryce, sir, and Sergeant Fodakis. If they didn't sabotage her we can go, but I hope you don't want to go too far. I'm low on juice."

"Can you manage sixty clicks?"

"Twice that, sir."

"Good. Check the bird and report to Pierre Coté, then move her up to the tracks for a getaway."

He was interrupted by a burst of shooting, mixed SMG's and rifles. He left the mess on the run, sprinting to his jeep where Laurin was hunched over the radio. "Well?" he demanded.

"Pas sûr, Monsieur. Some of Lieutenant Jones's men were fired at. They returned . . . un instant . . . four dead ALQ, two wounded . . . four running towards the tracks . . . . You can listen on this, sir."

Sloerill grabbed the extra earphone.

"One, this is two, roger my report of four ALQ your direction?" he heard Wayne Jones ask.

---

[3] Royal Canadian Dragoons (Armoured Corps)

"Two, roger that. We'll intercept, but they're yours until they cross the tracks. Roger-dodger, pip pip and out."

Sloerill gave an involuntary bark of laughter at the exaggerated takeoff of Brit radio proceedure, but he was pleased. Coté had defined areas of responsibility perfectly. He would be all right. He climbed into the jeep and unholstered his pistol. "OK, Zuke. Let's go to work."

Under a curfew the ALQ hadn't enough men to enforce, men and women from every Montreal regiment had trickled into the big armoury on Côte de Nieges all night. Armand Chantilly sat in his office, a phone in his hand, staring at Pierre St Pierre across the desk.

A half hour ago the phone had rung and on the rationale "What have we got to lose?" Chantilly had answered it. Once he identified the caller as Pierre Coté and had St Pierre confirm it, he had cautiously admitted that the ALQ were not in control. For his part, Coté revealed that he was not alone in Montreal and asked them to hold the line while he brought in Colonel Sloerill, his force commander.

When Sloerill came on, both St Pierre and Chantilly remembered his voice from three years ago—almost positively. Knowing that the phones could be tapped, they spoke in circumlocutions. Chantilly listened to Sloerill's terse account of activities, filling in the blanks as best he could. At the suggestion they join forces, he nodded. "It is the only option that we have, but how can we set a recognition signal over what may be an open phone line?"

As Sloerill spoke, Chantilly first made notes, then smiled. "Ah. I had forgotten that. Yes . . . it is quite clear. A bientôt." He hung up.

"What is the signal?" St Pierre demanded.

"About six years ago, Sloerill and I attended a briefing given by a Major Bacque. After he hit the area commander with his pointer—twice— I gave him the name Slapshot and it stuck. That's our recognition signal, SLAPSHOT."

"It sounds good, Armand. So why do you still look worried?"

"It may be a trap or a ruse to lure us out of here."

"I do not think so. The man *was* Sloerill. It *was* Coté—"

"That may be it. Coté knows more of vintages than tactics. I would rather hear from their Major Markos, despite his Ontario French."

"Do we have a choice, Armand? We can't really fight here either." Chantilly sighed softly, then made up his mind. "Eh bien, we go. What is the best route into Longue Pointe?"

St Pierre had moved to the large wall map of Montreal. "Over the mountain, east on Jean Talon and down Langelier direct to the main gate on Hochelaga Street."

"We don't have enough trucks for all the men." Chantilly checked his figures with a pocket calculator. "Private cars?"

"Yes." St Pierre knew the figures too. "But we can cram fifty men into a deuce-and-a-half. Three one-tonners and some jeeps must do traffic control and fight if necessary. Three men per jeep, an infantry section per one-tonner. No tarps. The lead vehicle flies the ALQ flag they had on the armoury." He shook his head. "Colonel Berkowitz should command. Over two hundred of his men are here. I have barely a hundred."

"Unless he arrives soon, we will be gone," Chantilly said grimly. "Raids to recover relics from an armoury are best left to younger men. You command—and remember, eight trucks will be towing my guns."

"Can't you get more at Longue Pointe? Towing will slow us."

"Guns are my colours, and I do not surrender them. Now, you organize the convoys. I will find a volunteer to remain in Montreal to contact more men. There must be hundreds of ex-militia around. We must be quick. The clock is ticking."

"By now they will have missed those they sent to arrest you last night. Sloerill's raid will stir them up even more. Our parade through the city may be costly, Armand."

"As you said, our alternative is to surrender, and we did not call our men in to do that. Many will fight even if we do not. We cannot abandon them, Pierre. We will fight for our homes—and theirs."

"You are right. Plan to leave at 0715." He glanced at his watch. "In one hour—and two days' work to do first. Ah well."

Lieutenant O'Brian, the artillery officer scouting ahead of Chantilly's convoy, was relieved to find Wayne Jones at the main gate guard post. They had taken officer training together and were both military and social friends. Wayne sent the codeword "SLAPSHOT" to indicate the patrol's arrival, then began to answer Kevin's questions.

"Hold on, Kev. Isn't your gang coming down Langelier?"

Kevin looked. "That's them. What's the matter?"

Wayne was looking west through the thinning snow at an approaching military convoy. A Quebec flag with a flaming sword fluttered on the lead vehicle. "Shit! Heads up, Sar'nt Luft," he told his platoon sergeant, "we have the ALQ in our face—or maybe not." He struggled into a captured ALQ sergeant's tunic. Like the Americans, the ALQ wore their stripes upside down.

"We may be OK, Kev. If they were turning in they'd be slowing down."

"I'll try to hold my gang back," O'Brian said, starting out.

"Too late, sir." Sergeant Luft saw the first jeeps of the artillery convoy approach the intersection from the north. They had the green light.

"Kev, lead your guys down the road to your left and outta sight. If you have to yell, yell in French. I'll stop that ALQ bunch. Luft? Tell our men to stay cool." Jones started out, running. "Wave to the ALQ going by. Don't ask the bastards in for tea, just look friendly!"

He dashed onto Hochelaga Street as Chantilly's convoy reached the lights a hundred feet ahead of the ALQ who now had the green. Wayne planted himself directly in front of the east-bound convoy, imperiously holding up his hand. The lead vehicle, after starting to accelerate, braked and skidded in the fresh snow. The bumper was a scant two metres from Jones when it finally stopped.

"Laisse-moi passer!" The driver roared, half out of his cab. "Il y a deux cent gars qui attendent ces véhicules!"

The artillery convoy was now crossing Hochelaga Street behind Jones. "Et il y a un autre convoi pour Longue Pointe qui a la priorité. Reste là," he ordered.

The ALQ driver began to get down onto the road. Wayne stopped him with a wave of his SMG. "Je me souviens?" he challenged.

"Un Québec libre," the man replied automatically, standing on the running board, watching the convoy charge through the gate. "Quelle brigade?" he asked, pointing to the trucks crammed with men, many in civilian clothes.

"Des renforts, pas une brigade," Wayne answered, looking to see how many of Chantilly's trucks remained. The civilian cars he could see might be the tail end. "C'est une priorité de les équipper pour aider dans la contrôle des réfugiés. C'est sérieux."

The ALQ driver nodded. He knew every situation was serious, but although he could see nothing wrong he continued to stare.

As the last car cleared the intersection, Wayne turned on the driver angrily. "Vous avez dit que vous êtes pressés?" he demanded harshly. "Pourquoi tu n'as pas commencé à avancer?" A notebook appeared in his hand. "Ton nom? Ta brigade?"

The driver scrambled back into the cab. "J'avance, j'avance," he called, clashing gears as he started to move forward. Jones kept his eyes on the driver as he put the notebook away, almost regretfully.

"A la prochaine fois!" he called warningly as the truck went past. He stood on the road staring at each driver as if making notes for a report. He waited until the convoy was a full block away before strolling back to his now applauding men.

Sloerill and Zuke were loading stores when Laurin gave Sloerill the SLAPSHOT message. They shoved four boxed Carl Gustav anti-tank weapons into a truck and headed for the main gate.

Passing the incoming convoy, Sloerill saw trucks gratifyingly crammed with men, but many lacked rifles, even uniforms. A jeep stopped ahead on his side of the road. Two men got out and began to approach.

The one on the right reminded George of Etienne, especially in the easy, athletic way he moved. Only the unruly red hair looked odd. He remembered St Pierre as the FMR training officer six years ago. A good man, impatient of delay and red tape. His contributions at training conferences had always been incisive and useful.

George knew St Pierre's companion better. He had a bias towards Gunners from his early militia days under Corporal Tom Bush, but Chantilly had always impressed him as being a superior soldier even by Gunner standards.

Both men were rich and influential. St Pierre was a lawyer; Chantilly had a seat on the Montreal Stock Exchange. Both were well connected politically. On the phone Sloerill had made suggestions. Now he had to give orders, and as he moved forward, he wondered if they would accept his unsubstantiated authority.

Chantilly and St Pierre had recognized Sloerill. Even if they had not, the air of command around his stocky figure was unmistakable. They habitually moved among powerful men and recognized their own kind.

"I remember that this one does not like people to stand too close," Chantilly whispered to his friend. "There is a wall."

"I remember, but I am in no doubt as to who commands here."

They stopped and saluted. Sloerill returned the salute; then he let the wall down and stepped forward to shake hands.

"Enough formality, we have too much to do. I can't believe how fast you reacted and how many men you brought. Do you have a nominal roll by regiment?" He spoke in the fluent French he'd picked up on the streets of Cowansville and in various hockey arenas. "What's the total? Five hundred?"

"More," St Pierre reported, not needing his notes. "Within a few either way, the Black Watch have two hundred and forty. My FMR number one hundred and three. Thirty-one Van Doos, twenty-six RMR and twenty-two R de Mais make up the infantry. We also have ninety-seven Gunners and eight guns, fifty-two Hussars, thirty Engineers, ten from the Communications Squadron, and about thirty service and medical troops."

"Awesome," Sloerill said warmly. "I'd hoped for two hundred, you've brought me six. Now, report to Captain Coté. Have your men draw rifles and ammo. Uniforms can wait. Coté will divide your people into loading parties and send them where they're needed. Your Hussars go to Major René, reg force Dragoon type who's cranking up armoured cars to protect convoys. No matter what, we depart at 1000 hours—sooner if we're attacked in force. What's your assessment of the situation out there?"

"Confused," Chantilly admitted. "We saw two ALQ patrols but they ignored us. I suspect they have too many jobs for too few people to go looking for trouble. All bridges out of Montreal are closed but jammed with cars waiting for the curfew to lift. How do we get through that?"

Sloerill checked his watch. "It is now 0811. My orders for breakout will be given at the tracks at 0830, but I plan to leave via the inbound lanes of the Boucherville Tunnel. It will be guarded but not heavily. In the meantime, everybody works till they drop. What we can't save we'll burn, a good job for the Engineers. Questions?"

"None that can't wait until 0830," Chantilly replied.

As he and St Pierre started away, George followed them. "Have you heard from Colonel Bosch and Colonel Berkowitz?"

"Colonel Berkowitz decided to raid his armoury. He will be along later." St Pierre answered the easy question.

Chantilly looked embarrassed. "I tried to call Bosch. He wasn't home and the ALQ are at his armoury. They tried to arrest me last night. Perhaps they were successful with him. That must explain it."

At 0950 Sloerill was at the railway crossing. Loaded trucks were double-parked on roads leading to the south gate. A few were still being loaded. The commuter train sat chuffing twenty metres behind Zuke's jeep. Two hundred and ninety men were crammed on board, the roof-mounted machine guns fully manned. The Voyageur helicopter waited in a cleared space near the tracks, its rotors turning slowly, rear loading ramp down. His officers gathered around him.

"Your convoys ready?" he asked. Chantilly nodded. "You are in overall command. Move five minutes after the commuter train departs. SITREP, Colonel St Pierre?"

"I allocated fifty men to clear the tunnel. With the password, my Fusiliers can capture the ALQ guards, not kill them. Two formed infantry platoons are assigned to each of the three convoys. I go with the one which takes the longer northern route. It is the most dangerous. We also have spare vehicles to block the tunnel after we pass."

"Thank you. Major René?"

The short officer shrugged. "I assigned four Grizzly's[4] and four armed jeeps per convoy. With good infantry fore and aft we should be able to handle most problems."

Sloerill shook hands with each man. "Go for it. There'll be rough spots but I know you'll overcome them. Good luck. Captain Coté? Why is that train still here?"

"Because Jim Fox asked permission to raid our armoury with two NCO's and I said I'd ask you. Secondly, the train is waiting for you."

"No, I'm with the rearguard." He thought for a moment. Would Fox have a chance? Was it worth it from a morale point of view?

---

[4] A wheeled armoured car

Coté was ahead of him. "We scrounged civvies for them and an old panel truck that was down here. The men want it to happen, sir."

"OK, they go. And I want you gone—now."

Coté sprinted for the train that was already moving as he reached the rear steps. Five minutes later a fake ALQ patrol left the south gate, and two minutes after that long snakes of trucks began to unwind from the streets to follow the advance party. In the still and now silent air, Sloerill could hear the muffled thumps as demolitions squads ignited gasoline bombs in the loaded warehouses.

"Shall I screw up this baby's motor?" Zuke asked, juggling a two-kilo bag of sugar in his left hand.

Sloerill nodded absently. Zuke poured the sugar into the gas tank and they waited until the engine choked and quit. Sloerill began walking back and forth, peering into the snow as if expecting some new force to materialize out of it. Finally he stopped. "Feel lonesome, Zuke?"

"Not with that chopper there. When do we haul ass?"

"Soon." The train had been gone forty minutes, the tail end of the last convoy, almost ten. He turned to Laurin. "Tell them to start thinning out at the gates. Pull demolition teams—" A burst of machine gun fire from the main gate interrupted him. "One, SITREP," he demanded. Jones didn't have machine guns.

"One, SITREP. Gate lost. Estimate figures one, zero, zero attackers . . . taking up . . . line parade square." Jones was obviously running and talking. "Over."

"One, hold parade square for now. Out. Two, SITREP."

"Two, all quiet here." Sam Armstrong reported from the south gate.

"Two, move to my location now, with demolition parties. Out."

Sloerill heard heavy firing, rifles and at least two machine guns, punctuated by the sharp cough of grenades. From the south ten Engineers straggled towards the helicopter, their uniforms singed and black from the fires. Behind them came Sam's men. George waved them into the helicopter. Sam left two men outside to help others on board and placed four riflemen at the ramp to support the retreat of Wayne's men.

From the billowing smoke of the burning buildings ahead six more Engineers came running into view. Sloerill grabbed a corporal. "Have you got all your men?"

"Yessir," the man slurred, wiping his shrapnel-torn cheek with his sleeve. "I mean I sure as hell hope so, sir."

"Get them into the chopper, Zuke. Well to the front. Give us room." Zuke led the men off and Sloerill turned to watch the thickening smoke in front of him. Now he could see a few tongues of flame in the black coils. "One, break off now," he ordered.

Almost at once ten men, bending low, dashed out of the smoke and took up fire positions along the track. "Are they holding?" Sloerill asked.

Sergeant Luft shook his head, his eyes checking the sprawled men and the curtain of smoke ahead. "No way, sir. They're over us like paint. They—Bernier! Target left! Two hundred metres!" A Guardsman swung and fired at two running figures down the track. Two more rifles joined him and the targets were tumbled into the grimy snow. Incoming fire began to rake the line of Guardsmen. "Where's Jones?" Sloerill demanded.

"Coming, sir," Luft answered. "Cormier! Baker! Watch to your right!"

Bullets were striking the abandoned jeep and ringing against the rails. Just as Sloerill decided he could only wait one more minute, five figures broke through the smoke and ran for the helicopter that was now clear of the ground. Four men ran on. Wayne flopped down beside Sloerill and emptied his SMG into the smoke.

"Sar'nt Luft. All men change mags, fire automatic until empty then fuck off."

The men obeyed and the level of fire rose. "This is all that's left?" Sloerill asked.

"Sir." Down the rail line, as each man's rifle emptied, he dashed for the helicopter. Four sprawled men did not move. Wayne had reloaded his SMG and began to run backwards, firing as he went. He and Sloerill reached the slippery steel ramp as the helicopter surged forward and Jones almost lost his grip as Bryce fed full power to the twin rotors.

The men braced by the ramp door began to fire at groups of ALQ running out of the smoke. As their weapons emptied, loaded rifles were handed to them as the helicopter clawed for enough height to clear the blazing warehouse ahead. They flew into the thick smoke, becoming invisible to the men firing at them from below, and Bryce turned sharply right to get out of the line of fire.

Sloerill picked his way to the cockpit past his exhausted and wounded men. Wayne Jones, his face black with smoke and gashed by a bullet, was swearing with unusual fluency as he cut away a man's pantleg to get at a thigh wound. The bullet-smashed headset of his radio dangled from the shoulder strap of his tunic. Sloerill clapped him on the shoulder as he passed. It was too noisy to talk.

In front, he put on a helmet and opened the intercom. "Any damage?" The helicopter was skimming trees and buildings as it zigzagged across the city. Behind them, a hundred plumes of smoke rose into the morning air from the burning warehouses.

Bryce's hands and eyes were busy as he coaxed the overloaded bird higher over the river. "We took a few hits, nothing serious. By the way, where's this Farnham?"

"Straight east and a bit right." Sloerill took the vacant co-pilot seat. His hands were shaking and he forced them between his thighs to conceal it. They'd pulled it off, somehow. Everyone had contributed to a near-unbelievable success.

To his left a stream of trucks and guns was emerging from the inbound lane of the Boucherville tunnel, and he wondered how long St Pierre's roadblocks would delay the ALQ pursuit.

"Can we swing a bit south to check on the commuter train?"

Bryce pointed to a gauge. "Only if you want this baby stuck in camp."

Reluctantly, George decided he could live without the information. He'd done the best he could with what he had. "Home, James," he instructed, took off the helmet and went back to help Sam and Wayne with the wounded.

CHAPTER SEVEN

The Van Doos

The helicopter landed beside the bullet-riddled drill hall in Camp Farnham. As Sloerill got out, Peter Forbes and Leo Markos met him. He leaned against the helicopter while Zuke went to find him a jeep and his officers reported.

"Ashworth brought back a hundred and sixty-three officer cadets, fifty-two instructors and forty-three recruits from St Jean," Forbes told him. "Most of them are guarding towns now."

"We have fights everywhere," Markos added. "My reserve is ten men." He watched the two small platoons leaving the helicopter. "I need those bodies."

"What about the fights? Who's winning?"

Peter shrugged. "Depends. I'd rate the ALQ about even with the Argies in the Falklands. If we're under cover, mostly we win. In the open they do. Tom Bush found a neat strategy. We set up ambushes near signs with English names or words on them. If the ALQ try to rip them down, we shoot them. Works well."

"What towns do we control?" George asked Markos.

"The Farnham–Cowansville–Bedford triangle is pretty solid. Adamsville, Foster and Knowlton are ours now, but we lost them before and may again. Sutton is OK. We had Bromont but they took it back. The roads are a shooting gallery."

Andrew Bryce had been listening from his cockpit. "If I can make the US base at Plattsburgh, and if they'll let a combatant fly out again, I can ferry men around in this."

"Can you pay for a load of avgas, Bryce?"

The pilot waved a small plastic card. "No sweat, colonel. Fly now, pay later."

"Do it. We need you ASAP."

Bryce checked that everyone was clear. The engines coughed and began to whine. The rotors swung lazily, then with a heavy, lifting beat. The downblast rattled small stones off the side of a truck as the helicopter hoisted itself into the air and heeled off to the south-west.

Sloerill had seen the two supply trains from Longue Pointe on a siding in town as they flew in. "Who's guarding the trains?"

"Sergeant Green unlimbered the tank guns." Peter laughed. "Nobody there knows how to shoot them, but they look warlike as hell."

The three men went to Markos's command post on the drill hall roof. It had to be on the highest building in camp to give extra range to the radios. As it was he could only talk through a fragile relay system that broke down every time a set was moved.

The snow had stopped, and the officers paced through the slush on the flat roof, listening to reports as they came in. Sloerill and Forbes shook their heads at the poor radio discipline and confused messages.

Canadian casualties mounted to fifteen dead and twenty-three wounded. The ALQ were losing men faster, thanks to Tom Bush's tactic: twenty-one dead, twelve reported wounded and seventeen prisoners. The number of towns with citizen defence forces was growing, and they were causing more ALQ casualties.

Heads came up at the blast of a train diesel horn. The commuter train had stopped across the road from the main gate, its metal sides ripped by bullets, windows shattered. The bodies of four Guardsmen lay sprawled across the torn sandbags of the machine gun nest on the first car. Pierre Coté unloaded his men and brought them into camp on the run. There were twenty-six fewer than the two hundred and ninety that had left Montreal.

"We had to fight our way across the river at St Jean. I formed this crowd into ten platoons. They're a bit of a salad, but they're ready to go and they've been shot at."

Sloerill looked at the mixed group of officers behind Pierre—
three Black Watch, one Van Doo, one Régiment de Maisonneuve, one FMR
and four Guards. "Welcome, gentlemen. You know the overall problem.
Here's our situation. We control most towns, the ALQ mostly control the
roads. You will put an end to that. Starting in the southwest, we will seal
off every inbound road, prevent ALQ reinforcements from arriving, then
eliminate the ALQ trapped inside our net. You're the net.

"Once your men have weapons and uniforms, we'll shut out the
ALQ from Pike River north to the Autoroute and east to Magog. Lake
Memphremagog is our right flank. I want a tight line Pike River–Autoroute–Bromont. We're not alone. Three convoys are coming with five
hundred men. Captain Coté, report to Ashworth. He has some roadblocks
out now. Don't worry about mixed units, we'll sort things out later."

"Sir." As Coté led his troops away, Grigson and his sergeants
weeded out the weaponless or civvy-clad men as they went past and took
them to QM.

As the first road-blocking platoon left camp, one Longue Pointe
convoy arrived. Twenty minutes later the second rolled in, and an hour later
the one led by Colonel St Pierre, the men standing in the trucks and cheering.

"I came in by Bromont," St Pierre reported to Sloerill, his face half
concealed by a bandage. He'd been hit by grenade fragments in an attack
on the City Hall. "The ALQ had it. They don't now. I took seventeen casualties but they paid more. I left a platoon of my FMR and an armoured car
to hold it. They will."

His key roadblocks placed, Sloerill began to take apart the crude
groupings he'd thrown together from the men available. Often five regiments were represented in one platoon. He began to build what might in
time become a brigade.

First he unscrambled the Guardsmen. He gave 1 Company to Leo
Markos. Peter Forbes had 2 Company, and Coté got the untrained 3 Company.[1] John Ashworth commanded Headquarters Company.

St Pierre had all the French-speaking Montreal infantry and the
bilingual RMR from Knowlton. His Fusiliers formed A Company. B Company consisted of a big Van Doo platoon, a small platoon of R de Mais and

---

[1] Guards companies are designated by numbers instead of letters

a third of the Regular Force recruits and staff from St Jean. C Company consisted of two RMR platoons. He also had nearly a hundred officer cadets, most of whom were manning road-blocks.

With no need for artillery and little ammunition for the guns he had, Armand Chantilly organized his Gunners into fighting teams to be deployed quickly to threatened areas. Tom Bush's men guided the Mont-realers and put them in contact with the growing network of lightly armed self-defence units he was organizing in the towns.

Maarten Pieters, an over-age Armoured Corps Lieutenant Colo-nel from Longue Pointe, was in charge of all armoured forces. It was a mixed bag of regular Dragoons, militia Hussars and a dozen infantrymen who could use machine-guns.

Jan Berkowitz arrived in mid-afternoon, driving a loaded panel truck, to take over his Highlanders. Behind him he trailed a convoy of thirty-two cars picked up while waiting in traffic at the Champlain Bridge. They were full of refugees, mostly of military age, whom he'd recruited under the noses of the ALQ.

His truck was crammed with concealed treasures. His regimental colours were behind wall panels. Mess silver rattled in the gas tank. A ram's-head snuff box (a present from the Guards) made the trip ignomin-iously wrapped in plastic at the bottom of a barrel of used engine oil. Pipes that had played at Waterloo were under the floorboards along with several venerable claymores. He wore the ancient leather air bag for the pipes on his back, taped under three sweaters to give his athletic body a humped look that discouraged any idea that he was a soldier. He had also brought the wives and children of six of his men, all of them concealing more loot.

His two hundred and sixty-six men cheered as he entered the drill hall led by a piper and brandishing a claymore. He quickly took charge, putting his best-trained men into two small A and B companies, and sending C Company for training. He gave A Company to Major Feldman, his lone field officer. B and C Companies went to captains, and he chose a regular force major from Longue Pointe as his second-in-command.

The last good news of the day came when Andrew Bryce returned with his helicopter refuelled and bringing the news that the Americans were friendly. With him came three ten-man Huey helicopters. Two had been at Mobile Command; the third had been on its way to Montreal from Ontario when the pilot heard about the war and volunteered to join in. The four helicopters could move sixty men to any part of the defence.

The area was too big to hold without help. As the new formations worked to become teams, Sloerill gave a report to a wounded Gunner officer to take to Ottawa via Plattsburgh. With it he sent the videotapes showing prisoners admitting they'd struck before independence and one of the actual attack.

Sloerill had called his O Group for 2300. In the past 72 hours he'd flown the Atlantic, attended a long dinner party, fought two battles and organized the defence of an area some thirty by fifty kilometres on nine hours' sleep. When his officers arrived he was snoring.

St Pierre smiled. "I doubt if he could tell us much tonight, and he has earned a rest." He looked at Ashworth. "Where?"

"There's a room down the hall with a bed. This way, sir."

St Pierre and Chantilly picked up Sloerill's chair and followed John out. In the hall by the door they met Corporal Zukrowski, squatting against the wall: an old soldier resting when he could.

"What's up with the old man?" Zuke asked Ashworth, slinging his SMG as he joined the parade of men carrying Colonel Sloerill.

"I can think of a dozen things wrong with that question, starting with the omission of 'sir' and the fact that a Guards colonel is not 'the old man', and I feel that one of us ought to have saluted somewhere. Forget it. Stay with him. When he starts to wake up, call me and make him tea. Steep the mug for about a cigarette, dump in six heaping spoons of sugar and put it in his hand. Can you handle that, corporal?"

"Sure." Zuke nodded. "I've done that for him lots o' times . . . sir."

On Sunday afternoon as Sloerill's convoys rolled into Farnham, a mixed civilian-military convoy arrived at the Citadel in Quebec City. The local ALQ commander had been demanding all day that the soldiers inside open the gates and haul down the only Canadian flag that still flew over the city. His demands had been refused.

The convoy, escorted by armed jeeps and Lynx armoured cars, had left the confusion at Camp Valcartier to carry the men, wives and children of the Royal 22ième Regiment, the Van Doos, to the Citadel. The regiment was coming home to die.

The Colonel of The Regiment had watched the declaration of independence in full dress uniform, his gold lace and glittering medals a sign of order amid growing chaos. Around him sat the Régie, ex-officers who looked after Van Doo interests outside the military, found jobs for ex-soldiers, administered a private welfare fund and used their influence to obtain promotion for certain officers or hold back those that the regiment considered unsuitable candidates for higher command.

After Cyr's speech, separatist and federalist soldiers had begun to fight, but not the Van Doos. They had sealed off their lines. The men inside that self-made island of tranquility were no different from those rioting, but the regimental determination to maintain order in a disintegrating world held them steady. Independence for Quebec had come, but for the Van Doo family it would come with dignity.

The Regimental Colonel spoke to the men company by company, with their families. "You have but three choices: Quebec. Canada. Home. Decide."

"A secret vote!" several soldiers demanded.

"The choice is too important to hide," the colonel ruled. "As Van Doos we stand and say what we believe."

Everyone voted: men, women, and children over sixteen. They knew what their votes meant. Those opting for independence would form the Brigade Royale in the ALQ. Neutrals could depart in civilian clothes. Those choosing Canada would be escorted to the New Brunswick border.

The one serious dispute centred on a site for the final parade. Lieutenant Colonel Frappier of the 3rd battalion (a separatist) wanted to "clear the rabble" and hold it in Valcartier. Lieutenant Colonel Fortin, 2nd battalion (a federalist), opted for the Citadel. The Colonel decided.

"The Citadel is our home, our sacred heart. We will parade there if we have to fight both armies."

On Sunday at noon the regiment came together on the small parade square within the walls of the old city. No weapons were carried. The battalions made solid blocks of green: the 2nd Battalion on the right, the 3rd on the left, the regimental colours cased in black oilcloth between them. The officers carrying the colours were Canadian. Their armed escort was ALQ. Providing one spot of colour, the royal goat-mascot Baptiste stood haughtily behind the colour party, brushed coat gleaming white, his keeper Goat-Major Seguin, beside him resplendent in full-dress scarlet. The wives and families of the men stood in two well separated groups against the fortress wall, the Canadian group nearest the main gate.

"Royal Vingt-deuxième Régiment! . . . Gaaaarde à . . .vous!" Nine hundred and sixty gleaming boots lifted and crashed down as the regiment came to attention before their Regimental Colonel. On the ramparts thirty heavily armed men ignored the command. Their job was to keep the regiment undisturbed until it had completed its business.

As senior serving officer, Frappier made the regimental report. "Monsieur! Mille trois soldats présents. Huit soldats font la garde du terrain. Trente soldats aux remparts. Aucuns malades."

There were no speeches, everything had been said. The need now was to disperse the regiment with the dignity befitting its traditions.

"Royal Vingt-deuxième Régiment!" The Colonel did not shout but his voice carried to the back rows and the men stiffened slightly. "Les Drapeaux. A moi. Par la droite. Marche!"

The colour party stepped out twenty-one paces to the beat of a drum and halted. There was no tradition to cover this, no drill to be learned.

"Régiment! A genoux!" The men dropped to one knee in a ripple of green, and as the muffled drums beat, the colours were marched down the ranks for the last time and into the regimental church.

"Gaaaarde à . . . vous!" The men rose and stood at attention again.

The next piece of regimental business concerned Baptiste. The original goat had been presented to the regiment after World War II by King George VI and replaced as necessary by the royal family.

Goat-Major Seguin tugged at the lead and moved up with Baptiste to stand in front of the Colonel. Two officers from the Canadian contingent stepped forward and halted behind the mascot. The Colonel touched the lovely animal on the silken hair between the polished horns. Thirty-five years ago he had been goat-major.

"Adieu, mon ami." The goat tossed his head at the unaccustomed familiarity. The Colonel nodded to the escort and the party marched off. The entire regiment had contributed to the cost of flying three men and the goat to England to be returned to the Queen.

It was nearly over. The Colonel, his voice so low that the green ranks rippled forward to hear, made his final remarks.

"To those who stay, I charge you to keep this place in honour. If your endeavour fails, I command you to surrender this fortress to any French-speaking regiment that demands it. Enough blood has been spilled. No more is needed to consecrate this soil."

The Colonel paused until the ranks stirred slightly. "I place one last charge upon you. Do not fight with bitterness. There is enough hatred and division in this land without . . . without . . ." When he realized that he could not regain control of his voice, he looked up and nodded blindly.

Colonels Frappier and Fortin turned smartly. The commands rang out and the regiment turned from line into column. The officers moved to the head of their men and they marched past one last time to the regimental march, "Vive la Canadienne". As each company swung by, saluting, the colonel returned the salutes, his face wet.

The lines snaked around the square; then, on the brittle October grass, the regiment ceased to be. Of the one thousand and three men in the citadel, three hundred and eighty-four had chosen the ALQ. Two hundred and ninety-seven stayed with Canada. Three hundred and seventy were simply going home.

The men loyal to Canada marched straight to the main gate and the waiting trucks, their families following quickly, eyes averted from those who were staying. After a symbolic coming-together behind Colonel Frappier, a platoon of ALQ prepared to escort their estranged Canadian brothers to New Brunswick. The largest group went to the barracks for their civilian clothes. Each man had a discharge paper signed by Colonel Frappier.

The Colonel of The Regiment waited until the last man disappeared, then turned away. His driver opened the car door and saluted.

"You should go too, Jean-Luc. I can drive a car twenty miles."

The driver pointed to an armed escort behind them. "We are told, monsieur, that you are to be arrested for not supporting independence. We of the Brigade Royale decided to guard you until the government understands that the parole you gave us is good."

The Colonel was driven away. He had joined this regiment at eighteen and now it was gone. He had served Canada around the world, policing many divided countries. Now Canada was divided and at war. He could not fight against Quebec. He would not break his oath and fight against Canada.

At the flagstaff on the Citadel ramparts an officer waited. The moment the Colonel's car disappeared from sight, he rapped out a sharp order, and the last scarlet and white Canadian maple leaf flag flying in independent Quebec began to descend the flagpole.

By Sunday night, thanks mainly to CNN, the world knew of the uprising. In the capitals of Europe, Africa, South America and Asia, the news spread like a timber crown fire. For years poverty-stricken nations had torn themselves apart with civil wars. Now Canada, one of the world's richest democracies, was falling. No nation was safe if Canada could break apart. Quebec delegations sent out to win diplomatic recognition were held off until governments decided if Canada faced revolt or revolution. Most adopted a soft wait-and-see position well short of official recognition. Some watched for the British, French and American reaction. All tried to find out what Canada's official position would be. If Canada accepted Quebec's departure, recognition would be almost automatic. If not, there would be no UN seat for Quebec. Recognizing a breakaway province in one country might encourage those in other nations to try and there would be chaos. After the breakup of the USSR nobody wanted that.

Around the world Quebec delegations sat in hotels and waited. In some they were honoured guests. In Commonwealth countries they were ignored. In a few they were followed by large men with conspicuous bulges in their jackets whose presence prevented people from speaking to the Quebecers.

In the United States the question of recognition posed immense problems for the White House. The president was engaged in the toughest election in thirty years. War in Canada could cripple his sputtering campaign, which was based on a peace dividend.

Having been warned on Saturday by his Security Adviser (who had a memo from an NSA[2] task force set up to monitor the situation), the President had authorized NEARPAC to co-ordinate intelligence flow to the Operations Co-ordinating Board. Next he asked his Special Assistant on Foreign Affairs, John Melling, to chair an emergency meeting.

---

[2] National Security Agency

The meeting had begun at noon Sunday, but despite NEARPAC's detailed damage assessments and communication intercepts, nothing like a recommendation Melling could take to his boss had surfaced.

"I trust you're aware there's an election next month?" He broke into an acrimonious debate between the CIA and the Secret Service. His midwestern voice, tempered at Choate and Harvard, showed an edge. "Need I remind you that the President will be campaigning in Vermont and New Hampshire next week? Can anyone tell me if that's safe?"

"I'm aware of it." The Secret Service chief was unintimidated by Melling. "I repeat, it should be cancelled. The area is full of former French-Canadians—some not so former—who came down within the last year. My people are assessing their reaction to Quebec's move now, and we're trying to check their reaction to the administration's policy towards Canada. It would really help if the administration *had* a policy."

"How can we, Jack?" the CIA Director interrupted. "The *Canadians* haven't got one yet, and it's their damned country!"

"Yeah, well, any way you cut it, we have an economics–security problem going. Vermont and New Hampshire are afraid they'll lose the cross-border shopping. There's a newspaper campaign in favour of Quebec independence in the form of articles on how well Quebec will do. And there's speculation on Canada's maritime provinces joining the USA, solving our fishing problems on the east coast. It's all well financed, and I hope the CIA has some information on that that we can use."

"The pro-independence money is offshore," the Director admitted, sitting up very straight. The table was big. He was short, and for some reason his special chair with the built-up seat wasn't there. "It's a French operation called La Rochelle. The penetration of their security was a combined British–Israeli–German–American effort. We're still evaluating the available data."

"May we hope to have a preliminary analysis before your experts torture the last shade of meaning from each word?" Melling asked softly.

"La Rochelle was mounted in 1988 when separation sentiment began mounting again in Quebec. It provides money. Its officers brief visiting Quebec officials on Canadian intelligence matters. They plant articles in foreign periodicals and in general try to speed up what has been snail-like progress. NEARPAC suggests that French agents but not DGSE itself helped plan the unilateral independence option. Most of this has come to us post-facto, and with an election on, it's stuff we should have had."

"We could have used a warning too," growled the general representing Military Intelligence. " MILSECUR isn't involved in those areas."

"We have two problems, really," the Secretary of State intervened. His normal diplomatic voice, lacking its customary lubricant of bourbon, rasped as if he'd been talking all day.

"Only two?" the CIA Director asked neutrally. While many considered the Secretary to be an alcoholic, those who were more astute knew that he often reliably expressed the President's thinking—often before the President knew those thoughts himself.

"First, the diplomatic problem. This isn't analogous to the Baltic States. Quebec was never independent, or subject to tyranny. How do we treat their application to join the UN? How do we deal with France if they sponsor Quebec? Finally, what international signals do we send?

"Secondly," the Secretary leaned forward, steepling his fingers, "we have a situation in Canada, good neighbour and occasional nuisance, that caught us short. Congress will come after us on it—not to mention the opposition candidate, who needs a good international issue to boost his domestic programme. If we aren't careful, he's got it."

"Quebec killed four American officers at Mobile Command," the general reminded the Secretary tartly. "If that isn't enough to justify an intervention, perhaps the bomb attack on your diplomat might light a fire under the striped-pants set."

"It's not a case of lighting fires," Melling soothed. "There's been too much of that already. That's why we're here. We must be sure we're lighting fires under the right tailbones. For that we rely on the CIA." The flattering admission was tainted by delicate reluctance. The acerbic CIA Director wasn't popular around this table.

"I have a few *constructive* suggestions," the Director said sharply. "I assume we will not come down definitively on either side today, so we have time. First, I want funds to reposition a spy satellite for voice intercept and near-real-time photo capability.

"Second, I want permission to start a full penetration operation. Until the situation clarifies, it has to be based on American soil. As a first priority, I want to insert agents in that proposed Canadian corridor area so that if we adopt the full Canada option we can organize a counter-revolutionary front for our government to support."

"Then send the army in as advisers?" the general asked slyly.

"I'll have some advice for the military in a moment," the Director replied with a smile. He had two suggestions, but one was anatomically impossible, even for a general. "Before that, I have an interesting bit of intelligence. Mossad was tracking several large arms shipments that didn't seem to be going anywhere; five ships effectively loitering around the Atlantic. Three days ago one headed for Montreal. On Saturday morning the others began to follow. There's a lot of stuff on those ships. Can this group give guidance on whether we notify Canada or not?

"Now, I suggest using First Army to seal the Quebec–US border, officially to control refugees flooding into Vermont and upper New York. At the same time, our ambassador to France can explain the Monroe Doctrine again and tell them that any French fingers we catch in the pie will get cut off. As a bonus, putting ten thousand eager young GI's into border communities will make up for losing Canadian shoppers."

The Secretary of State nodded reluctantly. "Your tilt towards Canada may be too strong. The President wants to take the position that he's concerned about Canadian and American lives and concerned about Free Trade. And while he prefers as already stated a unified Canada, it would be a pity if precipitate action by either side jeopardized UN efforts to resolve this dispute without more bloodshed. I also want him to call a special session of the Security Council."

"When?" Melling asked, pen poised over a notebook.

"Probably Tuesday," the Secretary replied, looking judicious. "There is after all no danger of this spreading, and nuclear weapons are not involved. Let's give them a few days to work out their own problems."

Melling shuffled his papers together. "I'll take this to the Man. Bear in mind, we're fighting for American votes, not a united Canada or a separate Quebec. Whichever side we support will pay in trade concessions and energy, and while I don't want to choose between Quebec Hydro and Canadian gas before what looks like a hard winter, we must also consider a growing need for water in California, a key state. Only Canada can supply it—the scenario of Canada joining us *with* its water is not on the table at this time." He cut off the expected proposal from State. "The President is not interested in adding twenty million new voters, all of whom will demand medicare.

"Now, I will approve or deny any covert operations at our next meeting, which will be at seven AM tomorrow, but start setting it up anyway. I believe the answer will be affirmative. General, crank up the First Army move. I think that adding spending power to three key states without its looking like a bribe will fly well." Melling closed his folder and put everything away in a slim attache case.

"Oh, Allan," he tipped a frosty smile toward the CIA Director, "your people might investigate a rumour I heard to the effect that a counter-revolutionary force already exists in southern Quebec and has carried out an interesting operation. Good day, gentlemen."

As the meeting broke up, the CIA and Secret Service Directors found themselves walking away together. "Rumours?" the Secret Service man asked sympathetically.

"Like hell. He must have had it in a bag ready to let out. I'd better have chapter and verse by tomorrow morning."

"If we hear anything, I'll call. Coffee?"

"No, I have to get back. Despite the fact I won't 'know' until tomorrow, we're reading a guy in for the Quebec job now, and we have to factor in the new development."

"Anybody I know?"

"I doubt it. He's been in counter-terror for three years, but that's getting dull. His cover will be light colonel, Special Forces. If the tilt stays towards Canada and if Canadian forces are operating in Quebec, especially with ad hoc formations, Clay Anderson is tailor-made for them."

"A specialist?" The men were standing by their cars now.

"Hell, no. Specialists are a dime a dozen. They tell me that this guy can do anything you ask. I intend to test that claim. See you tomorrow."

While American spooks met in Washington, the Canadian government was trying to devise a policy to unify the country and stay in power. The full cabinet met, forty-seven ministers in all. Every suggestion that pleased the Quebecers angered the rest and vice versa. The Prime Minister finally ended the debate by bringing in the Chief of Defence Staff to give a military assessment.

Pittman brought General Vinet to the briefing. They both had the necessary figures, but only an army man like Vinet had enough authority to calm a panicky cabinet. It was a risky move. The Prime Minister could replace him with Vinet, a loyal Quebecer *and* French Canadian; but the alternative was to risk looking bad because he didn't have the answers. Having Vinet around was safer—if only the bastard didn't look so *military*. Unlike Pittman in his greens, Vinet wore a beautifully tailored khaki summer army uniform though the order for winter greens had gone out weeks ago. Vinet was soft on unification and had to be gotten rid of quickly.

"Prime Minister, members of cabinet," Pittman began. "In a few moments General Vinet will give a complete briefing on the land situation. I asked for this because as a land element soldier and retired CDS he has a greater grasp of the fine details that I have not had a chance to familiarize myself with in my three weeks on the job.

"In brief, there is good news and bad news. The Canadian Airborne is deployed in Ottawa. First RCR in NATO is loading to return. Third RCR is taking up a position along the Quebec–Ontario border and the 1st battalion PPCLI will defend the Ottawa River up to Camp Petawawa as soon as they arrive from the west. Second RCR has the Quebec–New Brunswick border. This is not a defensive line I am describing. All we can do is patrol.

"3rd PPCLI is in Cyprus, on alert to return once we find air transport. The 2nd battalion is in Yugoslavia, also on standby to move. The Van Doo battalion in Germany will naturally remain there.

"Anticipating authorization from their governments, the German and Brit training establishments in Alberta are loading tanks onto trains for the move east. I spoke to both commanders. They will send instructors to assist in retraining. If as expected they get permission to roll today, we will have armoured forces again by Thursday.

"In the air we're tight. We lost a squadron of CF-18's at Bagotville and most of our F-5's. Since the CF-18 repair shop is in Montreal, severe restrictions have been placed on flying time for combat aircraft. Transport aircraft are in very short supply, and we need cabinet authority to commandeer civilian planes to move troops.

"The navy lost two destroyers in Montreal, one in drydock, the other waiting a refit. That one was scuttled by a very courageous crew member. Finally, I have sent a mobilization alert to all militia regiments in accordance with the Total Force plan approved by this government." Pittman looked around carefully. None of those present knew that he was adamantly against the use of militia or that he had, even before becoming CDS, used militia funds to support the regular forces. His news was the best that could be harvested from a pile of bleak reports. It was Vinet's job to explain how dark the picture was, while leaving hope that the armed forces could bring back the light. Pittman smiled. Most of the problems were structural, and Vinet had accepted them during his tenure as CDS. Now he had to defend them. "General Vinet?"

Vinet, though retired, had come deliberately looking every inch the fighting general because he wanted his job back. He knew that his chances were slim, but not impossibly so. Before this war was over, the government would need strong military leaders from Quebec, even if they had reached retirement age. He took a position behind his chair and began.

"The picture isn't entirely bleak. Within a week of your authorizing mobilization we can have five to six thousand militiamen in a crash training programme. Two weeks later most of them should be fit to reinforce the regular soldiers on the defensive line.

"As for armour, once our NATO personnel return to man the new tanks, we can field four squadrons. To get more will require several weeks' training for militia personnel in Canada. The problem is that the new Leopard tanks are more modern than our 1964 models, and none of us know the British Challengers. A lot of retraining is necessary before they're operational. I am sure General Pittman has that firmly in hand.

"There is also a problem of instructors for the militia. We had to strip training bases in order to bring fighting units up to minimum operational strength. We have little ammunition. I took the liberty of phoning General Blakeslee, Chairman of the Joint Chiefs in Washington, a fine soldier whom I've known for years. He promised swift action on vital supplies once he gets authority to send them. We have friends down there, sir. They remember our support in the Gulf War.

"In brief, we grow stronger every day, but we can take no offensive action now. In a month, however, we can field three CMBG's.[3] The ALQ will also have grown, but they must disperse their forces. Now, perhaps if

---

[3] Canadian Mechanized Brigade Groups

I answer questions rather than talk figures to you? You know better than I what information you need."

After the briefing, the Prime Minister broke for lunch and a word with General Pittman. The PM could count on his support no matter what policy was put forward, whereas Vinet insisted on putting things for his soldiers ahead of national concerns.

Having reached an understanding, the PM sent the generals away and reconvened the cabinet. The earlier sense of optimism had dissipated, and the afternoon news did nothing to change the mood.

The Solicitor General read a long report from the Canadian Security Intelligence Service that consisted of complaints about being ordered not to operate in Quebec, vague promises of what could be done once the rules changed and finally an intelligence summary based principally on information from MI-6 and CIA. It boiled down to a guess at how fast the ALQ was growing and the facts that several shipments of clandestine arms were on the way and that one ship was unloading in Montreal harbour now. The report mentioned the Bell Helicopter factory at Mirabel and the Oerlikon anti-aircraft-system plant in St Jean and recommended that they be taken out by air strikes.

The Prime Minister vetoed that proposal. Canadians would not accept such an act so early in the war. Then he created more gloom when he asked each minister to report on the state of his or her department.

The reports were depressingly alike. Quebecers at all levels of the civil service were gone, leaving or demoralized. A deputy minister at Treasury Board had broken into tears over the phone. He was a federalist who had written papers to show that Quebec was better off in Canada—but his home was Quebec, and his son was in the ALQ. Promising to take no part in the struggle, he was going to join his family.

Every department was facing unparalleled problems with a decimated staff. Canada had been ripped in two: communications no longer worked east-west. Telephone companies were frantically trying to lease American lines and satellite time. Ships were trapped in the Seaway; airlines had to be rerouted; Boston Air Traffic Control had been asked to take over Montreal ATC duties. Freight trains were blocking lines across the country as goods piled up in east and west coast ports, unable to move.

The Prime Minister listened with half an ear. What he was hearing was serious, but unless he put a resolute face on the situation in time for the evening news, world stock markets would destroy Canada before Quebec's separation could.

Two Quebec members had not returned after lunch. All afternoon he listened to his cabinet come together only to break into new warring groups. They were behaving like politicians in a fifth-century Greek city-state. As the afternoon wore on his course became clear. He'd lose some members, but it was time to enforce solidarity, not negotiate it.

He'd fire two leading peace-at-any-price members tonight. Most of the Quebecers were with him, but only two out of nine would support an invasion of Quebec. He had to hold them at all costs until time and events showed the necessity of reuniting Canada. His government's majority was based on the MP's from Quebec, but with their legal status open to question he had to prevent the opposition from challenging their right to vote. Also, before he met the scrum of journalists outside, the air of defeatism that pervaded the room like swamp gas had to be eliminated. If that showed on the evening news, his government was history. The Sunday papers and commentators were calling for his resignation. On Monday the financial sharks would be in a feeding frenzy, and he'd be lucky if the dollar was worth fifty cents when the market closed. Decisive action was the best defence, but without an army, he'd have to bluff until a national coalition unity government could be formed under his leadership.

As he listened to the Finance Minister's lucid list of the financial strategies he would employ to defend the dollar, a messenger entered with a red-flagged envelope. Nervously he tore the heavy paper open under the table and scanned the single sheet quickly. As he assimilated the information, all eyes in the room began to turn in his direction. Even the Finance Minister paused.

"Good news at last!" the PM exclaimed, rising to wave the paper aloft. "General Pittman is coming back to brief you, but I'm going to steal his thunder. We deserve to hear this now." He glanced quickly at the paper to make sure he had the name right.

"It appears that a Colonel Sloerill, an ex-regular force soldier, has led an extremely well planned and executed raid into Montreal. The long and short of it is, we have most of our lost equipment back again!"

The explosion of cheering could be heard plainly by the reporters gathered outside in the corridor. The PM knew that and made no attempt to quiet the room until it began to die down naturally.

"Colonel Sloerill has defeated the ALQ in several key battles. He has effective control over a major portion of the proposed corridor area— the area we agreed would remain Canadian in the event of separation," he reminded his Quebec Ministers sharply. "General Pittman will also bring the officer who carried this good news to us."

His eyes went to his Minister of Justice. "Good news, Karen. We're getting a videotape showing the ALQ starting to shoot before Cyr declared independence. I want a legal position on this tonight. Work with External. Canvass every foreign capital. Call in the diplomatic community tomorrow. Perhaps you can use the tapes to prove the declaration of independence was illegal. Say we'll withdraw recognition of any country that helps Quebec. I'll speak to the ambassadors myself."

The hubbub broke out again and the PM sat down. The feeling of being at a death watch was gone. He would end the meeting before the glow was dissipated by more bad news. He studied the note thoughtfully. When the American Civil war began, President Lincoln had needed a victory to prevent the doves in Congress from surrendering to the south. Like Lincoln, he now had a victory. Could he use it to prevent surrender? Sloerill. Odd name. Was Sloerill his General Grant? If so, what brand of whiskey did he drink? Neither Vinet nor Pittman was showing much stomach for fighting without overwhelming superiority. If Sloerill was a fighter, he'd get whatever he wanted.

CHAPTER EIGHT

Getting it Together

While George Sloerill slept for eighteen hours, his officers created an operations centre in the drill hall to get his forces under control.

The walls of one large room were covered in charts recording the location and strength of units. Lists announced times and places for QM issue. In the signals room next door, phone numbers and radio frequencies were taped to the walls. John Ashworth sat at a long table across from six clerks. Four phones, hastily installed by regimental handymen, crowded around him trailing long tangles of wires. One of them rang.

"Captain Ashworth, Corridor Force HQ." He listened, then cupped his hand over the mouthpiece. "Perkins," he told one of six lightly wounded men sitting along one wall who were being used as runners. "Get the Colonel. He's somewhere outside. Tell him Ottawa's on the line." As the young man got up, Sloerill came back in.

"Sir? General Thomas on the line." Ashworth held out the phone.

Sloerill seized it, his delight showing. The general commanding Mobile Command had escaped. "Good morning, general. Sloerill here." He listened for a moment.

"No, sir, not at all. I know how hectic things must be up there and I'm glad my messenger got through." He listened again. "No, sir, that SITREP hasn't changed to speak of except we're a bit more organized."

The phone crackled at him again. "A few more men have come

in." Ashworth, listening on another phone, held up a pad. "Our strength is now twelve hundred sixty-three . . ." Another paper was held up. "Plus two hundred seventy female personnel. "Of the total," he peered at Ashworth's notes, "about five hundred and thirty-two are recruits and I have a lot of ex-militia and some regulars. What do I . . . right, sir. Sign them up.

"That brings up a point, sir. I'm a civilian, so is Peter Forbes . . . Forbes . . . the Brit major mentioned in my report . . . no sir, I must have him. He's my best officer." The phone made discouraging noises.

"I hope in an emergency red tape can be cut, sir. Now . . ." he was interrupted by the roar of tank engines and the scream of iron tracks turning on pavement outside the window.

"Hold on, sir. Tanks coming in. Not theirs! Ours!" Sloerill bellowed over the noise. "Hold on!" He counted the monsters going past, sixteen Leopards and twelve ancient Centurions. He had recaptured fewer than half of the newer tanks.

When he returned to the phone, Ashworth made a victory signal as General Thomas confirmed Sloerill's old rank of full colonel and promised to expedite Peter's enlistment. He also wrote down the general's words for publication in Routine Orders.

"Colonel Sloerill, you and your men have performed a tremendous service for Canada. The entire nation is grateful. Your exploits are on radio, TV and in the press. We can't help you much, but I'll do what I can to support you. You have destroyed Quebec's claim to full control of its territory. You have no idea how important that is."

They said goodbye, and as Sloerill put the phone down a smiling John Ashworth saluted. "Congratulations, sir. Ready for a SITREP?"

"I guess I can take it. From a quick look-round, things seem to have been moving while I was lying dead. Is there much fighting?"

"It's picking up after a lull last night. I guess both sides needed sleep. Colonels St Pierre and Chantilly want to see you. Their men finally understand that it's civil war and that when they shoot ALQ they're shooting French Canadians. At the moment Colonel St Pierre has his FMR on camp security. That looks as if we don't trust them. Do we?"

"We have no choice. Half this force is French-speaking. If they quit, we're gone. Isn't Sam Armstrong in law at McGill?" Ashworth nodded. "Have him do a paper on the illegality of what Cyr did. Point out that we're not fighting Quebec, we're fighting rebels. Tell them six French-Canadian Guardsmen were killed in Bertrand's sneak attack. Tell them the towns they're protecting are mostly French-speaking, so indiscriminate firing by the ALQ is killing more French than English.

"Another thing. Cyr is accusing us of murder. Put the prisoners on camera, holding today's paper and telling their parents they're OK. Send it all to Ottawa."

He turned to the door again. "I'll talk to the men one on one. Once they see the ALQ don't ask who they're shooting at, they'll be fine. For now, let's hope that momentum carries them along. Also, message to all units. Find a friend of mine, Etienne Messier. He drives a grey Bentley."

The euphoria of independence had faded quickly, especially for ALQ soldiers at the borders. Young men who had been taught to hate "English domination" and had joined for the glory of setting Quebec free found there was no glory in standing on a cold bridge as streams of English and French Quebecers flowed by, fleeing their freedom. The unending tide of refugees, particularly from Montreal, had not slacked in three days. It was sapping their morale. Would anyone be left in their independent Quebec?

The constant stream of reports and casualty lists had sobered the exultant ALQ headquarters staff. They were now equipped with teletypes, faxes and phones. Bad news could circulate fast.

"Quebec City will call soon, mon général." His aide touched the old man's sleeve deferentially. "They demand more news. More good news."

"I had hoped . . ." the general began wearily, his red-rimmed eyes sweeping over a map of Quebec on the wall. At Sherbrooke, Cowansville, Farnham, Bedford, Dunham, Bromont and Sutton, red flags marked losses. The rest of the map was covered in triumphant blue flags. As they watched, a man placed a red flag at Ange Gardien, near Farnham. Another fight. Another loss. The general went into his office.

"It is not so bad, mon général." The aide tried to be cheerful. "We hold the major cities. Apart from one small area, we control our country for the first time in over two hundred years. We lost some stores but—"

"Unimportant," the general interrupted. "They got less than we feared, and by letting them escape we saved from burning most of what was left. New equipment is now being landed in Montreal harbour. Our agents disrupted NDHQ in Ottawa, and the computer virus we planned to activate on the original takeover date will now hit in time to destroy their new plans. The problem is Farnham."

"Are the seventy men we lost so important then?"

"Men's lives are always important, Jacques. Never forget that. Never!" The general shook his head fiercely. "No, we lost more than lives."

"But it was one small failure among so many successes!"

"Such small failures decide the fate of nations. Had the South captured Washington they might have won the war. We may have lost our war with that small battle. How did the Guards get live ammunition?"

"Our people at Longue Pointe say they had nothing but live ammunition, hidden in boxes marked 'blank'. We couldn't control every indent for supplies. We trusted in the order for militia units not to train."

"You can never plan for everything, Jacques. We never thought that a few artillerymen in Cowansville led by an overage major could harm us. But they, the Guards, Colonel Sloerill and one mistake have destroyed our whole plan for the corridor region. Worse, they effectively disprove our claim that all Quebec is under our control. Canada can use that to prevent our government from being recognized by the United Nations."

"Then let us get the land back. Our Valcartier men are professionals. We can destroy Sloerill's amateurs."

"The Canadians have invaded Quebec near Hull, we need our best men to hold them. Merde! I did not want to fight so soon . . . so much."

"The Townships brigades have lost many men in ambushes and we must strike before Sloerill becomes too strong."

"Send help, but remember such men will not be as effective as those who either live in the area or have been exploring it for two years. Replace casualties—but the priority is recruit training. Send men to Sherbrooke. The fighting there must be stopped very soon."

"Good. They can crush this Sloerill on the way."

"They will ignore Sloerill. If he is not crushed those resisting in Sherbrooke will take heart, and every newspaper and TV station in Canada will demand that he be supported. He is now a hero. To make him a martyr would be folly."

"We leave him alone then? Let him kill our men?"

"You don't understand, Jacques. Men die in war. It is our job to see they do not die for nothing. Last Saturday Canada was divided, and to lull his Quebec MP's the Prime Minister was rejecting force. Faced with a fait accompli, he would have accepted our demands. Now, in only four days, Canada has two victories, recaptured some tanks and guns, and part of the corridor. More important, they take heart. They think we frogs are not so tough. They think if they are strong we will surrender."

The general turned to his desk, his shoulders straightening. "Eh bien. Confine Sloerill to his present location. He is not strong enough to menace St Jean or Granby, and he is at a safe distance from Sherbrooke. Let that suffice. Before we eliminate Sloerill, we must safeguard Montreal."

In the Townships the ALQ were getting through Sloerill's lines, around the guarded roads through the woods to join the ALQ forces already there. Every man he could spare was assigned to plug the gaps.

Fresh snow had fallen Wednesday night, and patrols could track ALQ incursions. On a dirt road east of Farnham twenty-four men reluctantly climbed out of a truck into a biting east wind. Corporal Bishop's eight men huddled beside the cab. Corporal Weitz's eight vanished into the ditch and spread out, watching their front and flanks. He'd had his section since Monday, learned their names and trained them at every opportunity. Sergeant Luft's seven men did the same in response to his order. The nineteen-year-old lieutenant, his map flapping against the fender, called Luft to the front of the truck to show him the patrol routes.

Luft interrupted him. "Scuse me, sir. Bishop! Get a grip on your men. This is a patrol, not a sheep pen. Take cover!"

As Bishop got his section into the ditch, Cpl Weitz assigned arcs of fire to each of his men, then began to distribute rations from the truck.

"What're we getting today, Corp?" one Guardsman called.

"Same as every day, Baker. Road kill. Watch your front. Rations in your parka pockets. Odd number men put your packs in the truck. Even numbered men do the same once the first group is back."

"Ah, Corporal Weitz?" The officer was shaking his head. "Carry packs and sleeping bags. If the trucks miss us, we may have to stay out all night." Last year he had been chewed out in public by Colonel Bosch for leading his men through wet ground instead of going around. The message stuck: the men's comfort came before tactics.

"Sergeant Luft, you and Corporal Bishop patrol east. I'll go west with Corporal Weitz. If you find tracks, notify Company HQ. Does everyone know where to meet the trucks?" The men nodded. "Right, move out."

Weitz took his men across the roadside fence in two groups, waved them into arrowhead formation, himself on point, and began moving toward the wood. The officer followed, carrying a radio, his parka hood up to protect his neck from the wind.

One man pulled up his hood too but Weitz snarled, "Keep it down, you re-tard."

"Neck's cold, Corp," the man complained, but he obeyed.

"Next time, wear a scarf. You can't see balls with the hood up."

"Let the men have hoods up till we get into the woods, Corporal Weitz," the officer countermanded the order. A warm soldier can fight better than a cold one, he rationalized.

"Sir," Weitz acknowledged and the men gratefully pulled up their hoods. Weitz left his down, his head turning constantly, checking his men, his eyes sweeping the wood line for any sign of movement, selecting nearby fire positions in case he was shot at. The men did as he did, look left, right, check the corporal, do it again, but they didn't really believe that it meant anything. It was only a drill.

As they entered the woods Weitz halted the patrol, waving the senior Guardsman forward. "Take over, Pete. I'm going to check forward to see if I can spot any tracks. Take the men in a hundred metres and stop. All-round defence. Wait for me."

Weitz, not trusting anyone else to check the dangerous fringes of the wood, moved along an old logging road, pushing deeper into the pine and spruce forest. Behind him, when Pete Chiltern halted, the officer waved him on. The woods didn't provide much shelter from the wind. The hoods stayed up.

Nobody saw the flicker of movement before the ALQ opened fire. The three men who survived the first burst of shots tried to crawl to cover, hampered by the dark rucksacks that showed their positions against the snow. They died trying to shuck them off, their weapons lying uselessly on the ground.

The ALQ commander sent two men after Weitz, whom he had allowed to pass the ambush. There was a burst of firing but neither man came back. The ALQ officer cursed but he wasn't about to lose more men chasing one corporal.

George Sloerill was munching a ham sandwich as he stamped his boots at the headquarters door. Behind him his jeep took off for the mess hall in one of Zuke's gravel-scattering jackrabbit starts.

"How did it go, sir?" Ashworth turned from the big situation map. Sloerill had been talking to St Pierre's FMR soldiers.

"They're coming round," he grunted. "Some can't hack the idea of fighting other French Canadians. Five more will be released today."

"That's seventeen in two days."

"And the last, I hope. I was afraid there'd be more. The rest have been shot at—by French Canadians. Sam's paper on illegality helped. American TV news is making us the good guys. And every time Cyr rants about the 'English' killing Quebecers, he pisses off our French-speaking soldiers. He won't admit that *any* French Canadians are on our side. What's happening with the RMR? The men I spoke to want their own unit, not to be attached to the Fusiliers."

"They're trickling in. We got twenty-six in Montreal, the Knowlton company had seventy-two more and the new arrivals number . . . I think it's forty-seven and counting. Can we use them as a Headquarters defence unit?"

"Good idea." Sloerill shook off his parka and hung it over a chair. "Anyway, I see the lights are still working."

"Why shouldn't they?"

"Because the ALQ control all hydro and gas distribution, food and phones. If they want to, they can freeze us in the dark and incommunicado."

"Not us, sir, but the civilian population is vulnerable. Should we encourage people to move into Vermont?"

"Not yet. I don't want this place to turn into a . . . what's going on out there?"

It was an argument, and it was getting louder as the sentry was obviously determined not to let someone get past him. As Ashworth got up, they heard Peter Forbes's drawl.

"I say there, sentry. You'd best let that chap in. We've been trying to get our hands on him for days."

"Sir!" The sentry's feet banged and the door opened to admit Etienne Messier, fur collar turned up against the wind. His face was lined and grey, his face haggard as if he hadn't slept in days.

"Etienne!"

"George!"

The two men embraced. "Ah, Damon and Pythias," Forbes said from the door. "You've no idea how many man-hours we've used searching the highways and byways for you. We were beginning to think you'd fallen foul of the local gunplay."

George made introductions and led both men into his office. "Etienne! You've no idea how I worried. Your house was empty. Nobody knew where you were. Where's Andrée? Robert?"

"I suggest you let him answer those first," Peter suggested, hanging up coats. "Try this." He poured a tot of brandy from his flask into a mug. "Frankly, Etienne, you look as if you need it."

Messier swallowed the brandy in one gulp. "Ahhh. Thank you. I did need it." He turned back to George, his face less grey.

"When you did not come to Bromont I thought you had gone to see that Englishwoman and I did not worry—much. That night I saw armed men on the street. A boy I know told me what had happened. I came, of course, but the guards would not let me in.

"On Sunday the shooting was worse, so I took the family to Lac Brome. Andrée was afraid to stay alone and it was only this morning I could return. I met Tom Bush in Dunham and he gave me a pass to enter camp."

Messier held out trembling hands. "What are you doing, George? The hospitals are full of wounded and dying. Cyr says Quebec is independent. You cannot fight a nation, George. If you do not stop, you will be crushed. Thousands may die—and for what? To hold a small piece of Quebec isolated from the rest of Canada?"

Messier rubbed his face. "Was it only last Saturday that we discussed this in theory? Did we not agree that the citizens would suffer most? It is not theory now, George. Our friends are dying. Do you remember Claude Gabriel?" George nodded. "His funeral is tomorrow. He died in Bromont. There are others. Do you want their names?"

George shook his head. "I have lists of names too, Etienne. I knew Gabriel. He died fighting for the ALQ."

"Does that matter? What about the names of the men—the boys Tom Bush lost? They are as dead as Claude. Does the name of their army make a difference?" Messier was almost shouting, fumbling in his pockets and pulling out wads of crumpled notepaper.

"I have more names here. I regret I did not inquire as to what army they were in when they died. Look, George. These are the names of your friends!"

Sloerill didn't look. "I have longer lists," he said flatly. "If you wish, I'll give you a copy."

The callous, rasping tone hit Messier like a blow. "What has happened to you, George? I do not know the man I see now."

"What happened? My friends at Mobile Command, Frank Harris, Babe Trinker, Fred Scott, Marcel Laporte—you had him to dinner six years ago—were killed by people who prefer guns to ballots. My friends in the Guards were shot down with no warning. The only consolation is that we got the bastard who did it. Do you know what happened in Sutton and Knowlton last night?"

Messier shook his head, unable to break through his friend's rage. "I'll tell you. Five cars full of ALQ drove into Knowlton. Three more arrived in Sutton. They drove into town, spraying machine gun fire at every store with an English sign. No warning. In Sutton ten FMR and a dozen armed civilians killed or captured the whole gang. In Knowlton, only two got away. Three of our Cowansville Gunners are slightly wounded. As for the civilians—your list won't have these names yet—fifteen dead. Forty-three wounded!"

Sloerill's finger stabbed out. "Do I remember Gabriel? Do you remember Luc Marchand, the strongest separatist in the area? When the ALQ opened fire in Knowlton he tried to stop them. They shot him.

"That's what happened, Etienne. It's also happening to more than five hundred French Canadians fighting on our side against a bunch of murdering rebels."

"You go too far, George. Cyr is elected. The declaration of independence was passed by the National Assembly. Even the Queen's representative signed it."

"The killing began before that. Cyr is trying to make murder retroactively legal. Last night he called us 'English terrorists who refuse to bow to the will of the majority'. Battery Sergeant-Major Lessard—you know him—threw a boot through the screen and the whole sergeants' mess cheered. In the French units they've started to say 'Je vais cyrez' when they go for a shit. That's how the men see things here—and I'm proud of it!"

There was a long silence as the two friends stared at one another. It was Etienne Messier who looked away.

"Ah, well, I can see your point. We are in the corridor that, as I told you, I supported if it came to this." He paused to look beseechingly at the two officers. "But how many must die for it?"

"It depends on the ALQ. If indiscriminate shooting continues, the civilian guard units won't take prisoners. My men will, if they can."

"Very well, George." Messier seemed to sag. "I have said . . ." A thought struck him. "You say you have been looking for me? Surely not to give me this lecture?"

"Not at all, Etienne. In our talk on Saturday, one subject didn't come up. In a war like this, there must be tight civilian control—local civilian control."

"C'est raisonnable. I am sure Ottawa will send—"

"Ottawa doesn't know where the Townships are. I mean *local* government led by people with friends on both sides—and I want you to run it."

"Impossible!" Messier exploded. "I cannot. You have the wrong man. I will not supervise a war, even for you, George."

"Etienne, the man must be neutral and be respected. That's you."

"There must be others. I assure you, I am not the man for this."

"You're exactly the man for this. You care about lives. You just proved it. In this job you can do more than care, you can help them."

"Help kill more French—and English Canadians?"

"Help keep them alive. Look, civilians have to be fed. They need jobs. Factories must stay open. I can't do it. There are thousands of refugees. Who looks after them?"

"But why me?" Messier protested, weakening. "There are many here with more experience than I have."

"If you don't take hold, the man with the biggest mouth will get the job. Good Lord, do you want Sam Thackery? He'd deport anyone who wasn't English or wouldn't wear one of his 'One Canada' badges." George wheeled as John Ashworth came in. "We're a bit busy, John."

"Sorry, sir. A Cowansville civil defence group tore down a Quebec flag, pissed on it and beat up a man who tried to stop them. Sam Armstrong stepped in but tempers are high. He wants orders."

"Arrest the idiots who did it, take the injured man to a doctor, wash the flag and put it back up himself. The Quebec flag is legal, dammit." He turned back to Etienne.

"That's what I mean. A civil government can stop this crap. Hell, Etienne! You barge in all hot about French Canadians getting killed, and when I ask you to do something about it you go all coy on me."

"But I don't know where to start! I cannot go to Sam and say, 'I am in charge. George Sloerill has decreed it.' He will laugh at me."

Sloerill grinned. "No, call a meeting of businessmen and mayors. Elect a temporary governing council. Believe me, if you start the ball rolling, you'll be elected. Will you do it?"

Messier sighed. "For some reason I can never refuse this terrible man. I will do it. But I warn you. Power is seductive and you may not like some things I do." He began to put on the coat Forbes held. "In the meantime, will you be careful, George? I spoke of loving French Canadians. I hope you will not take it amiss if I include you among those I love. I do not wish to read your name on those lists of dead and dying."

"Don't worry. They can't get me now."

"Ah? You are finally taking some precautions? You will wear one of those bullet-proof vests we saw in the Gulf war?"

"We don't have any. No, I mean the team of Messier and Sloerill is on defense again."

Etienne shook hands. "It must not become a high-scoring game." He walked out, the lines on his face reflecting undiminished concern.

"I have a car dealer on the line," Ashworth went on. "He says you want to trade. Is Zuke's driving finally getting to you?"

"No, John. I want to move around and I don't want to be too conspicuous. Ask for a four-door Chev, three or four years old."

"What's your car?" Peter asked putting on his parka.

"Something I got a few years back. An Opel. Not suitable at all."

"I see what you mean about conspicuous," Ashworth agreed.

"That's not it, John. There's going to be a lot of hardship before this is over. The military commander can't be seen using opel-ent transport."

"Good God!" Peter exclaimed. "I've never heard you make a joke that foul unless you were feeling absolutely tops. Are you willing to share the cause of your optimism with us lowly foot-sloggers?"

"He does have an Opel, you know," Messier said from the door. "I suspect he bought it in order to make that joke." He sighed. "I have a thousand questions and only you have the answers. Have you the time to assist me in what must be done?"

"I have to meet André Taschereau. He and Bryce are looking for a training camp and supply depot. Farnham's too close to the front. However—" He waved at Peter who was starting out. "He did a paper in Staff College on government organization in a civil war climate. He's all yours."

Forbes unzipped his parka. "The past will ever haunt us." He sighed as Ashworth followed Sloerill out. "John? Tell Wayne not to hold tea. I'll be a bit late."

The dark briefing room at CIA headquarters in Langley, Virginia was lit mainly by a computer screen. Maps, photographs and intelligence summaries paraded across it under the watcher's control. Faces and facts were recorded in the man's mind to be recalled at will. When the final picture went by the screen darkened and the room lights came up.

"That's the info as of last night, Clay," the man seated behind the watcher said. "After this assignment we'll change that bird on your shoulder to a star. You've earned it."

"They don't hand out many stars to Special Forces people, Jeff." Clay Anderson stood up and stretched. His uniform was rumpled and he was unshaven. In three days he had assimilated most of what the agency knew about Quebec, which was a lot, and all they had on the rebellion, which was not much. "What day is is it?"

The man behind him laughed. "October tenth, 1500 hours, the day Colonel Anderson is to be demoted to light colonel, special adviser to Canadian Forces in Quebec. Congratulations."

"Thanks a whole heap. What's next?"

"Two more briefings, then you meet your Stateside control. He'll work out of St Albans, Vermont by special permission of the FBI."

"What about the border? I hear nothing's to get into Quebec."

"That's for public consumption till Mr Gallup tells the White House chicken-hawks how the great American public reacts to helping either Quebec or Canada. If you want something to get through, it will. Now, before the next briefer arrives I want your ear. I had breakfast with Melling, so this is the latest political poop."

"I've had the latest political poop four times. Each time it's different." Anderson folded his lean six-foot-four frame into the chair and lit a cigar. "What's the new version?"

"American policy has always been to keep Canada united. Usually we don't interfere, but when a rebellion and/or revolution coincides with an election, the President has to re-define the word 'interfere'."

"What's it mean now? I knew Wednesday, but I'm a day behind."

"That's what makes your job interesting. The Man's getting heavy flak. Some want to let Canada go and pick up the pieces after. Some favour Quebec, some favour Canada. The Boss wants to jump in with both feet. Leadership wins votes. What isn't clear is where to lead to. That's no evil empire. The Pentagon thinks Quebec might pull this off, depending on how good the Canadian military is."

Anderson studied his cigar ash thoughtfully. "They aren't bad, individually. Organizationally, echh. They have four combat groups, each which has an infantry battalion, an armoured regiment without tanks, some artillery and support elements. It's too unbalanced to fight. Also, the policy of rotating people through their system means officers are low on field command experience."

"Not bad. I'm told that on the signal 'play ball' they have about 3000 fighting men. The CIA calls the ALQ at about 5000, growing fast but low on training. With their NATO and UN troops Canada can match that, and calling up their reserves will double the number. We estimate they can be effective in about two months."

"Sounds good. The ALQ with half the men and three borders to watch can't do much against Sloerill with those odds."

"It's the organization, Clay. We threw out combat groups before Nam. The Brits did it even earlier, and if you think we're heavy on brass, hey—we run one general per two thousand. They're one per five hundred. One mistake and Canada's gone. As the Man said, 'If their Prime Minister folds, we deal with Quebec.' Nothing can compromise that position."

"OK. How does it tie my hands?"

"Lightly. Keep Sloerill effective. Get him what he wants when he wants it or sooner. I'm told he's a maverick with a long line of enemies, mostly generals, who'd love to cut his throat. In your spare time set up his intelligence unit. We can let you have some specialists, no real troops."

"Am I tied into the satellite observation net?"

"A bird was repositioned last night. We're testing now. The system is NSA to Langley, then to you via your control in St Albans. A twenty-four hour delay is about the best we can do until you're set to handle real-time stuff. Any thoughts on the kind of present you'd like to take into Canada?"

"I bet Sloerill's short of flak vests. Can I get a few truckloads?"

"No sweat. Remember, Clay. The Man's on top of this. Do OK and you get a star. Screw up and you'll be counting penguins until pension time."

Anderson didn't smile. He was from Tennessee, and his face, like his home county, was all ridges and rocky planes. His rare smiles always reached his pale blue eyes. He often wondered if the job specs for CIA senior management demanded an unfailing ability to deliver veiled threats during a briefing. They seemed to forget that if he really screwed up he'd win a plot in Arlington instead of a pension. He hoped they'd realize one day that the possibility of death was a greater motivator than penguins.

His visitor rose. "Time for your next session, Clay. You've got unusual flex on this one. I know you'll make the boss happy."

Anderson nodded and took his seat again, his mind starting to probe for the core of the man Sloerill. He sounded interesting. Men with generals for enemies usually were. Independence was a characteristic a man with Clay's mountain blood appreciated.

The parade square was full of recruits, marching or learning basic rifle drill. Sloerill watched with a professional eye until a Huey helicopter settled onto the half-frozen ground to his left. Captain Bryce waved from the dark glass cockpit as the rotors slowed to a drooping stop, then got out to check his bird. Two passengers climbed down looking grateful for the feel of solid ground and walked over to where Sloerill waited.

The man in front was Major Taschereau, the efficient officer from Longue Pointe who was running the embryonic brigade supply organization. He'd been looking for a new training and logistics base.

The second man was a short, dark, serious-looking captain with a round face permanently set in a mild frown. No one had ever seen him smile. Tony Manieri was one of the Longue Pointe regulars who'd stayed with Sloerill. Andrew Bryce loved flying helicopters; Manieri was addicted to radios. He was now Sloerill's senior signals officer.

"Bryce must be off his flying," Sloerill observed, returning the salutes. "You both look reasonably happy." Manieri was frowning less than usual and André Taschereau wore an enthusiastic grin.

"We have your base!" he cried with a wide sweep of his arms. "It is perfect! It is huge! In all of Canada there is not enough equipment to fill it. Our tank crews will vanish in it. There is even a railway line to Vermont, and wait till you see the view!" He whipped a map from his pocket and opened it with an extra flourish.

"Here! South of Sutton is Abercorn, almost on the border. There's a bypass around town so our convoys will not disturb the sleeping Abercornais. This," his finger drew a rough rectangle, "is for tank training. They can shoot into the mountain there.

"In addition, near the main road but up the hill is a perfect place for your headquarters. There is direct line-of-sight radio communication to main relay points, a huge rock ledge that is perfect for helicopter landings— in fact the site has everything!"

"Looks good," Sloerill agreed. "But what about Sutton?"

"It's not bad, but when Bryce picked me up, we detoured south because he had to resupply a relay station. I saw Abercorn and I fell in love!"

"We'll take a look. How about you, Tony? Have you solved all our communication problems yet?"

Tony shook his head, his frown deepening. Their sets had a range of about fifteen miles in flat country. Patrols often operated at twice that distance from headquarters, and the ground was mountainous.

"Unless we rent a satellite, we'll have to keep on as we are, sir. That means more fouled-up messages as people try to pass information from station to station. The best I can do is eliminate the dead spots. I figure we'll need eight major relays, three men each on an eight-hour shift. Call it a hundred men including spares."

"OK, Tony. See John about stores and men, but remember how short we are on trained sigs personnel."

Manieri saluted and left to find Ashworth. George turned to Major Taschereau. "Now show me the new base. If it's as good as you say, start setting it up tomorrow, because this place is about to bust a gut."

The two officers climbed into the Huey as the rotors speeded up. George put on a helmet and plugged in the intercom.

"Where to, colonel?" Bryce's voice even managed to bubble with enthusiasm over the tinny earphones.

"Abercorn. I want to see this sexy new real estate."

"Right you are, sir." The chopper surged into the air, spun on its axis and nosed down facing southeast as it surged across the camp, barely clearing the drill hall roof.

"Mr and Mrs Bryce's favorite son wishes to welcome Colonel Sloerill on board flight 763, Farnham to Abercorn. On your inaugural lift in this bird we will cruise at approximately five hundred feet, unless the colonel wishes to get a better view."

Sloerill, fighting to control his stomach after the headlong take-off, stared at the rapidly approaching Farnham water tower and made a gesture that said "go up—now".

"And away we go!" Bryce chortled, feeding power to the engine, banking slightly as the tower vanished under the skids. Sloerill felt the seat grab the base of his spine and haul him higher into the sky. He tensed, waiting for the deceleration that made his stomach churn. As he looked around for the barf bag he thought wistfully of his jeep below.

"Just what I've needed, a Zuke for a pilot," he muttered and reached for the white container. He wanted it close to his hand.

CHAPTER NINE

The UN

On Wednesday night the Prime Minister invited his key cabinet ministers to dinner at 24 Sussex Drive, along with the party's chief pollster, despite the fact that Allan Brewster carried almost unrelieved bad news. In order of rank, the ministers were Karen Ormsby, Justice and Deputy Prime Minister; Joe Gates, External Affairs; Gilles Leroux, Finance; Normand Descelles, Treasury Board; and Alfred Banner, Defence. They were a sombre group around the dining table.

The Prime Minister's overview of the problem had done nothing to relieve the gloom. "In short, while officially everyone's in favour of pre-serving Canada's boundaries under the 1970 UN Declaration on Friendly Relations, some accept Quebec's demand for recognition under Section 73 of the Charter. Therefore, while nobody will officially recognize Quebec, they'll support her indirectly through clandestine trade. On the other hand, the Brits and Germans have given us over two hundred tanks, and I told the President yesterday that Canada has more to offer the US, and more money to buy what we want, than Quebec has. Also, our Navy intercepted an arms supply ship today. Unfortunately they missed four others. General Pittman can't guarantee we'll stop more, and Karen's lawyers aren't sure if we have the right to unless we declare a blockade, which—and Justice *is* sure about this—is an act of war." Karen Ormsby nodded her close-cropped head firmly. "Also, only when it's effective will it be respected.

"However," he went on, trying to sound as if the worst was over, "we'll deal with international events case by case. The domestic scene is more serious, and unless we stay in power, who deals with whom over what becomes academic from our point of view.

"Allan." The PM turned to his pollster. "It's time to explain what your polls are really telling us."

Brewster, his garish sports coat belying a conservatively bald head, might look like an emaciated hippy funeral director, but his IQ exceeded any other in the room and, he suspected, could be matched against almost any two of them.

"Thank you, Prime Minister," he said formally, glancing at a single sheet of paper on the table beside his plate. "I did a poll last month. With 4322 respondents, it was very accurate. We intended to create a baseline group and return to them in subsequent weeks to detect opinion shifts. The coup fouled up the plan.

"On the Sunday after UDI we could only reach 1837 base respondents. On Monday, we got 2117, and today's figures put us back in the 4000 range.

"The baseline is a public that believed only a minor crisis was likely. Sunday's poll followed UDI, before the Montreal raid was known. The next three were taken as the news improved. Unfortunately, results did not.

"In brief, the big survey gave us a clouded point of departure. Those in favour of Quebec independence, 64 percent in Quebec, 46 percent outside; those in favour of retaining Quebec at any cost, 12 percent across the board. Satisfaction with the government, 10.6 percent. The percentage of people who want you to resign is 73 percent, up four points.

"The Sunday call-back dropped government approval to 8.3 percent; 'keep Quebec at any cost' rose to 26 percent. 'Let Quebec go' rose to a soft 51 percent with lots of undecideds. No Quebec polling was done on Sunday.

"Monday's and today's data are still under analysis, giving a fairly high bugger factor to these next figures, but government popularity is up to 19 percent. 'Take Quebec back' rose marginally to 30 percent, and 'let Quebec go' rose, but only two points.

"What the polls show clearly is that the government's in deep doo-doo. There's anger out there, but the opposition hasn't capitalized on it.

THE UN   155

People want leadership and they'll support any leader who has a clear policy on Canadian unity, Quebec *and* the economy. To give an idea of the confusion: half the 'Let Quebec go' crowd would switch sides if they thought we could keep Quebec without *major* fighting. Half the 'Get it back' bunch would cede Quebec if there *was* major fighting. In English Canada, 83 percent believe Quebec will not fight. The figures did not change after last weekend when Quebec did. In Quebec, only six percent believe Canada will fight. Their reason, cited by 76 percent of respondents, is based on Canada's failure to mount a counter-attack against the ALQ. The same cause is cited by most Canadians to justify letting Quebec go; they think we can't fight. On a brighter note, 47 percent of respondents would support us if we show strong leadership. In Quebec, you, Prime Minister, are perceived by 64 percent, up from 52, as the best man to negotiate fairly." Brewster's eyes skimmed the paper to see if he had left anything out. He hadn't.

"Canadians are bewildered by what they see as a mess they can neither understand or influence. War pits Canada against Quebec in an open fight. Canadians can understand that. They want a problem they can solve. The first party that puts it that way wins the popularity sweepstake."

"How did you poll Quebec?" challenged Gilles Leroux, the Prime Minister's Quebec Lieutenant. He had been unable to phone his home base for almost a week.

"Most phones inside Quebec work, sir," Brewster replied. "Lines from Ontario aren't good. We used New Brunswick and Hull."

"I want to remind you," the Prime Minister said quietly, "that if Quebec goes, the House of Commons is reduced by seventy-five seats. The new majority would be a hundred and twelve aside from the Speaker. We'll have one hundred. Our claim on the corridor's fifteen seats gives us a majority of two, but six are iffy. The one thing that can save our ass is a hard line against Quebec."

"Prime Minister," Normand Descelles interrupted. The man usually looked like a diplomat, impeccably dressed, imperturbable. Today his face was anguished, his feelings visible to all. "I cannot accept that. The Quebec caucus will bolt and we are lost. We must reassure them that at least most of Quebec will be allowed to go."

"That's true, Normand, but think of this," the Prime Minister replied. "Twelve Quebec MP's have left Ottawa. A total reunification policy may lose us forty-one more, but they'll go back to Quebec, not stay to vote against us. On the other hand, without a hard line, twenty-six other MP's will cross the floor. Losing MP's to Quebec gives us a chance to make deals with individual opposition members. Losing them to the opposition means we're dead in the water.

"In addition," he went on to forestall protest, "you heard Allan. If the opposition goes for simple solutions, that means a screw-Quebec policy. If we're defeated, Quebec's fate will be in *their* hands. You know our government will be generous."

"That might hold twelve Quebec MP's, Prime Minister."

"It will hold twenty-six *non*-Quebecers. In addition, I'll tell caucus tomorrow that any MP returning to Quebec loses all pension rights. That might hold ten more. Anyway, mull it over, Normand, while Al brings us up to speed on the military picture."

Alfred Banner presented another glum face. "Prime Minister, mobilization is not going well. Militia units that should muster two hundred trained men are sending a third of that. The missing men are teachers, students, farmers and factory workers. For some reason the regiments we called up as complete units, rather than as reinforcements, did better.

"The bases are chaotic. Most base staff left to join their regiments on day one. The militia are now running the camps as well as training. Civilians who want to join up haven't been able to because our policy is an 'off the shelf' war. I told Pittman to accept five thousand recruits—to reduce unemployment. The Regular Force desertion rate is 18.2 percent; Combat Arms, eleven percent and Support Services, 23 percent. Combat Arms are less affected than the 1980 study that predicted a desertion rate of 17.8 percent, but it's still high.

"On a positive note, training on the replacement equipment is progressing, though we still have people stuck with NATO and the UN. We tried to replace the PPCLI in Yugoslavia with the Van Doos from NATO. The Serbs wouldn't allow it for fear they'd side with the separatist Croats. Also, the Patricias on Cyprus can't leave until a Finnish battalion arrives in two or three days—I'm told. We could push, but we'll need allies in the UN and we'd better not get too many backs up."

"Good thinking, Al. Keep after Pittman. I knew his estimates were off, but I didn't think they'd be this bad. You might do lunch with General

Vinet, get his views on the desertion rate. If nothing else, it'll light a fire under Pittman's ass. Finance?"

Gilles Leroux had accepted political reality and would stay. Without the moderating influence of men like himself, the party could be forced by public opinion to adopt a policy that would destroy every vestige of French rights in the country.

"Prime Minister, my news is better. Our dollar has stabilized at seventy cents US. Our exporters love it, but to afford new military equipment we must get it back in the 80-cent range. The Bank of Canada can support the dollar now; however, unless we create confidence in our survival we'll be out of foreign reserves by year-end. Foreign bankers tell me unofficially that they'll feel confident if we move against Quebec—and win."

"I'm sure we can restore confidence soon," the Prime Minister soothed. "Now I believe Justice has a problem none of us had thought about."

"I have," Karen Ormsby said in her authoritative voice. "The Cree of northern Quebec want independence from Quebec. Their claim is based on the 1912 agreement. That territory includes most of Quebec's hydro development. They're not being subtle. They say that without our unequivocal support—including armed forces—they'll start bringing down power lines. They want a reply very soon."

"Wait," Banner said. "If they fight, the ALQ will have to react, and that will make our attack at Dorion even more likely to succeed."

" And scuttle us at the UN," Joe Gates stated in his flat, ponderous voice. "Native rights are big now. If we abandon the Cree we kiss a lot of support goodbye. My people are war-gaming this. Our best suggestion is to offer verbal support and create a native special force to defend their territory. We can, I assume, supply rifles?"

Banner flushed at the implied criticism and nodded. The idea had been discussed in his department, but Pittman was against it. He was insisting that his unified soldiers could do the job, because the more help he needed the weaker he looked.

"Very well," the PM said, standing up. "We'll take coffee in the library. In the meantime, think about these ideas. Joe will give our speech at the special UN debate next Monday. How hard a line we take will be decided later.

"Fly the pension loss kite, and suggest that if the opposition is irresponsible enough to defeat the government in mid-crisis, it will effectively break up Canada so *nobody* gets a pension.

"Find what likely defectors want and give it to them. Promise shipbuilding contracts to unhappy Maritimers. We need armaments factories, and we can build them anywhere. Allan." He turned to the pollster. "I meant to ask earlier. Will the Ontario–New Brunswick corridor idea still satisfy the anti-Quebec crowd?"

"Yes, if it's bigger. On the other hand, I'm monitoring this Sloerill. He's been on the National and CNN. He absolutely *drips* virile sincerity, honesty and moderation. Supporting him will help our image, and backing the Cree will let the rednecks stick it to Quebec while appearing to support the noble savage."

"What about West Island Montreal? Will we have to claim that?"

"You can blow it up for all English Canada cares. Quebec's the problem, and les anglais who still live there are seen to be as much a part of it as the separatists.

"I'd like to add that people believe that if the country's coming apart they deserve a piece of the pie before it goes. Ontario farmers want Quebec's milk quota. At least five boycotts have started, mostly against Quebec but some against the west or Ontario. You need a policy that will pull Canada together, stop anarchy and put Quebec in its place—soon."

"Thank you for sharing that with us, Allan. Nothing like a bit of sour cream in the coffee." The Prime Minister led them into the next room.

Near the main camp gate at Farnham an ambulance was parked beside a bullet-riddled green panel truck. A Guardsman and two Fusiliers were placing a stretcher in the ambulance as people came running. Sloerill arrived in a dead heat with Peter Forbes.

"Who is it?" he demanded, then saw the blood-stained face. "Jim Fox!"

A sergeant touched his arm. "He can't hear you, sir. We did what we could but I don't think he has a chance."

The ambulance growled off through the gathering crowd.

"You were with him in Montreal. What happened?"

Sergeant Demers looked tired and depressed. "We got out of

Longue Pointe fast, sir. The area was crawling with ALQ but they were too busy fighting fires to stop a civvy truck. We hid up in my apartment, planning to hit the armoury on Monday."

"This is Thursday. What happened?"

"On Monday the ALQ were taking weapons out so we had to hide again. Tuesday we got chased by a patrol before we even got close. Last night we broke in through the roof, tied up three guards and started piling stuff by the back door. The only problem, sir, the bastards had four guards on the place."

"Didn't you search first?"

Demers flushed. "We did, sir, but some rooms were locked and we didn't want to waste time."

"OK. How did you get away?"

"Shot the guard," Demers replied. "You know the stone in the officers' bar, the one over the fireplace with the carved Guards crest? Mr Fox said it always goes with the regiment in wartime, so we got it. The ALQ guy came in and opened fire. The rock's kinda chipped up and Mr Fox took a couple of rounds in the arms. I shot the guard and we split with the stone. Mr Fox wouldn't leave without it. Sar'nt Blok went for the truck. I bandaged Mr Fox, we loaded everything and took off."

"Are the bridges still guarded?"

"Sir, but they're letting people through real fast. Thing is, talk English. Tell 'em you're scared and are getting the hell out. My parents called my apartment on Tuesday with the word. They left on Sunday. The ALQ just want the English to leave. French refugees mostly get pulled over and given a hard time."

"So what happened to Lieutenant Fox? He has more than arm wounds."

"Right, sir. They made us take highway fifteen to New York, but we cut east above Lacolle and came through Noyan–Clarenceville. Mr Fox was doing fine and we were real happy—till we hit a roadblock."

"From the look of the truck, you ran it," Forbes observed.

"Had to, sir. They were stopping everyone. I slowed down, Danny started shooting and I gunned her. They chased us but we found an FMR patrol and were OK—except for Mr Fox. Near as I can tell, a bullet came through the back, took him in the shoulder and came out his right leg. He's real messed up inside. The FMR called for help but their radio was wonky. I'm sorry, sir. Mr Fox is a nice guy. A real good officer."

Peter looked into the truck. "You certainly were busy." The regimental colours lay across an ornately carved chair from the officers' mess. An oil painting stood against the chair, a bullet hole through the outstretched hand of a young naval officer. The chipped stone with the regimental crest lay near the back door. In a jumble on the floor lay uniforms, pictures and mess silver, some spotted with blood.

"They weren't searching cars so we decided to bring everything," Sergeant Demers explained. "We threw blankets over it at the bridge. Oh, yeah. Someone better take care of this." He picked up a plastic bag with some thin cloth folded up inside. "Mr Fox said it was delicate as all hell."

"Good Lord, the 1812 Colour!" Ashworth exclaimed as he pushed through the crowd. "It was sealed in glass in the mess anteroom."

"What's going on?" Regimental Sergeant-Major Grigson strode up, his highly polished pace stick tucked under his arm, the peak of his forage cap almost touching his nose. At his approach the outer fringes of the circle around the truck began to fade away.

"What's this?" he went on as he saluted. "Who's the driver? You!" His glance spotted Demers' guilty face. "Get it rolling, Sarn't Demers, you're blocking the road. The rest of you—MOVE YOUR IDLE FEET!" His voice rose to a sharp scream that dispersed the crowd as if by magic.

"Sarn't Demers," his voice returned to normal, "get rid of this— object, then report to me on the double. Your vacation's over and I've saved a job or two for you." He delivered another crisp salute to the officers, then wheeled away on his interrupted camp rounds.

On Thursday night the UN Security Council had called a full session of the Assembly for Monday afternoon to discuss Quebec's application for membership and a cease-fire which the Security Council (Canada abstaining) had voted for.

The huge hall was packed with uneasy delegates. Over the years they had debated famines, civil wars, terrorism, invasions and the status of break-away states, but these things had always happened in Asia, Africa or South America. Now they were faced with a similar dispute in the nation the UN itself had described as the best place on earth to live in.

Unofficially the Council President had conferred with Canada on the order in which speakers would be called. Major Canadian supporters would go at the end. Except for the Americans, who insisted on being last, most were members of the Commonwealth. The first speaker had been from Iraq. His violent speech had taunted the Canadians with undisguised glee, effectively asking, "How do you like a taste of your own medicine?"

The hall darkened as the Minister for External Affairs made his ponderous way to the podium. Joe Gates had flown to New York to deliver the speech in person rather than leave it to his ambassador. In his hand he held a thick sheaf of papers.

Emphasizing the solemnity of the occasion, he slowly spread his notes on the podium before looking up, his lined face lit by a single spotlight. He knew that in another room a Quebec delegation was watching. Eleven countries were ready to sponsor their admission. He wanted to prevent a vote on that and if possible prevent even a debate. To his left a huge screen glowed grey and empty high on the wall. It was on that screen that he'd win or lose the battle. The videotapes provided by Colonel Sloerill and a civil servant in Hull gave him confidence. Most of the nations represented in this room owed Canada favours, and his UN staff had been delicately reminding those with short memories of that fact as they canvassed for votes to be cast against Quebec's admission.

When he began to speak, his voice held only a trace of tightly controlled anger. His flat tone and relatively soft delivery with almost no emphasis struck a reassuringly solid chord after the impassioned Iraqi outburst supporting Quebec independence.

"I wish to begin," he said slowly, "by categorically denying the accusations being spread by the so-called government of Quebec. There is rebellion in Canada, not revolution. You know this, but I remind some states that the UN Charter guarantees *national* borders. If this were not so Iraq would have been destroyed. The national borders protected by the Charter are those of Canada, not of its component parts.

"My government welcomes the opportunity to speak before Quebec's official request for admission to UN membership is made because today we speak to the world and cannot be accused of saying one thing to one country and something different to another. Today you will hear the complete and fully documented Canadian position.

"I say 'documented' because we will here before the world examine public charges made against us by Quebec and expose them as lies with incontrovertible evidence. We challenge the rebel government of Quebec to match us in this regard.

"My first point covers the slander that Canadian soldiers murdered prisoners of war. This is a lie. The government of Quebec knows it is a lie, as do the prisoner's families; yet all week a videotape has run on Quebec television, a tape that graphically shows such executions taking place. This irresponsible act has inflamed feelings in Quebec and made the task of finding a peaceful solution very difficult. I now ask you to watch the scenes shown on Quebec TV because you must know the extent of that monstrous lie as you hear the rest of my testimony."

The huge screen lit up with the execution tape, skillfully edited. The UN delegates saw live men being dragged in, bound to posts and heard the "Ready—aim" commands. "Cuts have been made," the TV announcer explained, "to spare the population scenes of horror." The tape then jumped to show the bloody bodies being dragged away. When the screen went blank, the delegates were audibly shocked and the hall buzzed with protest.

"And now, certified by a Justice of the Canadian Supreme Court, here is the uncut tape made by the Canadian troops who participated in the event," Joe Gates continued. "This is the tape sent to the Quebec government by its spies. Scenes censored from the previous tape are marked."

This time the delegates saw shots going into the sandbags, men being clubbed, bodies smeared with blood and dragged away. The room was silent as the tape ended.

"In case some of you doubt what you have seen, I now call for tape three, interviews with the so-called 'murdered' prisoners five days after their 'execution'. Copies of the newspaper you will see them holding are in the kits to be distributed after the session."

The new tape showed well-dressed ALQ prisoners being interviewed and assuring their parents that they were well. Some were defiant. All agreed they had been well treated apart from the faked execution. All held Thursday's St Albans Messenger, the headline "CANADIAN CIVIL WAR!" clearly visible.

"That tape was sent to the family of each prisoner," Gates said evenly. "The British consul hand-delivered a copy to the Quebec government at the same time. Yet the vicious propaganda you saw is *still* being callously used to inflame public opinion in Quebec and raise fears in the hearts of prisoners' families that their sons and husbands are in fact dead. The rebels still claim that their men were murdered. This despicable charge is made by desperate rebels, striving to hold power by any means they can devise. I will return to the subject of murder in a moment. We have brought four of the 'dead' prisoners to New York to testify to the truth of what I have told you. After you question them, they will be released on parole.

"The officer who conducted the fake executions offered his resignation. It was not accepted by the Canadian government because we understood the stress that he was under and his absolute need to find out why his men had been murderously attacked without warning. Isolated, cut off from headquarters and fearing another attack, he took the minimum action necessary to safeguard the lives of his men. This brings me to the next point.

"As confirmed by outside sources, M Cyr began his illegal declaration of independence at 11:07. According to the signals log at Canadian Forces Headquarters, a teletype message was received at 11:11 from Mobile Command, a military base near Montreal, stating that they had been under attack for ten minutes. The final message at 11:53, as M Cyr asked Canadians to 'understand' Quebec's aspirations, stated that the signals room was being overrun. Official transcripts of the messages are available. Thirty-two Canadians, four Americans and two British liaison personnel died in that treacherous attack.

"On the next tape, I will show an even more flagrant violation of the international law this body is sworn to uphold. The militia regiment you saw on the first tape was in Camp Farnham. The ALQ killed fourteen unsuspecting Canadian part-time soldiers before they even knew they were at war."

The tape was short but graphic. A calm scene of men checking weapons and handing in ammunition wobbled as shots were heard. The camera swung to show Colonel Bertrand's men firing. With sound augmented, delegates clearly heard his scream "Kill the English bastards!" Added at the end of the tape was a portion of Forbes's interrogation of six captured ALQ who admitted that they had attacked almost two hours early.

In his seat, the French Ambassador, a Parisian aristocrat who was slated to speak after Canada, shook his head and handed his prepared speech to a senior aide.

"You must answer these charges," she protested. "We must support Quebec."

The Ambassador snorted. "Imbecile. With luck I may be able to raise the question of recognition again—in perhaps a year. I was betrayed by the lies those fools in Quebec told us, but I blame myself too. I should have known enough not to trust a people descended from Norman stock. They are Celts, not French."

Gates was not finished. "As you know, and I have copies of his speech, M Cyr claimed that the insurrection was a spontaneous outburst of Quebec patriotism. If that is true, why have over two hundred thousand people fled Quebec, sixty thousand from the Hull region alone? If that is true, why have most of the Hull refugees returned home now that Canadian forces have reoccupied the city? M Cyr also claims—and this *may* be true—that the revolt surprised him. I ask you to watch a final scene."

As the screen lit up, the British Ambassador turned to an adviser. "The Yanks may object but our SIS chaps handed the Canadians this tip. Considering their navy, I'm surprised that they even caught one arms-runner. Anyway, every day in every way, they owe us more and more. Are the additions to my speech ready? I want our gift of Challenger tanks to come at the very end. We're competing with the Yanks for arms sales, and I want to give Chester as little time as possible to think up ways to top our offer."

Delegates saw a freighter, low in the water. A smoking shell hole in the bow showed how the captain had been finally persuaded to stop engines. Armed figures were climbing the sides of the ship from a motor launch alongside. After a blurred scene on deck, the next views were of Canadian sailors tearing open packing cases of weapons and ammunition, and pulling coverings from artillery pieces and tanks.

The lights came on. "The ship is the *Lyons*, Panamanian registry," Gates explained. "We do not suggest that France is implicated. The ship manifests are clear, however. The arms were loaded in Algiers two weeks before the rebellion began. This ship and four others lurked in mid-Atlantic, waiting to make delivery on October twelfth. They were ordered into Montreal at 7:00 AM on October seventh—well before the declaration of independence. My government believes that the coup date was moved up by a week. If anyone will advance the argument that five ships, loaded with arms, sat in the Atlantic for several days and on hearing of a rebellion, albeit a few hours before it began, decided independently to make for Quebec, I will gladly debate the point."

There was subdued laughter. Gates felt the wave of support and built on it. "I have," he held up a paper, "a letter from M Cyr, dated last month, which acknowledges our right to a corridor connecting Ontario and New Brunswick in the 'unlikely' event that he is 'forced' to adopt a separatist policy. In that corridor three hundred Canadian civilians died or were wounded. Hundreds of millions of dollars in damage has been done by a so-called Quebec army—" the speaker leaned forward, and now his voice rang with passion—"operating in a part of Quebec Cyr had agreed would be ceded to Canada—*and they dare accuse us of murder!*

"This illegal attack is inexcusable. Yet if the Quebec people support M Cyr in a democratic election or referendum, we ask only for sufficient territory to maintain east-west links and to protect the language and culture of the indigenous people of Canada's North. This land will be held in trust because we are confident that Quebec will soon return to its proper place in our great country.

"I close with this. President Cyr refuses to talk peace in Ottawa because that would 'humiliate' Quebecers. Cyr's treachery humiliates them more. We have pictures of wanton damage to civilian targets in southern Quebec and in Hull. Each photo is attached to a notarized statement from a mayor identifying the town, target, date, and the casualties suffered. In over ninety percent of cases the mayors are French Canadian. I ask this assembly to refuse to consider Quebec's application for UN membership. I ask it to expel rebel delegations. I invite the UN to Canada. I assure full co-operation in any investigation they may make. I challenge Quebec to do the same. Canada asks you to set a cease-fire. We will abide by its terms— but we reserve the right to retaliate if we are attacked again. Our navy will continue to intercept arms shipments. This is not a blockade but a legal exercise of Canadian sovereignty.

"Finally, we call on you under the Charter to condemn this rebellion, rebellion Canada tried to avoid by painful constitutional compromise, rebellion that could spread. As a founding member of this body, one that has never made a territorial claim on any nation, we appeal to the international community we have worked with for five decades to support one of the oldest democracies of this troubled world."

Joe Gates returned slowly to his seat. The cheering of his staff was almost lost amid the standing international sea of supporters, waving papers and clapping. He permitted himself a small self-congratulatory smile as he acknowledged the rolling applause. The speech would play well back home. Such a reaction had never been seen in the staid hall before. The president of the Assembly deliberately let it go on. When it died he recognized the French ambassador, who merely supported a cease-fire (his audience declining as delegations followed the Canadians to their briefing), endorsed sending a fact-finding mission to Canada and Quebec, and closed with a plea for calm and understanding.

In the American section, a senior diplomat handed an envelope to his ambassador. It contained the two hundred dollars he had lost on their bet on what the Canadians would do and say. The Ambassador smiled and slipped the envelope into his pocket.

"You're too young to remember World War II, Doug, but I'm not. Despite Canada's new wimp reputation, when the cards go down they fight. If it's any consolation, I bet the President double. The way I put it, as I remember, is 'the Canadian speech will show more balls than the entire United States Congress'—or words to that effect."

He stood up. "Since we're not due to speak until after the British, let's go and congratulate old Joe. If there's any sign of the Quebec crowd, ignore them."

"Diplomatically or pointedly?"

The ambassador thought about it briefly. "What the hell, it was a great speech—pointedly."

Around Camp Farnham, everybody was moving with extra snap. For days they'd been inundated with reporters anxious to glean some detail the others had missed. What was special about the Tuesday after the UN debate was that ABC News was there in the form of their major news star. Peter Harrison, a Canadian who had made it big in the United States, had come to place his stamp of approval on the event, arriving with a full crew of cameramen, sound men producers and directors to record definitively the story of Canada's civil war.

He had been given the standard jeep ride close enough to the action to hear shooting but far enough away to avoid danger. They knew the ALQ would behave. It would be suicide for their cause if an important American TV newsman was killed by their action.

At a dirt crossroads in the hills east of Bromont the TV crew ran into a Guards patrol commanded by Sergeant Demers. Waiting to rendez-vous with another group, their armed jeeps were tucked into the thick evergreen woods lining the road. Demers let the TV crew shoot the soldiers behind the guns and explained how the camouflage was applied.

"We cover the jeeps with rubber cement, then press strips of bur-lap over it. After that we sprinkle it with sand, dirt and twigs. Looks good, and when you peel it off again, the jeep's shiny clean."

Demers had no objection to his men being interviewed so long as the guns were manned and they stayed alert. As Harrison talked to the sol-diers, Demers prowled the road, his eyes and ears open for the ALQ and for what interviewees were saying. Finally, despite orders to give all reporters as much of a free rein as possible, he stepped in. Harrison was asking one of his Guardsman about "the enemy" again.

"Wisebraugh, back to your jeep, get cocked," he ordered sharply. The Guardsman fled gratefully and Demers turned to face the reporter.

"Sorry, sir, but you're getting my man into trouble. I can't allow that."

"I wasn't getting anyone into trouble!" The reporter was angry and sounded it. "I was just asking where the enemy was and how well trained they were."

"That's the problem, sir. We don't have an enemy here. That's an order. If you'd got Wisebraugh to say the word, he'd have been in trouble with the Colonel. I see that, I stop it just like I'd stop him from stepping on a mine."

"What do you mean 'we don't have an enemy'?" Harrison de-manded. "Today I spoke to a dozen wounded men in the hospital. Who shot them, their friends?"

"No sir, those guys were shot by the ALQ, otherwise known as Sugar Delta Tangos, but never as enemies. Our guys are called Sugar Delta Oscars.

"See, sir," Demers went on before the reporter could speak, "after the war we gotta get ourselves back together. Start calling people 'enemy' and it's kinda hard to shake the habit after a bit. They say it took the Americans over a hundred years. We can do without that. The Colonel passed the word that 'enemy' is a no-no. So's anything else that puts us French-Canadians down. Now Wisebraugh's a Gretz, he even might be a good Guardsman in time, but he's no rocket scientist. You keep asking about 'enemies' and he'll pick it up."

The reporter was confused. "But you *have* to have an enemy in a war. Who are those Sugar Delta Tangos you mentioned?"

Demers looked embarrassed. "Ah, just a code name for the ALQ. We're Sugar Delta Oscars—phonetic alphabet for S, D, and O."

"I probably know the phonetic alphabet as well as you do, Sergeant. What do the letters stand for—or is that a military secret?"

Demers shuffled his feet. "Depends on what you can say on TV now. Well, I guess I've heard worse. OK. Sugar Delta Tangos are Shit-Disturbers-Theirs. Sugar Delta Oscars are Shit-Disturbers-Ours. It sort of keeps it even. A Gunner invented that, sir."

Harrison shook his head. "You've got your own language like we did in the Gulf and Nam. What's a Gretz?"

"Hockey, sir. Wayne Gretzky. A good guy."

" And 'cocked'?"

"That's 'ready to go', sir."

"Private Wisebraugh said that—"

"Sorry about this, sir, but Wisebraugh's a Guardsman, not a private. Well, he's enough of a Guardsman to be out here with us anyway. Believe me, sir, there's a difference between Guardsmen and privates."

" All right, *Guardsman* Wisebraugh said this patrol was supposed to be a wall jumper, then it started tapping. What did he mean?"

"Wall-jumping is from a bar game, you know, where you take a running jump at the wall wearing velcro pads and get stuck on? If we hadda bumped the ALQ, we'd've stuck to 'em till they were dead or we'd turned 'em into six-packs—ah, prisoners held with plastic beer can loops. Tapping is French, tapannage. It's like effing about but I guess on TV you should probably call it 'waiting'. That's what we're doin' now."

"Can you write a list of those terms so we can follow what you're telling us?"

"That's a lot to ask of slugs—infantrymen, sir."

"So you're a slug, sergeant?"

"Negit sir, infantry are slugs, tankers are rivet heads and the recce crowd in their dinky toys are dinks. Gunners are yuppies—baby-boomers, sir. I'm not infantry, I'm Guards. I hear the guys in lesser regiments call us toe caps."

"I'll ask for a dictionary when I get back. Thank you, Sergeant— ah—what's your name, anyway? You people don't seem to wear name tags."

"Nossir. The men know their names. Most can even write 'em. We sergeants—and officers—know our men. Only people who want name tags are Ottawa, the ALQ and you Tin Tins. I'm Sar'nt Demers, sir."

"Tin Tins are reporters? From the French comic strip?"

"Hole in one, sir. 'Scuse me, but I'd better get a grip on my crowd. You want another guy to interview, just pick him and go—but no 'enemy' stuff, OK?"

"I think I'll wrap this up now." Harrison signalled his cameraman for a two-shot as he caught Demers by the belt and pulled him close. "And so," he said looking into the camera, "in this war men kill one another but are not enemies. A new military language is invented to prevent the scars of war from going too deep. A country is split and, as in the American ex-perience, families are divided. But here on a lonely road, one small patrol of toe caps, led by Sergeant Demers, intend to win, respecting the men they're fighting and, just perhaps, avoiding the terrible schisms that shook America after its civil war. For World News Tonight, I'm Peter 'Tin Tin' Harrison reporting from a location near Bromont, Quebec, Canada."

CHAPTER TEN

Esprit de Corps

Zuke drove with less than his usual panache. In a training area you never knew when a group of men would burst from the underbrush under your wheels. Sloerill sat glumly beside him on his way to meet Dave Phillips, who was running the recruit training programme. Today Phillips would be either promoted or given an administrative job. Sloerill had reviewed the situation several times and still didn't know which it would be.

He needed more trained men. The ALQ were playing cat-and-mouse games now. They had the edge because many of them (though fewer than at the start), were local mice, and even aided by Tom's Gunners his Montreal cats didn't know where the mouseholes were.

Pierre Coté's eighty-seven Guardsmen were almost ready to fight. They were "trained", but George had agreed with RSM Grigson: "I wouldn't trust them with fireworks." They would be ready next week. Another hundred and fifty Highlanders, seventy-five regular force recruits from St Jean and thirty-six RMR from Knowlton would be ready soon after.

Sloerill also had eighty raw recruits. He had sent them to a regular force training school once he'd gotten a written assurance that they'd be sent back. In this war one local man was worth ten imports who didn't know the people or the territory.

The largest group in training consisted of the ex-regulars and militiamen who were streaming into camp almost daily. Now numbering over two hundred, they had been well trained in the past and needed only a refresher course to become so again. He had already sent thirty of them, mostly ex-regulars, to Colonel St Pierre.

Yesterday forty-two men had arrived from Sherbrooke, all that were left of one hundred and sixty militiamen who had taken on the ALQ without orders or military weapons. After Colonel Frappier's former Van Doos had broken their resistance the survivors, a ragtag mix of Sherbrooke Hussars and Fusiliers, had fought their way to Farnham.

They'd arrived angry over their losses, dazed with fatigue, but determined to fight. George had seen their red-rimmed eyes and dirty bandages and ordered them to rest and retrain, promising them a better chance of winning next time.

Zuke braked as a tank neared the road half-concealed in choking dust. The commander in the turret suddenly began talking urgently into his radio. As the tank rocked to a halt, almost from under the treads, infantrymen rose out of the brush and long frost-brown grass. Their officer raced forward, screaming insults at "blind tin-heads!" to be told with greater emphasis that his slugs were on the wrong map square.

"Kinda crowded," Zuke observed as he bypassed the confrontation. Sloerill grunted. The training area was too small. The tanks had to move to the Abercorn base as quickly as possible.

At the training area Dave Phillips, warned by a sentry, met the Colonel's jeep outside his tent with a report in his hand. Sloerill waved it off and led him inside.

Phillips was a handsome bull of a man, a physical fitness freak whose powerful body could be pushed far beyond the endurance level of most men. No one worked harder, but when Dave's lips thinned, it was easier to move mules than to change his mind. Now his lips were firmly pressed together as if he knew what was coming.

Stubbornness could be useful, but it could also limit the flexibility a field officer needed to lead and survive. Dave had come to the Guards as an officer cadet and had at first flatly refused to grow the obligatory moustache. George had ordered him to obey the senior subaltern, but the moustache had been shaved one year to the day after its birth.

"Relax, Dave, I'm not here to order you into another moustache," he began awkwardly, not quite sure how Dave would react. "This time I'm asking you only to grow one metaphorically, and to want to because you understand why it's the right thing to do."

"Sir?" Dave asked cautiously. Unlike many regimental quiffs, Guards verbal brevity was one he approved of because it was efficient.

"You're doing a good job, Dave, but I question your, ah . . . training philosophy, I guess. You aren't teaching regimental history. All platoons are the same size with men from every unit mixed in. That destroys regimental team spirit. Colonel Berkowitz wanted to see his men yesterday, and he had to chase down six separate platoons."

"Sir, if I divided platoons by units I'd need six more instructors. You asked me to crank these guys out ASAP. I'm doing it. As for regimental history, I can't believe a man's a better soldier if he can recite a lot of old battle honours."

"He is, Dave. He is. I'll get you extra instructors, but that isn't the real problem, and you know it." Sloerill paused. Dave had been stuck out in the training area from day one. He couldn't see and feel the spirit growing among the different regiments as they compared their record of successful patrols, prisoner bags, and reaction times with other units, rationalized their mistakes, and built unit pride on unit successes.

"Dave, I want you to visit HQ once a day to get a feel for unit morale. We couldn't have done half what we've done without regimental spirit. I see the FMR too tired to move and say, 'OK, you're at the wall, let the Guards take over.' They shake their heads, get up and start moving again. They won't let another regiment do their job because that would mean they aren't the best. They need to feel they're in the best unit with the best leaders anywhere. Nobody wants to die for a united Canada or a corridor. They *will* die, if they have to, for a buddy—or their regiment."

"Yes, but sir, every unit can't be the best."

"It can to the men in it, Dave. I don't mean they'll excel everywhere. There are no all-purpose units. But give a man a badge and something to show he's different; tell him how good his regiment was in the past and challenge him to live up to that reputation; call him Gunner, Fusilier, Highlander or Guardsman; and soon you get more than a trained soldier, you get a regiment that can do far more than a collection of trained individuals."

"Jim Fox was the most regimental man I've ever known, sir. Was his death worth the things he brought back?"

George had known the question was coming and knew the answer might seem callous. "Yes," he said softly. "I regret his death—but what he did was a tonic the Guards needed badly. Everything else had been forced on us. Jim's raid hit back. It was a gesture, but now he's a hero to the men. He set a standard they try to follow. When Guardsmen come in, they ask to see the Colours, the fireplace stone, the colonel's chair. Jim gave us pride. Now they divide wounds into Jims and non-Jims. A non-Jim wound doesn't require evacuation. I've heard seriously wounded men protest 'it isn't a real Jim' and ask to stay in action. What he did was more valuable in the long term than the Longue Pointe raid."

Phillips digested the speech for a moment, then to Sloerill's relief his lips relaxed. "I'll give it a try, sir—and perhaps I can make do with only four extra instructors."

George grinned and took two dull bronze crowns from his pocket. "Hole in one as they say. Put these on, Acting-Major Phillips. These are pre-unification Guards rank badges. I'm putting the whole regiment into them, starting today. You're the first."

Dave fingered the crowns, a pleased smile fighting his reluctance to wear anything unauthorized. "Boy, I've only seen these in our museum. I have two Guards ensigns in my HQ, and there's Pierre Coté's bunch. Do you have enough for everybody?"

"I hope so." Sloerill put down a bag containing two dozen bronze elongated six-pointed stars whose design incorporated the Order of the Garter ribband and the motto *Honi Soit Qui Mal Y Pense.* "I collected a set in case unification died. It's my present to the regiment."

"Will Ottawa let us wear them?"

"At the moment, they're so confused up there they're stabbing each other in the chest. By the time they get sorted out we'll have a system in place they can't touch. Tomorrow you'll get blue berets for the Guards, and Colonel Berkowitz has bonnets for his Highlanders. Colonel Chantilly wants khaki berets for his Gunners. If you're the best, you want something to show you're different."

Sloerill stood up. "The militia's mobilizing, and we're generally non-unified. Once we outnumber the regulars we can take over the whole damned war.

"By the way, there's a CTV crew coming out. Have the men talk up their units. If they question your new badges, say they link the regiment to the Royal Family. Plug unit traditions. Stress the *French* Canadian contribution. The whole country's watching us. Explain how regimental spirit keeps us going. If we get that message across, Ottawa won't dare mess up what we've done."

Ottawa had other worries. NATO had allowed Canadian forces to withdraw from Europe, but the UN Commander in Cyprus had blocked the airfield to prevent Canadians from leaving before the Finns arrived. The president of the UN, worried about the Balkans, had called to express the hope that in trying to solve its problem Canada would not create more difficulties for him. The Princess Pats were still in Cyprus and in Dubrovnik, along with a thousand Canadian support troops and engineers.

On the political front, the polls were showing impossible variations in public opinion. Hostility to the war and to Quebec was growing. The opposition, scenting blood, were reluctant to even discuss the idea of forming a war cabinet that would link them with government policy.

Seething from failure to form the needed coalition, the Prime Minister was trying to reach the Cabinet Room. A scrum of reporters filled the grey stone corridor with TV mikes, tape recorders, lights and notebooks. As his security wedge reached the door, a microphone managed to pierce the screen.

"Prime Minister!" a veteran of a thousand such scrums shouted over the din. "Is Quebec going to get away with this?"

Furiously, the PM seized the mike. "No!" he shouted into the avidly waiting recorders. "We didn't give in to terrorism in 1970 and we won't now!" The door to the Cabinet Room opened. The PM threw the mike back and escaped.

As the door closed, he paused to take stock. He had just committed the country to a war against Quebec, exactly what his pollster said would renew his popularity—and split his government. Allan had better be right on the first part and wrong on the second.

"Ladies and gentlemen," he began, slipping into his hand-carved maplewood chair. "We must state a policy. Delay will fracture the country and lead to defections that will force an election. If one were to be held today, most of us would become unemployed."

Those who had been around longest sat up, recognizing the tone. The first among equals was about to become the Leader, the man in charge.

"Our UN strategy worked perfectly. There's no chance of Quebec's independence being recognized. Also, as I said in the House, we're discussing a cease-fire, but with no great enthusiasm. General Pittman says we must move soon or the ALQ will be too strong for us. The Intelligence people say there are still some Quebec sympathizers in the Civil Service, not all of them French, so our plan may not be secret. Remember, in the American Civil War the South nearly captured Washington. Had they done so historians believe the South might have won.

"As I respect General Pittman's expertise, I also respect your sincerely held views, even though they may not be popular. They show character and represent our party's determination to debate fully and take tough decisions, not popular ones. However, now we must act.

"If you cannot support what we decide today, I do not expect you to compromise your conscience by staying. Ten Quebec Senate seats have come open. The war will require new federal agencies, many of a humanitarian nature that need chairs with a basic grasp of realpolitik." He paused to look benignly around the table.

"I have heard well-founded legal and moral arguments for Canada to make larger land claims on Quebec and also for allowing Quebec to separate. These are not narrow legal or constitutional issues; we are talking about Canada's survival."

Deliberately building suspense, the Prime Minister opened his briefcase, extracted two sheets of paper, placed them carefully on the dark table, and closed the case again.

"According to some polls, sixty-two percent of English Canadians support taking Quebec back, up from forty-eight last Friday. We had asked if this course should be followed even if it meant war. Seventy-nine percent expressed the opinion that such a war would last only a few weeks. On the other hand, fifty-nine percent described our conduct of the war so far as 'indecisive', and forty percent say we're too harsh."

He put down the first paper and picked up the second. "General Pittman sent what the military calls an 'Appreciation'. It deals with relative strengths of ourselves and the Quebec forces and with the numbers of ALQ that Colonel Sloerill is tying down in the Eastern Townships."

The PM deliberately looked around the table, engaging each pair of eyes. "General Pittman claims we can retake Montreal and end the rebellion." Considering what had gone wrong so far, he did not believe the rosy forecast, but his cabinet needed good news. "Mopping-up operations will probably take the rest of the winter."

"Why so long?" demanded Bill O'Hagen. "Sloerill is cleaning the ALQ clocks with only a few militiamen. Once we turn the regulars loose, it's game over."

"General Pittman states that Colonel Sloerill's success was due almost entirely to surprise. Many of the ALQ are also professional soldiers. He says Colonel Sloerill cannot hold out much longer without substantial regular-force help."

The Prime Minister knew it was time to confess his outburst. "When I arrived just now, I lost my temper and made an inflammatory statement to the media about our war aims."

"How far did you commit us?" Gates asked bluntly. After his UN speech, he felt safe from prime-ministerial wrath.

"I said Quebec won't get away with this," the PM said flatly. "The public will interpret that as recovering all of Quebec. My contact in Cyr's office says he's a prisoner of the radical element and unable or unwilling to act. He indicates that if we win a decisive battle, Quebec will negotiate. We'll call that a victory, make a few power-sharing concessions, and Quebec will be back in Canada again.

"The choice is clear. Win or surrender to rebels. Our military people say we can win. The polls say we'd better not surrender." He looked around the table. Six pairs of eyes refused to meet his directly, and for the first time that day he smiled.

"Do we need a formal vote? Good. The exigencies of the situation make a course of reunification clearly necessary. Any minister who does not agree may see me privately afterwards.

"Now, at Question Period today we'll be asked about a refugee compensation programme. This is Gilles's and Normand's territory, but I'm open to constructive suggestions from anyone. Also, Karen, get your legal beagles working up legislation to protect any Canadian who had his or her property seized after they left Quebec."

*

The expanded Farnham Operations Room, was for once filled with smoke. St Pierre, Chantilly, Pieters, Berkowitz, Forbes, Markos and Coté outnumbered the non-smoking Sloerill, Ashworth, Bryce, Phillips and Manieri. A window was open.

There was some good-natured banter with Sloerill about the new Guards badges, because as a full colonel and not on regimental strength, he couldn't wear them.

Ashworth reported on manpower and equipment, making references to the diagrams hung on the now pale yellow walls. Inspired by Peter Forbes, the Guardsmen slumped or sprawled in their chairs. Even the hyper-active Markos tried to look bored. St Pierre and Chantilly sat as at a Board of Directors meeting. Maarten Pieters (Armoured Corps) fiddled with a pencil, while the technical experts Andy Bryce and Tony Manieri waited impatiently for the group to discuss the helicopter guns and radios dear to their respective hearts.

Equipment was arriving slowly. Most was coming by truck, but a supply train from Ontario was now being unloaded at Abercorn under the supervision of André Taschereau.

"We keep two command APC's and six armoured cars," Ashworth announced. "All other APC's are to be shipped out on that Abercorn train."

Sloerill saw his officers didn't like that. "Glad to see the Dinky Toys go," he interjected. "I want our people out talking to people, not living in sardine cans."

"What about my tanks?" Pieters wanted to know.

"We keep twelve Centurions. The Leopards go with the APC's. The only battle we really won was the helicopters. We keep our wokkas and two more are coming."

Andrew Bryce beamed but Pieters snapped a pencil between his stubby fingers. "The Centurion was a good tank in Korea. Today it's an antique. It is foolhardy to try to fight from them."

Sloerill took over from Ashworth and looked disapprovingly at Pieters's name tag. "I hope I won't see that again," he said mildly, pointing to the offending item.

Pieters looked startled. "Sorry. I forgot. NDHQ requires everyone to wear name tags." He ran a hand over his greying brush-cut hair, and stroked his moustache.

An edge crept into Sloerill's voice. "My orders are that *no* name tags be worn. I will not have men showing their names so the ALQ can shoot their families. By the way, I trust you know the Leopards we're losing have a rated battle survival time of four minutes? Their only real advantage over a Centurion is better turret armour. Now, how many of your crews can fight—even in a Centurion?"

Pieters cocked his head in a way that told Sloerill he was considering a new idea. "Six or seven," he admitted finally. "Four are reg force, but in antiques like ours—"

"All but four antiques are going to Abercorn," Sloerill cut him off. "Start early tomorrow. Move openly. Civilians won't know they're antiques, they'll just see that these bloody huge things are on our side. At Abercorn, do driving, fire control and communications till you drop.

"Four tanks and crews go to Bedford tonight. I found a metal-working shop that can do a turret modification that may approximate modern spaced armour. Impress on everyone that speed is essential. I doubt that the ALQ will give us all the time we need or would like."

His eyes moved to Armand Chantilly, giving Pieters a chance to work through the idea of a new training area and upgrading his tanks. "How about your guns, Armand? When do we get covering fire from them?"

"One six-gun battery on Tuesday with God's help and Tom's Gunners," Chantilly said calmly. "A second comes on line—I hope Friday. Number three needs two more weeks at least." He spoke in English in deference to Leo Markos, whose Ontario French wasn't up to Chantilly's normal fast delivery.

"I hate to tell you this, Armand," Sloerill said ruefully, "but you won't get Tom's men back that soon. I need them as guides for another week. The Montreal crowd are improving but they still get lost."

"Eh bien," Chantilly said resignedly and started to make changes in his plan with swift, sure strokes of the pen. "With four-gun batteries, I can have two ready on Wednesday." He looked up with a quick smile. "It is done, but I must warn you that, while the guns will fire, I make no claims as to hitting targets. Only one officer besides myself has ever directed live artillery fire before."

"Hang in there, Armand. Manieri?" Sloerill looked at the signals officer.

"Cocked, sir." He'd been working on a new signals diagram that incorporated his latest relay stations. The normally reserved officer liked the new crisp military slang. "My net [1] went operational at approx 1023 hours this morning."

Manieri was a jewel without price. While improving the technical quality of his net, he ran an impromptu training course for all ranks. Manieri's now famous "Hello, last station, Control suggests—" was frequently heard before a devastating critique of the sender's message and a suggested rewording to cut it by half. Rank was no shield, and messages were now approaching the brevity and clarity Manieri demanded. Over forty radios were on the air at any given time; wordiness had to go.

"How goes the wokka patrol?" George turned to Andrew Bryce, the man who believed helicopters (and their pilots) could win the war alone.

The cropped blond head came up quickly. "I have a bird in the air at all times now. Vehicle recognition signals are set, but some slugs are slow in showing them. My wokkies need to know if it's a Delta Oscar or a Delta Tango down there. I sure hope they hang some weapons pods on the new birds so we can shoot back."

"Back?" Sloerill asked sharply.

Bryce shrugged. "When we pick up ground fire we just send a Hotel Foxtrot signal to the nearest patrol and fly cover till they wax 'em. Give me mini guns and we'll handle our own problems."

Sloerill grinned. "First of all, Hotel Foxtrot, Hot Fox or High Five is for an operational success, not a spotting. It's a new language, let's keep it simple. Don't use Hot Fox unless the ALQ die of fright watching you fly. Second, I want you to fly more than shoot. I'm not convinced you know the difference between running ALQ and farmers chasing the cows your wokkas have panicked." Bryce looked unconvinced.

"Cheer up, Andrew. Your shooting irons are coming. Once they arrive, we can fight about how to use them."

Bryce sat back, mollified. When the Colonel offered to fight with you, you could put your views forward as forcefully as you wanted without getting shot down.

"Very well, gentlemen. If there are no questions, you're excused.

---

[1] Radio network

Infantry stays. Colonel Pieters, I want your tank move plan tonight—and check with the locals. Not all our bridges can take tanks."

With the others gone, the infantrymen moved closer together. "OK, I won't hold you long. I want feelings, not reports. How's it coming together? How are the locals receiving you? Do your men really believe they should take risks to protect civilians?" He looked at his commanders one by one. "Jan?"

Colonel Berkowitz hadn't impressed him at first. Far below the intellectual level of St Pierre and Chantilly, he was slow in comparison; but he had compensating qualities. He was as brave as any man Sloerill knew. He took more chances than his men and in return got their unswerving loyalty. Jan also reduced complicated issues to street language his men could feel. When visiting the Black Watch, Sloerill had been amused to learn how few of his actual words had reached the men but how well they understood his intent. Berkowitz had placed a very personal stamp on his growing command.

Typically, Berkowitz didn't directly answer the question. "We have the best territory in the area, real highland country. The people are fine. I mention shortages and we get a flood of hand-knitted socks and sweaters. Pipe-Major Davidson started a piping class in Knowlton—you may hear from the parents on that one. The people around Magog are a wee bit nervous when we show up. They're on the front line, as it were, but they're bonny. We're making good friends there."

"Are they giving you information?"

"Well," Berkowitz said slowly, "indirectly. We ask about a place. If the ALQ are there, the locals evade the question—but very openly," he added defensively. "They're good people, and we can't always protect them. I get all I need."

"And you, Toupée?" St Pierre's men were stretched along the Richelieu River from the U.S. border to the Autoroute in the north, facing the ALQ base in St Jean.

St Pierre shrugged. "Unlike Jan's, my territory is like a billiard table with eight-foot side ditches. Farms confuse my city boys, but they're learning. My Fusiliers are also no longer defensive. They have seen too many French-Canadians killed or wounded by the ALQ. We have a home-visit programme. Patrols stop at all houses in their area. Every farm has now been visited at least twice, and we have reached almost every house in every town once. We keep a book on each family, what is said, impressions of reliability, visitors—that sort of thing. The dossier grows impressively, and I check to ensure that information is not entered creatively. Our campaign to persuade people to fly both Canadian and Quebec flags advances slowly. There is, for one thing, a shortage of flags."

"I'll order some. When they arrive, your men can hand them out."

"I believe, Colonel, it is better if people buy them rather than receive a gift," St Pierre stated firmly.

"Good point. Leo? What's happening on the Guards front?"

Major Markos uncoiled like a spring. Unlike Peter Forbes who looked relaxed at all times, Leo was always moving, impatient with delay. "Cowansville is now quiet. The local militia are under control. No more flag incidents. Visiting homes is taking too much of our time." He shrugged. "At least the ALQ haven't bothered us since we hammered them last time they crossed the autoroute. That's the way we'll finish this thing, by fighting, not taking a census."

"I suspect we'll get more fighting than we really want," Sloerill replied sharply. "If we get another week of semi-peace, I'll be happy. The UN cease-fire talks won't get anywhere. Canada can't give the ALQ time to train and arm. Keep up the visits. There'll come a day when you'll need to know where your friends are as well as who they are."

"Oh, I'll keep visiting," Markos grumbled, "but did you hear how we nailed that ALQ patrol? Bryce spotted them. Four Platoon humped in that night. For my dawn patrol, I only used five jeeps and five men. The ALQ ambush was right where we predicted. They hit us and Four Platoon hit them. Bryce landed a cutoff party. Three ALQ dead, seventeen sixpacks and it cost me two non-Jims. A pink!" He rubbed his hands gleefully. Pinks, from the paper on which the "right" training solutions were printed for umpires to use on exercises, were operations that went exactly to plan.

"Wayne Jones planned it," Markos went on. He always gave his men credit for their work and defended them when plans went awry.

"Keep it up. Variety may not only be the spice of life, it may be life itself. Now, when Peter's men come back from their training exercise Sunday, Three Company goes on battle course." He looked at Coté. "Then if your crowd are up to it I'll give you a job."

Coté smiled. His company had almost finished training and had a distinctive air, the tension of eagerness. "Cocked, sir. We've worked our tails off, and I tell them real ops will be a snap. We're ready when you are."

Coté still carried a flask for show. He claimed no Guards officer was properly dressed without one. He had taken eighty-three men at several levels of training, all disgruntled at being out of the action, and turned them into a cocky, well disciplined company that called itself JC Force. Drill-Sergeant Coutts had explained the term to Sloerill last week, wearing a broad grin. "Jesus Christ came into the world to save it, sir. We've taught our men the way, and now we'll come into the war to save the poor bastards who don't have our training."

"The job will fit your religious instruction, Pierre. You too are going to a mountain, where you'll find inordinate temptations in the form of new toys lying around Base Abercorn. Grab a wokka and do a recce, but I advise doing it on an empty stomach. Air Bryce has one inflexible rule: he who messes up the floor cleans up the floor."

John Ashworth put his head in. "When you finish, sir, an NBC crew's waiting for an interview. So's CNN. I have a pile of papers that require your signature rather than my reasonable facsimile. The Fus MR called from the border to say an American adviser is on his way up. They say his French isn't bad—for an American."

"Is that all?" George asked as he began to gather his papers.

"Good heavens, no, sir. An entire CBC Radio programme will die without the latest poop from the horse's mouth as opposed to the end they usually hear from—official sources. You also promised a decision on the women-in-combat question. NDHQ says go. My figures tend not to support their assumptions."

As the young major finished his briefing, General Pittman sat back, a worried look on his pink face. Like most people at NDHQ he wore greens, and although he knew the four officers with him intimately, like them he wore hard a black plastic name tag above his breast pocket. General Pittman believed in setting an example.

"Thank you, Major Winetka," he said formally, nodding at the door as he spoke. The major saluted and went out, clutching his briefing notes and wondering how the bad news he had delivered would affect his career.

"OK, let's get down to it," Pittman said slowly, looking around the plain oak table. His Air and Sea Commanders wore light and dark blue. The soldiers wore army combat. "General Thomas, I want good news for the PM when we have dinner tomorrow at 24 Sussex. General Overly, what in hell's wrong with your militia? The projected reinforcement figures aren't even close to what we're actually getting. As for Air," he turned to General Plourde, "I know you lost planes, but why can't we get more missions? I need photo reconnaissance of ALQ positions. I'd do better with a Kodak in a Cessna." He saw the Air Commander bristle. He hated to come down that hard, but as an airman he expected his former command to do better.

"Unfortunately, the Navy is as bad. We'll start there. Boarding that ship before the UN meeting made us look good, but since then, nothing. What's happening, Admiral Blake?"

The sailor wasn't going to let his service get savaged. "Point one, we lost two ships in Montreal. My best remaining one took an Exocet hit yesterday, leaving one destroyer and one new frigate at sea. Two usable destroyers are on harbour duty because I had to use their seamen to fill the holes left in Base Halifax when you pulled out the army-qualified people. With all that ocean out there, I only caught the freighter because one of my Orion surveillance planes spotted it. Now the army want them to spot ALQ movement. If I lose *any* I can't enforce our blockade."

"Keep the Orions, and I'll mention new ships to the PM. He doesn't know anything about navy problems. Give me figures on the number of square miles to be covered, ship speeds, radar coverage—that sort of thing. I think he'll buy it. If he doesn't—"

"If he doesn't he'll lose his Commander, Maritime Command," Admiral Blake said harshly. "My resignation is ready. If he shits on my sailors again the way he did in Cabinet, I'll advise him to learn bridge navigation and gunnery."

"Now, Terry, play it cool," Pittman soothed. "Our politicians are scared of losing their jobs and our country, in about that order. They say things they don't mean. You'll get your ships. Did you order the Pacific fleet back?"

"Fleet? I ordered four old destroyers to Halifax, one of which has a boiler that's only good for half-speed. They'll be in by mid-November— I hope."

"I'll mention that to the PM too. Give it to me in writing today. Do you know how that Exocet missile got you?"

"The radar picked up a blip at extreme range near a mountain. It turned away and vanished. It must have dropped onto the deck, gone wet-foot[2] at sea level, fired and run. I'd asked for air protection. I never got it."

"How often do you refit your ships, every five years?" General Plourde demanded hotly. "CF-18's need more maintenance. With the repair facility in Montreal gone, I can't keep more planes up than I do now. As for reconnaissance, General Pittman, the refit to take cameras would have been done in Montreal. The Americans can do it, but that level of support hasn't been authorized. They give us refueling stops and spare parts, and one base in Maine hands out ammo after dark. My CF-5's now belong to the ALQ except for two at Cold Lake. We're also fitting cameras into our air-demo Tudors. I should be able to give you pictures in two weeks—but if there's any ground-to-air defence system, we're gone."

"Are the ALQ flying the captured planes? Is there enemy air activity—opposition?"

"They fly mostly recce missions—they have the refit base, remember? So far, no shooting. The estimate on taking them out on the ground isn't good. Their F-18's and F-5's are at four airfields, dispersed, revetted and protected by ground-to-air missiles. If they come up I can hit them, but before I promise effective Combat Air Patrols, I need a repair facility and more planes. Let me tell you, admiral, if you think the ocean off the coast is big, take a look at the sky over Quebec. I had a CAP on your ship yesterday but it had to leave before the enemy appeared. Unlike your ships, when planes run out of juice they can't park in floating mode."

"OK, OK," Pittman said sharply. "The problem about getting more planes, apart from what they cost, is that the cabinet can't decide what to buy. The Brits are offering Harriers. The Americans have whole air fleets, and every arms salesman in the world is camped on the Minister's doorstep. Remember, we've been selling the government on a come-as-you-are war. Our credibility's on the line here."

"We only sold it because of financial cuts," Admiral Blake said quietly. "I hope we never promised it would work."

---

[2] Air force slang for going out over water

"They think we did, that's what counts," Pittman replied. "General Overly. Why aren't the militia turning out?"

The militia major-general, a portly individual with a permanent pout on his full lips, had gotten his job through political influence. "The plan called for each infantry unit to provide up to a hundred and fifty men for the regular force. We aren't getting them because, despite CDA [3] pressure, we never did define job exemptions. A high percentage of militia officers teach school. If we can't protect their jobs, they won't volunteer. Canada has surplus teachers who'll be delighted to fill in—and stay. It doesn't motivate a man to join up. Also, it's harvest time out west. I'll tell you unofficially that a lot of men don't volunteer if their regiments are going to be broken up. The nine we mobilized in their own name did fine."

"Job protection legislation is coming. The PM promised it by the twenty-fifth, next week. In the meantime, get out there and kick ass. The militia claims to be a vital part of Canadian Defence. They'd better damn well prove it or in five years there won't *be* a militia!"

Pittman turned to the Commander, Mobile Command. "I know you're operating out of temporary quarters and you lost some good men, General Thomas. Just the same, you have to do better."

"With what?" Thomas grumbled. "I appreciate General Overly's recruiting problem, though. Given a choice of being shot at or combining two sections of wheat, the combine wins eight times in ten."

Thomas was a rangy Calgarian who regularly broke regulations to wear a cowboy hat on field inspections. He wanted to forge the image of a tough infantry commander despite his known career as an Engineer. His role model was General Patton. He went on.

"We still haven't recovered from that computer virus. It ate manpower data, equipment serial numbers and supply records. We used to have twenty-three thousand French-Canadians in uniform. Most of them went to Quebec or resigned. I do have *some* good news. The desertion rate is lower than Major Cotton's paper predicted, probably because civil war pumps more adrenaline. Even so we're losing men. Is the cabinet still nixing a surgical strike? And did the PM buy the idea of evacuating Sloerill's men to fill my brigade groups?"

---

[3] Council of Defence Associations

"Negative," Pittman said quickly. "Our Prime Minister sees himself as President Lincoln and Sloerill as General Grant. Unfortunately, as the man with our one success so far he's in a damn strong position. That face and those eyes jump right off the screen at you, and you believe what he says. He wants to fight where he is, and the PM wants him to because that way Quebec cannot claim to control all of its territory. The up-side of the PM's delusion is that I sold a quick strike. He thinks weak commanders almost lost the Civil War for Lincoln. What's your preliminary plan for the attack on Montreal?"

"I'm using two small brigade groups. Each will comprise two infantry battalions, a regiment of armour but with only three tank squadrons, some artillery and support troops. Our other two regular infantry battalions, with four militia battalions, will form two more brigades, one in New Brunswick, the other on the Ontario–Quebec border. We tasked our four best militia infantry units for that: 3200 men. In addition, Sloerill will need two additional battalions for his break-out, so add 1600 more. I need 2200 individual militiamen to bring the regulars up to full strength. In addition, I called up three regiments for special tasks. I'll need damn close to nine thousand militia infantry, General Overly, plus every Gunner and tanker you've got. On D plus three the Airborne jump into Mirabel. The main force joins them on D plus five. It's tight, but unless we win before the cracks show we're in deep trouble. CSIS calls the ALQ to be at twelve thousand by December, and to get a big enough army to beat them we'd have to rebuild the militia structure and strip the regular force to provide officers and instructors for them to the point that we'd be vulnerable to an attack."

"Not good, General Thomas. What have you done to help the Cree up north? They want to secede from Quebec and us to defend their territory." Scattered fighting with the natives was growing as Quebec tried to secure the vital hydro dams. American money from electricity sales was needed to pay for their war.

"I tasked a Nova Scotia unit for that," Thomas answered. "We'll airlift them in next week after a bit more training. They're light on support weapons, but we don't anticipate that the ALQ can hit them with any real strength way up there."

Thomas paused, frowning. "An officer on my new staff was visiting the Quebec North Shore south of Labrador when the war began. He nosed around, then commandeered a fishing boat and got out. The people there do not support Quebec independence. They've formed a civil guard and they're thinking of their own UDI. He says they need help. I have, of course, passed this information on to Military Intelligence."

"Our best help for them is to attack Montreal," Pittman stated. "It takes pressure off the Cree too. For now, our forces must concentrate. If the ALQ go after the hydro dams, they'll have to weaken the force facing us. Send the Cree weapons and ammo. Do the same for the North Shore, perhaps with a small instructor cadre."

He looked around the table. "Put your backs into this, people. If we fail, Canada will flush unification down the toilet—and us with it. We must show it works, at least officially. To be frank, I don't give a damn how often we break the rules to create an impression of success. Do what you have to. I'm sending an officer to degloss Sloerill. Once the war's over, we'll go back to peacetime soldiering where *anything* works."

The Camp Farnham officers' mess was blacked out with plywood panels over the windows and heavy inside shades. The whole building was a prime exhibit of the army school of decoration, blue-grey paint and dun rugs. In the TV room, lit only by a single lamp in a corner, George Sloerill and Colonel Clay Anderson, U.S. Special Forces, were taking each other's measure. There were two kinds of chairs: government issue, and comfortable, the latter donated by local citizens. The room was lined with books in defiance of the TV. The men sat in the comfortable chairs. Sloerill sipped at three ounces of straight rye. Anderson puffed on a Cuban cigar and nursed a single malt.

They had taken to each other on sight. After John Ashworth's introduction, the tall American had saluted and the heavier, shorter Sloerill had returned his salute. Then they'd shaken hands, not as a macho finger-crushing test of strength but as a tactile reconnaissance before verbal exchanges began.

Sloerill found that the Special Forces officer spoke six languages and had been in most of the world's trouble spots. Anderson's air of quiet confidence was only found in people who were truly very good at their work, men like Armand Chantilly, Peter Forbes, John Ashworth, Pierre St Pierre—and Clay Anderson.

For his part, Anderson was amused to find that the celebrated Canadian commander did not present a heroic image. Instead he saw a broad-shouldered, almost squat, slightly bowlegged man whose eyes (hooded by massive brows and puffy from lack of sleep) probed him like an X-ray. The wide, thin-lipped mouth and heavy jaw completed an impression closer to a giant intelligent frog than a charismatic military leader.

After a preliminary exchange of traditional military tall tales, they began to talk seriously about the war.

"You know, sir, you've created something pretty special here. I thought that I knew the regimental system, but I've never seen quite such an extreme example of it. I was told you people were all unified."

"Some are, some aren't. I aren't," Sloerill replied with a grin. "What did you have in mind particularly?"

"A Fusiliers Mont-Royal patrol met me at the border near Philipsburg. They escorted me to Bedford and handed me over to the Guards with a big fuss while they expressed the hope I'd arrive in Farnham safely, considering what I had for an escort. The Guards officer wondered how I'd gotten so far without him. No hostility, they simply were making the claim that each in its own way was number one. For a non-professional army they're pretty cocky. What's your motto, Nulli Secundus?"

"We don't have a motto yet, but if we pick one it will be 'nulli'."

"None?"

"Why not? We're trying to be the people everyone else in the world usually claims to be second to. That's a warning. I confess to a weakness for bad puns."

"I've seen worse. Mine's Cuban cigars." Anderson rolled his eyes to the ceiling. "Unofficially I can say that while I am Special Forces, the spooks pay me. I mention this because I suspect you've guessed. Besides, the CIA can get Cuban cigars. I'd appreciate that information being limited to senior commanders—the first part. I don't care who knows about my passion for cigars."

Their eyes met again. "I had a chance to talk to John Ashworth for a few minutes. I'd like to know more about your admin and logistic set-up. From what John told me, I'd guess it's pretty close to being unique."

"Unique? It's old-fashioned. Unification was designed for peace, and I don't have time to experiment with it in a war. I keep my admin tail as small as possible consistent with supplying what's essentially a small infantry brigade with a few attached Arms."

"Infantry need help today," Anderson said carefully. "What happened in the Gulf War is what happens to ordinary infantry. They get smashed by technology, armour, guns and missiles. I'm here to give you a hand in that area—among other things."

"If I were fighting the US, I'd buy that, but the ALQ are lower-tech than we are. Besides, my aim is to keep casualties down, especially among civilians. As I keep telling my officers, we all have to work together after the war is over. I know about smart bombs and missiles. I also know they can be programmed by some remarkably dumb humans. There's also the fact that we probably can't afford the damned things."

"May I be frank, sir?" Anderson had asked that of a score of senior commanders. Without exception they asked for frankness and when his advice went against their own views tried to get rid of him. He felt that this man was different.

"If you aren't, I'll try to fire you. Be honest. I may get mad but I'll always listen."

"OK, sir. Your position here is too strategic. Limited war hurts your ability to control the enemy—sorry, Shit-Disturbers-Theirs. John briefed me on local language and I heard some coming up. Countries can afford anything they need to survive. Shoot now, pay later. However, in addition to the ALQ, there are those on the home front that may not appreciate your delicacy."

Sloerill shrugged. "Canada would lose, long-term, if we smashed the whole area flat. My force is more than half French, and they're fighting their brothers and cousins. It's only the idea that we're doing it in a relatively civilized way that keeps them going—and the fact that the ALQ *aren't* being as delicate. Now, what's my home front?"

"Ottawa," Anderson said succinctly. Sloerill laughed. "It isn't real funny, sir. You have to remember that a lot of generals don't look too good right now. They lost Mobile Command, a whole bunch of planes and two ships before they knew anything was in the fan. My people tell me they want a consolation prize. The one being mentioned is roughly the shape and size of your ass, sir. They want it in a sling and if necessary, framed."

George tossed back his drink and stood up. "I'm for bed. My ass is well attached and there's no handle. I don't want general officer rank. I just want to finish this as gently as possible, then go back to fighting editors—now that's *really* dirty fighting.

"Anyway, now you're here, spend a few days looking around. Talk to people. See the civilian structure we're building. That's important. After that, tell me what you think."

"I will, sir. Can I grab a chopper?"

"You can have one for a fast orientation tour." Sloerill gave Anderson a nasty smile. "Andrew Bryce will be delighted to do the job. You'll be a new victim of his flying terror. I warn you, though, one flight by Wokka Air usually cures any desire to travel that way. For the rest, draw a jeep or a humvee—for which gift, grateful thanks, by the way. My men are on the ground and officers are expected to visit them on the ground, not drop in for a chat from what looks to be a relatively safe airborne taxi. The men know that and they try to keep their areas secure. As for my ass, the ALQ will get it before Ottawa finds out that the screw in my navel is left-hand thread. Get a good night's sleep. We tend to go a bit short."

With a wave, Sloerill went out and Anderson sank deeper into his chair, thoughtfully turning the remains of his cigar between his fingers. Langley hadn't known the half of it when they called the assignment "unusual". How could he help a man who didn't want high-tech toys, wasn't after a general's star, ignored his enemies and thought that success was enough to protect him from them? It would be *very* interesting.

John Melling had gone to California to meet the President. He was now in the presidential suite and his boss was pacing the room, suffering from an excess of indecision. He was in the final weeks of the closest election campaign since the Nixon–Kennedy. His original plan had been to fight on his international record, winning the Gulf War and Middle East peace, but the Canadian civil war was now dominating the agenda. His opponent was raising the issue in every speech.

"Well, John?" The President paused beside his desk. "I hope you've brought some good news for a change."

Melling shrugged. "The usual bag, Mr President. News is neutral. It's what you do with it that makes it good or bad." He deftly administered the needed ego shot.

"For your speech tonight I wrote an ad lib that may be useful. Two days ago Garry Landsberg spoke at an L.A. Chamber of Commerce luncheon. When he expressed his hope that the US would support Canada, he got a standing ovation."

"Who's Garry Landsberg?"

"A Canadian hockey player with the L.A. Kings. A superstar. It's the reaction we listen to, not the speaker, but it won't hurt to mention the name. He's popular."

"Memo my speech writers. How is the UN playing it?"

"Cool. De Repentigny tells me that France has definitely backed away from any recognition of Quebec. We can thank Joe Gates's speech for that. On the other hand, they have no intention of stopping arms shipments through the various third-party channels that they have available. At the moment, the money that Quebec needs is coming in through a complicated system that starts in Syria and goes through at least four other countries."

"What about our cease-fire proposal?"

"It's popular in theory, Mr President. In practice, it's dead. Both sides need one but they're afraid they'll lose momentum. The fighting in southern Quebec keeps on in small unit actions. Chester is not optimistic that he can negotiate anything meaningful."

"Can we or should we be doing anything about that French supply system?"

"We can cut the money supply now, sir, but the CIA want to wait until the whole system is fully operational before they move in. A black operation or two—"

"I'm not in that loop," the President said quickly. "What are the military capabilities of each side? Dammit—who's going to win?"

"Too early to tell, Mr President. The Canadians are planning to make their big move sometime near the beginning of November. The boys at Langley say that thanks to Sloerill, Quebec is in no shape for a pre-emptive strike. They only intend to try and blunt the Canadian attack, then hit back with a counter-punch. I'm not sure they can handle anything that complicated. The Canadians plan to come at them from two sides with two mostly regular-force combat groups and a reserve of two more. They don't have enough tanks really, but they claim they do and what they have, weak as it is, is a powerhouse to throw against a brand new army."

"So what you're trying to tell me is that Canada will win?"

"Mr President, Canada's war is item one or two on the news every night, and what people see are Canadian refugees fleeing Quebec and Quebec soldiers chasing them out. Americans tend to side with refugees. On the other hand, if Canada loses a big fight anywhere they're up the creek, because to meet the threat posed by the ALQ, they're sacrificing military growth potential for speed. It could be a long, dirty war. Military Intelligence and that NEARPAC group say Colonel Sloerill's the wild card. Unless the ALQ nail him, Canada wins."

"And if they don't we're stuck with an independent Quebec. Why did they have to do this now? If I tilt to Canada, it's because Quebec screwed up my election plan. OK, push Canada into as many new defense contracts as possible and send semi-overt aid. I'll ask the Prime Minister to advance his attack to election day. If he wins we get the credit. If he loses our opponents won't have time to blame us. Now, this Sloerill guy. If he's the key, are we sending him what he needs?"

"A liaison officer was inserted yesterday. We'll feed weapons, ammo and vehicles to him across the Vermont-Quebec border. Sloerill will get what he asks for, but both the CIA and the Pentagon say he can't survive if the ALQ hit him full bore."

"Why not? Didn't Churchill say 'Give me some tools and I'll finish the job'? Sloerill has the tools, doesn't he?"

Melling didn't try to correct the quotation; it was closer than the President usually got. "He has tools, he's short of trained people to use them. I gave our man some leeway to help out in that direction. A lot of Canadians are serving in our armed forces."

The President started prowling the hotel suite again as he wrestled with the problem, his ideas emerging as a stream-of-consciousness that Melling would be able to turn into policy. "It sounds to me like the battle thing can go either way. Putting ten thousand GI's on the border solved Vermont's short-term financial worries, and defence contracts will win us a few states. The French are being coy, as usual, but if we don't choke off their money and arms shipments to Quebec—too much—we'll have a few markers to cash if Canada loses . . . Dammit, John, I *want* Canada united, and according to the polls, so do the American people. There's already an evangelist yelling about a Cuban Commy plot to build a new utopia now the

Soviet Union's down the tubes. Another problem. The Northeast needs Quebec Hydro. Remind Cyr that as long as the power keeps coming, we'll keep paying—cash. Warn Canada not to pull the plug on it. Can we tie help to fresh water? Another year of drought and Californians are going to be eating sand tacos. Is our best bet an independent Quebec selling us power and a Canada linked by a corridor through Quebec, and both of them being grateful as all get-out and selling us water and having to make more free trade concessions? Yeah. I think that will fly. Get working on it."

"Yes, Mr President."

CHAPTER ELEVEN

Laying Plans

Jacques listened as his general briefed the ALQ commanders. It was a tour de force, but he did not smile. His staff had worked hard to prepare the neatly stacked papers, colour-coded red for Canada, blue for Quebec, grey for Intelligence and green for equipment. Irritatingly the folders remained closed. The general had his facts memorized.

The general caught his aide's eye and his eye flickered in a suspicion of a wink as he touched the neat pile. "There is much information in these folders which cannot leave here for security reasons. I commend them to your study before departing. The knowledge contained in them is vital to the success of our cause."

Jacques felt mollified and noted the words so that the people responsible would know what had been said about them.

"Messieurs, I am almost done." The general hated formal briefings; he preferred to talk individually to men. "These are the salient points to consider in your plans.

"First, we underestimated ourselves. Ten thousand men are preparing. We who are trained must carry the load until they are ready to stand beside us.

"Our pre-emptive strike has been cancelled. The government feels that an attack would disturb the world community and alienate the Americans. In this I reluctantly concur because Canada's regular army has gone to Camp Petawawa to prepare their move against us. We could defeat the militia brigade now along the Ontario–Quebec border, but then we would be heavily counter-attacked.

"Our agents report that the Canadian attack will come about November tenth. We must defeat it. They intend to capture the western bridges into Montreal and occupy the West Island while other forces push east through Beauharnois and Chateauguay to meet Sloerill. Our men have moved into their real defensive positions, wearing civilian clothes. Our tanks are hidden, the surprise is set, and the decoy defence we are building is getting most of the attention from the few air reconnaissance patrols Canada can mount.

"Sloerill is still our bête noire. To destroy him would cost us heavily at a time when the main Canadian thrust is imminent. On the other hand, the longer we leave him, the stronger he grows. He has subverted over five hundred québecois, some of whom we had counted on our side. His civil government and his policy of avoiding battle in areas where civilians are at risk have won him much local support. We are now starting to test his defences."

The general paused to light a cigar. His new headquarters was air-conditioned and he could smoke whenever he wished. "I commend a paper," his hand touched one of the folders beside the lectern, "entitled 'La guerre civile dans une région amicale'. It was compiled by our staff from Sloerill's published work, intelligence assessments and observation. Use this to enter his mind. Many of his words have value for us as well.

"So." He rubbed his hands together. "We know what Canada intends to do. This is what we will do.

"The Canadians will be allowed to reach Dorion, where they will be destroyed by our forces on the Lachute–Ste Scholastique–Dorion defence line. Do not plan on air support. Our air force must protect supply ships in the Gulf of St Lawrence as their first priority. Only four aircraft were allotted to us, and they will be used sparingly.

"Just before the Canadian attack, we will strike Sloerill with infantry supported by tanks and artillery. This is to maul his forces so he cannot join in the main Canadian attack. After the Dorion battle, we will destroy him."

The general stepped off the dais. "Take a break. In thirty minutes

I will answer the questions that will occur to you." Jacques smiled as the general plunged into the crowd of officers. A hubbub of confident, animated discussion broke out in the room.

The birth of Sloerill's civil council had not been an easy one. October twentieth was the third date that had been set, but this time at least enough mayors and businessmen had come (under military protection) to make it an assembly that commanded respect.

The agenda optimistically called for electing a civil government, setting up essential services, and building an economy. The area was in chaos. Services had broken down. Heating oil was not being delivered. Gasoline stocks were almost gone. Road crews were refusing to repair damage made by tank treads. Farmers were selling some unpasteurized milk and dumping the rest. Factories were working only three days a week. The meeting which had started at 2:00 PM finally ended at 11:00.

Peter Forbes was dozing in the officers' mess, perversely wearing his beret as he watched the midnight movie on a Montreal channel. The combined mess permitted all regimental customs, even the more outré Guards practices. He looked up as Sloerill led Clay Anderson, Armand Chantilly and Etienne Messier to the bar for much needed drinks.

Forbes observed the American carefully. Anderson was wearing standard US Army uniform, pressed and starched to perfection. His boots would have passed a Guards inspection. The nose, Forbes decided, was out of place: button-like, incongruent among the harsh ridges and angles of the tough soldier's face.

Anderson poured a neat scotch from the night table, as did Messier. Chantilly took a small brandy. Sloerill took a large rye, straight, and signed the chits.

"Care for a cigar, colonel?" Forbes asked Anderson, offering one from the mess stock. "These are Cuban, rolled on the thigh I believe."

The American accepted the gift. "Now, Major, I dined out on that story for a month the first time I was in London." His pale blue eyes flickered in amusement as he lit the greenish tube. His accent had perfectly matched Peter's Oxford drawl.

"One for the Yanks!" Chantilly laughed. "Clay was a Rhodes Scholar, and he can speak as bad Canajan as you, Peter."

Anderson sat on a sofa and leaned back. "My strong point is regional accents. When I got back from a course in Scotland, nobody could understand me for a week. Give me a month here and I'll sound as québecois as the rest of you."

Chantilly, who had been swept up by Sloerill's party as it came in, was anxious to return to his guns. "You say you have a project for me?"

"I need two officers and two sergeants, inventive and flexible."

"I don't have a surplus of them," Chantilly said almost protesting. Sloerill waited, knowing Armand's mind was sorting through its files, tentatively rearranging his ever-shifting organization. "Most who fit the description are in training as FOO's[1] and GPO's,[2] learning skills you will be needing very soon, I think."

"Very soon," Sloerill agreed. "No, they'll train the mortar and machine gun platoons. We'll need infantry support weapons ASAP."

"I can see a Gunner with the mortars," Chantilly said slowly, "but machine guns are infantry weapons."

"Not these. I asked for them the day Clay got here. He found thirty-six complete with ammo and spare parts. They're Vickers water-cooled guns, Armand. They have dial sights. To handle them I need Gunners."

"Vickers?" Chantilly almost choked on his brandy. "They haven't been used in forty years! They're antiques—twice as old as the Centurion tanks!"

"They're lighter than our 50-cal's," Sloerill replied. "They can fire all day without a breakdown, and with Mark 8Z ammunition their range is a bit over four thousand metres. The ALQ won't even know where the fire's coming from."

"Let me think about it," Chantilly muttered as he sat back. How could he spark enthusiasm in his people for working with what were essentially weapons from 1914?

"What happened at the meeting?" Forbes demanded as Messier dropped into an easy chair beside him.

Messier shrugged elaborately. "First George made a speech which left everyone with the impression that unless I became head of the

---

[1] Forward Observation Officers
[2] Gun Position Officers

council the army would desert, plague would ensue and we would all be doomed. He donated Tom Bush as our liaison officer and sat back to watch the fun.

"We now have a council and a group—you will appreciate this, Peter—that I call my decemvir, an inner cabinet of ten to control housing, set up rationing, create and run a bilingual newspaper, establish refugee centres, invent a decentralized school system and create jobs for our regular citizens as well as the refugees. In short, our finger is on every pulse. To hear George talk, this should take but a week or two."

He turned mournfully to Anderson. "Colonel? I may need political asylum. When it is known that I lead this bureaucratic monster, I shall be taken out and hanged."

"It does sound like a jolly group," Peter offered brightly.

"Jolly!" Messier threw up his hands. "To know that mob is to know bedlam. Two of them you met, Sam Thackery and Terry Williams—and they are not the worst. I have never heard so much talk, talk, talk."

"I confess that for people who said they didn't want to stay late they didn't seem to be in a hurry to finish," George said, laughing.

"They were not." Messier finished his drink and stood up. "But I was. I am now going home to bed."

"Got a few men handy for an escort, Peter?" George asked.

Messier shook his head. "Among the many things you said to us tonight was that the civil authority must rule the military behind the lines. I have a chauffeur and I refuse an escort."

Sloerill nodded dubiously. "It isn't safe at night."

Messier gave his first genuine smile of the evening. "It is amusing to order soldiers about. I may learn to enjoy it. Now, before I go, will you consider what I said about Robert?" George promised and Etienne left.

"What about Robert? He isn't hurt, is he?" Forbes asked.

"He joined the FMR. Robert is Etienne's son," George explained to Anderson, "and Etienne isn't happy. He wants me to talk him out of it. Only son."

"He's over eighteen," Chantilly said with a shrug. "Intelligent and educated. Officer material."

"I know," Sloerill said, frowning. "He thinks this is a big romantic adventure."

"He'll learn," Anderson said. "But Colonel, I'm glad the troops didn't hear your speech tonight. It sounded like a lot of soldiers will get killed fighting with one hand tied behind their backs to protect civilians. Why not evacuate your civvies?"

"Because this is their home," Chantilly said forcefully. "We protect the people in them. As George says so often, in the end we must reunite. In order to do that soldiers must . . . how did you say it, George . . . take unpleasantness upon our own shoulders. I assure you, colonel, my French Canadians appreciate what we do."

Anderson's jaw set. "I haven't been here long enough to pick a fight." He stood and stretched. "But I doubt if my mind'll change much, no matter how long I stay. The Gulf was easy. The only targets were camels and a real enemy. Anyway. I'm for bed. My Intelligence section arrives tomorrow. I want to be awake enough to recognize them." He started out and Chantilly, after a "me too?" look and a nod from George, followed.

George and Peter sat back comfortably. After a moment's companionable silence, George sighed. "OK. When this started I gave you Gail Buckley as a platoon commander and you haven't said a word. I give up. How's she doing?"

"Her job like everyone else. No, a lot better than most."

"No static from the men?"

"Not her platoon, but there've been incidents which fortunately got stopped before I had to take official notice. Her men are a tad sensitive and tend to take umbrage if they detect a slur about their platoon commander. Am I about to lose her?"

"Yes. Ottawa OK'd women in combat, but it isn't working. I don't want men taking umbrage. I hear rumours that she and her signaller are lovers—I know it's crap, but it hurts her, the signaller, her platoon and your company."

"Perkins is the best radio man, admittedly of a bad lot, in the platoon. He's also a pretty fair cook, so Buckley's HQ eats well. The rumour-mongers are envious."

"I know, but in the military as in politics perception can be more important than truth. John gave me some figures. Fifty-six people engaged or married since this began. By next month we'll start losing female personnel through pregnancies.

"I can live with that, but six men have been charged with fighting over women. In one case, the woman didn't know she was involved and didn't like either man. We have over a thousand healthy young Canadians, average age twenty-two and bursting with hormones. Who knows if they'll be alive tomorrow? They're scared. Scared people take comfort and pleasure anywhere they can find it and damn the consequences."

"I studied the Israeli experiment," Peter admitted. "They found men were too protective, even though the women didn't want it. Men took risks for them and fought over them too. Is this another Ottawa order that goes into file thirteen?"

"It has to. I have no quarrel with women dating, marrying or screwing at the base—if the attraction is mutual. We don't have to pull them out when they get pregnant, and if the men are motivated to protect the women at the base that's a bonus, not a liability."

"Good. Part of the glue holding us together is a sense that everyone's shafted equally by the war. If some people seem to be getting special treatment morale falls. As you say, with all those hungry hormones milling about we'd soon have an epidemic of sex, jealousy and not to mention violence. Do I tell Gail or can I persuade you to do the dirty deed?"

"I'll do it. She goes up to captain and replaces Dave Phillips in the training wing. We need him at the sharp end."

"May I suggest her replacement be chosen with care? The poor chap has a hard act to follow." George nodded and Peter went on. "While we're debating personnel and who is best where, I gather that you are somewhat taken by this Anderson."

"I am," George said firmly. "He knows what he's doing and he does it well. He seems to have special pipelines into places most of us don't know exist. Damned handy."

"Hummm. I gather he isn't writing panegyrics about your minimum force operation?"

"He'll come round when he sees it work," George replied tartly. "I'm taking his bias into account. I expect the ALQ to switch to guerrilla ops soon. That's when Clay will prove his worth. We'll need electronic warfare stuff. He can get it for us."

"All right, but in my experience, men with strange pipelines tend to be spooks, and spooks are spooky. You might also remember that the

Americans just may decide that they can live with an independent Quebec as a private resource colony."

"I know what side he's on." George shifted uneasily in his chair. "Ahh, Peter?"

Forbes opened his eyes wider, an eyebrow arching. "Hello, hello. I haven't heard that tone since you asked to meet the erotically structured Lady Hamerfield."

George looked acutely uncomfortable. "That was different," he said defensively. "No, the problem is Betty. She's moved. British Airways refuses to tell me where. I have a letter I hoped you could get delivered, London being your turf. I suppose she'd get it sent via BA, but I'd rather it looked as if I'd . . . made an effort . . . ah, you know, tried harder . . . as if she were special. Well, she is."

"In other words, I make an effort and you look good. Give me the letter. I'll send it to Sir Barney at the home office. What are friends for?"

"You'll be discreet, won't you?"

"Never fear. My globe-trotting father invented a code to summon assistance when required—which was unfortunately often. It's handy when you wish to inform the home office that the sheik's eldest daughter is preggers and you're arriving in Cairo on flight 623 hotly pursued by chaps waving sharp scimitars. I suppose I can use it to keep your dalliance out of the tabloids. You're serious about this wench, aren't you?"

"Shouldn't you be doing something with your men?"

Peter rose, tugging his beret square on his head. "Faithful retainer departs, and if allowed, remarks that you should get your own head down from time to time. Your tan goes grey at the edges when you're over-tired, and it's been putty-coloured for days. The world will not end if you sleep more than four hours at a time, and your troops are quite prepared to carry out the inhuman program you established. Quite a few of us are even convinced that it might work."

They started out. "One of these days," Peter continued, "we will need your hand on the tiller or whatever the Canadian equivalent happens to be, and I for one would be happier if the hand were directed by a relatively clear head."

Sloerill knew Peter was right, and as they clattered down the steps to the floor of the drill hall he resolved to turn in early. Then he saw

Chantilly working with five of his Gunners, a 105mm howitzer stripped down and lying in neat rows along the wall.

Peter sighed as George went to help the men struggling to separate a leaking recoil hydraulic cylinder. "So much for good advice," he muttered and went to find his jeep.

On October twenty-third Sloerill's Command Post went into operation to free him from the confusion and administrative problems of Camp Farnham. Two M577's[3] formed the heart of the unit, supported by a dozen trucks, drivers, clerks, signallers and military police. For five days they had been practicing to achieve the level of teamwork that Sloerill demanded. Now they were ready. New and powerful American military radios could reach every unit, call down artillery fire, or control a battle. Under the administrative command of John Ashworth, the unit was now northeast of Camp Farnham, lacking only its commander.

Sloerill had been trapped. Major Taschereau, the supply officer, had reminded him that he couldn't escape the paper war simply by heading into the field.

Colonel Chantilly, commanding the guns, Clay Anderson as Intelligence Officer and John Ashworth tested the communications and found that for once everything worked as promised. Having nothing better to do the three of them left the centre, where unit positions were still being plotted on maps, and walked out into the crisp fall air. The first snow had melted two weeks ago, and they wanted to experience the brief Indian Summer day and inhale the clear air spiced with the scent of distant burning leaf piles.

Clay took a cigar from his seemingly inexhaustible supply and Ashworth stepped forward to light it. "Thanks. A lighter? Are you a secret smoker, Junior?"

"Lord, no. I'm simply the perfect staff officer, ready for any emergency."

Armand Chantilly watched the cigar smoke rise almost straight up. So far the rangy American had spent most of his time listening. "I am curious," Armand said quietly, "as to what you were told about our little problem before you got here."

---

[3] Armoured carriers equipped with powerful radios, designed as HQ vehicles

Anderson had been expecting questions and had made a bet with himself that the artilleryman would start. "To tell you everything, I'd have to talk for four days. They briefed me on the people involved, the political history, our assessment of your forces—that part is being revised, by the way. They also set up a private supply system I can tap into without bothering the bean-counters in administration."

Both men spoke French slowly for the benefit of Ashworth, who had a good vocabulary but an imperfect grasp of grammar. "Let me toss one back at you. They said that Quebecers were insecure because English Canada kept humiliating them. They weren't clear about the humiliation thing, but that was the main thrust of it. Comment?"

"Merde," Chantilly said succinctly. "That is what the separatists say; my God, how they say it! It is as if respect and equality were tax refunds to be awarded by some distant and anonymous 'they'. Have you discovered any of this to be true?"

"No, that's why I asked. The French-Canadians I've met, as a group or individually, are as self-assured as anyone I've ever met—people like yourself. Are you typical?"

"Of course not," Chantilly snorted. "French Canadians are much too individual to be typical. The separatists ignore that we have done well in Canada, they only magnify inevitable tensions—such as those between blacks and whites, north and south, rich and poor. They imply that only in Canada do such tensions occur and that such tensions are all anti-French. Merde, I say."

"You can say so, you have money. What about André Taschereau? He isn't rich, but he sure has all the confidence he needs."

"Of course. People may lack confidence if they're denied the right to advance according to their skills and talent—or because they are inferior. André is regular army and there's no discrimination there. French-Canadians often reach the top. There was prejudice in the past but not now. In fact, there are signs of discrimination against English officers."

"But surely, opportunities are only open if you speak English. Would a unilingual French soldier ever become CDS?"

"Of course not. Every serious scientist speaks and writes English. Pilots on Air France, Lufthansa and JAL fly in English, even in their own countries. Anyone who wishes to climb out of a local pond today must speak English." He looked at his watch. Noon. "George said he would be here for lunch?"

"Not a chance," Ashworth assured him. "I saw the pile of paper André had for him. My guess is 1500."

"1700, anyone?" Clay waved a ten-dollar bill invitingly, but before anyone could take the bet a radio inside the command centre came to life with an operational message.

"Hello, One. Eight Sugar Delta Tangos moving south, figures five, zero, zero metres echo my right flank. Out of rifle range. Do you have Delta Oscars to intercept? Over."

Ashworth was inside in a moment, his eyes studying the map and he pointed at a patrol position about a kilometre from the Headquarters.

"Send Call Sign 6 to block them," he told the duty officer.

"Wait," Chantilly said. "Last week my guns did a practice shoot on the road they'll have to cross. The code name is TRACK. I have a FOO at call sign One. He needs practice."

Chantilly moved to the gunner radio net. "Three, message," he alerted his Forward Observation Officer on the artillery net. "Engage Sugar Delta Tango targets at TRACK."

Ashworth gave orders to the infantry. "Hello six, block Delta Tangos from penetration south of TRACK. Maintain visual contact and report all movement. Out."

Colonel Sloerill was well on his way to winning the bet for John Ashworth but an unexpected visitor delayed him. He was just signing the last paper in the pile when he heard a rap at the door.

"Come!"

André Taschereau looked in. "Ah, bon, you are finished. A visitor from Ottawa has arrived. A friend of yours, I believe."

As Sloerill rose, a slightly overweight, round-cheeked officer bustled around the door and came straight in. George gaped.

"Fred? Fred Scott! I thought you'd been killed at Mobile Command. I might have known you'd wriggle out of weekend duty!" George gripped his friend's hand as if he couldn't believe his luck.

Scott pried himself loose and lifted a green sleeve to show a wide gold band at the cuff. "I am a brigadier general in Her Majesty's Canadian

Armed Forces, you ugly ruffian. I am not to be manhandled. Back, I say, back!" He stepped away from what threatened to be a bear hug.

"I'm alive due to an extremely virtuous life and because General Thomas dragged me up to Ottawa the night before all the shooting began."

Sloerill raked his hands through his hair, grinning hugely and not knowing how to express his delight. He and Scott had been in the same officer cadet class, attended Staff College the same year and taken command of their battalions on the same day. They'd got drunk together, lied for each other and trusted each other without qualification. At last George sat down and dug a half-empty bottle of rye from the bottom of a drawer.

Scott settled into a low chair opposite. At first he thought George hadn't changed. Then he saw the lines of fatigue around the wide mouth and the pouches under the bloodshot eyes. "You look a bit peaked, old scout. Is age beginning to grind you down?" George was a full week older than Fred.

Sloerill poured two powerful drinks. "At times, Fred. At times. You've no idea what's been happening."

"Nor does anyone else. That's why I'm here." Fred accepted the drink and took a deep swallow. "You may not believe this, but a report saying so many killed, captured and wounded isn't too illuminating unless we know what you did it with. Jesus, George! Pittman learns more about your ops from CBC and CNN than he does from you."

George opened his mouth to speak but Scott waved him off. "Silly Ottawa bastards thought that because we're friends I could get the straight poop from you. If I'd disabused them they'd have picked one of your enemies—much easier than finding a friend. So, in words of one syllable, George: what in hell is going on?"

Sloerill pointed to a slim file on his desk. "It's all there, Fred."

Scott ignored it. "I've seen your reports. I've even helped cook up one or two. Seriously, old scout," Scott leaned forward, "I want the full picture. Big stuff happening, and I have to know what you have going and what can be done with it."

George sighed. "I've got some of the hardest-working officers and NCO's in the world. We don't get an awful lot of sleep, but we're holding on and even improving. I think I'm set unless someone out there gets very mad at me."

"What does that mean?"

"It means I can fight platoon or company battles. I have two artillery batteries in direct support. My three-inch mortars are fairly operational. On the ground I have some Black Watch, FMR and Guards and a horde of recruits that are not up to speed yet."

"What about the tanks we let you have?"

"You let me have! You bastards'd be walking if we hadn't rescued yours from Longue Pointe!" Sloerill exploded. "Then I get the crocks, forty-year-old Centurions you couldn't sell for scrap. Thanks loads."

"Hey, they run, don't they? What more do you want?"

"A commanding officer. One troop is good, mostly reg force, and the second isn't bad, but Pieters is out of it. He hasn't had an idea in years. I've a good man on the admin side though. André Taschereau cobbled up a logistics organization that's weird but works, and my teeth-to-tail manpower ratio is half the Canadian scale. That's it, Fred. My reports don't contain org charts because you guys wouldn't believe them."

"Quality of infantry?" Fred ignored the jibe, all business.

"It's ninety-five percent militia or ex-militia. Quality? From about the bark level to as good as I've seen. They fight with a rifle in one hand and a pamphlet in the other, but they fight. In general, man for man we're almost as good as the ALQ now. In a month we'll be better."

Scott gave him an appraising glance. "OK. I've never known you to lie about training standards. Tell me, if your Guards were at full strength, could they work as part of a brigade in say . . . three weeks?"

"No." Sloerill said flatly. "If I got the men, and if my other units were reinforced, the Guards could start battalion training. Come on, Fred. You know this stuff. My men aren't up to that training level—and I don't like the look in your beady little eyes."

Scott checked that the office door was closed, then turned his innocent blue gaze back to his friend. "For your ears only, George. Our elected masters have decided that they want all of Quebec back and it's up to us nice boys in green to get it for them."

"With what?"

"Don't you watch TV, old scout? This is October twenty-third. By the twenty-seventh, our far-flung forces will be reunited. Even as we speak, a militia brigade stands on guard for thee at the Ontario–Quebec border.

Regulars are in Petawawa. On or about November twelfth, two full mech brigade groups, well, at least almost full brigade groups, will advance astride the Ottawa River, take West Island Montreal, link up with you and start a siege. Montreal should surrender by February. In the spring we'll push on to visit Quebec City, and lo! Peace will break out again."

Sloerill shook his head. "You've getting bad grass up there, Fred. A major river between two brigade groups? Hah!"

Scott looked away briefly. "Cabinet decision, old scout. There's some real estate in the area that belongs to influential government supporters. They want it back."

"Have you forgotten that the ALQ will not just roll over and play dead? You won't set foot on Montreal Island."

"The Ottawa view is that they aren't so tough. After all, you're zapping them with a rabble. Our attack is by a professional force—OK, thirty percent militia, but the best militia. For deception, we invade the Gaspé from Gagetown; a militia battalion goes to the Cree at the James Bay dams; and we fly troops in here as if this is our break-out point. The ALQ can't defend everything but they have to try. They're in a box."

"Have you got a trained militia battalion for the Cree?"

"Trained? These guys can march and shoot. That'll be enough for up there."

"And the link-up with me? What phantom regiments do that?"

General Scott finished his drink. "The militia brigade at the Ontario border. Wait," he said as George tried to interrupt. "You can't do this alone, even if that is your style. How's the airfield at Bromont? Assume a lot of men will fly in real soon."

"It's too near the front lines to be secure. With Buffalos [4] you can use a small strip near Cowansville once we improve it a bit."

"I'll look at both. Now, as the main attack goes in on the twelfth, we'll airlift two militia units in to you, the Royal Regiment and the Toronto Scottish. By the time we reach Dorion, the pressure will be off you, so your mob can head west. Between now and then we'll bring your Guards up to full strength. No new armour. Everyone who can fight a tank will be in a real one for the big push. Does that sound better?"

---

[4] Short take-off and landing aircraft

Sloerill sat back, hooked both thumbs under his front teeth and chewed on the nails briefly. "Who commands this brigade?"

Scott's eyes opened wide in mock surprise. "Now how did I forget that? There was quite a discussion, but we finally decided to go with one Brigadier-General Sloerill."

Sloerill's eyebrows shot up. "You're kidding, Fred. They'll promote me?"

"Have promoted you, old scout, so you can drop the obsequious 'sirring' that makes me feel so uncomfortable."

Scott leaned forward, elbows on the desk, his chubby face serious. Sloerill projected an image of deadly purpose; Scott looked like a schoolboy who had attached a stink bomb to the teacher's car. But on one night exercise in Germany, a cut hand dripping blood onto his map through the field dressing, Fred had led his battalion across ten kilometres of bog to a dawn attack against a British "enemy" which, had the umpires allowed it to go on, would have ended the exercise two days early.

"Let's get serious, George. I had to pull a lot of strings for this assignment. Scores of Ottawa denizens hate promoting you. Nobody actually said so because the PM asked for it. Politicians love you. You're on TV almost every night spreading glad tidings of success, hope and moderation. That wins promotions but not friends.

"On the big attack the regular force gets the glory, you're the side show. We want to wrap it up fast, award you a gong and a golden handshake, then send B/Gen Sloerill back to civvy street before we have to adjust his pension to his new rank.

"We can't ignore what you've done nor forget how you did it. Nobody will go out of their way to help you. There may even be a bit of creative hindrance, but not to fear. Your promotion will not be announced until the main push goes in. That way it gets buried in the big news—Canadian army takes all of Western Quebec—navy intercepts six more ships—valiant airmen shoot down ten Quebec planes—and oh yes, Colonel Sloerill is now a general, mumble, mumble. Do you read that message loud and clear?"

"A long time ago, Fred. Now watch carefully." George lifted an empty silex pot from the burner and reversed it on the desk. He picked up a camouflage scarf hanging on the back of his chair, wound it loosely round his head like a turban and held his hands over the pot, closing his eyes.

"I foresee trouble. I see armies vanishing into the mist. I see Montreal, but there are no Canadian flags there. I see soldiers held at bay by unknown forces. I see piles of shit and people running in every direction to keep it from sticking to them." He removed his improvised turban. "Now that the seance is over, who commands the division? Babe Trinker would be my choice."

"He said a few incautious things at the beginning and he's flying a desk at the moment. Never be right too early. Anyway, who said anything about a div? We don't have an HQ for openers. No, this is four individual brigade groups, five with yours, commanded by General Thomas in Ottawa-wa-wa." Fred grinned disrespectfully and stood up.

"Come on. Show me around. I should leave tomorrow, so let's get cracking."

Sloerill got out of his chair slowly. "Cracking? You're cracked already. You say I don't have to advance until you get onto Montreal Island proper?" Scott nodded. "I bet it never happens. What's this operation called, FOOLS FOLLY?"

"It's TALL THUNDERBOLT, and I'll take that bet. Something real big?"

"You're on, sucker. Five bucks." They both laughed. Five dollars had been a lot of money to poor officer cadets. They had bet often but that was their ceiling.

"Come on, George. Convince me your funny ideas work."

Sloerill grabbed his parka. "Only being flexible, Fred. By the way, on Mondays, Wednesdays and Fridays, everyone talks French unless they happen to be in a private office—and this is Wednesday. Crank up that Ottawa French of yours and let me show you how we administer this area with half the people Ottawa says we need."

Scott was so fascinated that he stayed three days. As General Pittman's personal emissary (he had wisely demanded elastic orders), his approval of anything made it official. He and George had argued endlessly about the merits and evils of unification. They had agreed that the system of short postings hurt military professionalism, and both had seen what happened when a hotshot new CO arrived in a strange unit with only two years (often less) in which to make a name for himself.

The difference between them was that while Fred Scott accepted the basic idea and worked from within to improve the system, Sloerill wanted to scrap the system and perhaps incorporate some unified features into the new.

Scott approved Sloerill's ultra-regimental recruit training. It was against current policy, but as he knew that could change overnight.

He disliked Sloerill's administration and logistics system and suggested change after change to bring it more into line with regular standards. In each case George could show that his system worked better. In the end it was approved, with General Scott muttering darkly about the tail wagging the dog.

What had not flown were the new Guards badges. Blue berets were one thing; on badges he was adamant. What began as a quiet discussion between two senior officers soon degenerated into a shouting match that almost emptied the officers' mess.

Pierre Coté waited until the bellowing died into baleful silence. Then he strolled over with a brandy bottle and a compromise. There were frequent rumbles of protest, but they finally agreed. Guards NCO's would wear cloth grenade badges over their stripes. Officers kept the unified rank, but over the gold bars, captains and below could sport a single garter star on each shoulder or sleeve. Majors and above wore crowns. Even Scott had to admit it had style.

General Scott left on October twenty-sixth, grumbling but newly appreciative of his friend's situation. He promised to send any help he could pry loose from the system.

In the following days, as the ALQ continued to probe, a steady flow of fresh soldiers began arriving. Ashworth dubbed the engineers, signallers, drivers, cooks and quartermasters "the flying trickle". When two full platoons of infantry came in, George added thirty of his best trained Guards recruits to create 4 Company and placed it in reserve at Farnham to learn to live and fight as a team. In Abercorn civilians and soldiers worked at the new base, but most of their new prefab huts lay in the half-frozen mud, waiting for roads, foundations, power lines and sewers.

Clay Anderson provided ammunition, tools, weapons, flak vests and computers. Most of these arrived at the border by night in unmarked army trucks that the waiting Canadians took over without any paperwork.

In Bedford twelve regular force Dragoons and four militia Hussars were running tests on the new tank armour plate that Sloerill had designed to protect the Centurions. The plates, welded onto turret brackets, had to be able to withstand an initial explosion long enough for the shell's effect to be partly dissipated in the space between the new armour and the original hull. This modification ws a crude but (Sloerill hoped) effective imitation of the expensive spaced armour of modern tanks.

The troopers' enthusiasm grew as they saw that the extra protection worked. Once convinced, they ignored the clock in the race to retrofit their four tanks with the ugly protective scales before they had to fight in them. The extra weight would slow a tank down, but it (and the troopers inside) would survive a few minutes longer in the battles that were coming.

CHAPTER TWELVE

The Test

Etienne Messier found Sloerill's new command post from Colonel St Pierre's directions. The Bentley bumped across the half-frozen ruts made by the armoured carriers backed into a copse of trees under a large camouflage net. Thirty-foot radio masts swayed above each steel top, the focus of the radio network essential to a modern battlefield. Deep in the woods stood four trucks and four humvees. One truck was fitted with beds where the dozen men of the tactical HQ took turns sleeping. A second provided a mobile kitchen; the other two were filled with stores.

Sloerill's humvee was parked in the open, facing west, a dark maroon and navy blue Guards pennon waving listlessly in the light air of a late October day. Corporal Zukrowski lay back against the windscreen, feet extended on the hood, parka open to absorb the sun. Across his lap lay the SMG that Etienne knew never left his side. A 9mm Browning pistol was in a shoulder holster under his jacket, and he carried a long fighting knife strapped to his left thigh. As Etienne went past, Zuke's eyes opened fully and he held up a hand.

"General's asleep," he said in his rough joual. "I heard you was coming but he ain't had his head down since two AM. You really want I should wake him up?"

Messier hesitated; it was important, but now he had a chance to talk to his friend's bodyguard.

"It can wait." He looked at Zuke intently. "Is he all right? I hear he takes too many chances."

Zuke patted the hood. "First jeep hit a mine, the second had too many bullet holes in it. This humvee's better, but it won't last. Yeah. He takes chances."

"A mine? He did not tell me. Why were you not both killed?"

"Fella in Bedford puts steel plates under the seats. Same guy as does the tanks."

Messier looked pointedly at a vivid scar across Zuke's right hand. "And that of course happened opening a can of beans?"

"Nope. Knife. Some frog jumped the general in Farnham. I slit him open but I'm outta practice. He nicked me."

Messier winced. "I thought we French are no longer to be called frogs," he said sharply.

Zuke shrugged. "In the Point, Frenchies were frogs, 'talians were wops, and we English got shit from everybody. You don't get upset too easy. My best pal was a frog. He called me tête carrée and we got along swell. Didn't mean you anyhow."

Etienne had to smile. "Our general is very dear to me, Zuke. I am glad it is you taking care of him. Does he eat well?"

"Enough, but not regular, you know?" Zuke grumbled. "He might eat when he wakes up, then go ten straight hours. I drive him past restaurants a lot."

"But you're also his bodyguard, Zuke. Why?"

"Well, he sure as hell needs one. He's a good CO, hard but fair, and he treats us right. Know what I mean? Anyway, I figured I'd better protect him real good because if he gets the chop we're up shit creek." Zuke, uncomfortable with this examination of his motives, changed the subject. "You want I should wake him up?"

"No. Tell him I want to see him at my home tonight. My problem is food. We have so many refugees, we cannot feed everyone."

Zuke nodded. "OK. I'll try to get him there round six, after he chews me out for not waking him up now."

Messier began to turn away, then turned back. "And how do you see this English against French war, Zuke?"

"Ain't English and French," Zuke replied roughly. "Lots o'

froggies on our side, prolly some English on theirs. Stupid politicians got greedy so we gotta fight. Then we start over. Like my mother says, a fair fight means a real good making-up party.

"Thing is, it's gotta be clean. If we start the old knee-in-the-balls stuff, nobody'll ever talk to nobody again. The sons-a-bitches who write the history stuff will make this look bad anyway, so why give 'em facts to use? Prolly only confuse 'em."

His speech finished, Zuke inspected his SMG. Two magazines were taped together, reversed, for quick reloading. He checked the tape and began to remove the bullets, one at a time, cleaning each round with an oily rag. His hands worked with unconscious skill as he watched Messier pick his way over the frozen mud to the massive grey Bentley and the chauffeur standing by the open rear door.

Ten men marched down the road from the Camp Farnham training area. They were led by the newly promoted Sergeant Weitz of 12 Platoon in the company of regular and militia that was coming together under Major Phillips. These men were regular force, but as new Guardsmen they had to tour the camp battleground as part of their indoctrination. Weitz knew where every man, ALQ and Canadian, had been during the battle, where they had fought and where they had died. To him regulars were still recruits until they had absorbed the Guards way of doing things.

After service in Germany and Cyprus, his men were disdainful of mere militia. But having been in combat, the militiamen had an edge in prestige. Weitz was forcing the pace because he was late and trying to catch up on his schedule.

"Halt!" A bellow came from the drill hall. "That twenty-two-legged object flailing like a centipede on a hot stove will be still! What are you doing galloping at such a pace?"

The men froze as Regimental Sergeant-Major Grigson strode up, boots gleaming, uniform impeccably pressed, pace-stick seemingly welded in place under his armpit.

"Sarn't Weitz. I am surprised. What do you mean careening around camp at such a speed? Is that how Kermit would do it? I'll have you in the book for reckless marching!"

Weitz knew lateness was no excuse. Guardsmen were not late. Good NCO's planned activities to start and finish on time. Lateness indicated bad planning and led to worse trouble.

"No excuse, sarn't-major."

Grigson looked slightly mollified. "I see you have more virgins." The new men had been given the name on arrival and it would stick until their first battle. "There's no excuse for galloping along like hysterical Riflemen." Grigson managed to infect the word with immense scorn without using the least inflection.

Weitz knew better to reply, and Grigson turned his attention to the men with him. "For your information, Guardsmen—which with divine help you are slowly becoming—do not dash about or stroll idly as do other regiments. We march at a steady, dignified one hundred and sixteen thirty-inch paces to the minute. I will see you get additional practice tomorrow. Understood?" The men stood frozen, mute and awed.

"Yes, regimental sergeant-major," one man incautiously replied. In five years with the regular force he had never met a man like this.

"You do NOT address me as regimental sergeant-major!" Grigson screamed. "I am THE sergeant-major! How can you fight if you don't know who you're fighting for? You are fighting for ME, you idle man. You will fight if only to survive the war and get me afterwards. Sarn't Weitz! How fast do the Black Watch march?"

"One hundred and twelve paces per minute, sarn't-major."

"Why so slowly, Sergeant Weitz?"

"Because they are content to let the Guards precede them into battle, sarn't-major."

"And what is the pace of line regiments, Sergeant Weitz?"

"One hundred and twenty paces per minute because they lack the discipline to move at the dignified pace that prepares men for battle, sarn't-major." The dialogue was a play that every Guards NCO had learned.

"What about the Riflemen you seem eager to imitate?"

"They march at one hundred and forty paces because, not knowing what battle is like, they are eager to arrive. They march out of battle at one hundred and eighty because, having found out, they are eager to depart."

There was a muffled boom to the west. Grigson's head came up as the blast was followed by a rattle of machine gun fire. Behind him, a

Voyageur helicopter settled dustily into the parking area to collect another load of stores for Abercorn.

"To your duties, Sarn't Weitz. Next time plan the tour with more care. I will not have Guardsmen turning roads into drag strips."

Weitz gave the order, but as the squad marched off, Grigson halted them with another bellow. One man was swinging his arms from the elbow, not the shoulder.

"Didn't they teach you how to march? Elbows stiff. With your arms pumping like that, you look like you're masturbating with both hands and I doubt if you need more than two fingers. QUICK MARCH!"

The men started again and after approving their arm and leg movements, Grigson fell in beside Weitz at the rear as they skirted a tarp-covered stack of ammunition boxes. "I'll be happy to see the last of this place, Tony," he said conversationally. "It's too much temptation for the ALQ, and if you ask me the buggers are getting set to come after it."

Grigson started to wheel aside, then turned back. "When you finish the tour I wouldn't be surprised if a truck was leaving for the training area from about here. Look for it. You'll get back faster."

In Abercorn, Herb Kerner parked his pickup in his mother-in-law's yard behind the big two-storey white frame house. Gloria was sweeping leaves from the walk and he rushed to take the broom from her.

"Silly girl. I'm supposed to do the heavy work here. All you should be doing is getting more pregnant."

"How did it go today, Herb?" Gloria surrendered the broom.

"Hey, great! The whole hill's turning into an army camp. A Major Taschereau hired me, over union scale and overtime. I start tomorrow.

"You know, honey." He leaned on the broom. "This is a great place to bring up a kid. Why don't we look for our own house? The local plumber left, and I hear they're sort of scarce generally. I can start my own business. Kerner Plumbing. Sounds OK, eh? Perhaps it will be Kerner and Son—or Daughter. Why not?"

Gloria laughed. "Sounds fine, Herb, but when I had the broom, the walk was getting swept."

Sloerill turned from the radio with a sigh. "The second tank refit troop is in Bedford at last. ALPHA Troop's back in Abercorn for training, but this is November first. We won't get much more time."

Clay Anderson looked up from his map board. "I've never seen so much ground held by so few troops. Is this the fabled thin red line?"

Armand Chantilly marked a mortar section location on the map. It was supporting Leo Markos at Bromont on their first operational shoot, and both his fire control sergeants were there to gain experience in correcting the fall of the bombs.

"Thin," he agreed, "but tough." He turned to George. "I'm concerned about Jan Berkowitz at Magog. I cannot support him from any gun position."

"That's why he got armoured cars," Clay reminded him. Anyway, I don't think he has to worry a whole hell of a lot. My INTSUM predicts the ALQ main attack will be from the west."

"Predicts or promises?" Ashworth asked.

"Take your pick." Clay reached for a cigar. "How's operation SHORT SPARK going, sir?"

Sloerill's code name for his breakout reflected his doubt that the main push TALL THUNDERBOLT would really work.

"The general plans are laid, so if the Toronto Scottish fly in on the fifth and if the Royals follow them, we'll start getting concrete. Can your guns follow us, Armand?"

"The guns are ready, but in defence you have time to plan. In an advance-to-contact battle I need better trained FOO's. General Scott promised them, but I have not seen any so far."

"They're coming down with the Tor Scots. Starting Sunday you can practice."

"I'll need to. The new men will not be familiar with my batteries; each works a little differently. We are not machines."

John Ashworth, listening to the radio reports, handed a note to the man maintaining the operations map.

"A Company, FMR, are getting hit near St Alexandre," he reported, "so's Markos at Bromont. If the ALQ are probing for weak spots, my map shows a score of them."

"If they find one," Sloerill said grimly, "they'll try to make us commit reserves, then smash in somewhere else. The one thing in our favour is that they're as short of men as we are, and their best are concentrating on the Ontario border—Clay says."

His reserves were Pierre Coté's 3 Company at Abercorn and Dave Phillips's company is in final training in Farnham. All the other fighting men were deployed, stretched around the defence like a frayed rubber band trying to hold in the sides of a cardboard box.

Anderson looked at the map over Sloerill's shoulder. "I know those tankers need practice, but can't they do it a bit closer to where we're going to need them?"

Chantilly nodded as he listened to his mortar fire controllers trying to engage targets for Leo Markos. "Good idea."

"It is, and we'll need them soon. With the new modification, if a squash-head round hits, the new plates are torn away, but there's no penetration. It's no good against sabot[1] shot, but not many tanks are."

"André Taschereau has enough flatbeds for eight tanks," Ashworth contributed.

"Send four to BRAVO Troop in Bedford just before their refit's complete." Sloerill stared at the status board.

"OK, time for changes. The ALQ have taken some prisoners, so they know where everyone is by now." He pointed to the map. "Jan has an independent command." They all nodded. Berkowitz was the kind of man who did his job without fuss, asking only for clear orders and almost enough men and equipment to carry those orders out.

On the previous day his Highlanders had been pushed back from Magog. At the height of the battle he had radioed for help. Twenty minutes later he'd cancelled the appeal, and two hours after that had reported that the line was again stabilized.

"They'll attack tomorrow or next day," Sloerill went on. "They have three options. Go for Abercorn, split us with an attack on Cowansville, or go after the symbolic goal of Farnham where they lost their first battle."

He stabbed a thick finger at the Black Watch position. "To get to Abercorn they'd have to drive thirty clicks through perfect defensive country. I think they attacked Jan to draw us that way. I won't fall for it.

---

[1] A small-calibre dense steel projectile with a wooden casing around it that disintegrates on firing

"The Bromont front is potentially the most dangerous. Peter and Leo have a large force in front of them with good roads leading into their positions from Granby.

"John. Time the virgins lost their name. They relieve Leo. Pull him back to Farnham in a reinforcement role. Peter commands all Guards, less Coté's company, and will maintain a line Ange Gardien–Bromont–Foster. The Bromont airport is vital to Saturday's fly-in.

"The FMR are stretched. The ALQ nearly took Sabrevois yesterday, and I had to send a dozen nearly trained recruits to replace casualties.

"Coté has a semi-independent command, taking over the line Noyan–Henryville up to Route 133. Toupée shifts north to concentrate his forces on the line Sabrevois–St Alexandre–St Brigide–St Césaire. The FMR boundary with Coté is the road between St Césaire and Ange Gardien.

"Armour. I want the refitted troop flatbeds, ready to roll on ten minutes' warning. We've dug a few tank-fighting scrapes around Bromont but we've only had time to recce hides in the FMR area.

"Finally, recruits. If the ALQ break through, on the codeword MARATHON get them to Abercorn fast."

Sloerill turned to Chantilly. "Give me flexibility, Armand."

"I have four troops in position. We've started registering targets on St Pierre's front. All is in train, mon ami. Gunners do not let you down."

George believed it. With untrained crews and inexperienced observation officers, Chantilly had managed to provide some covering fire from guns or mortars every time it was really needed.

The changes were made that night. Small convoys of blacked-out trucks crept along back roads carrying tanks, soldiers and guns, concentrating the defence at weak points and leaving others vulnerable.

At Farnham Leo Markos's men slept in the drill hall, fully dressed, weapons beside them. In the parking lot their trucks waited fully gassed and running. The intermittent snow that had been falling for two days stopped at dawn as fighting began in earnest.

First the ALQ hit the Black Watch near Magog. More, supported by mortars, came down the Adamsville road to Cowansville. The Guardsmen withdrew to prepared positions and held an attack that fell largely on the 4 Company regulars who had just taken over the line.

At 11:00 AM, Pierre St Pierre came on the net. The FMR were in trouble.

Sloerill took over the radio. "Hello Four, SITREP, over."

"Four, estimate figures three, zero, zero ALQ advancing axis Route figures one, zero, four with artillery and tanks. LOCKSMITH position under fire. Over."

The area was a network of roads, and LOCKSMITH was a key roadblock for Farnham. If the ALQ took it they could swing southeast and outflank the JERICHO position covering Ste Brigide. As Sloerill studied the map, St Pierre came on again.

"Four, new SITREP. ALQ force, estimated figures three zero men, moving down Highway figures two, two, seven towards JERICHO. Over."

"Roger," Sloerill acknowledged. "Hold JERICHO and LOCK-SMITH. More later, out." He turned from the radio. "I'm going up. John, send Leo to junction Route 227–Versailles Rd to support either LOCK-SMITH or JERICHO. He is under command of St Pierre. Tanks to same location. Can the guns support those positions?" he asked Chantilly.

"Two troops can do both, one troop, LOCKSMITH only. Number four supporting A Company at St Alexandre is out of range."

"Three troops should do it. Questions?"

"What do I tell Peter if he yells for help?" Ashworth asked.

Sloerill grinned tightly. "Say 'repeat after me, Our Father, who art in heaven'. . ."

Clay Anderson was talking to the US forces on his own radio. "Colonel, you promised gunships yesterday. When in hell *will* they be ready? Over." The reply was clearly unsatisfactory. "Well, get your ass in gear, colonel. Out."

"What was that about, Clay?"

"Two AH Apaches, gatlings and anti-tank Hellfire missiles, Canadian markings, Canadian crews, Canadian uniforms. They're supposed to be operational now. They're not, but when they are, they're yours, general."

Sloerill turned to the map. The roads in the area were lined with the homes of people who had moved from St Jean and Montreal. Most of them were inhabited by French-Canadians who had decided to stay with Canada. The town of St Grégoire was less than half a kilometre west of the LOCKSMITH position.

"I can use them," he admitted, "but I'm almost glad they aren't ready. In a built-up area, Clay, we have to beat the ALQ face to face. The FMR aren't a hundred percent committed to the war yet. If we turn this battle into a Gulf War turkey shoot, they might balk. Gunships will *only* engage targets in the open. Built up areas are no-go. This is a NODUFF [2] message. If they start a shooting gallery, *both* sides will shoot them down. I'll beat the ALQ my way."

"And how many Guardsmen and Fusiliers get killed that way, sir?"

"In the long run, a lot fewer." The American started to reply but Sloerill cut him off. "You have advised. I'll take the gunships under my rules or not at all.

"Stay here," he ordered as Anderson started to get up as if to follow him. "You and John have to keep the war on the rails while I'm with St Pierre." He turned to Chantilly who was putting on his parka. "Is the reserve artillery ammo still in Farnham?"

"Yes, but minimum level. André Taschereau has moved most of it to Abercorn. First line ammo stocks at the gun line are up to scale."

"The battle may require ammo in excess of scale. Your guns have to do the work of the infantry support weapons we don't have yet. John, this should be an ideal job for Bryce's wokkas. He can air-lift shells right into the gun line."

"He'll love it," Chantilly said and headed for his jeep.

Sloerill followed. "Let's find St Pierre. I think we'll miss our road kill today."

The critical road junction LOCKSMITH was a sharp bend in Route 104 just west of St Grégoire. Toupée's command post was in a farm east of the road with twenty-eight men of B Company's 5 platoon dug in with overhead cover, dominating Route 104 from a flank in a long wood two hundred yards to his left.

If the ALQ broke past LOCKSMITH they still faced JERICHO, weakly held by a platoon of twenty-two men. From there Camp Farnham was almost a straight run.

The LOCKSMITH position resembled an upside down Y. The

---

[2] A term indicating that the message is real, as opposed to one sent for exercise purposes

ALQ would come out of St Grégoire and either swing left to JERICHO (after pushing back St Pierre's men) or bear right into uninhabited farm country dotted with small woods and open fields. Their best tactic would be to bear right to the railway, then left to Camp Farnham. The flat, lightly wooded country was better for tanks than the built-up Highway 104 where they were vulnerable to ambush by concealed infantry.

When Sloerill arrived the position was under light artillery fire, but the ALQ were unsure of where the FMR were. A burning truck and two bodies on Route 104 showed where the attackers had been stopped.

Zuke parked in a farmyard near the junction of Lareau and Versailles Roads, behind the wood concealing St Pierre's men. Leaving Chantilly talking to his guns by radio, Sloerill, Zuke, and Laurin ran forward to St Pierre's observation point, using a ditch that offered some cover from view and direct fire.

"Greetings." St Pierre waved from behind the house. "The weather forecast is warm this morning, hotter in the afternoon. Much hotter, I fear."

Sloerill checked the position on the map, then on the ground, shaking his head.

"I know," St Pierre agreed. "The road angles make everything look wrong. Given a choice, I would not defend here." A shell landed a hundred metres to the right, destroying a planter on the house lawn.

"Are there still people in those houses ahead?" Sloerill asked.

"Only a couple in a basement who refused to leave. It's a stone house. They are safer than we are. Everyone else is gone."

"Do you have alternate positions ready, Pierre?"

"Some. My men grumble that they are soldiers, not moles. They've been digging for ten days. Leo's men occupy one such position. Wayne Jones is fifty metres directly ahead. Lieutenant Palozzi is across the road to his left. Lieutenant Cook is behind Palozzi. Leo's HQ is behind Cook. I hope we have guns and armour because the Tangos certainly do."

"Armand is calling in co-ordinates now." Two shells landed on the far side of the road in front of them, their effect muffled by the soft ground.

"I have an outpost in those trees ahead," St Pierre explained. "The ground around it is soft enough to bog down tanks, but without support those men are isolated."

"Where did you hit that ALQ truck from?"

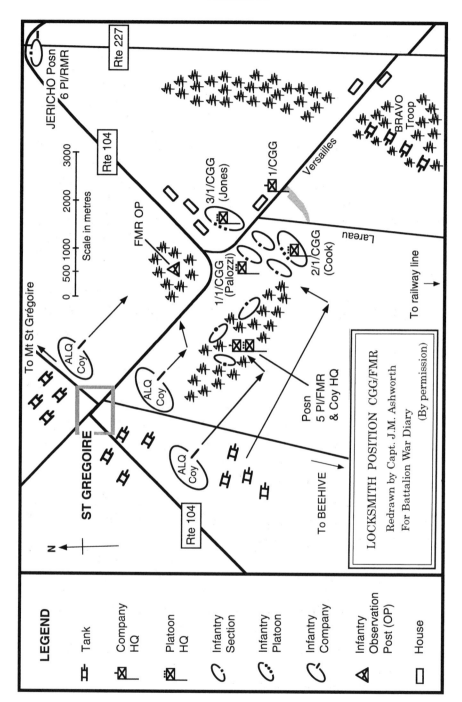

LOCKSMITH POSITION CGG/FMR
Redrawn by Capt. J.M. Ashworth
For Battalion War Diary
(By permission)

LEGEND

⚞⚟ — Tank

⊠ — Company HQ

⊠ — Platoon HQ

⌒ — Infantry Section

⌒⋯ — Infantry Platoon

⌒ — Infantry Company

△ — Infantry Observation Post (OP)

▢ — House

"The outpost. It was only a recce patrol, but with JERICHO so weakly manned I didn't dare let them pass. We shot them up, then went to ground. I tried to make the ALQ think it was our main position."

Sloerill studied the map. Tanks could advance down both sides of Route 104, and the defence was overlooked by Mont St Grégoire, a 730-foot massif rising out of an otherwise flat countryside to the north, the perfect if distant observation post for the ALQ artillery spotters.

St Pierre pointed west. "They are using St Grégoire as an assembly point. We see movement on the street and hear tank motors. If they attack my outpost, 5 Platoon can take them from a flank."

Sloerill nodded appreciatively. "We'll need tight fire discipline. Your men must not reveal their position until the last minute. If the ALQ attack the outpost thinking it's the main position, let Leo's forward platoon engage them. When the ALQ regroup to go for the Guards, your men can shoot them up almost before they start."

"Good, and what about an anti-tank defence?"

"M-72's are no good except close up. The Carl Gustavs are better, but nobody's had much practice with them. ALPHA Troop is coming up. They'll be in the wood behind us and will engage any armour that overruns us. Our job is to stop the infantry. How are your other positions?"

"JERICHO is holding an attack. BEEHIVE was hit earlier, but not seriously. They have tested all my positions and inflicted casualties. One platoon commander is dead, two are wounded but still in action. Altogether, six dead, twelve wounded. Ammunition is plentiful."

"I'll see Leo now. Move to your headquarters in with 5 Platoon. You're too cut off here."

"When do I pull in that outpost?"

"At the last minute. Keep the ALQ focussed on them. During the attack Armand can lay smoke to let your men get clear, then use HE[3] to discourage pursuit. OK?"

When Sloerill got to 1 Company's HQ in a ditch beside the Versailles road, Leo was off touring his three platoon positions. Only his driver, a Sergeant MFC[4] and two Guardsmen were there, all battering at the ground

---

[3] High explosive
[4] Mortar Fire Controller

to deepen a shallow drainage ditch into a real shelter. Zuke was swinging
a pickaxe. Laurin, on the radio, turned to Sloerill.

"Sir. An armoured corps officer arrived. Should he come here?"
Sloerill took the set. "Hello IRONSIDES. Come to my location.
Bring SHELLDRAKE.[5] Out."

Sloerill looked over the edge of the ditch. Some shells were falling
on the FMR outpost. Others probed towards the Guards. In the distance he
saw a church steeple. If it was an ALQ artillery OP, [6] the guns would have
to take it out.

On the left, a small party of men was approaching, concealed from
the ALQ by the woods. Chantilly and his signaller had two men with them.
One would be Lieutenant Brault, Sherbrooke Hussars. The young officer
was Sloerill's link to the Centurion tanks that were on their way—he hoped.

When the party arrived, Sloerill drew Brault aside. "Where are the
tanks? The ALQ will attack any minute."

"Coming, sir. ALPHA Troop was delayed by mines and is half an
hour away. BRAVO Troop in Bedford have finished their refit and want to
join in. In fact they're closer than ALPHA Troop is."

"Where are they?"

"On Rang Kemp, sir, coming up to Highway 227."

"Tell them to hurry. Unknown number of ALQ tanks to our front."

Brault grabbed his radio. "Hello, Tango Niner Niner Two, message, over." He paused briefly and began to relay Sloerill's orders.

Sloerill was looking over the battlefield again. The shelling was
getting heavier. The field around the FMR outpost was erupting in huge
gouts of flame and smoke but the soft ground there muffled the blasts. The
guns had also found the range of Palozzi's men. Two or three guns were
firing at them while another ranged in on Wayne Jones across the road.

Laurin touched his shoulder and pointed right. Markos and his
signaller were running towards them at full speed. They crossed Versailles
Road, their boots skidding on the cold pavement, leapt the shallow ditch and
plunged into the knee-high corn stubble. The screaming whistle of an incoming shell began to build. The men in the command post went flat. Leo's

---

[5] Designation of Armour & Artillery representative
[6] Observation Post

radio operator, lagging a few feet behind him, dropped to the ground. Less than three metres from the ditch Leo left the ground in a desperate hard running dive. He was too late. The shell landed almost under his feet. The explosion hurled his shattered body across the headquarters trench and threw it, rolling like a bundle of bloody rags, between the brown rows of corn stalks.

His signaller lay fifteen metres from the ditch, dazed but unhurt. Sloerill bounded from the trench, seized the man by his arms and began to drag him to safety, vaguely hearing the muffled plop of exploding smoke grenades. He dragged him into the ditch as Zuke threw a last grenade. Chantilly pounded on his arm.

"Tanks! Tanks ahead, twelve o'clock!" His normally calm voice was high with excitement.

Sloerill looked. Two Leopard tanks had come out of St Grégoire to the left of Route 104 and stopped, their long guns swinging slowly in search of a target. Two more emerged from the town, followed by a hundred ALQ infantry. The soldiers passed the first two tanks and moved up until they were opposite the FMR outpost. As the tanks opened fire on the position with machine guns, the infantry swung left to the roadside ditch and began to fire into the copse of trees.

"Sir? There." Laurin pointed right. Four more tanks, this time on the right of Route 104 were moving directly towards the FMR outpost position. Behind them more ALQ infantry, at least a full company, advanced to the attack across the open field. "Poor bastards," George said softly. "Armand, smoke in front and to the left of the FMR outpost. There are four men in there who are going to have to run for it."

Armand began talking to the guns, his voice again under control, calling cryptic figures and code names to assist the Gunners in bringing down fire where it was needed.

The MFC sergeant crouched two metres away, face blank with shock. "Sergeant!" Sloerill snapped.

The man shook his head hopelessly. "I can't touch those things," he replied, his eyes wide as the tanks' machine guns shredded the supposed FMR platoon position.

"Fuck the tanks, hit the infantry!"

The sergeant nodded, and began to talk into his radio. Behind the line men began to drop bombs into the upraised mortar tubes as the second group of four ALQ tanks moved forward in support of their advancing infantry. The tanks on the left fired into the FMR position from right angles as the main attack began.

"Sir?" Brault crawled closer. "BRAVO Troop is ready to dismount from their transporters. Do you wish them to come right forward to engage those tanks? They are now on your battalion net."

"I want them in those trees behind us to engage any tanks that get through. Tell them to engage targets at about a thousand metres."

"Roger." Brault acknowledged. "Tango Niner Niner Two. Eight tanks your front. Delta Oscars around crossroad. Present range, approx five thousand metres. Engage tanks that pass our position at figures one zero, zero zero metres from your location. Over."

"Tango Niner Niner Two, dismounting now. Roger eight tanks. Roger range. Roger friendly slug location. Out." The reply was reassuringly calm and professional. The officer might have been acknowledging ten enemy tanks or a ration resupply.

Sloerill risked a quick look at the attack. The first mortar bombs had hit St Grégroire. Now they were creeping east towards the FMR outpost, hitting the rear of the attacking ALQ company. The sergeant, who had been ranging with one mortar, ordered rapid fire for all eight weapons.

An explosion ahead of the HQ sent smoke billowing over their position, half-blinding them.

"Sorry," Chantilly said grimly, then barked into his radio. "Stop. Add eight hundred . . . right four hundred. Go on." The next smoke shell landed beside the outpost. "Close," he muttered and spoke into his radio again. "Add one hundred. Battery shoot." Moments later a wall of smoke began to build between the outpost and the ALQ tanks and their accompanying infantry which were now being hit by the mortar fire. The tanks ignored the bombs but the infantry was vulnerable to shrapnel even though the soft ground swallowed much of the explosive effect. As Sloerill watched, three Fusiliers appeared from the little stand of smoke-shrouded trees, and sprinted for the relative safety of Wayne Jones's platoon.

Sloerill nodded. "Armand, switch to HE when their main assault goes in. Mix in some airbursts to make it interesting."

"Hello, Four," he called the FMR. "Your orphans now at my Call

Sign 3. Let ALQ Ironsides pass, then engage infantry on my command."
St Pierre acknowledged calmly although his slit trenches at the edge of the
wood were less than a hundred metres from four ALQ tanks.

Leo's signaller was still huddled at the bottom of the trench, his
nose and ears bleeding from the blast. Sloerill took the radio handset.
"Laurin. I'll talk to the Guards and tanks. You pass everything on to the
FMR. Got it?" Laurin nodded.

"Hello all stations," George called to what had been Leo's company. "Enemy tanks to be engaged by M72 only at range figures one, zero,
zero metres. Fire in groups of two or three at same target. Primary target,
treads. Secondary target, hull side. Tertiary target, rear of tank after it
passes. Acknowledge."

The three replies came swiftly: Wayne Jones, Alfredo Palozzi (a
Collège Militaire officer) and Grahame Cook (regular force) understood.

"All stations," Sloerill continued. "Allow tanks to pass. Do not fire
except at sure target. Following infantry must, I say again, must be stopped.
Acknowledge." The three replied quickly.

In a pause between explosions a man dived into the ditch in a flurry
of snow and dirt. Weapons swung to cover him.

"Company Sergeant-Major Fortey." Sloerill lowered his pistol.
"Glad to see you."

"I was distributing ammunition, sir. Where's Major Markos?"

"Dead." Sloerill pointed to the bloody heap in the corrn field.
"You're in charge now." He briefed the young regular-force warrant officer on what he'd done. Fortey took the company radio as it began to crackle
at him.

"Sir? Mr Jones says ALQ tanks and infantry are moving past the
FMR outpost and towards his position."

"Thank you, Fortey." Sloerill looked over the edge of the trench
again.

The ALQ were advancing; but they had no choice. The mortar fire
was driving them relentlessly into the shellfire from Armand's guns falling
on their objective. Desperately they ran through the empty FMR position
and took cover in the low boggy ground in the bend of the road. The rear-
most platoon had been hit hard, but of the hundred men who had begun the
attack at least sixty were unhurt by the time they reached Route 104.

Their four tanks roared through the shellfire, machine guns raking
the ground ahead, finding no suitable target for the 120mm main guns. A
shell struck the rear tank on the side, smashing its tread. It slewed to a stop,
machine guns still firing. Three others plunged on towards Wayne Jones's
position on the other side of the road.

On the left the ALQ company that had been providing covering
fire for the attack now continued its eastward advance. Two platoons were
spread between the road and the trees; a third followed a hundred yards to
the rear. The tanks ahead of them cleared the way. Palozzi's men in deep
slit trenches were invisible to the buttoned-down tankers rolling over them.
Fifty metres behind the tanks came the first wave of infantry.

"Now, FMR. Hit them now!" Sloerill ordered, then snapped an
order at Fortey. "Tell Palozzi to hold fire until I give the order."

The ALQ company, moving close behind their tanks, were totally
unprepared for the raging rifle and machine gun that erupted from the trees
to their right. The major and a signaller were the first to die; then others began to fall as the ambush was sprung. Officers desperately tried to turn their
men in the middle of an attack to send them in an unexpected direction
against an enemy they couldn't see. They failed. Some men went to ground,
firing blindly into the trees. Others tried to run for cover. A few pressed on,
seeking protection from the tanks that had moved past Palozzi's position,
unaware of the carnage behind them.

Sloerill pointed at CSM Fortey. "Palozzi to open fire now."

Palozzi's men engaged the surviving mob of about fifty infantry
with rifle and machine gun fire at point-blank range. The leaderless ALQ
company, hit from two sides, disintegrated as a fighting force. Individuals
fought for possession of a slit trench or a dip in the ground. Grenades
bounced over the rutted field and exploded, sometimes killing both the
target and the thrower who had been too close.

The tanks passed through the artillery fire now falling on Lieutenant Cook's position. Two Guardsmen tried to fire M-72's at the nearest
monster and died under the machine guns of the following tank.

To the right, using the tanks as cover, the ALQ infantry, pushed
towards Wayne Jones by the relentless mortar fire falling on their rear and
torn apart by the shells Armand's guns were dropping on them, began to
cross Route 104. One tank bogged down in the soft ground, but the two

survivors pushed on, their steel treads tearing gouges in the bank of the ditch and ripping off chunks of pavement as they reared up out of the marshy area in the bend of the road.

As they exposed their bellies, guns pointing uselessly at the sky, Jones and three Guardsmen stood up to fire shoulder-held anti-tank rockets at the monsters. Two exploded against a tread of the left-hand tank. It rocked, then killed the Guardsmen with a burst of machine-gun fire. Jones's rocket hit the second tank in the soft underbelly and it blew up, the massive turret lifting high into the air followed by a blast of flame as two hundred gallons of fuel exploded. The fourth tank roared through Jones's position and, seeing friendly tanks on the right, veered that way, converging on the four that had overrun Palozzi and Cook. The five tanks advanced into the cornfield, leaving the infantry to fight.

Jones's men engaged the faltering ALQ infantry, who stopped trying to follow the armour and took cover around the houses lining the road.

A tank commander in the open field behind Sloerill risked opening his hatch for a better look and saw the confused battle behind him. With no Canadian armour in sight, he ordered his troop to assist the infantry.

In the woods, the four tanks of BRAVO Troop were now taking up fire positions. Their commander saw the ALQ tanks turning ponderously in the field in front of him and ordered his men to engage. They fired almost together. At a range of 2000 metres, two rounds missed. One sabot shot ripped a deep gouge in a turret but did not penetrate. The fourth struck the ALQ troop leader's tank, smashing a tread bogey wheel.

The ALQ tank turrets swung, searching for targets. The Canadian position was spotted by the surviving tank of the right-hand attack. The commander had seen them shoot and fired a HESH [7] round. It hit one Centurion on the side and burned its way through the armour to blast a spray of molten metal throughout the interior. By the time the tank's ammunition blew up, the crew had been dead for several seconds.

Laurin hit Sloerill's arm. "Message from Colonel St Pierre, sir."

Sloerill took the headset. "Four, send, over."

"Tangos, figures one, zero, zero men, entering wood from west. Also figures four tanks south of wood. Can SHELLDRAKE engage?"

[7] High Explosive Squash Head

Chantilly shook his head. "Not if I can't see them."

"Four, negit SHELLDRAKE. Withdraw eastward. Call Sign One will support you. Out to you. Hello One," he called Cook's platoon. "SITREP, over."

"One, four non-Jims; taking fire from right. Ammo good, over."

"One, move to support FMR position. Tanks to your left. Engage infantry, over."

"One, support Budgies. Roger, out."

Sloerill turned to see what had happened behind him. One ALQ tank was burning amid the corn stubble, but four others, including the disabled one, were firing into the woods where his Centurions were. As he watched, a second Canadian tank blew up in a display of fireworks that set twenty fires in the woods.

"Tanks left!" Fortey yelled, and Sloerill turned to see four Leopards emerge southeast of the wood, their turrets turned to fire into the trees concealing the FMR withdrawal.

Twenty of Cook's men had been running to their new position as the ALQ tanks appeared. A crew commander saw them in his telescope as the turret cranked round and opened fire. Eight men died in the stream of 50-calibre bullets while the survivors dived for whatever shelter the irregular ground offered.

"Armand, HE on those tanks. Now!" Sloerill ordered, but Chantilly was already talking to his gun line, switching fire to the new target. In his platoon position, Lt Cook ordered smoke grenades to be thrown to mask the machine gun fire while he got into the woods. Sloerill saw what he intended.

"One, no move till SHELLDRAKE engages IRONSIDES. Out to you. Hello, Four, friendly forces entering woods behind you. Acknowledge."

"Four, acknowledge." St Pierre's voice sounded ragged as if he was running. "I am withdrawing. Casualties heavy. Over."

"Roger Four." He turned to Laurin. "Send MARATHON to Captain Ashworth. I want the recruits out of Farnham, now."

"I've kept him informed, sir," Laurin replied after sending the codeword. "The recruits have been in their trucks for an hour."

Sloerill grunted and turned his attention to the battle on his left.

The new ALQ tank troop was shooting up the woods without opposition. Machine-gun fire interspersed with powerful blasts from the main armament was tearing the trees to shreds.

"Fortey! Where's the Carl Gustav?" Sloerill asked as a few artillery rounds landed beyond the ALQ tanks. As Chantilly called corrections, Fortey handed Sloerill the short ugly weapon.

"The only man here who'd fired it is dead, sir." Fortey pointed to a Guardsman lying at the left of the ditch, half his head missing.

"I used to be called the Gustav Sniper," Sloerill lied, seeing the frightened faces around him. "Let's discourage that lot." He aimed carefully at the side of the nearest tank. It was at maximum range, but he fired.

The slow rocket arced away, rising slowly, then plunged to strike the exposed side of the Leopard. The long projecting post in front of the bomb ignited the charge on impact. The explosion from the shaped charge focused on a section of armour less than an inch wide. It burned through the steel, expanding as it went, and a third of a second later a lance of flame and globs of molten steel burst into the tank. One struck a racked shell and the tank blew up, smoke and flame pouring from the blown-open hatches.

As artillery fire thickened around the new tanks they began to move out of the danger area. Between explosions, Sloerill heard the constant rattle of light machine guns in the woods where the ALQ and FMR were fighting hand-to-hand. He saw Cook and a dozen men dash into the trees, briefly hidden from the terrible gunfire from the Leopards.

On his right Wayne Jones was also in trouble. Two disabled tanks in front of him were raking the area with gunfire, as almost fifty survivors of two attacking ALQ companies, having found a leader, the one surviving platoon commander, prepared to attack.

"Hello, Two," Sloerill called Palozzi. The firing from there had diminished. "SITREP, over."

"Two, the Tin-Heads rolled right over us, nine casualties, about half Jims, ten six-packs, ammo low. Over."

"Two, support Call Sign Three with a counter-attack. Out."

Two of the last-arriving ALQ tanks churned across the rutted corn field to support the three already advancing on the tree-line where the Centurions were hidden. Both fired together and a third Canadian tank exploded in the trees.

"Fortey, grab ammo for the Carl Gustav and follow me. All HQ personnel get into the woods!" Sloerill ordered. "If we stay out here, we're dead." As they gathered for the near-hopeless four hundred-metre dash to cover, they heard the now familiar crack of a tank's main gun, immediately followed by an explosion. The lone tank still supporting the ALQ infantry in the woods had blown up.

"What the hell—?" As Sloerill looked for the cause of the explosion Armand hit his arm and pointed south down Lareau Road. "There! Tanks! Ours! Centurions!

Sloerill stared as the four Centurions of ALPHA Troop, made gloriously hideous by the carapace of welded-on armour, attacked. They moved in bounds, two tanks advancing while the other two fired at the ALQ tanks facing them. The ALQ armoured rush ended as their Leopards swung to face the new enemy. As they did so, the last Centurion in BRAVO Troop advanced to the edge of the blazing wood and blasted the tank nearest it with a sabot shot into the engine. Almost immediately the ALQ squadron commander's tank blew up, hit by two HESH rounds fired by the just-arrived ALPHA Troop. The surviving tanks broke and fled. Turrets facing south, smoke bombs flying from turret mortars, they raced for the relative safety of St Grégoire.

The pursuing Centurions swept past the wood, blasted the untracked tank on the road in front of Wayne Jones's position, then ran into a hail of accurate artillery fire. They scattered and pressed on, zigzagging to confuse the artillery spotters. Two other disabled Leopards and the one that had bogged down stood empty. Their crews had escaped to the town. The tank Wayne Jones had destroyed was still burning.

"My, my, and don't they look nice!" Zuke said admiringly.

Four tank transporters were roaring up Lareau Road, each one carrying twenty or twenty-five men. Near the crossroads they slowed. The men jumped down, shook themselves into formation and ran past two blazing tanks into the woods where the Guards and FMR were still battling the last ALQ infantry.

With fresh troops coming towards them and their tanks in retreat, the ALQ broke off. Those in forward positions threw down their arms and surrendered; those further back began a fighting withdrawal through the woods.

Zuke and Sloerill ran forward to intercept a platoon of the mystery company. "What unit? What unit?" Sloerill yelled at the passing men.

Sergeant Weitz jumped a small ditch, knelt and fired at a running figure ahead, missed, and cursed fluently. "Odds and Sods Company, sir. Captain Ashworth is OC[8]—You!" he bellowed at a pair of soldiers. "Berthiaume! Caporetto! That's a prisoner! Take his rifle, don't hit him, you ding-dongs!"

Sloerill ran towards the three men moving between the spread-out platoons. They must be Ashworth and his signallers.

"John? Where in hell did this crew come from?"

Ashworth grinned hugely. "Well, sir, from what we heard of the battle, things didn't look too promising, so Colonel Anderson and I began forming a camp defense. After listening to the battle over the radio, Clay decided that ALPHA Troop needed infantry support more than the camp did. You won't like the way we're mixed up, sir. They're cooks, storemen, drivers and about forty FMR recruits that mutinied and refused to bug out with the rest. Sergeant Weitz had brought in a dozen prisoners from the Bromont fighting and he effectively stowed away in one of our trucks. His story is that he thought that it was going back to Bromont."

"Under the circumstances I won't press charges. OK, clear the woods, then see if Wayne needs a hand. He has about a platoon of ALQ in some buildings to his front. Palozzi is about to counter-attack them. Once this area is clear, we'll push any remaining Delta Tangos out of St Gregoire and chase them right back across the Richelieu River. After that, they won't feel like coming for us again for a while." Artillery rounds were still arriving from the ALQ gun position but less intensely than before. Obviously the ALQ guns were pulling out with their infantry.

"Armand, can you drive that lot away faster? Do you know where their gun line is?"

"Only in general terms. I lack both radar and spotters."

Laurin came forward. "Sir, Mr Bryce is overhead. He can see their guns and will spot for you." Laurin handed Chantilly the mike. "His radio name is Barf Bag, sir."

George roared with brief laughter and trotted away. There were

---

[8] Officer Commanding

wounded to see, dead to bury—too many dead—on both sides. He could see fires burning in St Grégoire that would have to be put out, and somehow he had to find enough men to repair his fragile defence until the Toronto Scottish flew in. He started to swing past Ashworth's command post, wanting to say something particularly regimental. Then it came to him and he turned.

"John, tell the recruits they have permission to walk out—once they get a day off." Traditionally, Guards recruits were confined to camp until they reached a training standard that allowed them to be seen in public without reflecting badly on the regiment. "And thank you. I was never so glad of company as today. Well done."

CHAPTER THIRTEEN

The Toronto Scottish

The first political result of the battle came when President Cyr learned of it on Friday morning. The loss of eight expensive tanks (and crews); two hundred men dead, wounded or captive; and word from France that there was now no hope for a cease-fire shook the little confidence he had retained after the Cree had captured the James Bay dams and English separatists had seized part of the North Shore. Nothing was going right. He'd believed that Canada would not fight: Canada was fighting. He'd believed international law protected Quebec's territorial claims: regardless of law, international opinion was with the Cree. In a panic, he dictated a letter to the Prime Minister of Canada offering to end the war in exchange for having Quebec powers acquired through custom written into the constitution. This, as he said, would enable him to claim victory because they had never been written down before. He sent the letter with a trusted aide instead of the government mail.

At ten in the morning he walked into the party caucus room to be greeted by a stony silence. His MNA's listened impassively to his report on the battle, the cost to Quebec, and the danger of prolonging a war when massive Canadian forces were assembling to crush them. When he stopped, his Intergovernmental Affairs Minister attacked him for the "humiliation" of allowing foreign governments to negotiate with Quebec through the back door without demanding that they first recognize the new state. Then he took the secret letter to Ottawa from his breast pocket. He read it aloud and moved a terse motion of non-confidence that was quickly seconded and passed with three abstentions. The Minister of Finance proposed Lionel Bouget, Leader of the Opposition, as President. This passed with but one abstention. At 10:45 ex-president Cyr left the caucus room without power or any vestige of pride with which to cloak his nakedness. He'd been accused of failure to defend Quebec, cowardice in the face of danger, and treason. Nobody understood that everything he'd done had been to promote Quebec—without risking its economy.

No government car met him on the street, no journalists to whom he could pour out his puzzled anger at events he did not understand. For several minutes he stood irresolute at the street door, then waved at a passing cab. He still had powerful friends. The people who had staged this coup would pay dearly. The cab he'd waved at went by, but one in the taxi rank pulled out.

As Cyr stepped forward, the rear window went down and two men opened fire with Uzi submachine guns. Cyr staggered back, briefly held up by the force of the bullets tearing into his body, and collapsed in a twisted heap. One assassin, his face hidden by a stocking mask, leaned out as the cab accelerated away.

His cry "Death to a goddam traitor!" was heard by fifty shocked spectators who later reported that their president had been assassinated by "les maudits anglais."

After Thursday's battle Sloerill's force was left in relative peace for two days as the ALQ recovered. Then they struck back cautiously. From Magog in the east to Noyan in the west small ALQ patrols slipped in to probe and attack. Sloerill's men fought looking over their shoulders, their inner eyes on the Bromont airport where the Tor Scots would arrive. They counter-patrolled and ambushed, nerves already stretched almost to the breaking point by almost a month of constant action. By Monday, all that held them together was numbing fatigue, pride, and the desire to show the Toronto men that they had things under control.

Sloerill knew that if they relaxed they would fall apart, and he was everywhere, challenging, praising, leading, taking risks. Fortunately more humvees arrived; he used up two in two days. One hummer was shot into charred junk by a machine gun. The other (in a repair shop) rested on three wheels, its frame bent from running off the road after George, Laurin and Zuke had all fallen asleep returning from an inspection tour one night.

That afternoon some help arrived: a scratch force of militia and regulars rebadged to the Guards to form a support company with machine guns, mortars and TOW [1] anti-tank weapons. The additional firepower stiffened the defence but gave no relief to the men crouched in frozen slit trenches up front.

Conditions got worse. Freezing rain fell as often as snow. Any exposed group larger than five men attracted mortar or artillery fire. Men patrolled, added overhead cover and sleeping bays to their trenches, and tried to sleep. Then sergeants and officers crawled forward to inspect the work and demand improvements.

After the evening 100 percent stand-to came the one good hot meal of the day, a chance to shave and wash (two litres of hot water per man), and every two days a forty-ounce bottle of rum or whiskey for each platoon. Then they began their evening work. They carried stiff rolls of razor wire to stake in front of their positions. In front of that they constructed low-wire entanglements at ankle to knee-height above the ground to snare the feet of unwary infiltrators. They also braved the artillery fire to go out to booby-trap their work and add trip flares. The next night they usually had to repair wires cut by ALQ patrols or artillery.

In the first month of the war the men had become fighters. In the week following the battle of St Grégoire they became soldiers. Every moment of their day was programmed to ensure that they ate, improved defences, washed, patrolled, shaved, ambushed, slept a little, and got fresh clothing.

Pride grew with fatigue. The Black Watch clung to their hills around Magog and refused the offers of assistance they knew would rob other units. The Guards, now near full strength, insisted on taking extra duties, and the smaller FMR demanded an equal share of the line to prove they were as tough as (or tougher than) les anglais.

On Wednesday more help arrived. Two hundred and twenty French-speaking soldiers flew in from New Brunswick, nearly doubling the

---

[1] Tube launched, Optically tracked, Wire guided

size of the FMR. St Pierre fed them into his defence and withdrew the most exhausted men, who then had to stagger a kilometre out of ALQ artillery range before getting into the trucks that took them away. Even on hard benches, the men instantly fell asleep, and two died when they slid over the tailgate to fall under the wheels of the following blacked-out truck.

On the morning of the tenth, before going to visit the Black Watch, Sloerill ordered B Company of the FMR, the St Grégoire men, to meet the the 800 incoming Toronto Scottish. At Magog he found that Jan Berkowitz, supported now by mortars and a troop of guns, had the ALQ under control and was making their life as miserable as they had made his a week ago.

After the tour George responded to a prickling in his back hair and flew Air Bryce to Bromont. They touched down at the same time as the first of the seven Yukons in the airlift. Each carried over a hundred men. As Sloerill emerged from the wokka, a door in the first Yukon opened and a tall, broad-shouldered man appeared in the gap, jumped from the sill, and made a parachute landing roll as his muscular body hit the snow-covered ground. Sloerill moved towards him, spotting the three broad stripes of a lieutenant-colonel [2] on his epaulettes.

"Terry Gascoigne?"

"General Sloerill. We're a bit late, but we're ready to roll, sir."

The new man was regular force with jump wings and UN medals. His face was tanned and lean and he looked like a pusher. As they moved off the tarmac, Gascoigne's dark eyes flicked from the men starting down the loading ramp now in position to a second plane just touching down.

The remaining five followed, each stopping on the runway and swinging halfway around to park off the strip, where they waited for landing ramps to be placed in position. Two fire trucks stood by, and the FMR began moving trucks closer to receive passengers. Others were pushing heavy loading ramps down the paved runway.

Gascoigne saw the FMR tac signs [3] on the trucks. "I heard our trucks had arrived from the States. I'd like to have my own transport." He spoke in a neutral tone, but his voice still had an authoritative snap.

"Your trucks are in camp. This way is quicker. We're in range of

---

[2] Usually abbreviated as L/Col
[3] Vehicle markings individual to a unit

ALQ guns, and I want you out of here fast. I had suggested using the Sweetsburg airport because I have only two gunships for air cover."

"There weren't enough STOL aircraft available," Gascoigne explained. "Now that we're here, what happens next, sir?"

"You take over the Guards line so they can rest and train a bit." Sloerill watched the seventh Yukon turn off the runway and come to a halt.

"My orders are not to get involved in any local fighting," Gascoigne said, his eyes also on the last plane.

"You haven't had your orders yet, colonel," George said mildly. "My Guards have been in action for a month and they need rest and training. You'll give them the rest part, and the FMR will be your guides and mentors until you get your feet firmly on the ground."

"FMR? They're a French-Quebec militia unit, aren't they?"

"No. They're a Canadian regiment that speaks French. Be advised. Terminology is something that we watch carefully around here."

Gascoigne shook his head. "Sorry, sir. I mean my men are from Ontario. About twenty percent speak French at some level and I've scattered them around, but we sure don't qualify as bilingual. I'd like Guards or Black Watch guides."

"Look." Sloerill turned to face Gascoigne. "We're starting badly. Our population here is mostly French-speaking and on our side, but the ones who aren't let you know in very direct ways. I intend your first contact with French-Canadians to be positive. That means the FMR, some of my best fighting men. A few days with them and—"

He was interrupted by the explosion of a shell half-way down the field. A second screamed in to land a hundred yards closer to the planes.

"Tor Scots! Take cover!" Gascoigne roared at the eighty-odd men scattered around the first plane. One group was moving across the tarmac to the waiting trucks, the last few were coming down the ramps.

Seven transports were on the ground. One was nearly unloaded; one had its ramps in place but no men had emerged yet; three more waited, doors open, for the ramps; two were still buttoned up.

The hidden ALQ observer on one of the surrounding hills directed fire at the line of helpless aircraft. Men scrambled from the second Yukon, scattering into the flat field, looking for non-existent cover. A shell burst near one group, flinging a dozen of them flat.

"Come with me!" Sloerill grabbed Colonel Gascoigne's arm and ran for the helicopter. The blades were already turning as Bryce got ready for an emergency takeoff.

"Andy!" Sloerill shouted through the open door. "Get up there and nail those bloody guns!"

"Cocked, sir! The Apaches'll blow 'em out of the water!"

The Huey surged up, its newly installed gatling gun swinging out from the right-hand door. Bryce swept low across the field away from the shells and his chopper clawed its way into the sky, already swinging to look for the artillery blasting at the airport.

Sloerill turned back to the landing zone. Four Fusiliers were calmly lobbing smoke grenades to hide the dead and wounded Scottish from the ALQ spotter while the rest of their platoon dashed forward. The officer slung a man over his shoulder, waved to his men, and ran. Moments later two shells fell on the blood-spattered but now empty ground.

From the side, the FMR company commander raced past, standing in the back of his jeep and waving a line of ten-wheeler trucks towards the parked Yukons. He used hand signals to direct them in groups of four to the planes that had no unloading ramps.

"My men'll be butchered!" Gascoigne yelled, trying to break Sloerill's grip. "Let me go, dammit!"

Sloerill saw what the FMR were trying to do. Gascoigne couldn't do better. "Leave it to Captain Gendron!" he yelled over the crash of shells and screaming men.

A cluster of four shells burst by the last two transports. One began to burn. Gendron directed trucks against the hulls of the planes under the open doors, two per side.

More trucks lurched through the smoke of the exploding shells and into position. The trapped men began leaping from the aircraft onto the cabs and canvas tops of the trucks, then onto the ground. One driver saw a burning plane's emergency door jam half-open, restricting the exit of the heavily laden men. He seized a fire axe, climbed to the back of his truck and with a few savage strokes cut the door from its hinges to let the men escape.

Gendron's jeep raced down the field to the Air Traffic Controllers' base. The ATC officer sprang into it with his radio and they tore back to where Sloerill and Terry Gascoigne were crouched.

The jeep skidded to a stop. "Monsieur! Des compliments du Capitaine Gendron," the begrimed driver shouted. "Un cadeau pour vous aider à parler avec Barf Bag."

The controller vaulted out of the jeep as it turned and roared back into the shellfire.

"I have Bryce on the line, sir. He has guns in view and is ready to attack." He handed Sloerill the headset.

"Barf Bag, this is SUNRAY.[4] SITREP, over."

"SUNRAY, figures eight guns hidden in trees." To his left, one helicopter exploded in a fiery ball. "It seems they have triple A,"[5] Bryce continued calmly. "We'll have to take it out first. The Apache's call sign is Gemini. Are we go? Over."

"You're go, Barf Bag. Do it fast."

They listened to Bryce direct Gemini to the ALQ anti-aircraft guns, the helicopters popping up from behind a hill, taking a look, and vanishing before they could be fired on. On one pop-up, the people on the ground saw the flare of a rocket salvo being fired.

"Got the bastards!" Gemini's crow of victory came clearly over the radio. "Four Hellfires right down their throats! Let's get those guns."

Bryce whooped and began to describe what was happening. On the first pass his gatling gun killed a dozen ALQ gunners and damaged two of the 155mm howitzers that had been firing at the airport. Gemini followed, landing his remaining twelve Hellfire missiles along the gunline to smash the guns to fragments. Then the two pilots began strafing the woods to kill more of the fleeing Gunners.

At the airport, shells rained down for another minute as the rounds in the air continued to arrive. Then they stopped.

Two Yukons were burning, so were six of the eight trucks jammed against their sides. Firemen were spraying foam to contain the fire as four empty planes taxied with agonizing slowness away from the flames. The seventh was stuck, its landing gear and tires riddled with shrapnel. Men emerged from its doors slowly, many helping wounded comrades. The FMR helped carry the injured to ambulances. Around the field, Tor Scots

---

[4] Codeword for a unit commander
[5] Anti-Aircraft Artillery

were standing up cautiously, looking for their comrades and trying to assess the disaster they had survived.

"Move out," Sloerill advised. "Find Captain Gendron. He knows where you're going. He speaks some English, his driver doesn't, his radio op is bilingual. Your men did well, Terry. If they'd panicked, we'd have lost a lot more. Pass on my compliments. I'll tell them myself later, but the Scottish will make a fine addition to our little army. I hope the Royals will prove to be as good when they arrive tomorrow."

Gascoigne didn't turn away. His NCO's were herding the men into overloaded trucks each of which left the moment the last man was crammed inside.

"What's the matter, colonel? Don't tell me you still object to the FMR as guides?"

"No sir. I'll follow those men anywhere now. I just want to say that this isn't what I expected—what they told me to expect. I guess I got started wrong, sir."

"The whole war got started wrong." Sloerill was watching the burning planes. "What did they tell you to expect?"

"They said this was a one-man show, a bastard organization that deviated from everything we professional soldiers believe in. I was told to avoid local fighting and when we broke out to push west as quickly as possible so your force could be brought under the standard command structure." He stared straight at Sloerill.

"And?" George turned to face him.

"And . . . after today . . . watching an FMR captain get my men out of those burning planes without orders . . . well, I'd like you to forget we met here. We can have our first meeting in Cowansville. I want to shake a few ideas loose in my head."

Sloerill put out his hand and they shook. "I've never seen you before in my life," he assured him. "I warn you, though, this Sloerill's a mean son of a bitch who'll make you do things you never thought of before."

"Any hints on how to get along with an SOB like that?"

"Run a good regiment of men who think they're the best in the world because they're Toronto Scottish and don't want to serve in any other regiment or with any other colonel."

Sloerill pointed to the smouldering, foam-covered planes. "The

FMR got you out because they think *they're* the best in the world. Your job's to prove that you are. See?"

Gascoigne gave a soundless whistle. "Hey, he *is* an SOB. I haven't had much practice along those lines, I've spent too much time in an HQ. I'd better get busy."

Sloerill headed for Bryce's helicopter as it settled onto the field. Gascoigne walked toward the last few of his men on the field. As a regular, he was used to doing the impossible. How to pull his unit together? Perhaps twenty percent were original Tor Scots. The rest had come from militia regiments from all over Ontario. They'd met a training standard and been pronounced ready to fight. After seeing the FMR in action, he had his doubts, even if most of his officers and senior NCO's were professionals.

He passed a platoon of men boarding a truck, miners from the Algonquin Regiment at North Bay. They climbed in silently, heads turning to watch a party of FMR laying out the dead in a neat row.

Gascoigne suddenly rounded on them. "What's wrong?" he demanded fiercely. "You're alive! Did you think nobody got hurt in a war? Put some snap in it! If you don't move like Tor Scots, I'll tear your cap badges out by the roots! Platoon Sergeant Hruska!"

"Yes, sir."

"Get these bloody sheep moving. I want to hear singing. I want to know that the Tor Scots don't get the runs when the shooting starts. Carry on! That's our motto in case you'd forgotten—Carry on!"

Gascoigne headed away from the startled sergeant, aiming for the knot of officers waiting for him. "That was easy," he muttered. "Now to light a fire under my company commanders."

President Bouget used the battle at Bromont to consolidate his new position and build confidence among the people for his vision of the new Quebec nation. Details of the defeat at St Grégoire had leaked swiftly and too accurately. He had to claim that Bromont had been a victory. Solemnly, wearing a black armband in memory of President Cyr, he went on TV to speak to all Quebec.

He told them that the assassins had been found and killed resisting arrest. They had been English, but he asked the people not to blame all English Quebecers for the actions of a few. He went on to announce curfews, temporary rationing of scarce goods and a call-up of more men to defend the sacred homeland. Then he leaned forward.

"We have been naive. We believed that a democratically elected government would be allowed to carry out the people's clearly expressed wishes. We were wrong. President Cyr trusted his friends in Ottawa. They betrayed him with a war that no Quebecer wanted. I still offer a hand of friendship to the Canadian people. But if their soldiers keep trying to crush our democracy, if they continue to invade our land and seize our cities, our open hand will turn to a fist of steel that will destroy them.

"That fist has struck. In Bromont, eight hundred Canadians died or were wounded as they landed in violation of our offer of a cease-fire if Canada stopped reinforcing the mercenary Sloerill. Their defeat was far more serious than our setback at St Grégoire.

"Québecois! Only a few more sacrifices must be made before we can bask in the glowing rays of the first freedom our people have ever known. If some doubt that we can win this national struggle, I say this. Already we have done what people said was impossible—but not for us qué-becois. We lost a skirmish last week because we were attacked while our main force guarded our borders from invasion. I say to Canada, let us build our country in peace. Let us talk of a right of free passage, not a corridor. Let us talk, not shoot . . . but if you shoot, if you invade to crush our national aspirations with force, I say, make more coffins for your sons than are needed tonight at Bromont. Quebecers, roused from a sleep of centuries, will never surrender their new and priceless liberty!"

Sloerill missed the speech because he had invited his senior officers to a dinner in a Cowansville hotel to meet the Toronto Scottish. Only St Pierre had been late. He had had to schedule each FMR/Tor Scot patrol past the St Grégoire battlefield to avoid the traffic jams that would have ensued had he left it to his proudly competitive company commanders.

After a long dinner and a short speech, they moved from the dining room into a lounge to continue fraternizing over drinks. As they entered, the eleven o'clock news had just started. The set was tuned to ABC's Channel 22 in Vermont and the story was St Grégoire.

"According to an Ottawa spokesperson," the announcer read, "the ALQ lost over six hundred men, a dozen tanks and several guns in last week's battle. Canada lost thirty men and two tanks. The victory secures control of the part of Quebec held by Canadian forces since the civil war began. In an interview with our reporter, General Sloerill said—"

"Switch it off!" came the cry from a dozen voices.

"I don't feel secure. Not half I don't," Peter Forbes complained. "What's the other side saying?" He switched to a Montreal channel.

The picture showed eight guns firing. "Yesterday our soldiers destroyed a Canadian regiment landing in Bromont. The provocative move defied the offer of a cease-fire made by both President Cyr and President Bouget. Later tonight, M Bouget's address will be rebroadcast in full."

The picture changed to a studio shot. The announcer looked up, his face suitably grim. "A riot in St Boniface, Manitoba, left three French-Canadians dead and many others wounded. The riot began when anglo-phones attacked a store displaying the Quebec flag. We will bring you further details as they are available.

"Next, an interview with Mme Adèle Chantilly, Minister of Domestic Services, who will explain the rationing system outlined tonight by President Bouget. Here is our reporter Jacques Leblanc in Quebec City."

Peter quickly switched off the set. "My wife," Armand said calmly. "A family tradition. In the war of 1812 one side supplied the Americans, another fought for the British. No matter who wins, la famille Chantilly survives."

"I gather that neither of those reports was exactly accurate?" Gascoigne asked.

"ALQ casualties were two hundred and eight, including prisoners," Sloerill said. "We lost eighty-six, wounded and dead, plus four tanks. The local people here have the true figures." George turned to Jan Berkowitz who was nursing a very large Scotch.

"Tell Terry about your battle," he invited. "He got pushed away from Magog," George said to Gascoigne, "and yelled for help. I didn't have any, but an hour later he was in control again."

Berkowitz looked up with a bland smile. "The trouble wi' ye Sassenachs," he said, "is ye niver learned that hielanders take care of their ane." His stagy "Scots" accent was a popular comic turn in his own officers' mess and among his Highlanders. "We didna *yell* for help, although I may have admitted that if there were men standing aboot wi' their thumbs up their arse, I'd noo ha' objected ta having them. We saved ourselves. My pipers ooped muskets and hae at the buggers from a flank."

Sloerill brought them to order when the laughter died down. "Now, gentlemen, real news. The big attack is on the thirteenth, which is also US election day. Two companies of Royals fly in tomorrow. The rest arrive Monday. The FMR will be glad to hear the airhead is Cowansville.

"In Ontario, 1 CMBG[6] is positioned behind the Ontario–Quebec border at Hawkesbury. They'll pass through the frontier militia brigade, and push on to Dorion–Vaudreuil. On Monday, the Mohawks at Kahnawake will block the Mercier Bridge and roads on the South Shore to protect the militia units crossing the St Lawrence at Valleyfield to join up with us.

"Yesterday 2 CMBG moved out of Hull north of the Ottawa River. They are now strung along Highway 148 from Buckingham to Grenville. The task of 2 CMBG is to clear the area Lachute–Ste Thérèse–Oka–Laval. Air recce indicates the ALQ have not completed their main line of resistance, Beaconsfield–St Eustache–Lachute."

He started for the door. "Don't bend the new boys' ears too much, they had a rough introduction this afternoon." His eyes found St Pierre. "Toupée? I want names from you. A lot of your men earned gongs today, Captain Gendron and a Fusilier who chopped open a door on a burning Yukon for openers." At the door, Sloerill paused.

"Today the FMR set a performance benchmark," he told them. "Guards, Scottish, Black Watch—look to your laurels." The door closed.

By Sunday night, the two mechanized brigades were in laagers. Eleven thousand one hundred fifty-four men and three thousand three hundred and sixteen vehicles were stretched back along both sides of the Ottawa River from the outskirts of Ottawa–Hull to Pointe Fortune and Carillon. The fighting force, nearly seven thousand men, was concentrated at the head of the columns.

On the Quebec side of the river, 2 Brigade was spread from Montebello to Grenville. Its light armoured patrols to the north and east occupied all positions that the ALQ might attack them from.

The militia brigade allowed 1 CMBG to pass through their lines.

---

[6] Canadian Mechanized Brigade Group

Then it shifted southwards to concentrate between Highway 401 and Alexandria, ready to cross the river the next day.

The moves were made with professional skill, although militiamen filled thirty per cent of infantry and artillery units and fifteen percent of the armoured regiments. Once the defensive positions were manned, tanker trucks moved through the parked convoys, topping up vehicles with gas and diesel fuel. Helicopters chattered overhead, searching for enemy activity, and men stared into the darkness with night scopes and infra-red scanners, watching cattle and horses graze.

Twenty miles behind them brigade commanders listened to a steady stream of reports on their radios as the refuelling progressed. Contact with Ottawa was at best sporadic. Teletype machines fresh out of storage had not yet been properly worked in. About fifteen percent of the messages each way arrived garbled and unreadable.

All day the massive convoys had rolled through Ontario and Quebec villages, greeted with cheers and flags. Now the children came, English and French, infinitely curious. Then parents, older children and young women came looking for them. Regimental commanders allowed limited fraternization, but forbade the men to enter any house, even for a meal. In at least two towns there were impromptu street dances.

The senior officers remembered pictures of Allied troops entering Holland near the end of WW II. The scenes were the same, and now they were the conquering heroes.

Children and women scrambled onto tanks to talk to crews or wandered amid the armoured personnel carriers, full of questions. Old soldiers remembered their days in uniform and compared the modern sinews of war to what they had had to fight with.

The parties lasted until nearly midnight when the MP's went around to usher the last civilians out of the lines, banging sharply on truck bodies and steel hulls when they suspected non-military activity. It was the best night of war imaginable. In fact it was not war, it was a parade.

On Monday as engines coughed into life at dawn Canadian flags flew everywhere. Windows and porches filled with faces, and mothers had to restrain children from cycling after the slow lines of armour, guns and men who had liberated them.

As the brigades moved towards Montreal, slim high contrails

showed pairs of Canadian CF-18's flying cover. 1 Brigade advanced on Vaudreuil and Dorion down the four-lane Highway 417. The westbound lanes were reserved for their administration vehicles. Two infantry militia companies moved forward to secure the bridge to Valleyfield.

From Ottawa, General Thomas ordered the brigadier of 2 Brigade to send 1st RCR and a squadron of tanks to Lachute while the Patricias headed for Oka. Everywhere their reception promised an even better party than they had enjoyed the night before. Near Lachute, the Colonel of 1 RCR, having met no resistance, detached A company in APC's with four tanks to capture the ammunition factory at Brownsburg.

1 Brigade crept through Rigaud, Hudson and Vaudreuil, liberating that rich area of government support. The brigadier was cautious. His men waved to civilians, but at each stop they fanned out defensively. At Dorion, a company of 3 PPCLI dismounted from their six-wheel Grizzly carriers and, with a squadron of Cougar armoured cars, cleared the way for the troop of tanks edging carefully down the deserted streets behind them.

At 1500 hours K Company and eight tanks crossed to Ile Perrot as Engineers searched for demolitions. One platoon with TOW missiles began digging in on Montreal Island. The colonel send the success signal, BINGO ONE. To the north at Vaudreuil two more companies, supported by sixteen tanks and preceded by Lynx armoured reconnaissance vehicles, crossed the longer bridge onto Montreal Island and sent BINGO TWO. General Thomas radioed Sloerill to prepare his breakout.

Brigade commanders conferred with Ottawa. There was no resistance. Bridges were not set for demolition. Quebecers were friendly. The main ALQ positions were still ten miles away.

3 PPCLI with tanks and TOW anti-tank guns were across the river or securing the bridges. 2 RCR halted outside Vaudreuil. They had advanced forty miles since dawn, but most reconnaissance vehicles had travelled three times as far. It was nearly dark when General Thomas decided to delay 2 Brigade's crossing until next day. The brigadier only grumbled.

As the fighting men took up an all-round defence, the long administrative tail began to replenish the force with with gas, diesel fuel and oil. Some units used civilian outlets. Every Petro-Canada station carried the sign "Welcome Canadian Army! Fill up on the house!" By 1700 the job was done.

At 1720 the ALQ attacked. First they hit the Patricias on the Montreal side of the bridges; then they began a series of attacks against the widely separated brigades. The brigadiers assessed the reports and began to adjust their defences and send reinforcements where they were needed. Soldiers moved into their carriers and tanks. Junior officers checked maps and issued orders. Tank engines coughed into life and, screened by infantry, crept through the dusk to new defensive positions.

By 1800 on a cloudy November night the countryside around both brigades was littered with dead trucks, APC's and tanks, their engines fouling one after another as the doctored fuel took effect. While the soldiers were assimilating the fact that over half a billion dollars' worth of equipment no longer worked, the ALQ attacked in force.

The RCR company at Brownsburg did not have to cope with doctored fuel. It was ambushed. The convoy's first and last vehicles were hit with rockets; then the ALQ began picking off the trapped men. One tank and three APC's escaped. As the ambush was sprung, the tank commander swung left and smashed through a white frame house, crushing the ambushers inside. A platoon commander and two sections of infantry followed, leaving a fourth APC blazing on the street. The twenty-five men fled north into the hills and eventually emerged eight days later near their starting point at Hull.

In every "liberated" town and hamlet, the ALQ came out of the sympathizers' cellars where they had waited for a week. They closed roads, blew bridges and culverts and took as prisoners the small groups of soldiers who had been left behind to control traffic.

A stream of disaster reports poured into Brigade HQ and trickled to Ottawa over the faulty teletypes. Spans of the Dorion and Vaudreuil bridges had been blown by the plastic explosives the Engineers had not found in their hasty inspection. All tanks were lost. Eighty percent of the APC's no longer ran. Only a few hundred trucks were operational, all in the administrative tail of 1 Brigade.

Unit CO's somehow managed to retain control. In section and platoon and company-sized groups, men struggled back from forward positions and came together. Near the Dorion bridge a platoon commander (until October a chemical engineering student at U of T and part-time militia officer) kicked a wheel of his immobile Grizzly, tucked a fuel sample into his pack for analysis, and led his heavily loaded men back along the road to join his company. The tanks and infantry across the bridges were lost, but the remaining men were well armed and disciplined. Once they had drawn together they began to inflict heavy casualties on the ALQ. Gunners manned their immobilized M-109 self-propelled howitzers, firing at targets their FOO's identified until they became the front line. Then they blew up their guns and retreated. Tankers, engineers and drivers fought as infantry or carried the sparse stores of ammunition, radio batteries, rockets and grenades that had been saved from the debacle. The remnants of 3 PPCLI (HQ, one and a half infantry companies and most of support company) fought on foot through Dorion to the 2 RCR position at Vaudreuil, and together they retreated towards the Ontario border.

They quickly learned to stay off the roads. Every junction and bridge had been registered by ALQ artillery and mortars which lashed out with savage gunfire whenever a target was found. ALQ machine guns stuttered from barns and woodlots, and the flares their mortars threw up kept the retreating targets brightly lit.

The Ontario border was twenty miles behind 1 CMBG. As soon as the defeat was known the militia brigade poised to attack Valleyfield the next day drove east towards Dorion and north to Hudson in a rescue attempt. The move was not professional. Platoons and companies got lost in the darkness; but they followed the order, "Go east till you find somebody to rescue or fight." They often had to do both, but as the militia began to engage them in force the ALQ started to withdraw. Despite the help, 1 CMBG had lost a thousand trucks, fifty tanks, artillery, most of their APC's and nearly two thousand men, dead, wounded or captured.

Across the river it was worse. 2 Brigade did not have a convenient refuge defended by fresh troops behind them. The Hawkesbury bridge had been blown up at the first shots, and the river had not frozen enough for men to cross even one at a time.

The Brigade HQ at Carillon came under attack almost at once. The brigadier defended it with cooks, signallers, drivers, clerks and staff officers until two companies of infantry fought their way back to establish a real defence line. All night men struggled into the expanding position. Fifty Gunners arrived towing four light howitzers with ropes. Men staggered in weighed down by 50 calibre machine guns, mortars and ammunition. With his position more or less secure, the brigadier set his engineers to building a bridge across the Ottawa River in what remained of the darkness. When light came, ALQ machine guns swept the hydro dam clear while their artillery hit parties working in armpit-deep freezing water. The brigadier called for air support. There was none. At dawn, four ALQ F-18's had streaked across Ottawa to hit the airfield. They left nine Canadian jets burning. One that had already taken off was shot down, though not before it had destroyed one attacker and damaged another. Fortunately, the two last ALQ planes were refueling after the raid when the Canadian Airborne, diverted from their attack on Mirabel, parachuted into Carillon.

Unaware of the unfolding disaster, Sloerill gave provisional orders for the breakout and went to see Etienne Messier, leaving his commanders to plan in peace. His move was contingent upon the arrival of the rest of the Royals who were supposed to be in the air between Kingston and Cowansville. He couldn't move until they landed.

The Civil Affairs Council had adjourned when he arrived. It was a mini-parliament with a cabinet, back-benchers and an opposition. Etienne was prime minister. George realized how much he owed to his friend. Messier got everything done quietly, never issued orders and always sensed friction in time to avoid it.

Messier chatted briefly with several mayors and councillors, taking longest with those whose ideas had not been accepted. Then the CAC members were escorted back to their towns by soldiers of the Tor Scots, led by their new FMR friends.

The language barrier barely existed. The FMR understood more English than they spoke, and the shared battering had bonded the men of the two regiments. Many conversations began "how do you say—".

In the council chamber George sat at the head table beside Etienne. "Well?" they both said together, then laughed. They'd always done that.

Messier shook his head. "You were safe in Magog—why go to Bromont?"

"I thought the only risk was in flying Air Bryce," George said. "At least you have everything running like a Swiss clock."

"Yes, a cuckoo clock. First the good news. With heating oil scarce, electricity cuts and danger on the road, people go to bed early. There will be a baby boom. Also, the American food we receive is not taxed and so it is cheap."

"And the bad news?"

"Refugees. Most Montréalais pass through on the way to somewhere peaceful. But some stay, and our population has tripled. Unemployment is thirty percent. It would be higher but for the hundreds of young men and women who join up. Nobody is actually starving, but morale is terrible. That is where you can help."

"How?" George asked suspiciously.

"When I visit your camps I see soldiers driving trucks and stacking boxes instead of carrying rifles. I want you to hire civilians for that. Hire typists and filing clerks too. You need filing clerks, George. I have never seen so much paper."

Sloerill shook his head slowly. "You're asking the impossible, Etienne. Get the factories that are shut down to open again. That's work."

"Non, mon ami. Raw material used to come from Montreal and go back as finished goods. Now Montreal is lost to us. Won't Ottawa authorize you to hire civilians?"

"Easily," George grunted. "They're begging me to."

"Then what is the problem?"

"Security. Civilians in clerical jobs will learn military plans. There may be leaks to the ALQ. Admit it, there are still people around who want Bouget to win."

"And you say they will spy on you?"

"Yes. Take Friday. The ALQ have shelled the airport before with a few guns. On Friday they had a battery. They knew the Scottish were coming and they knew when."

"It was hardly a secret, George—certainly the date was not."

"I know. We have to tighten up security. The thing is, the men have accepted the idea of protecting the civilian population—all of it. Since Friday, some have wondered how the ALQ knew so much. I blamed their own careless talk, so they'll be more careful. But if HQ was full of civilians, every time there was a foul-up we'd blame the civvies, and there goes trust. Sorry, Etienne. You'll have to find other make-work projects."

"I am trying for some of the war work that is making other Canadians rich. Plants to make uniforms, trucks, helicopters, ammunition and guns are being built everywhere but here. We are too close to danger to be an attractive expansion area. In any case, even if I am successful nothing can be done in time to help people in time for Christmas."

Sloerill thought for a moment. "Well, I need a truck repair facility. At the rate we use them up, it'll take fifty men to keep us rolling. Sam Thackery's in textiles. Why can't he make the white camouflage parkas and pants we need? Ummm . . . are there any mechanics around who know helicopter motors? They'd have work. Is that enough?"

"No. I must have more than bits and pieces. Think, George. Working people become federalists."

"Construction is labour-intensive. We're building an air strip at Abercorn, we need labour to build the base. The brains in Ottawa say the war will be over by spring. If we get a guerilla war instead, we'll need traffic control forts outside every town with parking, bomb inspection bays, machine gun posts, reinforced huts for the guards. Lots of them. How's that for jobs for the boys?"

"I think that will do it, George. I knew you would think of something. Will the expense be authorized?"

"I'll work on it. I have an idea for you too."

Messier smiled. "I thought they were all for me."

"This is more in your line. Hundreds of houses are being damaged in the fighting. In a war zone insurance doesn't apply. But why should a family lose its home simply for being at the wrong place at the wrong time? Request funds to pay for repairs. It will save us from repeating what we had to do last week."

"I am almost afraid to ask what that was."

"Two houses near Ste Brigide got shot up too badly to save. I had Toupée burn them. Fire insurance is still in force if the fire isn't war-related. The local agent accepted the claim without inquiring into the cause too deeply afterwards. I gave him an affidavit saying that no fighting had taken place on the day noted in the claim."

"Now you are an arsonist. How war changes us. I will ask, and your construction idea is good. I am told that Abercorn is the one prosperous place in the whole area."

"André Taschereau believes in local hiring. For a Montréalais he's adapting very well. He put a young man, I think the name's Kerner, in

charge of hiring civilians. Perhaps we can expand his job specs. Why don't
you talk to him?"

"I will. Now I suppose you have to run instead of coming for a late
supper with me?"

"I'd like to but I can't. The big attack is on and the rest of the Royal
Regiment is due about now. They'll have a lot to learn before . . . that reminds me. How's the school system running?"

"Badly at the moment, but a team from Massey–Vanier and some
McGill professors who live out here are re-inventing the one-room school-
house—linked by computers and visited by science teachers. If it becomes
a reality, you and I will be fighting for every loose computer in the region."

George laughed and reached for his parka. "Take them all. I'd like
to bring up the subject of your personal protection again, though."

"I still refuse. However, my chauffeur now carries a pistol, and he
tells me that with a few more lessons from Zuke, he will be able to use the
weapon for shooting, not throw—"

He broke off as a door banged hard enough to shake the building.
They heard boots pounding down the corridor; the council room door was
flung open. "Sir!" Zuke charged into the room. "The shit hit the fan at
Dorion. Colonel Anderson says they're gettin' their ass kicked and Cap'n
Ashworth wants you. The Royals ain't comin'—and the big cheese Pittman
called." He shouted the last few words at Sloerill's back, then shrugged at
Etienne. "Never changes. Always at the trot. G'night sir. If I don't get
down there he'll drive the fuckin' hummer himself."

CHAPTER FOURTEEN

Aftermath

Across the country Canadians were riveted to TV sets as war came into their homes live. This was not the high-tech Gulf War they had seen in 1991. Now they saw their sons and husbands fighting and dying in a brutal battle of men and machines. Every province and city and almost every county had sent their men and women into a war that they had been told would be over in a month.

A CBC TV crew with 2 Brigade sent hourly live reports, the most dramatic being the Airborne's drop into Carillon. Viewers were able to watch as sixty-two men were machine-gunned in the air. Canadians saw the desperate fighting in the small town. They watched groups of ten and twenty men fight their way into the defensive position, their dazed faces turning away when asked about other formations. They saw ALQ shells destroy houses and barricades. Very occasionally they could see ALQ tanks burning. Mostly they saw the few Canadian tanks and light armoured vehicles that had escaped refueling lying as burned-out hulks.

The brigadier held the area around Carillon for three days, hoping more men would get back to his protective circle. By night his surviving engineers built footbridges across the Ottawa River. By day ALQ artillery tore the bridges apart before more than a few non-fighting personnel and wounded could escape. The RCR battalion at Lachute, cut off and surrounded, held out for a day before having to surrender. Of the seventy-six men who escaped, forty-eight got back to Ontario a month later to report that they had been hidden and protected, mostly by French Canadians. By then nobody wanted to hear that.

After three days 2 Brigade (no longer mechanized) fought its way across the river. The last troops out were the Airborne, dashing over a fragile bridge of planks and doors, outlined to the men waiting on the Ontario side by the burning town and a string of blazing cottages along the river front as the water around them erupted with shellfire. The ALQ let them go, glad to be spared the necessity of making another expensive attack.

When the cost was totalled, 1 RCR had ceased to exist; 2 PPCLI was reduced to fifty percent effectiveness. The Airborne had lost a hundred and eighty-five men. Armour and artillery had suffered almost as heavily. The brigade left six hundred and twenty-two dead, four hundred and sixteen too badly wounded to be evacuated and almost two thousand prisoners. In all, more men were lost in the invasion of Quebec than at Dieppe.

The ALQ, shocked by their own casualties, still managed to keep fighting. Using commandeered helicopters, five hundred men flew north and in a surprise attack at dawn destroyed the scattered West Nova Scotia regiment guarding the James Bay dams. Next the Mohawks blocking the Mercier Bridge were hit. Fewer than a hundred escaped to the St Regis reservation in New York. In that battle the ALQ, remembering Quebec's humiliation by the Warriors in 1990, fought with ruthless intensity and took few prisoners.

As President Bouget trumpeted the victory to Quebec and to the world, the force designed to smash Sloerill's enclave in the Eastern Townships had to be diverted to the Gaspé when Canadian forces converted a feint into a real attack. Lines of communication through towns with large English populations were being cut, and vital bridges were being blown up.

In a week, despite the failure to crush Sloerill, Quebec had built a fighting reputation, maimed the Canadian army, regained control of its north and contained the English separatists on the North Shore. Bouget's emissaries redoubled their efforts to gain international recognition, claiming that their victories demonstrated the new state's power to defend its territory. Foreign governments began to listen.

*

Sloerill tried to help but found it difficult. The rest of the Royal Regiment that he'd expected had been diverted to Ottawa. On Tuesday night Pierre Coté led his Guardsmen across the Richelieu to open the Noyan bridge in a diversionary attack. As as the Guards streamed over it Sloerill was ordered to prepare his brigade for immediate evacuation to Ontario.

He replied that he was too engaged to evacuate. Six hours later an order came to send back the Tor Scots. Sloerill countered with an offer to threaten a breakout at several points (using the Scottish) to tie down any ALQ reserves. His nerve somewhat restored by the ALQ's failure to attack Ottawa, General Thomas agreed. Pressing his luck, Sloerill asked for reinforcements, in particular the recruits he had sent off weeks ago. To his amazement, over the next six days ten helicopters and over five hundred men arrived, some as formed platoons, most as individual soldiers. Few officers came with them. Dorion and Carillon had drained all surplus junior leadership from the system.

As men came in Sloerill expanded his territory. The Black Watch, having already ingested the two hundred and forty Royals that had arrived on Monday, took a hundred of the new men and with the Toronto Scottish pushed east to establish a new line east of Lake Memphremagog.

A hundred and sixty French-speaking men went to the FMR. St Pierre, short of officers, formed them into a fourth infantry company of four platoons of forty men and began raiding across the autoroute. The ALQ in Granby soon had to be reinforced from St Jean and Montreal.

Once the St Jean garrison was weakened, the Guards drove north from Noyan to the edge of the city to shell a factory that made the Swedish ADATS ground-to-air missile system. The ALQ had deployed it at Dorion, making Canadian pilots nervous about low-level air support until their ability to give any support had been wiped out in the dawn air raid on Ottawa.

After ten days of continual fighting both sides settled down to lick their wounds. Over-extended again, Sloerill pulled the Guards back to the Richelieu River but held his ground in the east. Terry Gascoigne's Toronto Scottish stretched north from the U.S. border to Lake Massawippi. The Black Watch held northwest from the lake to Foster, where the FMR responsibility began.

The Tor Scots–Black Watch position was the only real defensive line. The FMR stayed out of artillery range south of the autoroute in platoon-sized groups with only forward patrols to warn of an attack. The Guards did the same in the west. The tactic worked because the ALQ were too weak to attack, and home guard units effectively protected the towns. Sloerill's reserves were two infantry companies that he had put together from the reinforcements.

By November 20th, with the stalemate confirmed, George held a briefing. Clay Anderson had the part of it they all wanted to hear.

"The ALQ had a well prepared plan. The doctored gas trick was made more effective by the warm reception our forces received as they advanced. Analysis of the additive used shows that vehicles were not put out of commission permanently, and most of them are back in service on Quebec's side."

Clay looked up from his papers. "You'll be relieved to learn that General Sloerill does *not* intend to mount a raid to recover them." After the laugh died down he went on more seriously. "The ALQ now have tanks for two armoured regiments and enough recce vehicles for two more. About the only big things they didn't get were the self-propelled M-105 howitzers which were destroyed by their crews."

"What about casualties?" Peter Forbes asked. He was acting CO of the Guards.

"Not firm yet. People are still straggling in, but the total will be four thousand plus, mostly captured and wounded. ALQ losses were high too. In fact, it's clear that after Dorion, the north and stabilizing the Gaspé, they must remain on the defensive until their new recruits come on line. Their worst loss was in leadership. Their regulars took heavy casualties, and in fact they let the Carillon force escape for fear that another attack would wipe out their professional cadre.

"Unfortunately, Canada's in worse shape and close to panic. Some government functions are moving to Toronto—by train. With smoke still rising from burning aircraft at the airport, few civil servants want to fly. This is disrupting all government functions.

"Militarily, the militia brigades were relatively unscathed, but militia in regular formations got hammered. Their casualty rate was double the regulars', and of course the West Novies up north are out of it.

"At the moment, the regular infantry consists of two PPCLI battalions put together from the survivors, two weak RCR battalions and the

Airborne. To rebuild, all militia units will be mobilized. However, since the militia has no trained men left, regular units must be stripped to provide instructors and a command structure. If the ALQ recover before we do, and they may well, Canada's in deep trouble.

"Now," Anderson said, turning a page, "intelligence reports indicate that the ALQ will not attack us in force. In the first place, they aren't strong enough. Second, the main threat to them is still the Ontario and New Brunswick border areas. Third, experience has made them very cautious about taking you on. I believe they'll start a guerrilla campaign to make you guard the towns, then raid out of Granby, St Jean and Sherbrooke till your line cracks. In fact, they may have started. Today's Brigade INTSUM reports snipers operating at Noyan, Cowansville, Bromont and Magog. We expect more."

"Can you read their signals traffic?" Tony Manieri asked with professional interest.

"About half. They use cellphones a lot, but we can't be sure if they're using them to feed us disinformation or if they're unaware that we can listen in."

"All right." Sloerill stood up. "The guerilla war *is* on. The Noyan sniper nearly killed Dave Phillips today. He's out of danger, but he'll be hors de combat for a month. Peter, I want that man dead ASAP. I also want your paper on anti-terrorist drills. Pierre, Jan, get the snipers in Bromont and Magog. Clay's off for a few days to find people for an anti-terrorist squad. Before you go, what's the picture on the Quebec civilian front?"

"Not as bad as we'd hoped. They have rationing. They confiscated homes of non-domiciled people and instituted tough monetary controls. English has no status, and vigilante groups enforce the rules with an enthusiasm that will set off more emigration now that the fighting's stopped."

"Too bad, Armand," St Pierre called across the room. "I wonder which cabinet minister will claim your house?"

"Look out for your own," Chantilly retorted. "Adèle has mine."

George stood up. "Right then. Start thinking guerilla war. Our local separatists quieted down after St Grégoire. Dorion has them ready to start trouble again. Next week we'll start protecting towns and searching. We'll have to be both efficient and polite."

"The Cowansville sniper?" Ashworth reminded him.

"He's odd. Twice he's fired at trucks full of men and didn't hit anyone. Such inefficiency almost has to be deliberate. Don't take chances, but I can't get excited about him. Any questions?" Sloerill looked around the room. "OK, gang, back to work."

As the meeting broke up, George waved Terry Gascoigne over. "You're invited to dinner at Etienne's tonight. He likes to meet new officers. Since it seems you'll be here longer than planned, you should start plugging into the local culture."

The first week in December was mild enough to allow construction crews to pour cement bases for car inspection forts outside major towns. What had been a make-work project was now vital as the expected bombing campaign got under way.

Messier looked idly at the operations map in Sloerill's Farnham headquarters. Scattered across the map were coloured pins and flags that marked patrols, platoons, companies, battalions, tank troops and gun positions. He was shaking his head as the door opened.

"Hi, Etienne. Sorry I'm late. Been here long?"

"Long enough to realize that this," he waved at the map, "is beyond me. Would it violate military security to learn which of those pins represents my son?"

Robert was now a Rifleman in B Company, FMR. George pointed to a triangular flag near Bromont. "This one. St Pierre says he's doing very well and may be recommended for a commission. How's the council going? Are the delegates still fighting for turf?"

Messier shrugged. "It is less fractious. Employment is growing. People are becoming used to war, and Sam Thackery and I have reached an understanding about treatment for frogs and traitors." There was a rap at the door. "Ah. We are not alone."

Clay Anderson looked in and saluted. "Just reporting back, sir. If you're busy, the new Major Ashworth can entertain me with stories about the prestige of power."

"No, come in," Messier urged. "Were you successful in finding men to combat these bomb throwers?"

"Yes." Clay's eyes inspected the operations map. The pins, flags and symbols told him exactly what was happening. He frowned at the over-extended defence and turned. "I have sixty-three personnel: ex-Mounties, ex-soldiers, two ex-FBI, eighteen Special Forces people, Brits and Americans, a good mix." He pointed to the map. "I see we're still in stretched rubber band mode. I thought Ottawa had sent reinforcements?"

"We're not a rubber band, Clay, we're a swamp," Sloerill said. "Extra men are swallowed up on arrival. I've been asking for recce units. I need the mobility two squadrons of Cougars would give me. From the reception I get, you'd think I want them gold-plated."

"Two plants in Ontario are working round the clock seven days a week turning out armoured cars. Only a couple of dozen survived Dorion. It'll be a while before they can feed you any. What do we do until then?"

"Damned if I know," George said cheerfully. "I used to think generals knew it all. We don't. We just hang tough and, as they say at Kodak, see what develops."

Messier ignored that. "There is, of course, the nightly sound of explosions to keep one from being bored."

"It's bad?"

"Four or five a night so far," Sloerill admitted, "and growing. They even planted one on me the other day."

"What?" Messier's head snapped around. "You did not tell me that! When did it happen? Where did it happen?"

"I sent Zuke to bring in my Land Rover. There was a package in it."

"Zuke was killed? Dieu!" Messier said savagely. "I relied on him to keep you at least relatively safe."

"Relax." He turned to Anderson. "Zuke found a pound of plastique wired to the radio to detonate when I tuned to a French station. Bomb disposal was towing it when she blew. Zuke's humvee was too close and he broke his nose going into the ditch."

Anderson laughed but Messier didn't. "Soldiers may think this is funny. I do not. George, you *must* tell me such things. The Garde Civile can watch your house more closely. This is not to be permitted!" He put on his coat. "I am, as you know, an elitist. I do not share your ideas of taking more risks than your men, and I insist that we need you at the head of our army, if only to have a minimum of sanity in an insane situation."

"Take it easy, Etienne. Nobody was really hurt."

Messier turned at the door. "This time. But consider my position.

Andrée would leave me if an omission of mine resulted in your death, and Robert would probably shoot me with his new rifle. Will you arrange to let me out?"

Anderson called into the hall. "Duties!" No civilian was allowed to move unescorted through the new headquarters building. A corporal who was recovering from a light wound appeared at the door.

"Sir."

"Show M Messier out, please," Anderson said.

Sloerill sat down at his desk and leaned back. "OK, let's have the stuff you really want to tell me about this intelligence setup you've been busy creating."

Anderson pulled out a notebook. "We start with local police who know their citizens. Then we build a network of informants. That will take a while because informants mostly inform when it's safe.

"Information flows into my Intelligence Co-ord office for evaluation. Then we turn the anti-terrorist people loose where they can do the most good. I have specialist groups to help them."

"What specialist groups?" Sloerill asked suspiciously.

"First, CI, Creative Intelligence. Some call it Propaganda Analysis. They read Quebec papers, listen to radio and TV and collect rumours. Nothing spectacular, but they can often make a pretty good guess about long-term operational trends.

"Next DD, Disinformation/Deception. They feed the ALQ good stuff to prove their reliability, then the disinformation. We have to give them some real info, but not often, and when we do our people get cocked. Some can't accept that DD will protect an ALQ agent from arrest by other agencies because he's a conduit into their Intelligence. We hope for long-term gain from short-term pain."

"I can live with that if we evaluate the levels of pain from time to time. What else?"

"Once started, we need an Operations Section. These are the boys who snipe terrorists while they're planting bombs, recce suspected terrorist camps and mount special ops against ALQ infiltration. The final group are my own boys. The Technical Section."

"That sounds innocent enough to make me suspicious."

"Wrong, sir," Clay said firmly. "Your message is loud and clear.

No black operations. Tec Sec is in charge of placing, monitoring and servi-
cing the anti-intrusion hardware I've ordered."

"Such as what?"

"Seismographs, telespectroscopes, bomb sniffers, infra-red detectors, parabolic mikes, that sort of thing. We call 'em sneakies. When they're
deployed, people can't waltz into an area and plant bombs in the boss's car."

"OK. Keep me posted. Now, will you ask John to step this way?"

A moment later Major Ashworth laid a thin folder on the desk.

"What's this?"

"A paper from St Pierre. He likes his four-section platoons and
four-platoon companies and wants the idea to spread. More men controlled
by fewer officers, which given our shortage of same, is a bonus. He notes
in particular that in anti-terrorist ops a platoon can operate normally yet have
ten spare men to patrol or as a reserve. Makes sense."

"I know. If it works with the FMR and, say, the Guards, we'll make
it a standard organization . . .Yes, Clay?"

"The Sutton Civil Guard authorized a road repair at West Brome.
In December? Are we sure there aren't any mines being planted along with
the new pavement?"

"I'll handle it." Ashworth turned to leave.

When he'd gone, Clay came fully into the room to stand in front
of the desk.

"Something else?" George asked blandly, knowing from the Brigade Routine Orders in Clay's hand what was coming.

"Perhaps this is none of my business, sir, but this message will not
get you fighting men. When the Lord said to love your enemy, he didn't
have terrorists to deal with."

"No, he only had the Pharisees, the Roman Army, the Zealots and
crucifixion. Is this what's bothering you?" Sloerill closed his eyes and re-
cited from memory. " 'We are not enemies, but friends. We must not be
enemies. Though passion may have strained, it must not break the bonds of
affection forged by two hundred years of our shared history. The mystic
chords of memory stretching from every battlefield and patriot grave to
every living heart across this broad land, will again swell the chorus of
Union when touched, as they will surely be, by the better angels of our
nature.' "

"That's it, sir. You told me to be candid, and to be candid, that's a real crock of whatever you want to put in it."

"Do you know where I got those lines, Clay?"

"Yessir, you rewrote Lincoln. Pretty good too. But look how our civil war turned out. Not much talk of 'friends' when the casualty lists hit half a million. Not a hell of a lot of reconciliation afterwards either."

"Because you shot the man who could have made it work and the rednecks took over. I hope we can do it better."

"Rednecks on the other side shot President Cyr for going soft. Matter of fact, our intelligence people and yours agree that if the Canadian PM tries to end the war short of total victory, he might not live the week."

"People are still in shock after Dorion. When they realize what the final bill in lives will be, they'll ease up."

"Haven't you been following this Prentice guy out west? Before the war he had a small redneck BC faction that was anti everything non-white and non-English. He's made the war a crusade. The 'French' are responsible for everything from piles to constitutional constipation. He started small. Now he fills halls. He wants to crush Quebec, and every French-Canadian who survives will be put on a boat to somewhere. I know how you hate black ops, sir, but this man might be an exception."

"Are you volunteering?"

"Nossir. Got enough grits on m'plate right here. I'm just suggesting that, apart from not being one of the world's great morale rousers that makes the history books, your speech makes you another enemy, one that unlike the military gets more powerful every day. I know you need the locals and FMR, but if you aren't careful your friendly civilians will bury the last Canadian soldier with genuine regret and welcome the ALQ in because they won."

"Take another view, Clay. We had a rebellion in 1837. The Patriotes barricaded themselves in a church in St Eustache. We shelled it and killed a lot of them. Today, nobody remembers there were English and French on both sides, and for me this war started then. I do not intend to start another one by anything I do around here."

The men locked stares for a moment, then Anderson looked away. "OK, I'm just an adviser, but if we're all good friends, why do we need rules about saying 'frog'? A lot of Tor Scots have been fined for anti-French remarks, and they don't like it. They came here to fight an enemy. Their friends are in the FMR or back home."

After Clay left, Sloerill sat thinking, tapping the folder Ashworth had left until he realized that there was something bulky under the cover. He opened it and picked up a blue envelope, running his fingers over the bold pen strokes across the front.

Slowly he drew the letter out of the envelope, prolonging the pleasure of finding out what Betty had written this time. In her last letter she had bubbled with elation at having persuaded a friend of hers in the BBC to do a documentary on the war featuring one Brigadier-General Sloerill. In his reply he'd tried to tone down her enthusiasm, indicating that he didn't really need a film crew in his hair while fighting a war—what he really wanted was his hands in *her* hair.

A dark curly brown lock dropped to the desk by his elbow. He swept it up, inhaling its fragrance, and placed it on a pile of books where he could see it while he read. With the hair catching the light from the window behind him, he opened the letter.

"Dear all conquering-general," she began. "Don't be foolish. Dan won't bother you because he knows what I'll do to him if he does. If in spite of everything he does get in your way, give a hard tug at the enclosed in retaliation. Best I can do for now!

"Dan will also feed stories to the CBC to help put your ideas on fighting the war across to the Canadian public. From what we see, your methods could stand some good PR. A few people I've heard interviewed were frightening in their calls for vengeance against Quebec. At least you're all the rage in London, but you'll never know how sick I was until I found out you weren't involved in that Dorion fiasco. Of course, if you had been involved, it wouldn't have happened."

George stopped reading for a moment. This was Betty's third letter. They followed no form; they seemed illogical, flicking from subject to subject, yet with a pattern of concern and support that made a letter from her as good as a night's sleep. She constantly delighted him by her understanding of his problems, however guarded he was in expressing them, or by detecting his tension even though he was careful never to mention anything specific. Smiling, he returned to the letter, hearing her voice in his mind as he read.

The letter was signed as usual with a sketch, the letter B on its side making a logo of her initials. Each loop of the B had an eye and the whole converted to a giant frog on a lily pond being kissed by a butterfly. He read it a third time, then reluctantly set it aside and turned to St Pierre's staff paper on big battalions.

Five days later at 0812 hours a light plane landed at the improved Sweetsburg airport, and Sloerill's friend Fred Scott and the new Minister of National Defence came down the steps. The Honourable Richard Bartholomew had replaced Alfred Banner two days after the Dorion fiasco.

Before boarding the waiting helicopter the Minister spoke to the airport guards, four men from each unit. He said little, but what he said made the soldiers stand taller. Sloerill sensed that this man, unlike so many of his predecessors, had a visceral understanding of what a soldier's job entailed.

At the rough new Abercorn HQ, the Minister met the staff and again impressed Sloerill by listening more than he talked. After an hour Bartholomew, Scott and Sloerill went to a conference room and shut the door. The Minister came straight to the point.

"General, you have the only successful organization we've seen so far. If possible I want to clone it and issue it to my department. I'm not hung up on former policy. The PM hired me to help win the war and that's what I intend to do. You've had three days to prepare for this visit. Tell me how you win."

Sloerill talked for three hours. John Ashworth and André Taschereau had prepared the facts and figures he needed to demonstrate his methods and document the results. The Minister listened, made notes and occasionally interrupted with questions until he understood the point Sloerill was making; then they went on.

At the end, Sloerill began to list the men and equipment he needed. The Minister cut him off. "Give that to General Scott. If we have it and don't need it to keep the ALQ off Parliament Hill, it's yours." He looked at his watch. "Now it's time to feed me. I hear your men call their rations 'road kill'. I hope you ran over something tasty today."

After the meal a few off-duty officers collected at the far end of the mess. The Minister, relaxed after a filling lunch, leaned back and accepted a liberal shot of cognac in his coffee.

"Now, General. Bottom line time. You read the Dorion battle reports. Tell me how you'd have done better."

George shook his head. "I wouldn't have done better." Fred Scott looked amazed at this unexpected false modesty.

The Minister frowned. "I didn't expect you to say that. You'd have lost too? Why?"

"Because of my orders, sir."

"Fine, move up a couple of ranks. If you'd run the show, what different orders would you have given?"

"Probably the same ones, sir. And I'd have lost the same way."

"Don't play games with me!" the Minister snapped. "The careers of those who tried that at NDHQ are in the toilet. I can smell bullshit at half a mile. Forget military etiquette. How could we have avoided that mess? That's not a question, it's an order."

"First of all," Sloerill replied equally sharply, "I'd have told politicians to stop telling me how to run a war. That means I wouldn't have had to worry about rescuing the estates of rich government supporters around Hudson.

"Second, I'd have tossed the entire military structure overboard on day one and sent a workable fighting force into battle."

"I'm looking for military answers out of you. Unification is a political decision, general."

"You can't separate them. A political decision in Ottawa to reclaim specific areas dictated military planning. So did the political decision to have a bigger air force than army."

"Point taken. OK. How did the unified system lead to Dorion?"

"Centralization," George said calmly, not wanting to make an enemy out of this man. "Each brigade group is self-contained, all components integral. Each one has the same resources as the other. But in action, 1 Brigade barely used its Combat Engineers. 2 Brigade was desperate for them from the start."

"So the commander of 1 Brigade should have let his Engineers go?"

"The only person who could order that was in Ottawa with no feel for the battle. Since they were organic to the brigade, the brigadier owned them. In war you don't let anything you own get away except by a direct order—and perhaps not always then.

"It was an organizational, not a command failure. I know both brigadiers. They're good men applying bad rules. The Americans and Brits tried combat and brigade groups. They failed operationally and cost too much. We adopted them because they looked impressive enough to hide the faults—in peacetime. Unification does that well. The damage it did to the army stayed hidden, asses stayed covered—and a hell of a lot of men died."

"General Pittman said our brigade groups have more firepower than a conventional 1945 division," the Minister offered invitingly.

"And more than the whole Roman army. Everyone has new firepower. What we needed was a 1945 division of three infantry brigades of three battalions each with attached armour and artillery, but with 1990's weapons and a commander who could shift his assets around to where they were needed.

"The division's third brigade could have rescued the men at Carillon. There'd have been fewer tanks forward for the ALQ to salvage once the engines gummed up. Div Engineers would have built a bridge at Carillon instead of the poor bastards who had to build and fight too."

The Minister digested that for a moment, then turned to Fred Scott. "You're unusually quiet. Do you agree with the diagnosis?"

Scott cleared his throat carefully. "What George says is substantially correct. A division is more flexible. He might have mentioned en passant that we don't have third battalions for brigades, a third brigade for the division or a trained div HQ. You don't put those together in a week or even a month."

The Minister nodded thoughtfully. "Thank you, gentlemen. For your information, General Vinet, who has replaced General Thomas, told me substantially the same thing. Tomorrow, show me around, let me talk to your people and get my snout in the pen to see what it's like. Tonight I'll give your papers a once-over, and before I go back tomorrow afternoon I'll give you some guidelines so that you will have at least a rough idea of what you can expect from us."

When the Minister left George took a bottle from the bar and led Scott into the book-lined TV room. "How was I?" he asked, passing over a four-ounce shot of straight rye.

"Convincing," Fred admitted. "Bartholomew got rich the hard way. He works his ass off and expects you to do the same. He spent three days nosing around, and then went through NDHQ like a dose of salts. I hear Pittman only survived by going to the PM. Those two see eye to eye on important questions like personal survival.

"You made a good point saying we can't afford combat groups. I've been saying that for years. You also hit the mark when you waxed eloquent on the values of individual identity and the need to build regimental pride and spirit with special perks."

"You think so?" George looked pleased. "I thought I was going a bit far with that one. After all, he's a civilian."

"Yeah, but this one turned a big corporation around by building pride and putting divisions in direct competition with each other. He used productivity, sick-days, quality control, strike days, profit, innovation and a bunch of other stuff to measure success. Quarterly winners got rewarded, and in two years each division was lean, mean and beating the competition hollow. He understands the regimental idea better than most soldiers. Your offer of using this private army as a test was particularly sneaky. You'll end up with more freedom of action than any commander in Canada."

"Which you think is wrong, eh?" George was an expert in reading the shades of meaning in his friend's voice.

Fred took a long swallow of the rye. "Ugggh! Vile stuff, George. I must send some Scotch before my next visit. Look, old buddy. Let me tell you something. I think you've managed a cabinet-level policy change. People will sulk. You have enemies from back when you only wanted to de-unify the army. Now you have new ones, a surprising number of whom hate to be proved wrong. Today you threatened the power of our senior officers and what's worse, a clique of deputy ministers. Bad news, old buddy."

"So let them fire me."

"Not while you're winning—but lose one and you'll think British Columbia landed on your head." Scott finished his drink and stood up.

"We pros have careers, even if you don't. The brass in Disneyland North came up through the unified structure. They won't thank you for mining the foundations. Remember, the natural condition of Canada is peace, and unification works in that mode." Scott opened the door. "I'm off to the Minister with my considered advice. I will not screw you. In fact, I'm curious to see how far you get before you self-destruct." He raised a hand. "Keep your head up and your ass down."

The door closed with a scrape on the poorly fitted wooden frame. Then it rasped open again and a five-dollar bill folded like an aeroplane sailed in.

"I always pay my debts, old buddy," Scott said from the hall. "I depart with a final bulletin. In the reinforcements arriving tomorrow there's a new CO for the Guards—Lieutenant-Colonel Victor Bosch!" The door slammed hastily shut as George angrily threw a book at him.

In the morning Sloerill, Scott and the Minister toured the area by helicopter. At each stop Bartholomew showed his understanding of Sloerill's system. In stilted French he complimented the FMR for their loyalty and their civilized style of fighting. He praised the Tor Scots for their contribution to national unity. He called the Black Watch colonel "MacBerk" and promised funds for a bigger pipe band. At the Guards he stressed steadiness and duty. To Sloerill the tour was worth a hundred men in raised morale and confidence.

Next day before the plane took off Bartholomew promised that Sloerill's armoured cars would get priority. Then Scott drew Sloerill aside for a private word.

"George, be careful of Bosch. He's no super-soldier like this Kermit guy you're looking for. Bosch is a spy, and I had to collect more than one favour to keep him off your headquarters staff. You owe me for that, old buddy."

"OK, I owe you," Sloerill acknowledged, and Scott walked to the waiting plane.

Zuke slouched by the humvee, a piece of plaster across his swollen nose. He and the machine gunner in the turret watched the government plane begin to taxi down the strip.

"Lucky the sniper didn't try to dust off the high price help," Zuke offered. "Not that he'd 'a' hit'm."

"Has he started up again?" Sloerill asked sharply. Three snipers had been killed and another, operating near St Brigide, had been turned in by an informant. Only the curiously inaccurate Cowansville shooter was still active.

"Yesterday. Took a shot at a tank, fer Gawd's sake. I figger he's some retarded."

"Or smarter than all of us. He's been at it almost two weeks and hasn't hurt anybody. OK, gang. VIP's gone. War stayed. Holiday's over."

On a short drive to the Guards CP the next day, Sloerill picked up a surprising bit of information. Peter Forbes had not been made Bosch's senior major; instead he had been demoted to company commander. The whole regiment seemed to be walking on tiptoe.

The man who'd replaced Sam Armstrong as adjutant wore a unified green beret, not the Guards navy blue. His name tag read "Webster". He led the scowling general to a basement room of the house Bosch had appropriated. Sloerill left John Ashworth with Captain Webster and went in. Remembering Fred Scott's warning, he controlled his anger; but he intended to show Bosch who was in charge.

The moment he appeared, Bosch rose to his feet from a makeshift desk fashioned from a house door laid between two trestles. "General Sloerill," he exclaimed. "I was just leaving for your HQ to report in, but the helicopter I called for is late."

Sloerill shook Bosch's hand. It had been three years since their last meeting, but Bosch hadn't changed. The thinning blond hair was cropped close. His skin was still slightly sallow. At five ten he was two inches taller than Sloerill, but they had the same stocky build. One difference: in greens Bosch had been immaculate. In the shapeless combat uniform he looked like a becalmed ship with all sails set.

Waiting until Sloerill was seated, Bosch sat almost nervously erect on his chair. "I must congratulate you on the promotion, sir," he said, smiling. "Another Guardsman makes good, eh? I had intended to report in at once, but Colonel Anderson said you were with the Minister so I decided to settle in until you were free. I hope that was all right?"

"Don't worry, we tend to be a bit informal here," Sloerill said mildly and saw Bosch relax a little. "You're invited to dinner at the Brigade Mess tonight to meet my staff and get a feel for what we're doing and how we're doing it. Say 1900. By the way," he asked casually, "when did this house become your HQ?"

"That Major Forbes had his command APC in the yard. The house was vacant, the family's in Ontario, so why be uncomfortable, right?"

"Wrong," Sloerill said evenly. "For your information, all houses

are off limits to all military personnel at all times unless the house is specifically assigned to you by the civil authority which rents from owners and
allocates to refugees."

"Right, sir. At the first sign that the place is needed, we'll be gone."

"You'll be gone in an hour, colonel. *All* houses *all* the time are off
limits."

Bosch flushed at the rebuke but his smile never faltered. "Right,
sir. Sorry I misunderstood. Anything else, sir?"

"Several. Your adjutant is wearing improper head dress—so are
you." Sloerill pointed to the green beret on the desk. "Next, name tags are
not worn here ever. *Anyone* caught wearing one twenty-four hours after his
arrival is charged. Also, your helicopter isn't late, it was cancelled. We call
them wokkas, incidentally. The word 'helicopter' marks you as a new boy.
They're only used as transport on my authority—which I seldom give. I'll
hold my other points until you've read Brigade Standing Orders.

"Finally, a question. Why isn't Peter Forbes your senior major?
He'd provide continuity, he knows the men and the territory, and he has
more experience than most."

"Well, you see sir, I didn't know that, so I brought a regular force
deputy commander and an adjutant from Ottawa." Bosch paused carefully,
then went on smoothly. "As a matter of fact, I wasn't impressed by Major
Forbes. I don't know him well of course, but he seems a bit . . . slack? Yes.
That's the word. He was acting CO but he actually heard Major Coté call
him by his first name and didn't take action. I see I'll have quite a job here.
I've started by switching officers around. They were in a rut, running their
companies to suit themselves."

Resolutely, Sloerill closed his mind to the effects of Bosch's command. A CO had full authority over his unit unless operations were affected.
With Bosch he'd have to see. One thing was evident: the style of leadership
in the Guards had changed.

He stood up, effectively ending a flow of thinly veiled complaints
about various officers. "Victor, be happy with them because you're stuck
with them. Good officers are in short supply. You can't post one out without my permission and you won't get it. People say we're a 'make-do' army,
and we are. Forget training pamphlets, we're writing new ones. Forget
unified organization, we don't use it. Forget unified rank badges. What

your Guardsmen wear is officially approved. All new people will con-
form." Sloerill smiled bleakly. "Don't think I'm picking on you. All new
boys spend their first few days forgetting so they can start to learn. You have
days to forget, not weeks. People catch on fast or they're gone."

He turned to leave. "See you at 1900, and don't forget to rehang
that door."

In the outer room Sloerill patted John Ashworth on the back when
he saw that the new adjutant no longer wore a name tag. They stepped out
of the house into a snow squall. As they climbed into the humvee, they heard
Bosch's voice.

"Adj! Grab a couple of junior officers and make them useful. We
have to move out of here."

Sloerill's teeth gritted as the humvee started. Beside him, John
chuckled. "Plus ça change, eh? Officers as go-fers, poor buggers. I may
pay attention to complaints by Guards ensigns now—or as he no doubt still
refers to them, second *loo*tenants."

On the day Sloerill visited Bosch, leaders of francophone groups
from communities across Canada were meeting to find a solution to the
growing anti-French sentiment that was manifesting itself in vandalism,
insults and fights. There had been two riots in which French Canadians had
been injured (and one killed). The conference was held in Windsor so that
the delegates could land unnoticed across the river in Detroit.

After two days of talk the fifty-two delegates had founded a new
association, Francophonie Canada. Maurice Lafontaine from Manitoba as
first president summed up the results of a long and often angry debate.

"The bill introduced in Ottawa this week to permit Quebec separation will not pass. English Canada will not allow it. The Prime Minister only
agreed to it to please his Quebec caucus. He is now close to forming a
coalition government. With that in place he will not need his Quebec MP's,
and the legislation will be withdrawn.

"I need not remind you of the pressure on our community or of the
fact that we owe no loyalty to a Quebec that has consistently opposed our
every attempt to win protection for our language and culture. Quebec has
claimed that Quebec and Quebec alone is the defender of French in North
America. I understand this, but they cannot now expect our support.

"CoR[1] is demanding an end to bilingualism in New Brunswick. In Ontario the racists of APEC[2] are demanding an end to *all* bilingualism. In the West the Reform Party is looking moderate compared with the movement started by the bigot Prentice.

"The matter of our people joining the army was debated by all groups, and it was unanimously decided that not only must we volunteer massively but we must make our effort visible. One group designed a flag, a 'V' on a maple leaf, to fly at a home where a son or daughter is serving Canada. Pins will also be available.

"Some want new French-speaking regiments. I am glad we decided not to ask for them. If we join existing regiments, after the war thousands of English-Canadians will remember the French-Canadians who served with them in a tank or trench. Make no mistake: to survive we must be united among ourselves, and we must be united with Canada. It is my hope that part of Quebec will remain independent as a focus of anger for the rest of Canada. Without that, anger may focus on us."

He raised his hands in the air, palms out. "Go home and tell your friends: French Canada joins the war not against French Quebec, but against greedy Quebec, against rebel Quebec. Canada has been generous to us but unless we support Canada without reservation, Canada will destroy us. Tell your people. Make them believe you. Now, let us rise to sing 'O Canada'."

---

[1] Confederation of Regions, a New Brunswick political party
[2] Association for the Protection of English in Canada

CHAPTER FIFTEEN

The Frog

For the exhausted men on both sides Christmas was an unofficial time of peace. In the Gaspé a Canadian fighting patrol "lost" four cases of scotch by a road. Later that night an ALQ "reconnaissance in force" reported two dozen turkeys missing in action.

In the Eastern Townships the truce was formal. Through Etienne Messier, Sloerill arranged a ten-day vacation from war with the local ALQ commanders.

The Guards withdrew for a leisurely Christmas dinner. The FMR, Black Watch and Tor Scots were more interested in celebrating the New Year, and Jan Berkowitz kept asking about Operation OAT BAG (fifty pounds of haggis that Clay Anderson had promised to get).[1] On New Year's Day there was a formal "levee". Armoured cars escorted revellers to the edge of town where they were met by sleighs organized by Messier (no municipal roads had been plowed). A Christmas snowfall had turned the area into a series of Currier & Ives prints in which only the soldiers carrying guns were anachronisms.

Bosch took advantage of the lull to complete another Guards reorganization. Officers lost sleep as they tried to learn the names of their

---

[1] After the war, a CBC documentary cited the use of a jet to collect the haggis from Edinburgh as an example of "how military commanders abused their rank to obtain special perks."

new men, wrote endless reports, prepared inflexible patrol routines, reduced training (Bosch claimed the men were already trained) and looked
after kit (they'd lost their batmen on his second day). Despite the soft
routine and the holiday the battalion mood was almost surly.

After the end of the truce on January third, Sloerill's anxiety about
the Guards increased. All units were being ambushed, but the Guards were
being hit more often and were taking more casualties. The number of men
reporting on sick parade, the best morale barometer Sloerill knew, was
growing.

He had meddled in the unit once. RSM Grigson had come to Abercorn as Brigade Sergeant-Major, and he'd made Bosch promote Drill-Sergeant Coutts instead of bringing in a regular force man.

On the sixth of January, after breakfast, Sloerill left the unpainted
mess building and stood looking across the valley towards Abercorn. It
seemed only a few hundred yards away in the clear frosty air. To his right
a series of explosions shook the ground as the day's blasting began. An
underground headquarters was being built deep in the mountain.

"Morning, sir. I was just about to go chasing you." Andrew Bryce's
jeep skidded to a stop behind him. Bryce was now a major and in charge
of all helicopters.

"Morning, Andrew," Sloerill said, returning the casual salute.
"Your birds all awake?"

"Cocked, sir. Want a ride anywhere?"

"You know I hate those runaway horses of yours."

"Runaway, sir?" Bryce asked innocently, the natural straight man.

George, with a new letter from Betty in his pocket, was feeling
bubbly enough to ignore his nagging hangover headache. "They're un-
stable, Andrew."

Bryce grimaced. "Just once I want to see one of those coming and
fly out of range. By the way, sir, the sniper's working near Bromont today."

George thought for a moment. The man worked a Tuesday/
Thursday/Saturday schedule. This was Saturday. "Why shouldn't he?"

"Well, he took a crack at Colonel Bosch, who spent twenty minutes
in the ditch while his driver shot up the whole hillside."

Sloerill grinned. "He doesn't trust our tame sniper yet." The man,
known to the police by name and to the army as "Deadeye", had never hit

anyone. He was from a prominent separatist family and under pressure to take part in the war. Brigade orders were that he was not to be harmed, and to maintain his credibility, from time to time John Ashworth officially designated him as the one who had destroyed a vehicle or had wounded a soldier (just before he was about to go on a four-day pass, for example). The system was well known (and accepted) by everyone in the brigade.

"Trouble is, sir, he called in a gunship. Steve Canyon—ah, Lieutenant Symbalewski took the mission." The new man was notorious for his willingness to take on any task.

"If you're reporting a successful strike—" Sloerill began ominously.

"No way, sir!" Bryce held up his hands. "I like him. He's the only guy in Canada who's making a totally ineffective contribution to the war. He'd split by the time Symbalewski got there. I don't blame him. He hadn't been shot at in a month, than all of a sudden boom booms all over. Can I drop a message at his house saying all is forgiven?"

"Better not. Instead, make sure *no* missions are flown against him."

"Done sir. Symbalewski's grounded for a week. Well, back into the old wild blue whatnot. The moles are disturbing my sleep." Bryce waved a hand in the general area of his cap and shot off as the engineers detonated another series of charges.

"Say the word and I'll handle this for you, general." Clay Anderson and John Ashworth had been listening. "Nothing fatal. Say six months in hospital?"

"No thanks, Clay. Besides, Bosch isn't that bad."

"Wa'al, mebbe not, sir," Anderson drawled, "but if we wuz back in Tennessee, I wouldn't tell him whar the still was hid."

"You figger he's a revenooer?" George tried to match Clay's mountain twang.

The American shook his head. "Revenooer spy." The word "spy" came out as two syllables. "But if he's a Canadian problem, I'll pass."

"Ah, but is he classified as a federal or a provincial problem, eh?" Ashworth asked, poking Clay's ribs. "Laugh, dammit. I just told *the* Canadian joke—but speaking of problems . . ." He pointed to a group of workmen coming towards them on the road.

Sloerill blinked. "What's wrong with the construction crew?"

"Not the crew, their boss, Herb Kerner. He wants a house away from his mother-in-law. He's after André and me every day."

"Isn't his wife pregnant?"

"More and more. April, I think. He wants that one." He pointed downhill and across the main road to a small, neatly painted wooden house with a detached garage. A line of smoke was rising straight up from the chimney.

"A refugee family has it. Herb wants to warn them of the dangers of living near a military base. I turned him off, but he may try voodoo."

The first meeting of the new coalition war cabinet took place on January eighth. The Prime Minister was in a good mood. His threat that a new government would prosecute the war against Quebec more harshly had kept most of his Quebec MP's from bolting, and with a coalition in place he no longer feared defeat. For the first time in months, the polls showed his government had an approval rating of over fifty percent.

To form the coalition he'd had to give the Leader of the Opposition the post of Deputy Prime Minister as well as six major cabinet portfolios. The NDP, officially anti-war, had agreed to take on Labour, so they were more or less on side. Life was rosy.

He still faced the difficult decision on how far to prosecute the war. They needed a strategy to combat Quebec's new drive for recognition. They had to prevent riots or other actions against French-Canadians. At least that zealot Prentice was some help. The government needed a war tax, and Prentice was claiming that Quebec must be beaten at all cost.

The polls were showing that Canadians believed him. In January, eighty percent of all Canadians put winning the war first, and forty-eight percent believed his government could do the job best. Even provincial premiers, normally guardians of their baronial fiefs, had ceded powers to Ottawa that they'd won in the 1960's. If the war lasted another year Ottawa would be at a level of power not seen since 1945—and after the war, there'd be no more "decentralized federalism" or similar power-draining schemes designed to emasculate the national government.

The key was to win quickly. Public opinion in Canada was demanding victory, and international opinion (after Quebec's successful defence of its territory) was swinging towards negotiation.

"Attention, please." The Prime Minister brought his war cabinet to order. "Later today we're posing for a photographer. This is, after all, an historic event. Every political party in Canada is in the front rank of our war to maintain our nation sea to sea. Sir John A. MacDonald would have been proud to sit among such distinguished colleagues.

"You have the agenda, and so, with a hearty and sincere expression of thanks in the name of all Canadians for joining us, I welcome the former opposition. I suggest we start with good news. I call on Jason McKay, Minister of Intergovernmental Affairs. His report also concerns Defence, but I want you all to hear this now."

McKay, an opposition MP and former virulent government critic, coughed. "My news will give you something to smile about." His barely noticeable Scots accent burred lightly at them. "Provincial premiers are delighted at the balanced way we awarded war jobs. Unemployment rates are dropping faster than predicted. Much of this is due to the jobs we've created. Part is due to army recruiting. I must also add that, contrary to popular belief, the enlistment rate for French Canadians in Ontario, New Brunswick and Manitoba is higher percentage-wise than for the English. I know Dick will speak to this later," he nodded at the new Minister of National Defence, "so I won't dwell on it. New Brunswick has dropped the demand for French-speaking regiments—Acadians want to join existing ones. I take this as a hopeful sign that the post-war period will not be as traumatic as you had feared. Will that do, Prime Minister?"

"Thank you, Jason." The Prime Minister took note of the way McKay took credit for the new jobs but laid fear of post-war trauma at the feet of the old cabinet.

"You'll find the stats in your folders, and I hope you'll carry the message to your constituents. Despite what Prentice says, French Canada is playing a full and honourable part in the reunification of the country. At the moment it's futile going head to head with him. He makes up statistics and fires them into any open microphone. What we have to do is peel away his support, then strike. Justice? Can we get him?"

Karen Ormsby nodded vigorously, the white lock at the front of her dark hair falling forward. "That son of a bitch has broken every slander and libel law in the book," she boomed. "But if we arrest him, we'll create a martyr. We have to discredit the bastard first."

"Work on it," the PM said. He'd brought the hawkish woman into his cabinet to pay a political debt, but she'd become an indispensable ally. From now on, though, he'd have to watch her carefully. His own popularity was lagging behind the party's, and she could be an attractive pole around which opposition to him could gather.

"Now, Richard, what have you found out about our military situation that the generals were afraid to tell us?"

Richard Bartholomew leaned forward, his hands flat on the table. After Dorion he'd been recruited from the business world to run the war and wouldn't have a Commons seat until after a by-election in June, but the lack of a political base was no handicap to him.

"Too much, Prime Minister," he said in his authoritative boardroom voice. "In a nutshell, we're back to square one. I've ordered every militia regiment to recruit up to full strength—to the sound of outraged screams from Pittman. At least my predecessor recruited five thousand men at the start to help the unemployment stats. Those men are now starting to fill the ranks of some very depleted regiments.

"I'm asking for a special grant to buy regimental caps and belts for the soldiers and equip regimental bands. Bands build morale and the members double as stretcher bearers or fight if they have to. I've authorized wearing the new khaki army uniform all year round. In a month, the only people you'll see in green will be fossils on their way out.

"What I'm fighting isn't the ALQ, it's Hellyer's idiot system. Cost-effective interchangeability of manpower prevents unit pride—and there's a concomitant lowering of professional standards because nobody stays in a job long enough to learn it. It works in peacetime, but I've closed factories that were marvels on paper and disasters at the shop level. I suggest that if a military isn't organized to fight, somebody should be hanged."

"Are you and Pittman getting along?" the PM interjected. "It's important to me."

"We are, now he realizes that when I say do something, he has to find more ways of doing it than reasons why 'the system' prevents it. We reached an understanding once I commented that he'd be retiring next year and prospective employers might ask me for a recommendation. I make no bones about it, Prime Minister, I'd prefer someone else, but as long as I don't catch his foot on my brake we'll get along."

"Glad to hear it. What about plans for a new offensive? International pressure to recognize Quebec is growing. A number of countries are sending weapons to them, and frankly, I'm not sure how long we can hold off the UN from recognizing Quebec's independence."

"I hope to be able to start some limited operations by next month. Supporting General Sloerill is my first priority. Retaking the hydro dams and helping the Cree is next. Then we have to defend the stretch of the north shore of the St Lawrence below Labrador. Fourth, we build a capability of invading Quebec effectively. To do this, I told General Vinet to form three infantry divisions: one for the Maritimes, one in Ontario and one for General Sloerill. A fourth may be needed. We'll see."

The FMR still had the Bromont front, but their forward area was defended only by a light screen of troops, supported by six new armoured cars. The main parts of the regiment were held in reserve for counterattack or to assist the civil guard in their battle against the multiplying number of sniping, bombing and guerrilla incidents.

St Pierre's headquarters was on Oak Hill southwest of Cowansville. He stood by his log-and-sandbag bunker as two humvees lurched along the rutted track and stopped.

"Quite a view," Sloerill called as he strode across the field. From the hill he could see most of the town and its surrounding grid of snow-covered fields. Armand Chantilly waved to St Pierre from the second humvee.

"Nearly as good as yours at Abercorn, sir," St Pierre replied. "How many of my guards on the road did you see coming in?"

"Two. One is two hundred metres from the main road on the left. It's a good position but his radio antenna shows. The second's two hundred and fifty metres along on the right. I saw his tracks."

"Ah, well," St Pierre sighed. "I will speak to them again. They're snipers. We have twenty-three now. Last night they shot a man attempting to plant a bomb and two more who drove through Dunham firing automatic weapons. Competition to join is keen. For one thing, snipers don't do drill or have to cut their hair short."

"Glad it's working. Is the big battalion still popular? General Pittman called to say it's almost authorized officially."

"C'est merveilleux!" St Pierre enthused. "At first we could barely cover the area we had. As we grew, so did the territory. My big battalion makes it possible for me to cover more ground more efficiently, and when we take casualties, it reduces our effectiveness less."

All Sloerill's infantry units were now "four-square": four companies of four platoons of four sections of ten men. A full company numbered one hundred seventy-one men commanded by six officers. A standard infantry company had one hundred fifteen men with five officers.

In the bunker George reviewed St Pierre's dispositions, made a few suggestions to improve them and in ten minutes was ready to leave.

"By the way, Toupée, isn't it time to send Robert for officer training? Etienne was asking last night."

St Pierre's face grew serious but he did not reply until they were outside, away from the clerks. "I must speak to you about that one. I know Etienne is your friend, but I cannot recommend the son."

"It's your call, Pierre. Mind telling me why?"

"He has become too . . . too fanatique—you understand?"

"No. I thought he was doing well."

"As a fantassin—an infantryman, I wish I had a hundred of him. He works like two men . . . but he is . . . I can only say it this way, he is anti-French. It is the bombs. He sees a terrorist in every civilian who gives him a sour look. Twice he was restrained from hitting people who thought soldiers were to be laughed at. Such an attitude in one private soldier is tolerable. But I will not give him power to command."

"When did it start?"

"After the bomb in your car. To him that was not an act of war but treachery. Every new bomb confirms his idea."

"Keep working on him. Remind him that the bombing can't last much longer. Between Clay's anti-terrorist squad arresting them and our men shooting them, there can't be many left."

"I hope not, but I will not send him for officer training."

"Your call. Is there anyone else you want to promote . . . anyone special?"

"No, no one special. Why do you ask?"

Sloerill shrugged. "Just checking. I'm going to visit the Guards next. I haven't been down that way in days."

St Pierre gravely watched Sloerill's two vehicles lurch across the broken field. George had looked tired. The news about Robert had added to his worries, and a visit with Bosch would not improve his day either. There were reports that the general was drinking too much—only rumours. He turned and went inside.

Fortunately Bosch wasn't at his HQ in Henryville when George arrived. He spoke instead to Carl Bates, the senior major. Bates blamed the extra ambushes on the local people; sick parade was up because of the cold; and his men were shooting more than other units because they had more terrorists to shoot at.

Instead of going back, George headed for Clarenceville and found, as he'd hoped, Peter Forbes lounging beside a jeep and smoking. Zuke stopped and Sloerill climbed out of the humvee.

"You look awful, George!" Peter greeted him cheerfully. "Or if you prefer—sir, you look bloody awful. Your face has more lines than an octopus fishing through the ice."

"They give me the look of weary ineffable wisdom essential to senior command," George replied. "How are things? As the absent bishop said, long time no see."

"First rate," Peter replied, wincing. "Colonel Bosch let me keep Wayne Jones's superbly trained platoon, and I love the extra men in the big companies. Could have used them in Ireland."

"On the subject of men, are there any Guardsmen doing an outstanding job? I'm asking company commanders because CO's don't seem to know what I'm talking about."

"Nor does this company commander. Who are you looking for?"

"Don't know. I keep hearing about an outstanding soldier, but when I ask who he is, he fades away. He's apparently a great leader, the ALQ are terrified of him, he works his ass off—I don't know. If half of it's true, he should be running the brigade, not me."

Forbes was fighting a grin. "Does the paragon have a name?"

"More a nickname. Kermit." He looked more closely at Forbes. "What's funny, you damned Brit? No you don't!" He hauled Peter away from the jeep. "I am a general and you are a major and this is an order. Who—is—Kermit?"

Peter leaned against the jeep choking with laughter. "Very well, sir. Actually he's everything you've heard and a bit more. Did you ever watch the Muppets on TV?" Confused, Sloerill nodded.

"Well, the Muppet MC was a green frog named Kermit, and frankly, old boy, unless you manage a bit more rest you'll be as green as the original Kermit was."

"Me?" Sloerill exclaimed, thunderstruck.

"The very same. The nickname was secret due to brigade order number one, 'the term frog is not to be used.' " Peter laughed again. "And when you look like that, brows beetled, jaw out, the resemblance to—shall we say a batrachian—is uncannily accurate."

George broke down. For weeks he'd been chasing his own tail. They stood on the street roaring with laughter, making passers-by wonder what could be so funny in the middle of a war zone.

"God! What an idiot I must have sounded," George gasped, tears running down his cheeks. "Telling everyone what a great soldier this Kermit was. How did Toupée keep a straight face?"

"He didn't have my problem. The FMR name for you is even better." Peter climbed into his jeep.

"What is it?" Sloerill asked, wiping his eyes with his sleeve.

"It's Ouaouaron,"[1] Peter said hastily. "Driver advance. Get thee gone from this madhouse." The jeep rolled forward and as George stepped back, Peter leaned out. "It means bullfrog!" he shouted. "I believe they hibernate from time to time!"

In the second humvee, Armand Chantilly sighed in relief. It had become almost impossible to keep the secret as George became more determined to find this nonpareil. Once they were rolling again, Armand picked up his radio handset. "Hello all stations, this is SHELLDRAKE. Kermit is on the prowl." That told everyone that the frog was out of the bag. From the humvee fifty yards ahead, he heard George's bellow. Armand smiled. It had been too long since they'd heard that raucous laugh.

Sloerill's last stop was Pinnacle Mountain. The humvees picked their way up a logging road, skirting boulders and windfall trees. They

---

[1] Pronounced wah-wah-ronh

entered a small valley and stopped, waiting for a guide. It wasn't safe to walk around the hidden camp unescorted.

In a few moments a figure emerged from a tangle of brush and rock that was in reality a machine-gun position. To his pleased surprise Sloerill recognized Captain Gail Buckley.

"Hi, general," she said cheerfully as she came up to the hummer. "Come to check on Kirby's Commandos?"

She hadn't saluted, but nobody in the special force being created here did. Describing it as a Long Range Patrol Group, Sloerill had put Desmond Kirby, an ex-British commando major in charge of what he hoped would become something like the British Special Air Service Regiment.

"Where is everybody?" Sloerill asked.

"On the mountain, sir. There's just me, four halt and two lame minding the store."

"Odd. From what I hear, you're usually leading the pack, not minding the store."

"Sir, I laid *out* the track, and even Desperate Des complained. I'm resting on my laurels." Her bright brown eyes sparkled with health and enjoyment. "You know, sir, when Colonel Bosch fired me I was even madder at him than I was at you for stealing my platoon. Now I'm glad. This stuff is lots more fun."

George left word that he wanted to see Kirby and climbed back into the humvee. Armand Chantilly had transferred from his vehicle to the back seat.

"That woman is truly remarkable," he said.

Sloerill nodded. When the commando was formed Captain Buckley had volunteered to escape the administrative job Bosch had put her in after taking away her recruits. Kirby had pressured Sloerill to accept the application. "Our job is long-range penetration, sir," he'd argued. "Gail's fully bilingual, and a chap and a girl on the street attract less attention than two men together." A month later he'd called to say, "If you have any more like her, send them along." There were now eight women in the unit.

"I might ask her to visit my Gunners," Chantilly mused. "Even *seeing* a woman with that much vitality would boost morale."

"Huh?" Sloerill shook his head. He'd gone half-asleep. "What about morale?"

Chantilly shook his head. "George, we worry about you. You command, organize, fight Ottawa, assist Etienne and create special commando units in your spare time. You are not Superman. You need to rest."

There was a sound from the driver's seat. "Did you speak, Corporal Zukrowski?" Sloerill snapped.

"On this road I wuz just sayin' my prayers and you heard the 'amen' part," Zuke said, turning dangerously in the seat.

"Keep your eyes front."

Armand didn't relent. "Even more than sleep, you need to relax, to let go. The pressure you are under demands an inhuman reining in of emotions that need to be released in small doses every day.

"We have not bothered you with this, but fights are growing among the men. They cannot take out fear and anger against the ALQ or our invisible terrorists. So they fight men in the next platoon or company. This affects all regiments. We have forbidden inter-regimental fights but we allow some local fights to work off tension."

"Your Gunners seem well adjusted," Sloerill shot back. "Are they immune or merely superior?"

"The latter is an interesting idea, but no. The Tor Scots are the least affected. Their poor French insulates them from some of the insults made by civilians, and because they are not québecois they do not have our emotional problems.

"My Gunners are next. We are not as involved as infantry. There is less danger but perhaps more frustration. Also, we kill by remote control and seldom see the results of our work. Finally, we have pillow fights."

"Pillow fights!" George roared. "My God! If the press got hold of that—Army Holds Pillow Fights as Terrorist Bombs Explode!"

"In the first place, they are not real pillows but bags with rope handles and stuffed with chunks of foam. Teams attack swinging as hard as possible. The winner is the team with the last unbroken bag. There are minor injuries of course, but it works off steam."

"Do you play, Armand?"

"Play? I am captain of the headquarters team, present holder of the Purple Privy."

"The *what*?"

"The Purple Privy. When I first suggested my idea, Major Dupras of 66 Battery said I was full of shit. When it worked out, he donated the prize, a purple toilet bowl."

Sloerill shook his head in wonder, a trace of a smile twitching at his lips. "I'm not sure if after this conversation I should visit troops more often or stop entirely. What about the other units? Do they participate in your pillow fights?"

"In different ways. Half of Jan's Highlanders are Ontario men from the Royals and they're in a strongly English area where terrorism never really got started. They feel somewhat ignored by their general, but I understand that enthusiastic Scottish country dancing relieves tension as well as pillow fights."

George nodded thoughtfully. Because Jan was so capable, he did tend to leave the the Black Watch alone too much. "The FMR?" he asked.

"One advantage, one liability. They fully endorse your limited war; on the other hand, as Quebecers they are called traitors who kill québecois. I doubt if any man alive could have held them together and united for Canada the way Toupée has done.

"The Guards were among the best," Chantilly went on, slowly. "Now they are the worst. Colonel Bosch does not approve of horseplay, especially among his officers, and in addition the men feel the conflict between their colonel and their general as Bosch tries to take away the regimental things you told them were so important."

When Sloerill didn't reply, Chantilly continued in a lighter tone. "You too, my friend, need relaxation, perhaps more than all of us. Why not come to Regimental Headquarters tonight and referee a match? My team is taking on 7 Battery. But I warn you, the referee must sit on the Purple Privy until the fight is over."

"When I told people, when was it, a hundred years ago? When I said we had to keep a sense of humour, I didn't . . ." George gave a short barking laugh. "What the hell, Armand, I'll make time for it somehow."

The pleasure of hearing Sloerill laugh quickly faded as Forbes drove to meet Wayne Jones. His platoon had the Noyan bridge and two other posts to watch, and it was time to relieve the guard. He had not lied when he told Sloerill that he liked commanding his present company, but he had no idea how long it would last. Bosch didn't like him, and he had a habit of shuffling officers around in accordance with a plan designed to break up teams of officers whom he thought might plot against him.

Wayne was located on a hill in a field east of Clarenceville. When Peter arrived a half-platoon was leaving to relieve the bridge guards. They rolled out onto Highway 202, but at the entrance to Clarenceville they were stopped by a civilian.

"Road's blocked," he shouted. "A huge bomb right in the middle of town."

"Are you evacuating people?" Peter asked.

"Yeah, but nobody knows how long it's been there."

"Come on, Wayne. You can't get around the bomb so we have to deal with it first. Radio the bridge guard to be patient."

The Guardsmen raced into the town centre and dismounted. As Wayne profanely divided twenty men into four-man teams to move people out of the blast area, Peter went to inspect the bomb. It was in a metal garbage can, and the crumpled papers placed on top for camouflage had blown away to reveal at least a hundred kilos of plastique.

"Any idea when it may go off?" Wayne asked as he came up.

"Not the foggiest, but they'll hear it in Ottawa when it does. Did you tell the colonel that a bomb disposal squad was required?"

"My request was acknowledged and he began a message that almost sounded like an order to clear out right away. The static was so bad I had to sign off. What's next?"

"Take that apart." Peter pointed to a sandbagged fort at the intersection that the civil guard used as their command centre. "We have to confine and direct the blast. Like mobs, explosions need a way to escape or they'll tear your head off."

"OK. Will you, me, our signallers and four Guardsmen be enough?"

"Have to be. Once the civvies are clear the others can pitch in, but I want as few people working in the immediate area as possible. Form a chain. I'll do the placing."

"It's my fucking platoon, sir. My job."

"Don't swear at your elders, Wayne. Move." Forbes stripped off his parka and combat jacket. It was a chilly day, but nobody was going to get cold slugging eighty-pound sandbags.

The men tore into the guard post, dragging down the carefully interlocked sandbags and passing them to Wayne who in turn handed them to Forbes. Peter stacked them around the container on three sides, three sandbags thick, leaving a gap pointing down the highway. Once the wall reached above the level of the plastique, he began to double the wall's thickness to six sandbags.

The tin roof of the guardpost came crashing down as the Guardsmen worked with desperate speed to beat the clock ticking inside the deadly pile. Two hundred people lived within a block of the bomb and less than half had been evacuated so far. Many were old and had to dress warmly or at least find warm clothes to carry. Once outside, the refugees had to be herded to the safety of a distant basement.

The circling wall grew to nine bags thick and five feet in height. Peter stepped back to look at it.

"I think . . ." he panted, "it's . . . high enough . . . but the . . . gap's . . . too wide. Have to narrow it down."

Wayne was gasping too. "Look . . . we're pooped. Some evacuation teams . . . are back now. Why not let them bring up more bags . . . so we can take a breather?"

Wordlessly Peter nodded. Wayne gave the necessary orders to Sergeant Luft, and the two officers sat down on the curb. Forbes pulled out his cigarette case. "Smoke?"

Wayne started to laugh. "Why not? This won't hurt my lungs as much as if that thing blows." He lit up, and both men lay flat on the pavement, almost in the gutter.

"Oh, my aching back!" Forbes groaned, arching his body upwards.

Wayne's reply was lost in the roar of the bomb as it exploded. Both men vanished under a mass of torn sandbags and loose sand, only their jerking feet still visible. The blast, channeled by the retaining wall, roared upwards and along the ruler-straight Highway 202. One sandbag that had been placed on top of the front corner was hurled aside. A guardsman in the carrying line looked up; it struck him full in the face, hurling his body twenty feet away.

Sergeant Luft picked himself up and looked around. He saw men moving but couldn't hear a sound. When he spotted two pairs of boots kicking weakly, he shouted at the dazed, shocked men around him but he

couldn't hear his own words. Five men of a relief team did hear and staggered forward to start digging out the two officers.

Peter and Wayne sat on the curb a few minutes later, spitting out
sand and bits of cigarette and recovering their senses. Sgt Luft helped
Forbes up and he looked around the square. A wood-frame store was
burning, its second storey having been ripped open by the blast. Two brick
buildings, now glassless and doorless, had withstood the blast relatively
well. In the distance he could hear the sing-song wail of ambulances, inter-
mingled with the more insistent honking of the bomb disposal vehicle.

Forbes's radio operator came up to them. He was shaking his head
and grinning. "Major, sir? Colonel Bosch says to report to him at once. Mr
Jones? You have to relieve the bridge guard now. You're late."

Peter took a step and groaned. "Oh, Lordy, what a day. First the
sides blow out, then the roof starts to fall in."

At the eastern end of the brigade area, nestled in the hills surrounding Ayers Cliff, Lake Massawippi was an important part of the Black Watch
defence. ALQ infiltrators often tried to slip across it at Baltimore Bay, so
they could vanish into the woods around the lake.

To prevent them, Colonel Berkowitz had assigned two Vickers
machine gun sections to the area, and Clay Anderson's men had installed an
electronic fence of anti-intrusion devices. On the top of the cliff, helicopter
landing pads had been cleared to allow troops to land minutes after their
presence was requested.

While Forbes was explaining about the bomb to a furious Colonel
Bosch, fifteen members of an ALQ patrol crossed the lake under cover of
a snow-squall, landing at the mouth of a small stream where it tumbled its
icy way down to the lake. A kilometre away, a technician watching his
screens and dials made a note and called the duty officer over.

"Looks like about a dozen, Captain. Up near that crick, say two
hundred metres north of sneaky niner-seven. If they were any farther, I'd
get a twitch from niner-six."

The duty officer picked up the direct line phone.

"Vickers!" a cheerful voice answered. "MacIntosh here. Is this call
for fun or do you actually have a target for me?"

"Target, Charlie. We're calling it two hundred north of point niner-seven. About a dozen men. They won't hang around long."

"Must have sneaked in with the snow," MacIntosh muttered as he checked his map and signalled his gunners to take position. "Hey! We're cocked on this one. We shot a target up there last week, BALTIMORE THREE. A hundred metres from that will be right on. Am I getting an ammo resupply tonight?"

He nodded at the reply. "OK, we'll do a major shoot." He hung up the phone and picked up another, his direct contact to the gun line.

"Sergeant Brown, BALTIMORE THREE, plus 100 metres. Four belts per gun. Two rapid, two normal rate."

The sergeant relayed the instructions to the gunners and they put the corrections on their dial sights. One by one the gun commanders raised their right hands. "On!"

"Guns ready and laid, sir," the Sergeant reported.

Charlie thought about the terrain. The guns were laid on the shore but the land rose steeply from there. At the range of 3150 metres, bullets from each burst of fire would land in a pattern fifteen by sixty-nine metres, approximately half of them in the water.

"Lay left two taps," he ordered.

Brown relayed the order and each gun commander banged the left-hand grips sharply twice with the heel of his hand, swinging the barrel exactly one degree left each time. The men checked their sights again. "On!"

"On, sir."

"Right and left, two taps, two belts, rapid fire!"

The four guns began hammering, sending bullets over the trees to plunge down without warning on the patrol that had just finished hiding its boat. Each gunner fired for three seconds, stopped, tapped right one degree, fired, tapped right, fired, tapped left, fired, tapped left, fired and tapped again, the gun barrels moving across two degrees of arc.

The ALQ patrol had no warning. They could not hear the guns nor tell where the fire was coming from. The pattern of bullets swept over the shoreline relentlessly, driving the invaders into the creek bed where their feet began to freeze in the icy water. By the time 8000 rounds had been fired, a section of Highlanders was descending the cliff. The four unwounded ALQ soldiers looked on them more as rescuers than captors.

At the gun position, the sergeant relayed congratulations from the company commander. The men drained a few cups of boiling water from the barrel jackets and went back to their shelter to make coffee and shave.

André Taschereau was sitting very erect in his chair. The general was upset again—the third time this week. This time the problems were money and promotions, and he was expected to do something.

"All the CO's say the same thing," Sloerill waved a sheaf of papers. "People get promoted, they can't handle extra responsibility, they screw up, and we're stuck with them. Why can't we promote someone to acting rank until we see how they do?"

"Acting ranks went out a long time ago, sir."

"Then bring them back. Right now, if a man's a good corporal I don't dare promote him. If I'm wrong, we lose a good corporal and get a lousy sergeant."

"I agree, sir," Taschereau said quietly, "but I don't know what more I can do about it. I've sent up three staff papers on the subject this month. They keep saying no."

"Can't they see it will save money? And, on the subject of money, Ottawa has to stop paying us by cheque. It's goddam ridiculous to have to give a man time off during a war to go to the bank."

"Ottawa mentioned theft problems with cash and the lack of pay-master staff to handle pay parades, sir."

"They never let up on control, do they?"

"I don't follow that, sir. Control?"

"Damn right. Control. Here's just one example: Guards privates are Guardsmen, artillerymen are Gunners, and the Armoured Corps have Troopers. On the other hand, cheques are made out to 'private' so-and-so, their official unified rank despite regimental use. This very simple ploy makes any officer or NCO who's foolish enough to use regimental titles look like a fossil. If I say 'Guardsman' and the pay cheque says 'Private' who do you think the poor slug is going to believe?"

"I don't know, sir, but I was told on a course that unification allows you to reduce all elements of a military force to quantifiable units for admin-istrative efficiency. Maybe this is part of it."

"This brigade is *not* a goddam quantifiable unit!" Sloerill exploded.

"Efficiency? Is it efficient to let men be killed because the wrong man is leading them? Why is the wrong man leading them? Because it's administratively convenient for him to be there—so he gets the 'combat service' entry on his record that he needs to be promoted . . ." He stopped.

"What is it, sir?" Taschereau asked nervously.

Sloerill was grinning like a shark. "Why, nothing. Get figures on what each promotion costs. Estimate the savings if two months of a new rank was acting/unpaid and what we'd have saved if we hadn't promoted people who should never have *been* promoted. Work up a cost analysis of time wasted in banking runs we make so men can get cash, number of ambushes on those bank runs, the cost of the paper-work when cheques get put into the wrong account—and anything else you can think of."

Taschereau shook his head. "I'll do it, sir, but the answer will be the same."

"Not this time," Sloerill said firmly. "Your paper will go to the Minister. He asked me to let him know what I needed. I think he really meant tanks and guns, but I need this too. The next thing NDHQ will hear of the matter will be in the form of an order to do it."

He saw André's worried look. "Don't worry. The paper will go in my name. You're reg force, but the militia have operated this way for a hundred years. Get it done one way or get it done another."

"I understand, sir, but we're starting to dig out foundations of the unified system now, not just changing the paint job like before."

"Right. People who said unification wouldn't function in a real war knew what they were talking about. Hellyer built a system where if you tear out one thing, it affects everything so as to stop anyone from changing some things back to the old way. It's like a balloon. It has to be whole or it goes poof! Once I prove some things *have* to change, *everything* will change because there's a hole in the fabric. Got the buggers!"

CHAPTER SIXTEEN

Explosions

One sure sign of spring in the military is the cascade of Personnel Evaluation Reports that begin flowing like sap from maples. A PER evaluates a man's performance for the past year and leads either upward to promotion or downward to early release. Each is made out by the man's immediate superior and checked by an officer above him, often with additional comments. The final PER becomes a permanent part of a man's record.

Sloerill had the latest batch on his desk. Once he had finished reading, he would carefully write the PER's for his commanders and HQ staff. As he was finding out, his battalion officers approached the task in highly individual ways.

Jan Berkowitz graded his Highlanders fairly but with a high degree of regimental bias. Sloerill smiled as he read that Captain MacIntosh, an officer he knew as having a keen mind trapped in an awkward body, was reliable and did his duties in an exemplary way but was incapable of learning the steps of a highland schottische.

Armand Chantilly graded his men by Gunner standards; a hint of praise meant a high overall grading. Despite minor grumbling Armand was content with his officers, but occasionally Sloerill added a few words to flesh out Chantilly's spare style.

Terry Gascoigne projected another image. As a regular officer, he knew that PER's were read years later by men who didn't know the writer's quirks, and he rated his Tor Scots meticulously in every category. Three officers were below the standard he'd set, but he noted that two of them had improved.

St Pierre's were a delight, full of obscure literary references, written in beautiful French, revealing the best mind in the Brigade and a man who knew and loved each of his men, even those who failed him by performing at less than their best on occasion.

Sloerill first frowned, then cursed when he came to the reports on the Guards officers. Bosch's PER on Peter Forbes seemed to be a commendation, but on closer reading George saw that it questioned his style of command, Forbes's loyalty and his military judgement.

He tore up the PER on Wayne Jones. Wayne was probably the best platoon commander in the army. His men loved him; their standard was "Would Mr Jones do this?" In return Jones swore at them, cursed their mistakes, occasionally used his fists to solve discipline problems; fought for them, stole beer and extra rations and showed them how to stay alive. The ALQ units that had met his men had been considerably chastened, captured or killed. Peter had graded him "outstanding". Bosch had reduced that assessment to the minimum acceptable grade, claiming that his foul language injured morale and that he risked men's lives needlessly. The PER suggested that he'd avoided dismissal only because the men were too afraid of his fists to complain.

Ashworth, Anderson and Zuke were drinking coffee in the outer office of the bunker when Sloerill's door smashed back against the wall.

"Going to the Guards!" he snarled as he strode into the twisting sandbag-lined hall. At the end of the maze, a sergeant stood in a concrete niche, his SMG aimed through a slot into the ten-foot square room beyond.

"Going out, sir? Let me kill the lights first."

The room on the other side of the steel door was a dazzling display of flashing lights. The walls, covered in hanging polished metal plates, shimmered and reflected the brilliance of the ceiling strobe lights in a coruscating show to blind and disorient an intruder within seconds.

In the office Zuke snatched up his beret and paused. "You figger I should talk to the old man, sir?" he asked. Ashworth nodded. "OK, I'll do it goin' down. He's always fangy after he leaves Colonel Bosch— comin', sir!" he yelled in reply to Sloerill's bellow.

Once past the main gate, Zuke looked back and cleared his throat. "Can I ask a question, sir?"

"What is it, Zuke?"

"Was you plannin' to transfer me back to the Grenadiers, sir?"

"God, no! What put that idea into your head?"

"Colonel Bosch said he wants me back to spy for him and he'd fix it with you."

"He did, did he?" Sloerill said grimly.

Zuke wanted a clear answer. "Is that right, sir?"

"No it isn't. You're stuck here unless you want to go back. Do you?"

"Nossir, but he seemed real sure, and if I don't, he might mention a couple of things he knows about me to the military police."

"I control the MP's, Zuke. Relax. All I want you to do is try to take corners before they're halfway behind us."

Ten minutes after they'd left Etienne Messier was passed through the dazzle room by the guards and escorted to Ashworth's office.

"Good evening, Etienne." John looked up from his papers. "You should have phoned. The general just went out."

"Such is the lot of the casual visitor." Messier shrugged. "Is his location a secret or would I be permitted to follow him?"

Ashworth grinned. "That might be a good idea, secret or not. He was steaming when he left. Do you know where the Guards are?"

"Regretfully, no. George tries to explain what the square flags and pointed flags and coloured flags mean, but it is too confusing. Can it be explained in simple terms in either official language?"

John reached for his new Herbert Johnson khaki forage cap, which had just arrived from London. "Explain? I'll show you. I want to talk to you about him anyway."

Zuke pulled up at the Guards' command post, a partially dug-in sandbagged prefab hut, and flicked his lights to warn the guards. The sentries' snapping to attention as Sloerill went by angered him still more. The function of sentries was protection, not ceremonial show like the summer guard on Parliament Hill.

Bosch's adjutant leapt to his feet, boots crashing together. "Good evening, sir. Colonel Bosch is occupied at the moment, but I'll tell him that—"

"I'll tell him," Sloerill gritted as he bulled past the young captain. He rapped once on the door and pushed inside.

Bosch was talking with a civilian, a man that Sloerill knew well. Both looked up as he entered, Bosch's annoyance smoothing over quickly to simulated welcome.

"Ah, a pleasure, general. I was just arranging to buy fresh beef for the men when we move to Bromont next week. May I present the area's largest beef grower—"

"I know Cliff Bailey. We went to school together for a while." The smoky eyes turned from the hard-faced farmer in the folding chair to Bosch. "I wasn't aware rations had to be supplemented."

There was a hint of defiance in the return stare although the voice stayed respectful. "I make it a practice when possible to obtain fresh rations for the men. Their opinion is quite clear. They call rations 'road kill'. An officer assessment pays for well hung aged beef that Mr Bailey provides at special military rates."

"I bet." Sloerill turned to Bailey who was nervously licking his lips. "Still buying every disease-ridden cow you find and flogging it as an A-1 steer at a 20% premium?"

"Just a moment, sir," Bosch protested. "I've seen his Herefords. They look in fine condition."

"They are, but if you buy three cows from him today he'll have just as many tomorrow. What you see grazing at Cliff's and what you get as beef are two different cows." His eyes flicked to Bailey again. "Get out, Cliff. If I ever catch you selling anything to the army again I'll have you arrested."

"You got me all wrong, George. You try to shut down a legitimate business and I'll sue you, that's for damn sure."

"Sue for what? Defamation of character? You'd have to go to small claims court. Get out. Now." Bailey scuttled away.

Bosch had recovered. "You must realize, general, that I didn't know the man's reputation or I never would have—"

"Shut up and listen very carefully. Everyone knows his reputation. All you had to do was ask any of your officers." Bosch started to speak. "I said, shut up. You gave him classified information on the move to Bromont. I've fired people for less than that."

Bosch went pale as he realized the magnitude of his mistake, but Sloerill had only started. "You're a pain in the ass, Bosch. I spend more time correcting your mistakes than anyone else's in the Brigade. Starting tomorrow you will restore officers' batmen. I want officers thinking, planning and leading their men, not working on kit and cooking."

He leaned over the desk, hands firmly planted on the edge. "As for your spy system, I find the idea of having men report on their officers is despicable and disgusting. It reflects on *your* inability to judge men. I intend to feature this weakness in your PER. Now get this. Keep your sticky fingers off Zuke or I'll chop them off at the elbow, and if you so much as *approach* him again, you'll get your PER in Ottawa because you'll be back there so fast you'll have windburn. Do you understand me?"

Sloerill took a deep breath, then continued more quietly but with no less anger. "Your PER will show an unsatisfactory rating. It will show you have no understanding of your officers' abilities. You call Pierre Coté barely competent. You damn Major Forbes with faint praise and reject his assessment of Wayne Jones—the man who gets more out of his men than any officer I know, the man who knocked out a tank in battle, the man who's first into danger and last out—and you call him incompetent to lead? If he isn't competent, nobody in this *brigade* is!"

Bosch stood up, his face sullen. "I will judge my officers as I find them, general. Their mistakes reflect on me. I don't want hard-working Guardsmen acting as servants to officers who can't take care of themselves. As far as my *information net* is concerned, my officers lie to cover their mistakes. True information is a basic management tool."

"You manage a store, Bosch, you *lead* a regiment and its men. When you do it well they respond by doing what has to be done—and a bit more. The Guards were doing that until you arrived."

"Perhaps, sir, but I hear you did most of the work. I have a bunch of losers, sir. About the only good thing that happened before I got back to *my* regiment was that that clumsy idiot Fox and that hot-shot Major Markos were out of the way so I didn't have to fire them."

Sloerill had a mental flash of Jim Fox dying slowly in the back of a truck full of Guards treasures: another of the short, intense Markos, leading his men fearlessly against the ALQ in Farnham and in a dozen smaller battles, only to die in a ditch less than a month later at St Grégoire.

Messier and John Ashworth had just entered the HQ when they heard a crash that shook the whole building. Ashworth looked in. Sloerill was smashing Bosch against the wall, holding him by the throat. His face was impassive, his eyes an expressionless flat black. John dashed in to pummel the general's powerful arms, but they were locked like steel bands, the short fingers buried in Bosch's throat.

"Excuse me." Messier pushed John aside. The military policemen's club he'd borrowed from the sergeant outside cracked sharply across Sloerill's shin. It took four more blows before Sloerill's arms lost some of their rigidity. Suddenly he shuddered and threw Bosch aside like a rag doll. Bosch crashed to the floor retching, his hands massaging his battered throat as he desperately gasped for air.

Without a word Sloerill strode from the room and through the outer office, ignoring the shocked staff. He stopped on the steps and looked around for Zuke. His humvee was gone.

In the office, Messier returned the club to the sergeant and tipped his homburg to the gaping adjutant. "I believe your colonel has need of medical attention," he said quietly. Taking Ashworth by the arm he steered him out, talking in an instructive, dispassionate way.

"I have not seen George so far gone in years. If it happens again, you must do as I did, strike his shins. Pain cuts through the fog of anger and brings him back to sanity."

As they reached the landing he released John and without stopping, took Sloerill's arm. "I took the liberty of sending Zuke home, George, in order to have the pleasure of your company. There is a small matter to discuss. I in fact followed you to pursue it." Messier rattled on as he guided Sloerill into the Bentley. Ashworth got in front and the car glided off.

Back at the base Messier broke off his chatter to direct the chauffeur to the half-finished mess building. Inside the one completed area, Ashworth poured two scotches and a double rye from the night table, and they sat in a cluster of chairs at one side of the deserted room.

Slowly animation returned to Sloerill's face. He shuddered again and put his drink down in one gulp. "Thanks, Etienne. I haven't done that in fifteen years. How did you happen to come by?"

Messier shrugged. "On a whim I decided to follow you to discuss a matter. I can't remember what it was now."

Sloerill shook his head. "Come on, Etienne. It must have been important, and it will help to talk business instead of . . . going over . . . that."

"If you insist, then. It's your commandos. The council thinks things are improving. There are fewer bombings. There has not been a kidnapping in weeks. We ask why such a . . . how shall I describe them . . ."

"Murderous outfit?" George prompted, the start of a weak smile on his mouth.

"That is your description. Do we need them?"

"They're for across the line, Etienne, not for here."

"Does that not invite a reply? I thought you only intended to maintain the corridor. If you intend to widen it, the council must prepare for new responsibilities."

"No, no, nothing like that." George yawned widely. "Dammit, my shins hurt, Etienne. The commandos are retaliation. With every attack here, the ALQ get one back, and unlike them, we only hit military targets—but we hit them hard."

"And so a counter-terror campaign escalates the war," Messier mused softly. "I had hoped it could be confined and resolved here, hard as that is to—" He broke off as Ashworth touched his arm and pointed. Brigadier-General Sloerill was asleep.

They got him to bed in the sleeping quarters. As they were putting on their coats, Messier turned to Ashworth almost fiercely.

"Why does he not get rid of this small man? He has sent many away because they were not good enough. How can Bosch defy him?"

"He has friends in high places. Can you—?"

"Ah non. I am not of the government's political persuasion. Armand Chantilly and Colonel St Pierre could help, I suggest." He smiled bleakly. "If Bosch were not afraid to move without an army of personal guards, he might meet with an accident." Messier gave a mock shudder. "Dieu! Even I become bloodthirsty—as far as my friends are concerned.

"Good night, John. Watch over him. He needs friends such as you and Clay. I will think about what you told me tonight. He needs . . . what does the army call it, leave? He must get away or the pressure will explode again, and not against such a deserving target. As for the Mme Marsh you have told me about, I do not know what can be done, but I will see. I will see. Bon soir." He walked quickly to the Bentley and was driven away.

The original ALQ headquarters in the barn was being abandoned. It was moving to the more civilized surroundings of Quebec City with its restaurants, theatre, civilized life—and government control. Under the barn, rotting sandbags leaked sand onto the floor, and wires dangled from holes in the ceiling where displays had been torn away.

The general kept his doubts about the move to himself. He would appreciate the comfort, but it brought him within the grasp of Quebec's second army, the horde of bureaucrats that were slowly attenuating his command with insidious suggestions that thus and so be done and in this or that administratively convenient way—to serve him more efficiently, of course.

"And so, Jacques," he said to his aide as they watched the desk he had used for over a year being carried out. "After all, it comes down to the fact that we surrender the corridor and withdraw. Too bad."

"Why 'too bad', general? Once you thought it was a good idea."

"In a way I still do, but then the land was ours to be exchanged for peace. I even admit that it is reasonable, but reason is becoming hard to find. Each death spreads unreason as ripples on the ocean can grow to destructive tidal waves in a hurricane—and there have been too many deaths that people can use against reason, Jacques."

"Use, monsieur? You mean the racist Prentice?"

"No, our people. Do you know that Colonel Bertrand committed suicide in prison? This man, the man who may have lost us the war, the man who attacked early, the man who cried racist commands into Canadian video cameras to be shown at the UN, he is to be made a hero of Quebec! Our government demands the return of his body, and our soldiers, the men Bertrand betrayed, must give the fool a military funeral. In February! I protested, but they no longer listen to me. An affair of state, they say. Bah!"

"Shall I prepare the order to evacuate the corridor, monsieur? We do not surrender it all at once, do we?"

"No, no, we retire as they advance, and Jacques—we go cleanly. No booby traps. No mined bridges. To paraphrase this Sloerill, after the war we must be able to live together, no matter what the result."

"I suggest he bears more responsibility for our problem than does Colonel Bertrand."

"Much more, Jacques, and for that reason as well as for our future good he must be eliminated. I take it that the forces we have in the corridor area cannot do the job?"

"There are barely twenty effectives remaining, general."

"Have Colonel Frappier report to me. He is about to become a general himself, but first I want him to do a job in that corridor."

"I am told that it is almost impossible to predict where Sloerill will be at any given moment. Many of our men have died trying to ambush him."

"Sloerill's career began with a raid. It will end with one. We still have resources. Sloerill can be held in his new headquarters for a few hours if necessary. Let Frappier know what I want, Jacques. He must give me a good plan."

It was one of the largest houses in Bedford, set in a wide lawn and partially hidden by large spruce trees and ornamental shrubs. Beside the paved drive, shrouded in shadow, a once purely decorative stone well housing now provided direct access to the basement via a tunnel.

In the furnace room a man was working carefully with wires, detonators and plastique, creating a new bomb to be planted by the members of his cell. He stiffened at the rap on the door, a coded series of taps and scratches. Pistol in hand, he opened the door.

"Bonjour, Guy," He looked past the man. "Where is Yvon?"

"He was arrested this morning."

"Merde. We move again. At least there isn't much. I am almost out of supplies."

"Is that the bomb?" Guy pointed at what seemed to be a leaky paper garbage bag.

"Ten kilos of plastique for the Torrington Ball Bearing plant. It will stop work there for weeks."

"If a patrol doesn't discover it."

"I want them to. The Guards are predictable. Their colonel insists. When they find the bomb at ten-thirty, the fake clock setting will make them think they have time to disarm it. When they lift it, a pressure-release switch sets it off in their hands and we get a factory and a patrol."

"They do not lift, they slide a bomb away on an aluminum sheet and then muffle it with sandbags."

"Behind Torrington the ground is rough, and I put in my last tremblor switch. If the bomb tips even a quarter of an inch—boum!"

"I need a lookout when I place it. You must come with me."

"Non. I must move. If I am caught, there will be no more bombs. Get someone else."

"There's no one. Gérard and Thérèse are being watched by the police. Look, if you help me I will help you move. I have an uncle who will hide you for at least a few weeks."

Housing to take care of the new workers needed for three shifts had been built around the Torrington plant in Bedford. The buildings, sited by military engineers, allowed surveillance over the back and sides of the plant.

At six PM two workers, long-haired and scruffy, came home to their apartment. As they came in two others departed, exchanging rude suggestions with the newcomers. While the shorter of the two heated a can of beans, the other went into the dark bedroom. A table covered by a blanket faced the window overlooking the plant. He went to a rack and picked up his rifle, an Accuracy International PM equipped with a Schmidt & Bender 6 x 42 sight. He sat down, opened the bipod, stood the weapon on the table and took aim at various objects along the back of the factory. Next he inserted the box magazine with twelve specially loaded 7.62mm rounds, fed a bullet into the chamber and extended the spike set into the butt so that the weapon was supported by a tripod.

In the other room his partner checked in by radio and stuck his head through the doorway. "The last patrol was at 1730. We can expect 'em every hour on the dot. Bosch's babies are more reliable than a Swiss watch."

The man with the rifle nodded. "Yeah, so we have a better chance for a target. Watch the beans, and Stan? Try to remember that when I smell burning, it's too fuckin' late to turn down the heat."

After the confrontation with Sloerill, Bosch had gone into hospital. The official explanation was flu with laryngitis to explain the fact that he couldn't talk. He could still write orders, but his sore throat reminded him to write fewer of them.

After three days of relative peace Peter Forbes decided that since the cat was away it was time to hold a party. He was still smarting from the rocket Bosch had given him after the Clarenceville bomb had killed a Guardsman and cracked two of Wayne Jones's ribs. Bombs were the job of civil protection. Bridge guards must be relieved on time.

Things began slowly. The officers were hesitant and little bit defensive. The newer ones weren't accustomed to the free-wheeling scope of a Guards party, and except for Pierre Coté the old hands had been cowed.

When Ashworth arrived with three helicopter pilots and a Black Watch captain it began to perk up. Wayne Jones limped in and the atmosphere became decidedly lively. Peter, a gleam in his eye, proposed a simple game to break the remaining ice.

On one of his unscheduled unit tours, Sloerill decided to visit the Guards' temporary mess in Bedford for a drink. From the front steps he heard the roar of voices and the crash of bodies. It sounded like a fight. As he wrenched open the outer door he found three junior officers trying to throw John Ashworth out of the room.

He jumped aside as one man judo-chopped John's braced right arm. Now that John's grip on the door frame was broken, the three of them pitched him head first into the foyer. "That's twice!" one of them yelled.

Ashworth sat up. "The hell it was. Clear track! I'm coming back in!" He looked up and saw George. "Just in time. A senior officer."

"I suppose you know what you're doing," Sloerill said, helping John up. "What's the game and what are the rules?"

"Peter calls it 'Boopsy Daisy'. Senior officers against subalterns. Aim: throw your opponent out of the mess. Since we're in short supply, majors must be thrown out twice. Wayne Jones is referee—look out!"

They jumped back as Forbes propelled a lieutenant through the door. An ensign tried to shove Peter out at the same time, but was deftly spun around and tripped. He missed a frantic grab for the door and ended in a heap on top of his friend.

"Hi, George. Come on in. Coté just went through the window for the second time, and we're getting a bit thin on the ground."

George dropped his combat jacket and rank badges, his fatigue melting away. He hadn't played games like this since his junior officer days. "Come on, John. Charge!" They burst into the mess together.

The junior officers, throwing aside caution, advanced in a phalanx with the war cry "Get the brig!" Sloerill went down under a dozen bodies.

An hour later the mess had calmed down, and the subalterns had learned a strategic lesson: never concentrate on one objective while leaving dangerous opponents like Peter Forbes and John Ashworth in the rear.

While waiting for the losing team to deliver the drinks, George, Peter and John sank onto a surviving sofa with grateful sighs. George dabbed at a cut lip: he ached all over and was supremely happy.

Lieutenant Gerry Bascombe (ex-Royal Westminister Regiment) who had arrived as reinforcement to the Guards and who had been posted to Peter's company, brought the drinks on a tray. As he went for more, he passed two helicopter pilots near the bar door.

"Hey, Gerry, we'll have a drink on that! Pistols in the mess?" one of them called.

Pierre Coté looked at the weapon Gerry was wearing. "Why not?" he asked. "This isn't the kind of place where a chap would get drunk and misuse his weapon. As you've seen, a Guards mess is a model of decorum. Officers wear side-arms if they choose because, being Guardsmen, they can be trusted—unlike denizens of junior service drinking holes."

"Hah!" an airman snorted. "I've seen more decorum in a mad-house—"

"And being an airman, you've seen lots of those!" someone called.

They were joined by the Black Watch Captain. "Ignorant young man. If you complain about this decorum, wait till you attend a party at my own esteemed regiment, the Royal Highlanders of Canada."

"Quite right," Coté agreed. "You infantry chaps throw wonderful parties."

"What do mean, 'you infantry'?" an airman demanded. "Guardsmen are infantry too. You certainly look grubby enough to be slugs."

Wayne Jones leaned forward. "Infantry? Horseshit. Never were. Never will be. We're simply Guards."

"Guards!" the airman snorted in disgust.

"No, no, no," the picquet officer scolded as he passed behind them. "If you Robins are going to drink with us, at least learn to pronounce the name right. You don't whine it through your nose. It's spelt G-u-a-r-d-s, but it's pronounced 'gods'."

"With a slightly longer 'o' sound . . . as in very g-o-o-o-d," Coté added with an airy wave of his hand.

Three airmen and the Highlander emptied their drinks over his head, and the brawl started again.

Five hundred metres from the mess, Guy placed the bomb against the rear wall of the Torrington plant. The workers on the night shift, ninety percent of them French-Canadians, were at work inside. Too bad, he thought, but they were traitors to work for les anglais. He laid the bomb gently in an angle of the wall and carefully eased out the trip lines that activated the buried trigger mechanisms.

In the bedroom overlooking the factory, the man with the rifle braced his elbows on the table and took aim. The figure of the bomber was divided by the illuminated cross-hairs into four sectors. As the target moved back, the sniper let out half the breath he'd been holding and squeezed the trigger. The bullet caught Guy at the base of the skull, cutting the nerves to his body. He pitched sideways into the dirty snow.

"Where's that patrol?" the sniper complained. "I got my man, but there'll be a lookout somewhere."

Company Sergeant-Major Green led his men forward at a stealthy half-run, alerted by the snipers' radio call when the bomber appeared. As he rounded the corner of the plant he crashed into the bomb-maker who had frozen at the unexpected shot. Without breaking stride, Green smashed his rifle butt into the man's jaw and kept going.

A few moments later he was kneeling by the bomb, his eyes on the dial of the ticking clock as he carefully pulled the surrounding garbage away from the explosive.

"What kinda bomb's that?" Lance-Corporal Sutherland, his new stripes obvious on his sleeve, peered over the older man's shoulder.

"The dangerous kind, Sutherland. She's due to blow in sixteen minutes. Get the plant evacuated."

Sutherland spoke to his eight Guardsmen, then turned back to Green. "Think we can move it, company sergeant-major?"

Green was gently carving bits of plastique from the bomb with the plastic knife that everyone carried for that purpose. With the clock wires exposed, he sliced more of the dull grey explosive from under the mechanism.

"Shit," he whispered. Something buried in the main charge had two wires leading from it. "Tremblor switch, I bet, and if what Colonel Anderson said on the bomb-disposal course is right, probably a pressure switch too. See any sandbags around?" Sutherland shook his head.

"OK, here's the drill. This baby will blow before the bomb squad can arrive. Evacuate the building. I'll slide the bomb away, then cut the red clock wire."

"You need a bomb shield, company sergeant-major."

"*Very* good, Sutherland. Did you forget your hip-pocket model like I did? I thought so . . . wait a bit. We *do* have a shield."

Sutherland's eyes widened in surprise at Green's orders but he nodded quickly and tip-toed away. Green unrolled the aluminum sheet that all patrols carried and carefully worked it under the bomb. He spent three minutes of the fourteen left in making a smooth path across the packed snow. Then he gently slid the package about two metres clear of the corner and into a slight depression that he hoped would hold it steady.

He sat up as Sutherland and another Guardsman returned with the unconscious bomb-maker between them. They put the man on his knees in front of Green and strapped the men's bodies together with rifle slings.

"How come we're aren't using him?" Sutherland nodded at the dead man's body as he tied the terrorist's ankles and pulled his legs between Green's.

"And get blood all over my uniform?" Green snapped. "That's my bomb blanket afterwards. This guy's alive and he can take the same chances I do. Now get outta here."

He reached for his pliers and Sutherland left hastily. A bare two millimetres of wire protruded from the plastique under the clock. He gently placed the open jaws of the cutters around the wire, ducked his head, contracted his body behind the frail human shield and after a steadying breath, gently squeezed. He felt the wire separate—and nothing happened. Sweat pouring down his face, he twisted the cut wires apart.

"Now for the tremblor." He reached for the plastic knife, and hesitated. "With the clock disconnected, this baby's safe until the experts get here." He stood up. With his human shield still in place, he awkwardly arranged the dead terrorist's body in a semi-fetal position between the bomb and the factory so that the main blast would be taken by the man's chest.

Explosions always took the path of least resistance and the body would offer some protection for the plant. He straightened and began to step carefully backwards. At the fourth step, the terrorist's left arm, balanced on top of the body, fell forward onto the package.

In the mess Bascombe and the picquet officer were using brooms to demonstrate the correct manner of carrying colours at a trooping when the explosion shook the building.

Glasses crashed down as officers raced for the door. Bascombe went out the shattered window. In the moonlight he saw a column of smoke rising in the east. "Bomb, Torrington!" he called back. "Tell Ops. I'm off."

A few minutes later those officers not concerned with the cleanup straggled back into the mess. Sloerill waved Pierre Coté over.

"Huge bloody thing," Coté mumbled. "Not many windows left in this part of town. It's unfair. I know war's hell, but I'd put together a poker game and my pigeons have flown."

At the factory Bascombe knelt beside the bloody body of Company Sergeant-Major Green. Part of the factory wall had caved in and there were a dozen wounded inside. He could hear the approaching sirens as he examined Green. The sergeant been thrown twenty feet by the explosion. His left arm was shattered from wrist to elbow and his left ear seemed to be missing. It was difficult to determine his other injuries because he was plastered with blood and charred pieces of the terrorist, whose body had absorbed the main force of the blast.

As an ambulance skidded to a stop and stretcher bearers came forward, Bascombe got out of their way. He turned to Sutherland.

"You're in charge. Check for damage and casualties, then finish the patrol. I'll want a full written report as soon as you get back." He clapped the shaken young man on the shoulder. "Tell your men they did a fine job of evacuating the plant. Now keep your eyes open. There could be more of these things around. The night's still young."

"The Hermit" was the last survivor of the ALQ brigade that had begun operating so confidently in the western Townships at the start of the war. One after another his friends had died, been taken prisoner or had fallen sick. Other men had filled their places, but they were city men. They didn't know the local sympathizers, the safe roads, the good escape routes through the hills, the hidey-holes. The new men called him l'Ermite, the Hermit. He found food for them, scouted routes, arranged safe houses for the sick— always alone.

Three days ago he had been in an ambush position in the hills when a plane dropped supplies to the men hunting him. The lazy Canadians had missed one container hung up in a tree. It had provided him with 5000 rounds of the rifle ammunition he was running short of. Now he was hoping to ambush a patrol. His base, with four sick men inside and two guards, was in a cave about a half a kilometre to his right. If a patrol came by, he'd kill one or two and let the others chase him a while. War had curbed his youthful impatience. In the early days he had actively hunted his enemy; today he lay unmoving on a rocky ledge, concealed by a screen of brush, with a clear view of five hundred metres of track any patrol would have to come along. A pale rock, a broken branch and a clump of light grass marked the various ranges he could use. After the ambush, he would have a choice of three hidden escape routes from the cliff.

Sergeant Hruska of the Toronto Scottish led a patrol along a twisting mountain trail. The sergeant, a miner from North Bay, ruled his platoon firmly. His idea of diplomacy was to give a man a half-second warning before punching him, but he treated them all alike. Intelligence claimed that a dozen ALQ were hidden in these hills, and weeks of patrolling hadn't found them. He intended to. The patrol was small enough to attract an ambush, and back at base two platoons of men were sitting in idling helicopters on radio call. His job was to stir things up for them to stamp flat.

The patrol moved down into a narrow valley, ten metres separating each man from the next. Half the men were Indians, but since they were miners like himself they were no help in tracking. Once he'd asked the platoon signaller about a mark on the path. Johnny Pinetree had squatted, stared at it for a minute, and shrugged. "Dunno, sarge. Looks like a broken twig to me. That the way you figure it?"

As the patrol entered a straight stretch, Hruska reported in. "Hello Three. Now at last position plus figures two, zero, zero, zero metres, northwest. No Delta Tangos. Over."

There was no reply and Johnny Pinetree took the radio handset back. "Must be metal in the ground like at home," he said. "Damn radios don't work as far's a man can yell." Hruska waved at the point man, indicating he was to bear left at the bottom. According to his map, there were steep hills that way that looked like an ideal place for a cave.

The Hermit had watched Hruska use the radio. "Good, an officer," he muttered. Range, 460 metres. He sighted carefully, the rifle resting between two sandbags. The tall foresight seemed to support the head of his target. He dropped his aim to the center of the man's chest then checked the position of his next target, the radio operator, to make sure he could get his second shot off quickly. He let out half a breath and squeezed the trigger.

The patrol heard a muffled explosion and dived for cover. Before the echo died, the patrol had vanished. Sergeant Hruska lifted his head and scanned the cliff face from left to right in his glasses.

"Target. Two o'clock. Cliff, halfway up, Range four hundred." He'd seen a movement in the brush screen along a ledge. He held up his right hand, aligning the forefinger with a clearly visible rocky outcropping at the left side of ledge. "Reference! Sharp rock! Left of ledge! Three fingers right! Covering fire!"

Five men opened up with their rifles as Hruska and six others dashed from rock to rock and tree to tree to close with the sniper.

The Hermit lay flat as bullets snapped over him, cutting small branches from his cover. He could not see because blood was flowing into his eyes. He fumbled for his rifle. The exploded breech was a jagged flower of torn metal that cut his fingers. The ammunition he'd "found" must have been loaded with an overcharge.

Dimly he heard voices calling for his surrender. It was over. He reached for a handkerchief and holding it above his head, began to get up.

The men in the fire section spotted him first, a lean, slight figure rising out of the low bushes near the top of the cliff, waving a rag. "I can pop him real easy," a private said looking through his rifle scope. "He's got a head wound. Prolly die on us anyway."

His corporal pushed the rifle up. "Cool it, Janke. The guy's surrendering."

"Jeeze, Corp. After that shit-kicking we got at Bromont, you said we'd shoot every fuckin'—"

"Bromont was a long time ago, Janke. Shut up." He saw the sniper rise fully to his feet and start to move forward. Perhaps he couldn't see.

"Arrettay!" the corporal bellowed, using a tenth of his French. "You'll fall, you silly bugger!"

The patrol watched Sergeant Hruska and two men scale the cliff and take the man prisoner. The corporal brought his men down to the fork in the trail. "OK, Janke, you want action. Take the point with Williams. Keep an eye open for caves. Sarge figures they must be holed up round here. And Janke, we want six-packs. If there are any bodies to hump out, guess who'll carry the heaviest one."

John Ashworth sat in his office in the bunker, a phone tucked under his left ear. His pen moved down a long staff memo, underlining and noted at the bottom, "Rewrite in either official language. TV military jargon not official at this HQ."

As he wrote, he was nodding his head agreeably. He looked as if he was going out, his khaki Herbert Johnson forage cap pulled sharply down over his nose.

"I do understand, sir, but I'm afraid the general did not authorize your helicopter request today, colonel." There was a short pause. "No sir. Not on Saturday either." This time the pause was longer.

"With all due respect, sir, the sniper is harmless. He even misses the general." A short pause.

"Of course he comes close, he has a job to protect. I assure you that a successful operation against him would not be well received. On that subject, we will require the names of two lightly wounded men to credit him with by Sunday. May I suggest that one be Sergeant Weitz? He hasn't had a good five-day pass since we started . . . Whatever, sir, but names *are* required, and may I congratulate you on your recovery from laryngitis, sir."

Ashworth saw Clay come in and waved. "Excuse me, Colonel Bosch, a security matter has just arisen and I have to go. Good afternoon, sir." He hung up firmly and for three seconds sat unmoving; then he removed his cap, placed it carefully on the desk beside the tray marked "Cat" in which a small black-footed tortoise-shell kitten was dozing, sighed and shook his head.

"Is the Guards custom of wearing hats at breakfast related to wearing them during phone calls?" Clay inquired as he swung a long leg over the visitor's chair and sat.

"At breakfast we wear them if we're hung over and do not wish to be disturbed. In the office, if we're talking to Colonel Bosch. A cap reminds me that as an officer and gentlemen I can't say all the nasty things that my mind invents. Can I help you?"

Anderson scratched the kitten at the base of her tail. "Hi, Sergeant Burlap, got the bunker mice under control?" The cat, a bribe or present from Herb Kerner, was official brigade mouser with the rank of drill sergeant. The name came from her habit of sharpening her claws on any handy sandbag wall.

"I'm glad I saw that, John. Perhaps you're human after all."

"And what does that mean?"

"Most HQ's these days are tied to computers. We're tied to a John Ashworth."

"I'll take that as a compliment—I think."

"Do, but why be so self-effacing? You even get drunk quietly— and don't give me the standard crap about Guards style." He let Burlap nibble on his finger.

"I suppose there's a point to all this?"

"Patience, Junior. Most people like you like to get patted on the head for a good job done now and then. They're go-fers, but they get re-membered at promotion time too."

"I'm not a go-fer, I'm a no-fer. That's the difference."

"I'll bite, what's a no-fer?"

"The general gets a dozen ideas a week. On average, three are brilliant, five need work and four are impossible. I'm the one who says, 'No, fer God's sake forget it.' "

"John, people who cultivate 'grey' shouldn't make jokes like that, wear a hat to talk to nasty colonels or have an out-tray labeled 'Cat'."

"At the risk of sounding non-grey, what do you want, sir?"

"I want that computer mind scanning my spy problem. The info being fed to the ALQ is very high-level stuff. Has to come from here."

"Do you have anyone particular in mind?"

"Armand Chantilly's wife is a senior member of their war council."

"And I have two cousins who may be in the ALQ. Armand organized the entire militia collection in Montreal. Without him we'd be dead— literally."

"He should have been arrested Saturday morning. His name got taken off the list. Why?" Anderson handed over an envelope. "This is a list of information on us that the Tangos have on file. Is there anything on it that Armand couldn't know?"

"That's sweet, Clay. How do you feel about Pierre Coté or André Taschereau?"

"They aren't high enough—but St Pierre and Chantilly are."

"Toupée held off the ALQ a dozen times when he could have let them through. Armand always complained that he couldn't guarantee his artillery, but every time we needed guns he delivered even though he'd built a perfect excuse."

"People have done that if they have a bigger goal in mind. Think about it, John."

"I'm surprised you don't have Messier on the list."

"Who says I don't? Anyway, he's clean. We have nothing on him."

"Nor on Chantilly or St Pierre either, I bet."

"Smart-ass." Anderson got up slowly. "For all I know Etienne would sell Canada for a plugged dime, but I'd bet my career he wouldn't do anything to hurt Sloerill. George represents Canada to Messier. Messier is the Quebec Sloerill wants to protect by his limited war. If Sloerill goes I'll watch Messier. Read my lists. If anyone has access to every piece of information on it, I want to know who he is." The door closed quietly, putting a neat period to the conversation.

CHAPTER SEVENTEEN

The Bunker

The clerk whistled his way down a hall at NDHQ and into an office. "Afternoon, Colonel Jenkins," he said cheerfully. "Just one today." He laid a thick manila envelope on the desk. A red tag on the flap suggested that someone in the upper echelons was annoyed.

Jenkins opened the sealed inner package and swore. The information block had "Sloerill" written on it. That Man again.

Quickly he scanned the memo, noting the request for information needed before the end of February, initialled and time-dated it under the signature. He was putting on his jacket when he heard a single rap at the door.

"It's open. Come in." Jenkins turned, stiffening to attention. "Sorry, sir. I was just coming round to see you."

"Relax, Don. My office is a three-ring circus today. Here we can have a chat without interruptions."

They sat down, Jenkins's visitor was a major-general. Instead of a regulation nylon shirt his was custom tailored in Egyptian cotton. Next to it Don's government issue shirt looked cheap.

"Your message just came, sir. It'll take a few days to get everything you want."

"Do it fast, Don. General Pittman's in a foul mood, and I have to get something to him pretty soon. This phony war can't last much longer.

Let's kick this Sloerill thing around the field a few times and see what we come up with."

"Reference his cash pay and acting ranks plan, why don't we just shoot it down as being against DND policy?"

"Because it isn't now. He got somebody to approach the Minister on his problem. The Minister asked Sloerill, as the man on the spot, to make recommendations. Sloerill did, the Minister bought them, and we're end-played. He's got to go, Don."

"Can't Bosch give us the ammunition we need?"

"Bosch is a broken reed. He can only do one thing at a time, and he needs every brain cell to fight Sloerill. What about Terry Gascoigne? He's reg force, and his opinion pulls more weight than Bosch's anyway."

Jenkins shook his head. "Sloerill got to him. Terry won't help."

"Are you sure, Don? I thought we'd put a good man in there."

"He and I go way back, sir. He was OK at first, but now he says Sloerill's system works. He's a convert."

"He's just blown his career. This war has to be kept on the rails despite Sloerill. You're Personnel. Bring Gascoigne back here."

"Can't, sir. The Minister's policy is firm: Sloerill's people stay. Why not ride it out? When the war's over, Sloerill will be a hero for a week, then he'll be forgotten."

"General Pittman doesn't believe that—and what if the hero decides to stay on?"

"I'm told he's a very hands-on type. Now that we're expanding the army—did I say something wrong, sir?"

"No, but expansion's a sore subject. When we got word to do it, we tried to open the recruiting depots, get the people in and train them the unified way. Mr Bloody Bartholomew vetoed the plan. We had to let militia regiments do their own recruiting and then train as a unit. Pittman was in orbit for a week. Anyway, what were you suggesting, Don?"

"Can we turn Sloerill's force into a division under a general who'll keep him in line?"

"Possibly," the general mused. "Babe Trinker's working up 1 Div HQ now. Fred Scott's doing the same with 2 Div in the Gaspé. Putting Sloerill the hero under an unknown commander is bad PR, but if he's the Div commander he'll turn the extra units around like he did the Tor Scots."

"Why not send good green regular units? The Tor Scots were mostly militia."

"We don't *have* any good green units after Dorion. I tell you, Don, there've been very pointed questions asked in the House about how the unified forces let Canada down. After the war's over we'll have a real fight on our hands to keep the system going."

"They can't throw out twenty-five years' work just like that!"

"Politicians will do anything to get elected. Remember, Hellyer tried to ride the military into the Prime Minister's job by unifying us. After the war there'll be a major shift in political leadership, and a hotshot like Bartholomew might decide to go for the brass ring and base his campaign on de-unification. It's being seriously discussed."

Jenkins shrugged. "Not much we can do about that."

"Don't kid yourself. Sloerill's the Minister's prize exhibit. If he fouls up, the Minister loses his healthy glow."

The general stood up. "Whatever we do has to look good on TV. Something he can't handle the way he did Gascoigne. It has to reduce his influence on troops. I can see a danger in this, but your idea may fly. Make the bastard a major-general, give him Three Div, and he won't have time to fight the system, he'll be part of it."

He adjusted his old RCAF tie pin across his green tie. "You may have found the answer, Don. Why not drop round for drinks on Saturday? The wife was saying she hadn't seen you and Gwen for too long. Can do?"

"Can do, sir." Colonel Jenkins saw his visitor out, then began to gather his papers. The general had been pleased. If he stayed pleased, star rank would follow.

It had been three weeks since the Bosch incident, and people were seeing changes. Bosch had allowed officers to have their batmen again. He had also relaxed his obsession with rigid patrol timetables, and as a result the Guards' bag of prisoners and the number of successful contacts with the ALQ were rising while the Guards were suffering fewer casualties.

At the evening intelligence briefing Clay Anderson reported that the ALQ seemed to be planning a major operation so far undefined, and that all troops were to be on the lookout. Andrew Bryce was using helicopters equipped with infra-red scanners for night surveillance.

"Speaking to the broader picture, gentlemen," Clay finished up. "While the ALQ grow stronger, they're also being more cautious and concentrating their defenses at Dorion and in the Gaspé. They sent reinforcements north, but they can't support them. Our CF-18's prevent regular resupply by air, and the Cree are interdicting overland routes. Having let the ALQ wither on the vine last winter, Canadian forces will retake the area in ten days. Are there any questions?"

After the briefing, Sloerill lingered to speak with Tom Bush, now L/Col Bush, his military spokesman on the Civil Council.

"Tom, that ALQ operation Clay mentioned has to happen either here or in Ottawa. They need a success, so tell your civil guard types to really keep their ears to the ground."

"Will do, George. The council also told me to complain about the Guards again. There's been a big improvement, but they still have the reputation of being trigger-happy. A couple of our own patrols got shot at. You remember Sergeant Wilson?"

Sloerill nodded. The man had been a godsend in the early days.

"He has a lot of friends in the Guards. The word comes from the top, George. Bosch is pushing a 'shoot first shoot faster' doctrine. Peter Forbes' and Pierre Coté's companies are OK, but the other two need some reining in."

"I'll tell Bosch. Is there any good news out there?"

"Oh, lots. Three new factories opened. Construction crews are working full out now that February's providing some good weather. Dairy farmers are smiling. We may become the yogurt, butter and cheese capital of Canada. Not only are we turning out a good product, we're beating everybody on price because the government is giving us tax breaks . . . and oh, yeah. Kerner finally had his housing request approved. His new kid gave him the extra points. He got that house by the base."

"At least somebody's getting a good rest at night."

"You should too, George. Go on, take a break. Things are quiet."

"I'd love to, but I promised Toupée I'd come to a special party his officers are throwing in their wing of the mess—a secret party, yet."

"And I keep telling him not to promise to be anywhere at a specific time." They turned to find that Clay Anderson had cat-footed up behind them.

"Clay's afraid Toupée will ambush me," George explained wasp-ishly. "He can't explain why he didn't take me out on any of the fifty or sixty other times he's had the chance—but now he says to watch out."

"All I asked was, why such a big deal tonight?" Clay said equably. "Every regiment has its own wing in the mess. Every unit has a real weird collection of relics they brought from their armoury and installed with a wing-dinger party. The FMR lost all their stuff. What will you do tonight, sit around listening to the glue on the new wallpaper set?"

"Well, whatever it is, I'm going and going alone!" Sloerill snapped. Without waiting for a reply, he stamped off through the late April slush. Zuke opened the humvee's rear door. When the boss walked that way, he wanted to be as alone as possible.

After supper, in a slightly better mood, Sloerill left the command bunker to walk to the sprawling brigade mess. Every unit had a room, decorated to suit its taste. Regiments lived mostly in the field, but this was their home. Conduct in each was governed by old rules and by improvisations, a few of which would survive long enough to reach the status of tradition. The one bow to commonality was the central bar with a serving window for each mess. (The Guards in addition had a night tray with a book of chits to be signed by thirsty visitors after hours.)

As George rounded the corner of a stores building he was startled by a familiar bellow. Lined up before Brigade Sergeant-Major Grigson was an RMR platoon. That mini-regiment had provided security guards for Sloerill's HQ from the beginning. This group was going out to form part of the outer security ring of patrols. Sloerill stopped in the shadow to see what horrors Grigson had discovered.

"You lot are going on patrol?" Grigson snarled in a lower tone from that first outraged bellow. "Listen to you! You sound like a wandering junk drive!"

He stepped back, hands on hips. "All right, start jumping." A few men started to hop tentatively. "JUMP! I said. Higher! I'll tell you when to stop! UP! UP! UP!"

The thirty men were leaping with fervour and even fifty feet away, George could hear the clatter of equipment.

"All right, stop cavorting and tune in." Grigson had become serious. "You're all idle. Fourteen of you have loose rifle sling swivels that clatter with every step. On patrol you don't need slings. Take them off and tape the swivels down tight.

"Next, you're carrying enough junk to open a store. I heard coins clanking. Coins? What do you expect to buy out there? Half of you are wearing rings—one more thing to bang against your rifle. Why are you wearing helmets?" Grigson went on, ticking off his points. "Helmets are noisy and cold. Stocking caps are quiet and warm and your heads are already protected by a double thickness of bone encasing a tiny target.

"Did you all eat tonight?" The men nodded quickly. "Then why are you carrying road kill? You can't build a fire to cook it, you won't have time to eat it, and if you try, the food will end up on your lap when the ALQ slit your throats as you attend to creature comforts.

"You have five minutes to get presentable. When you get back, I don't want to even hear your shoelaces rustling together—but before you go, Otis. Step out here."

The tall soldier stepped forward.

"What's that string tied to your left-hand jacket pocket button, Otis?"

"Church key, sergeant-major. Never know when you'll run into a beer—and it's plastic, sir. Safe. No rattles."

"Safe, is it? Permission to touch you?" Otis nodded. Grigson opened the pocket and pulled out the opener. It was attached by a wire. Then he removed a grenade from the same pocket and slipped the safety ring into the notch of the bottle opener.

"Now, Otis. It is dark. You're behind a tree. A small ALQ patrol stops near you. A perfect grenade target. You reach for one and you pull it out . . . no, don't look. It's dark, Otis. Feel for it." He spoke softly but the entire platoon could hear him.

Grigson turned the grenade so that Otis's hand wasn't properly holding the spring release handle down. "My hand is your pocket, Otis. Pull the grenade out of it."

Otis was sweating. "If I do, the grenade will go off, sir."

"Astute, Otis. The opener will pull the safety pin and the grenade will go boom in your hand. This will make you even more awkward. You will have to eat more slowly and for years you will set off metal detectors at airports.

"Do you know why there are mountains, Otis?" Grigson asked in an apparent abrupt change of subject.

Otis looked confused. "No, sergeant-major."

"Because after the Lord created Adam and Eve, he realized that *you* were in the future. His shudders created them." Grigson replaced the grenade in the man's pocket and stepped back. "What are you waiting for? Five minutes, I said. MOVE!"

Sloerill lurked in the shadows until Grigson moved away. Then he resumed his walk, realizing that while he had been concentrating on improving fighting standards among the combat troops he'd let things around the base go slack.

St Pierre met him at the door to the FMR mess, throwing it wide as Sloerill approached. "Bonjour, mon général. Bienvenu chez nous!"

Inside the room, George was struck dumb with astonishment. He knew the old FMR mess and museum in Montreal. All the regimental treasure that he'd thought lost was here. By each trophy case or display, an officer stood at ease.

"Where did this come from?" George exclaimed. "Duplicates? I thought you'd lost everything."

St Pierre was smiling quietly as he took Sloerill's coat. "Other regiments had to mount raids, all so unnecessary if one is prepared."

"Prepared? For a rebellion?"

"For those with eyes and ears it was not such a surprise as the blind men in Ottawa claim. My Régie discussed the problem, found money to duplicate things, replaced the real with replicas over two years, and sent the real relics into safekeeping in Vermont. Now that we have a home again, les violà! Will you honour us with an inspection, sir?"

Sloerill nodded dumbly. "We start with our founders," St Pierre began. The doorway was flanked by two bronze busts. "On your left, Colonel Forget, father of the regiment. On the right, General Labelle, the first Fusilier to become a general."

They moved through the mess. At each stop an officer came to attention to describe the exhibit at his post.

"The Regimental and Queen's Colours, sir. Beside them the colours of the 65th and 150th battalions of 1914. Next the wartime colours retired in 1952, and finally, the colours retired at our centennial in 1969."

"The regimental silver, general," a captain said. "It is the same pattern as that of our sister regiment in England, the York and Lancasters."

"The bronze Fusilier crest on the bar," a young second lieutenant explained nervously, "was presented by General Sauvé, an ex-Fusilier and at the time Prime Minister of Quebec."

"The three paintings at the bar, sir, are gifts. The one on the left, from the Molson family, represents the battle at La Ferme Beauvoir. You recognize the portrait on the right: General Dextrase, a Fusilier and former Chief of Defence Staff. Few militia officers rise so high." Major Gendron smiled as he spoke.

Sloerill took over. "Louis Riel," he identified the third painting to St Pierre's pleasure. "The first FMR action was in Saskatchewan, 1885, against the Métis at La Butte aux Français. I know of no regiment with a prouder history of fidelity and loyalty to the country they serve so well."

After the applause died down St Pierre pressed a drink into his hand. "Now, general. A toast to make the opening official."

Sloerill raised his glass. "Aux hommes valeureux de ce régiment. Je déclare cette messe des officiers officiellement ouverte!" The whole mess downed the drinks together and smashed the glasses in the fireplace.

"Hah!" George cried, rubbing his hands together. "Now for the serious drinking! First round is on me . . . then you," he pointed to St Pierre, "then Major Gendron, and we'll see how it goes from there."

Wait till that suspicious bastard Anderson hears about this, he thought gleefully as he moved away from the bar to let the junior officers get at it.

John Melling had called in the CIA Director to spell out the administration's new policy and receive an intelligence estimate of Canadian intentions. After a comprehensive review of the military strength of both sides, the Director summed up.

"Canada is definitely taking a harder line in response to pressure from the agitator Prentice. The government is also trying to undermine his position with planted rumours suggesting that the real reason for his crusade is based on business incompetence that let a Quebec company outmaneuver him. The rumours have the value of being almost true. The government is still nervous, however, and it's flying trial balloons about retaking all of

Quebec. What's holding Canada back is their failure so far to agree on a post-war policy. Disagreements about reconstruction and the degree of bilingualism to be allowed in the new Quebec have almost shattered the coalition three times.

"There's little middle ground. One side is against any but the most elementary reconstruction programme unless Quebec becomes a unilingual English province. The other side wants Quebec to return to the Canadian fold in a near ante-bellum status quo."

"Outstanding, Jack. What's Canada's reaction to our delay in selling them six destroyers?"

"Frustration, sir. They desperately want to choke off the arms getting in to maintain their military advantage over Quebec, but they don't have a prayer with that antique navy."

"I'm afraid their frustration will grow. Officially, we are experiencing problems in finding mothballed ships sufficiently modern to meet their demands. The fact is, we don't want their navy to be in too good shape with the navigation season opening up."

"They're also talking new ships to the Brits, Germans and Japanese, sir."

"I know, but if they go too far, they know it'll jeopardize our deals. The Man is still pissed off they bought British tanks instead of ours. Now, on Operation Garotte. The President would like the noose on Quebec arms supplies loosened a bit."

"What does he want let in, sir?" Melling handed him a paper and after a quick look, the Director whistled. "Have we switched sides?"

"Not at all, Jack. We start negotiating a water treaty next month, and we're looking at changes to the Free Trade Agreement. If Canada gets too feisty we lose our edge. Once the ALQ gets this stuff, Canada will have to rein in its war aims. Also think about France becoming a more important player than they've been to date."

"Well, I don't see much problem with this. We passed the word that Uncle would not be happy if certain things were delivered—we never tried to restrict *buying*. In fact, a lot of things on your list have been purchased by Quebec, they just haven't been able to get shipping. Their credit rating isn't very good."

"Right. If Quebec loses, their war debt has to be written off because

Canada sure as hell won't pay it. Open the net." Melling began to replace papers in his attache case. "The president wants to know how long it will take to tighten up again if we need to?"

The Director thought a moment. "Ball-park guess, a month, not counting what's in the pipeline at the time. Question?"

"Shoot, Jack."

"How does this affect the help we're giving to General Sloerill? My man up there has been sending new lists every week. Some of them have been pretty strange. He started with a request for antique machine guns."

"No problem. Sloerill wants what we want, a simple corridor, and from what I'm told, if Canada wants more they'll have trouble with his French-Canadians. Support Sloerill, open the pipeline, but be prepared to slam it shut again if necessary. Easy stuff, Jack. You can do it in your sleep."

Sloerill was in his bunker office waiting for a phone call. On his desk was a signal from Ottawa requesting him to stand by for an urgent message that evening. The phone rang and he snatched it up.

"Hello, George," Messier drawled. "I am sorry to disturb you but we have a most delicate problem at Civile. Tom Bush is away, and he would only push the problem onto you in any case. We are meeting informally at Sam's place in Sutton. Can I expect you in half an hour?"

"Sorry, Etienne, I can't get away." Sloerill looked up as John Ashworth came in with a pot of fresh coffee. "How about tomorrow?" As he spoke, Burlap sprang onto the desk and sat purring softly in the middle of his blotter.

"I am afraid that will not do, George. There has been a rape, a rather nasty one. The citizens are very angry, and we suspect Colonel Bosch will try to protect his soldier. There is also the question of his men being too trigger-happy still. I am afraid I must pull rank on you and insist."

"You can't pull rank on NDHQ, Etienne," George said irritably, caught between his orders and Messier's obvious concern. "Umm, just a minute." He looked at John, who had been making hand signals. "Yes?"

"We'll patch your phone through to Sam's, and if a call comes through before you get there, I'll tell them to be patient, you're in the crapper."

Sloerill grinned mischievously. "Good enough. OK, Etienne, I'll be there in about fifteen minutes." He hung up and grinned. "Who's minding the store tonight?"

"Clay and myself, sitting in for Armand who wanted to go and see somebody about a gun. No sweat, sir."

After waiting for the week of unsettled weather the meteorologists had predicted, Colonel Frappier had infiltrated a hundred and eighty men into the hills around Abercorn. Most had slipped across the border from Vermont, masquerading as returning refugees. A few, including Frappier, had parachuted in the week before. Moving at night, always under cover of snow or rain, they had moved close to Sutton Mountain. Two nights previously they had left their scattered bases and were now ready to strike, their backs to the US border, less than 500 metres from Sloerill's headquarters.

The raiders were bearded and nearing exhaustion but ready and willing to make a last push. Frappier had been told that after the raid his men would be evacuated, but he didn't believe it. The new French armed helicopters were too valuable to risk this deep in Canadian territory. He was planning to lead the survivors across the border, surrender to the Americans, and wait to be exchanged.

Now he and his officers were huddled under a blanket covered with snow and brush to hide the light as they made a final review of their plans.

"René?"

"My men take out the gate guard and delay reinforcements from Abercorn. On your success signal, we hold for fifteen minutes to allow your force to cross behind us, then we break for the landing zone."

"Remember, only fifteen minutes. If we are late, that is not your fault. Laurent?"

"I attack the main base," Captain Tétrault replied. "We burn what we can. Shoot up the camp. Draw off the guards on Sloerill's bunker. Then escape across the Abercorn road to our designated helicopter landing zone."

"Bon," Frappier approved. "When you draw off the guards, we attack the bunker. Henri will lead the entry party. Henri?"

"There are thirty-one steps down to the entryway. We blow the door with a shaped charge. Throw smoke bombs into the mirror room, then a satchel charge to destroy the guard post. Two teams of four enter the bunker. My team will find and kill Sloerill."

"Very good. Now, move into position. Do not let the men sleep. They are so tired that sleep will dull them. Bonne chance."

The four men emerged from under the blanket and collected their men. As they began to move off, they heard the fluttery sound of a night-hunter helicopter prowling the sky to the north of them.

Fifty-eight minutes later a roving patrol spotted movement in the trees and opened fire. The ALQ returned it. Leaving six men to deal with the patrol, Captain Tétrault broke for the main camp at a dead run, feeling the clock ticking away the scanty minutes he had to fulfill his task. As they had practiced, his men ran the zig-zag clear paths through the wire and mines and struck the RMR defenders mercilessly.

The sergeant at post number 7 grabbed his radio. "Hello, seven. Raiders, estimate figures seven zero, through wire and mines. Will—" The message broke off as a grenade exploded in the sergeant's trench.

In the bunker the operations staff had snapped alert at the first report of shooting. Klaxons sounded from every building. Men seized their weapons and ran for their positions. At many trenches, the marauding ALQ had arrived first, and around the base a dozen fires were already blazing.

John Ashworth called the Guards. "Sugar Delta Tangos attacking base. Main gate lost. Require two companies to assist defence now, a third company on standby. Over."

The reply was prompt and satisfactory. Pierre Coté was duty officer that night. "Roger. First troops moving in figures three minutes. Remainder to follow." The Grenadier Guards were on their way.

Grigson didn't hear the shooting or the klaxons. Deep in the pistol firing range, he stopped shooting, removed his ear plugs and meticulously cleaned his pistol. After checking that the range was now deserted, he turned out the lights and went upstairs. The door was blocked. He put his shoulder to it and shoved. The obstruction gave slightly. Now he could hear the shooting.

Through the half-open door he saw the glow of fires and dim shapes of men running through the smoke. He hit the door with his shoulder and it opened enough to let him out. A man's body lying across the threshold rolled over. Otis.

Carefully Grigson looked around. His post was in the Operations Room at the other end of camp. Heavy firing was coming from that direction so he was probably cut off, but if he could get behind the attackers he should be able to damage them.

When he stepped fully out, he realized the full extent of the raid. Buildings blazed everywhere, and in the flickering light he saw twenty to thirty bodies strewn over the thin spring snow that had fallen that afternoon. Holstering his pistol, he picked up Otis's rifle and began to move towards the command centre, darting from one bit of cover to the next, angling left to approach it from the south.

In the command centre the staff were trying to plot the ALQ attack from the fragmentary reports coming in. Over half their defensive positions had been overrun by the attackers, who had unexpectedly come from the south. The explosion of the main camp fuel tanks brought down bits of ceiling in the bunker a thousand metres away.

Peter Forbes reported that he'd left one platoon to deal with a block on the main road and was leading the other three around it on foot to clear the camp gate. The second company was being ferried by helicopter to a position below the main base and would move forward as soon as they had two platoons deployed. It would be thirty minutes before either force could assist the defenders.

A signaller looked up from his set. "Sir. ALQ approaching the ammo dump. They are crossing Dieppe Road now."

Ashworth studied the camp map. Dieppe was within four hundred metres of the ammunition dump. "Are we holding them?"

The signaller shook his head. "Only a dozen guards there, sir, and they're under heavy fire."

Ashworth agonized for a moment, then came to a decision. "Send three sections of the headquarters defence platoon to assist them. If that ammo goes up, half the base will go with it." The bunker defence was now reduced to ten men.

In the camp, visibility was improving as the fires spread. Frappier knew that perhaps half his attacking force was dead or wounded, but they were doing a magnificent job and would have done even better if they hadn't been surprised by the patrol. He moved up to the officers' mess, a hundred metres from the bunker. A man suggested burning the mess but he vetoed it. Fire would alert the defenders and his men would be outlined against the flames as they attacked. As he watched the bunker, a full platoon of men climbed out of their slit trenches and began to run towards the threatened ammunition dump.

Frappier waved his arm. "En avant!" he commanded and they dashed forward. The last man in the assault group tripped over a length of telephone wire and fell heavily.

Grigson, in a ditch near the mess, watched the attackers. He counted about thirty men. As soon as they were in the open, they came under fire from the remaining bunker guards. Ten raiders returned fire while the rest charged. Grigson took aim at them and pressed the trigger of his rifle. It moved slackly. Otis hadn't gotten around to cocking it! Cursing, he jerked the lever and was taking aim again when the last ALQ soldier ran by, firing as he passed the kneeling man and raced on without a backward glance.

"Here comes trouble!" Anderson pointed to the TV monitor. The camera showed fifteen men coming down the steps into the bunker, pausing on the landing to let a man with a package go ahead. On another screen they watched him hang a box on the door handle, press it firmly in place and step back around the corner. A moment later they heard the bang of a shaped charge as it blew the door open.

The attackers gathered outside the dazzle room. The leader threw a canister through the shattered door and smoke began to fill the room.

"The radios are dead!" Ashworth's signaller reported in panic. On the roof, Frappier's men had blown the tall radio antennas off their mounts.

"Guard the passage, I'll take the Claymores," Anderson ordered. John took two men and dashed forward to the first turning of the hallway leading to the dazzle room. Back in the operations room, Anderson saw a heavy package sail into the smoke-filled room. Then his TV monitor went blank as the explosion shattered the steel mirrored walls and blew in the concrete box around the two guards.

The first ALQ attacker came cautiously around the corner. A signaller beside Ashworth killed him with a burst of automatic fire. Anderson heard the shots and pressed a red button on a panel in Sloerill's office. The twin battery-powered Claymore mines covering both jogs of the passage by the entryway exploded and filled the area with slashing steel fragments.

From the former dazzle room, Lt Henri Rancourt waved his men forward. He'd suspected other defences and had sent forward the minimum number of men. They were dead, but the passage should now be clear.

Just as Rancourt rose to follow his men, Anderson pressed a second button on the panel. Under the entryway, a mine exploded. The dazzle room and the steps leading down to it were blown into rubble, sealing the bunker completely and burying Rancourt and his men.

Colonel Frappier heard and felt the underground explosion and for a moment thought that his men had succeeded. Then as the dust boiled up from the stairwell he realized that even if they had, they were now trapped. Over the radio he gave the order to withdraw.

It took over an hour for the Guards to secure the base. André Taschereau, his left leg shattered by a grenade and running on nerve and morphine, directed rescue operations from a stretcher near the ammunition dump. He concentrated on controlling the fires and collecting the wounded. He had no spare resources to start digging out the bunker.

The Guards began hunting down the surviving raiders. Bosch had taken command and was directing his men from a helicopter. The night-scanning devices showed every movement of the fleeing ALQ through the sparse, leafless trees, and he sent his men in careful pursuit.

Because he had been late crossing the Abercorn road, Frappier and his seven survivors were behind the line of Guardsmen driving the main ALQ body west into the hills. Lying beside the road, unable to advance, he saw several vehicles turn into the base. One was Sloerill's, but for the return trip Zuke had removed the commander's pennant from the radio mast, and Frappier, unknowing, let the man whose death had been the prime object of the raid pass by.

Shooting was dying down in the hills as the first streaks of light appeared in the east, and Frappier looked for a hiding place. Two hundred metres away he saw a small square frame house. The neatly plowed driveway made it possible to approach without leaving tell-tale footprints in the snow.

He and his men dashed from cover and up to the back door. They forced it and crowded in. Herb Kerner was in the kitchen, staring up at the base in the dark, wondering what to do. They quickly bound and gagged him. Gloria, who was in the next room, soon joined her husband in the basement. The two soldiers detailed to search the house found the baby girl upstairs and brought the child down to her mother.

"Block the windows. We will remain here until nightfall," Frappier ordered. "If we are discovered, we surrender. We do not make war on civilians or children." His men agreed. They were exhausted.

They dragged mattresses into the basement for the family and untied Gloria. Colonel Frappier, who had three daughters, went to the kitchen to heat some formula on the stove. As it warmed he watched the light grow stronger, listening to the sound of a circling helicopter.

Colonel Bosch had seen the party run to the house but had been too far away to intervene. Most of his men were hunting the surviving raiders in the hills. He diverted one platoon to secure the house, and the officer, now in position, wanted permission to attack.

Bosch hesitated. The ALQ were desperate and well armed. Twice his helicopter had been fired on, and the plexiglass above his head was starred with bullet holes. The fact that the helicopter's mini-guns had killed both raiders did not make him feel safer.

As they circled, he saw how isolated the house in the clearing was. His men would have to cross two hundred metres without cover against a determined enemy. He pressed the intercom button on his helmet radio.

"Are your mini-guns effective against houses?"

Lt Symbalewski nodded. "Yes, but no can do, sir. General's orders, and base doesn't answer radio call."

Swiftly Bosch explained the tactical problem, sure that given a good excuse "Steve Canyon" would bend the rules.

Symbalewski was still shaking his head. "I see the problem, sir, but my orders are clear. How about when the attack goes in I do a simulated shooting run? That should divert a lot of stuff from your men."

And onto us, Bosch thought. "Look, the refugees moved out a week ago. All we hit is a house full of ALQ. The general may be dead, and look at the lives we'll save."

"I can go back to the base to check." Symbalewski suggested. "Must be somebody there can give the OK."

"We don't have time," Bosch insisted. "I will make this an order, Lieutenant. On the grounds of operational necessity, attack that target!" He saw Symbalewski start to waver. "Go on. It's only got the enemy inside!" The helicopter heeled abruptly over and swung in a fast low circle as bullets from the mini-gun in the left door began to chew into the house.

Bosch was astounded at the result. He had expected to see something like the houses he'd seen hit by machine gun fire before. Instead, the building imploded as a fire storm of four thousand bullets per minute poured into it. The house seemed to collapse into the basement. As the propane gas tanks exploded, igniting the shattered wood, the helicopter spun on its rotor axis and raced back pouring fire into the rubble from its right-hand guns.

In the bunker Ashworth and Anderson, still dazed from the blast, were checking to see who had survived. The door guards were dead, their bodies deep under the rubble along with those of their attackers. The six duty clerks and signallers had sustained shock, broken ear-drums and minor wounds. The air sparkled with dust in the harsh emergency lighting and the floors were ankle deep in sand and plaster, mixed with water from the fractured pipes.

Anderson found that three of the six emergency air ducts were open and went back to the general's office. John was trying to sweep sand, plaster and bits of rock off the big desk, a handkerchief tied over an oozing slash on the back of his right hand.

"You were OK when I left you, Junior, how did that happen?" Clay tied the bandage more tightly in place.

"Never mind," Ashworth growled. "How did Burlap get into the general's safe?"

"Oh, shit. Did I forget to tell you that? Before I set off the mine, I tried to save her from the blast. I take it she was some scared?"

"The safe was unlocked so I looked in. When Burlap saw the light, she took off, using my hand as a launch pad. Since you put her there, *you* can tell the general that a lot of his records are now a kind of muddy yellow colour—a *wet* muddy yellow."

"Ah. *That* scared. OK, I'll—look out!" They jumped aside as another piece of ceiling fell.

"I hope that's the last of it," Ashworth muttered, trying to brush the latest dirt-fall out of his hair. "This place is like a French cheese factory."

"Cheese factory?"

"Damn right, and we're getting buried in de brie." Ashworth gave him a grimy grin. "How does that grab you?"

Anderson winced. "I'd give it about a five on the old rictus scale." He thought for a minute about what he'd said and shook his head. "Let's make an agreement, John. One like the general is enough, and since he outranks us we swear off. OK?"

They shook hands. "Speaking of the general, he will not be pleased. The sugar bowl his English lady sent him is broken."

Anderson laughed. "The ALQ have gone too far." He half-turned to go. "You know, I figure we won't be out until at least noon. Want to spend the time usefully?"

"Designing a better bunker?"

"Don't be sarcastic, Junior. Think about this. Why was the general ordered to wait for a call that never came? Why did the ALQ attack while he should have been waiting? How come they knew our defences—at least, most of them?" He stretched gingerly. "I'll excavate my desk and find my notes. You too. It might be handy if we double-check each other and try to find connections that shouldn't be there."

"I've been working on connections," John admitted. "Mostly I hit a blank wall." He sniffed at the sour reek of cordite in the room. "What else can I do?"

"Think, Junior. If a name keeps cropping up on our lists, we may be onto something. This raid makes me think someone out there has a real peeve against George. I'd kinda like to find him or her before they get lucky." Ashworth nodded. "Now, by the time you dig out your files the air may be good enough to let us light a stove, and with a bit of luck the bottle in my desk survived, so we can reinforce the coffee a tad or two. OK?"

"It's a deal, mainly because if somebody bumped the general, I'd be out of my cushy job and, heaven forfend, I might even have to go up to the grubby sharp end of this war."

"There you go, Junior. I like highly motivated types. See you in fifteen?"

CHAPTER EIGHTEEN

Blow-up

By noon of the next day the fires that had not been extinguished were under control. As Sloerill watched, men dug at the bunker entrance, their work recorded by the three members of a visiting CNN crew who had survived the attack. Behind him a truck pulled up and stopped. An FMR sergeant got out, looked around at the devastation for a long moment, then came over to Sloerill and saluted.

"Bonjour, monsieur. Une lettre pour vous de mon colonel."

Sloerill opened it. St Pierre congratulated him on his escape and reported that the FMR had captured one raider. Attached to the formal report was a personal note. Robert Messier had had to be physically restrained from shooting the man. Toupée asked George to speak to him. Sloerill looked at the truck and beckoned Robert over to him.

Robert's face had toughened; life outdoors, hard work and personal animus had given him a harsh, hawk-like appearance, the face of a man who could kill too easily.

"Why, Robert?" Sloerill asked. "We don't shoot prisoners."

Young Messier did not relax. "The man was no better than a spy," he said harshly in English. "He had stolen civilian clothes."

"Isn't it better to have a live spy than a dead one?"

"No. Spies are cowards. I can meet the ALQ in battle. That is soldiers' work. But these who smile at you by day and plant bombs at night are scum. They do not deserve to live. They make me ashamed of being French-Canadian. Even my father—"

"Your father," Sloerill said sharply, "is trying to preserve the country. He knows that we have to live together afterwards and that every drop of blood we spill makes it harder."

"He works too hard at that," Robert shot back. "I know times when we were prevented from killing terrorists because of his stupid rules."

"Am I also stupid, Robert?" The boy's eyes flickered and dropped. "I want those rules. Your father helps me and I help him, and because of *our* rules the terror campaign has failed. Why? Because people see what we are doing and turn in the terrorists. Your father—I couldn't get along without him. He saved my life last night."

Robert looked startled. "He did? How?"

"He made me attend a meeting. If I'd been here I'd have been fighting and, as we found out from the men we captured instead of killing, we know that I was the target of the raid. Go back to your company, Robert. The ALQ attack last night was legitimate, like ours on Longue Pointe, and almost as successful. You can't blame them."

Robert shook his head. "I have told Father that after the war I will go to Ontario. I no longer believe in French Quebec. We must become Canadians with no hyphen to divide us or we will fight again."

"It's that attitude that got this started!" Sloerill shouted. "The goddam Manitoba School Act started this war as much as Cyr did. You can't screw twenty-five percent of the population and not have trouble. What you do after the war is your business. Winning is mine, and I need your help—but not if you're a bomb ready to go off. Now get back to your company and help win this war my way. Your way will prolong it."

Robert saluted formally and returned to the truck. Sloerill watched it out of sight, knowing that he hadn't gotten through. He felt a touch on his arm. "What?" he growled.

"Food," Zuke said succinctly, offering a mess tin of steaming beans.

Sloerill sat on the bumper of the humvee and scooped up a mouthful, then heard a ragged cheer from the bunker entrance. He looked and saw men helping the grimy figure of Tony Manieri out of the partially excavated entryway.

Zuke glared at the mess tin rocking on the hood as Sloerill took off. "Shoulda made him a sandwich," he grumbled. "Well, no use wastin' it." He sat down and began to eat the general's lunch.

It took three days to restore power and communications. While the staff moved back in, Sloerill attended a funeral for the eighty-five of his people who had died: sixty-two soldiers and twenty-three civilians, including the three Kerners. Colonel Frappier and his men were buried in the same cemetery in fifty-seven additional graves.

Sloerill's face was grim when he returned. "John. Bring Bosch in by chopper and get me his file. I want Symbalewski's statement on the attack and those of his IR [1] operator and door gunners." Ashworth nodded. Everyone knew an explosion was coming.

"Will you need a witness at the . . . ah . . . interview?"

Sloerill shook his head wearily. "No, Bosch isn't worth getting mad at. He simply isn't fit to command."

"What happens to him, then?"

"He's relieved as of now. Peter takes over, and I won't take any shit from Ottawa about it this time."

"What about the senior major, Carl Bates? He isn't back from the trip to Ottawa Bosch sent him on."

"He isn't coming back. Being made second-in-command in the reg force proves you aren't good enough to command, and Bates—" Sloerill saw Clay stride past the door. "Has he got a hornet in his boot?"

Ashworth briefed him on Clay's spy theory. Sloerill grunted dubiously. "Help him if you want, about priority six. Now, get Bosch here and cut those orders. Where's the Guards CP?" [2]

"Bondville." Ashworth grinned. "Bosch will love getting a wokka. The sniper's working the Bondville road today." Sloerill didn't smile. "I'll get on it right away, sir."

Two hours later Colonel Bosch came into the bunker, saluted and stood just inside the half-open door of Sloerill's office.

---

[1] Infra-Red
[2] Command Post

"Shut the door, Victor, and sit down. I won't bite." Bosch shut the door and sat nervously in front of the desk. Sloerill tapped the files in front of him. "I won't prolong this. You're relieved of command."

Bosch's mouth tightened in sullen anger but he did not speak.

"Some reasons are in my report," Sloerill continued. "Officially you are fired for disobeying gunship use orders, thereby causing the death of Herb Kerner, his wife and baby. You forced Lt Symbalewski to disobey orders too. That has to go on his record, despite the extenuating circumstances."

"I deny it!" Bosch said hotly. "I've never disobeyed an order. Symbalewski said he could attack the house and save a lot of lives. If he says anything different, he's lying!"

Sloerill sighed. "Don't be stupid, Victor. The door gunners and the IR operator heard everything you said." His icy stare silenced Bosch's attempt at a reply.

"You may have friends in Ottawa, but if they try to get you reinstated I'll bring the following information to the Minister. You nearly destroyed the Guards command system by shuffling people around and spying on them. I'll prove men died needlessly due to your inflexibility. I can prove you're a coward. When I forbade you to fly above the shooting, you sucked pilots down on the pretext of briefing them on a task, then bummed rides with them." There was a rap at the door. "Later. I'm busy."

The door opened and Anderson looked in. "Sorry to interrupt, sir, but I assure you this won't wait."

"It had better be good. What is it?"

"Not here, sir. In my office, if you please?"

Puzzled, Sloerill followed the American down the hall to the Intelligence wing. Clay had never broken into his work like this before. He shut the door to Anderson's office and stood, arms crossed. "Well?"

Anderson handed him a thick folder. "You'd better eyeball this before you make a final disposition of Colonel Bosch."

The file contained photocopies of his written orders, letters, transcripts of his radio orders and memoranda. He read Bosch's interpretation of them, querulous words ripping his policies to shreds, quoting orders out of context and blaming him for everything that had gone wrong. He looked up. "How did you get these?"

"When I discovered Bosch was reporting to Ottawa via the US Mail, I had the FBI do an intercept. What you have there is what Bosch sent." Clay tapped an equally thick file on his desk. "This file contains what Ottawa received from him after the reports did a tour through a few very specialized departments at Langley.

"We fuzzed his figures and qualified his opinions, and as a result the brass are not happy with one Victor Bosch. Their letters are full of useful hints on how he can improve himself. Useful because it tells how dedicated your enemies are and what information they need to screw you."

"Why's he doing this, Clay? Before the war I didn't know Bosch well enough to *be* his enemy."

"Sir, Ottawa showed him your report charging that he'd ordered three hundred Guardsmen to surrender to sixty ALQ. They asked him to do a little job for them here in exchange for a battalion command."

"I didn't make a charge, I only repeated what John told me. Bosch claims that he'd only given orders to surrender if necessary. Ottawa must have believed him."

"They didn't, sir. D/Secur [3] in Ottawa knows Bosch told John to surrender because the alternative was for him to drive to Farnham and join the war. D/Secur's the one running Agent Bosch."

"Come on, Clay," Sloerill said weakly. "You can't prove that."

Anderson grinned tightly. "Sir, officially this war was a big surprise to everybody. Unofficially, the CIA, with some deniable covert help from your CSIS boys, was on top of things. If the war had been delayed six months we might have stopped it. We had taps on every military installation in Quebec—including Farnham. We recorded Ashworth's calls to Mobile Command and Bosch. Nobody thought they were important once the shooting started. Canadian Military Security cut the Bosch bits out of the transcript they circulated. I've heard the original. You can hear his voice shake when John practically ordered him to take command."

"John never told me about that."

"John never says anything unless it's useful. He didn't know he could prove it so he kept quiet."

"So if I send Bosch back to Ottawa, what can they do?"

---

[3] Deputy-Commander, Security

"Sir, before the war you were a gadfly. Suddenly you're grabbing all the headlines and telling the country that you owe your success to the fact that you brush daily with anti-unification gel. Then you preach the Gospel according to the Regiment and the politicians listen. Let Bosch go back and find out how I fudged his reports and they'll screw you into the ground."

Anderson leaned forward. "Sir, with Bosch's help, they'll cook up a story that can sink you. I know there are lots of fine officers up there, but there are some who wouldn't have made it past major in a real army. They have a vested interest in the system, and in addition to you the new Minister's starting to make waves. Two weeks after they get you, your brigade will be so scattered that even satellite technology won't keep them in touch, and the green boys will settle down to win the war their own way."

"But to get me they have to use Bosch, and my report will destroy him, especially with your tape added in."

"Tape, sir?" Anderson was staring at a point above Sloerill's head.

Sloerill put the folder down on the table. "I'll have to think about this, Clay. I won't keep the man in command but—"

"You'll figure out something, sir. Just let me know if I can help." His cold blue eyes met Sloerill's again. "With an executive action."

Back in his office, Sloerill sat preoccupied. Bosch had recovered from his shock and now poured out his defence. Sloerill barely heard the stream of excuses and thinly veiled threats. The thin, penetrating voice was preventing him from concentrating on the problem. He stood up.

"All right, Victor, you've said your piece. For now you're attached here. I still have a few things to say, but this isn't the place. I'll drive you back to your CP. We'll talk on the road."

Ashworth blinked when Sloerill led Bosch out of the office, explaining that they were going to Bromont. Puzzled, he headed for Anderson's office. Something had happened during the interview, and he had an idea that Clay could tell him what it had been.

Zuke was in the parking lot talking to another driver when a jeep shot by, the general driving, Bosch beside him. Zuke left his friend in mid-sentence. At the bunker door he met Laurin coming out at a run. They looked at each other, then Zuke pushed past. "We better see Major Ashworth before we do something stupid."

Sloerill drove silently. A warm sun was melting the thick-flaked spring snow that had fallen the day before. In normal times, steam would be rising from fifty sugar shanties on a day like this.

Bosch was still frightened. He gave Sloerill no chance to speak as he chattered nervously about his ideas on how to fight the war. He wanted to make the general see that he was right. To ensure the promotion he'd been half-promised, Sloerill must be prevented from making a report on the unfortunate Kerner affair.

Even half-listening, Sloerill got an all-too-clear picture of Bosch's war. All woods and fields would be free-fire zones. Towns would be controlled by rigid curfews at night and road checks by day. The civil council would become a rubber stamp for military operations. All known civilian separatists would be arrested and sent to special camps.

His anger grew. The stupid man was planning a war that would keep his own skin safe. It was even possible that the crap being spouted represented NDHQ policy. Clay had been right. If Bosch got him fired, the new man might—he broke off the thought, his knuckles white with tension on the wheel. Bosch must be stopped.

It had been a mistake to think that Bosch would say anything incriminating. He should have sent him back and gone into a huddle with Clay until they worked out a way to neutralize the man. He would have ordered Bosch to shut up but he didn't trust himself to speak. Even a word could shatter the tenuous control he had over his rage.

They were only five kilometres from the Guards CP now but he wasn't sure he could finish the trip without exploding. He had to get away from that nagging, high-pitched voice to regain control of himself.

Savagely he cut onto the wide, slushy gravel shoulder and jammed on the brake. The jeep stopped, slightly nose down in a shallow ditch.

"Why did you stop?" Bosch broke off his monologue. "That sniper's near here."

Sloerill wasn't listening. As he swung his legs out of the jeep, the flap on his pistol holster caught and pulled open. Sloerill yanked it free and stalked a few yards in front of the jeep, seeking relief from Bosch's complaining voice.

Bosch fumbled his way out of the jeep. Unable to see the flat black stare of Sloerill's eyes that would have warned him, he kept on about the sniper, his face beaded with sweat.

"We'll be killed!" he called to Sloerill who was standing a few yards away, dragging in deep breaths, his hands clenched at his sides. Bosch remembered the stories about this man, the ALQ interrogation, his threat to kill Colonel Bennet at Longue Pointe. He was capable of anything. He had almost choked him to death once, now he wanted his tame sniper to finish the job.

"He'll kill you!" Bosch half-screamed. "And once he does and I'm in charge," his tongue automatically formed the words he had so often rehearsed, "we'll wipe out every traitorous Frenchman here!"

The words hit Sloerill like blows. Quebec turned into another Lebanon—burning buildings—a paradise turned into a desert—he swung around. The pistol, loose in the holster, seemed to leap into his hand as he reached out to seize Bosch and silence his raving.

Through Sloerill's mind flashed a series of pictures: men dying, unable to return ALQ fire because of the crowd on the street; a guard post machine-gunned from behind a school bus; on the next day a tight-lipped French teacher telling them where to find her brother's cache of weapons; a council meeting that, despite threats from separatists, voted to add "de Sloerill" to the town's name; men in hospital with the people they had guarded coming to visit, giving blood, praying for them, taking them home to convalesce.

He hardly felt the pistol buck. He didn't see Bosch's body, the face half-torn away by the bullet, thrown across the gravel, spinning and collapsing into the now-bloody snow. He took another step and his knee smashed against the sharp steel bumper. He grunted in pain and as his eyes began to focus, he saw the gun . . . the body . . . the blood on the snow.

Sloerill holstered the pistol automatically, and drove off, his mind deliberately blank except for a picture not of Bosch but of the first ALQ soldier he'd killed in Farnham. Finally he had been defeated, not by his enemies but by himself.

In the bunker Laurin and Anderson were on the radio demanding reports and calling for helicopter patrols over all routes the general might have used. Zuke was in Ashworth's office, cursing himself for letting the general get away. Sloerill stamped in without a word, hung his pistol belt on the peg and went into his office, closing the door solidly behind him.

"Bryce reports a body on—" Clay broke off his announcement as he saw the closed door and Zuke sniffing at a pistol in his hand. "He's back? Was that fired?"

"Yeah," Zuke said and started to strip Sloerill's weapon.

"Jesus," Ashworth breathed. "What do we do now? Isn't this your private ball park?" he asked Anderson.

Clay nodded. "Yep. Has he got another gun?" Ashworth and Zuke shook their heads. "OK. Don't leave him alone. Divert him. Get Chantilly to find a problem. Wind up Messier to throw some more stuff at him. Keep him busy." He tore a page from his notebook and scribbled a number on it.

"John, call this number. Identify yourself as GO BIRD DEPUTY. Tell whoever answers that GO BIRD needs deep cover by tonight at the latest. Then burn the paper."

"Can I ask what that means?"

"No. Make the call and forget it. Zuke, come with me."

Zuke finished exchanging Sloerill's pistol barrel for his own, wiped the weapon, replaced it in the holster and followed Anderson out.

In his office Clay picked up a phone and dialed. The ring was answered almost at once. "Hello, chief, is this still your private line?" He nodded at the reply. "Warning Order. You're about to pick up the Cowansville sniper. He will resist. Send a good man—one of mine by preference."

He listened for a moment. "Sorry, chief, this takes priority over 'nice'. I can't explain now, by tomorrow you can put it together yourself, but he has to be dead . . . have I ever steered you wrong?"

He hung up. "OK, that's the cops on-side. Can you get your hands on a .303 rifle, Zuke—like in ten minutes?"

"One in my room. Did I kill the colonel?"

"Listen up. The sniper did. Meet me in the parking lot in a jeep, not the general's humvee. I'll tell Major Ashworth to have the sniper arrested, then we go to work." Zuke went out, and Clay opened a locked steel box by his desk. "Damn amateurs," he muttered.

The Quebec cabinet was meeting in the capital, and Bouget, after trying for ten minutes to lighten the depressed atmosphere, began asking for reports. He asked for the worst ones at the start because there was some good news, and he wanted it to come last.

The gloom around the table deepened as the news piled up. Unemployment was at twenty-six percent and moving higher on a curve that would bump thirty-five percent by year-end.

Government approval rating was down to twenty-five percent and sinking. Travel and shopping in the United States was impossible. Delivery of Canadian pension cheques was sporadic. The death toll continued to mount. People were fleeing, many on forged exit visas. The attrition rate was two thousand a month and growing.

The Minister of Agriculture reported that reducing all milk quotas to equalize the loss of Canadian markets had dropped farm income to below the subsistence level, and the number of bankruptcies were growing.

The Minister of Finance bluntly stated that Quebec had to print its own money. The supply of Canadian dollars was almost exhausted and no new bills were available. He estimated that a Quebec dollar might trade at thirty cents against the American, but any military reverse would drop it below the the ruble. The effect on inflation was incalculable, but a rate of four percent per month would surely rise to two percent per week.

Madame Chantilly managed to wring a few hopeful notes out of her department. A programme of food rationing combined with an aggressive food-growing drive ("Turn your apartment into a garden") was keeping people fed, but it only slowed the rate of decline in the food supply. She ended her report by stating that unless the war ended soon, the people would rebel against the government and declare allegiance to Canada again.

She was booed by six hard-liners, but Bouget noted ten others looked thoughtful, even nodding slightly at her words. The nationalist glue that held them together had softened and there were fewer true believers.

Adèle waited for silence, then turned on the six with icy fury. "Are we children? This is reality, and reality is that without peace our dream will fail! Your stupid boos do not put one potato on people's plates. When your departments have some good news, then you may boo me. Until then be still lest your foolish ideas condemn you." She pointed at the group's leader, as if to impale him on one work-roughened finger.

"Was it not you who cheered the statement that we must put a knife to Canada's throat and make them bleed? We did. Now they have guns to our heads. Have you another brilliant statement or will you go on sounding like one of our cows being sent to slaughter for lack of food?"

Bouget stepped in quickly. "I'm sure, Adèle, that no one questions your dedication or success. Yours is the first good news we have heard in several days. Now, Paul-Joseph, how is the Defence Department doing?"

"The Canadian blockade is, as we know, ineffective. Supplies are reaching us regularly, and we now have enough F-18 spare parts so that we can fly more boldly. France is trying to reduce American support for Canada in the UN. That encourages the arms merchants to give us longer lines of credit. But they are still nervous, and we must use our remaining Canadian dollars to pay them. They will not accept a Quebec dollar at any discount unless France underwrites it. That France will not yet do.

"In the north, we must surrender the dams. Our army can protect them but we can't supply the army. We are restricted to air drops, and of the last three flights two were shot down: one by fighters, one by Cree missiles. An attack is coming soon and I want to withdraw all but token forces from the area. If two thousand men are defeated, our new international support will melt away. If a few hundred are lost, well, that is war."

"Thank you, Paul-Joseph. We will vote on this later, but I agree with you. International support is vital. I think that we can apply again for UN membership by autumn. Finally, I wish to announce that we have hit General Sloerill hard. His base was destroyed and he cannot take action against us for months." Bouget saw Adèle Chantilly's lips twitch, and he wondered if, perhaps through her husband, she knew the raid had failed. Almost two hundred highly trained men were dead or captured, Sloerill's ammunition supply was intact and Sloerill had not even been wounded.

Two weeks later Sloerill sat in Fred Scott's room, a forty-ounce bottle of rye open between them, its level seriously depleted. Fred had accompanied a hard-eyed investigation team from Ottawa to look into the untimely death of Colonel Victor Bosch. The team had returned to Ottawa that afternoon by plane.

Fred lifted his glass. "I could have stayed home, old buddy. Your people had them flummoxed all the way. Perhaps a long time from now you'll tell me what really went down."

Instead of replying, George took a long pull at his drink. He had only testified that he'd fired Bosch for incompetence and had had him driven back to the Guards to pack.

Zuke had stuck to his story of the shooting through hours of grilling. The sniper couldn't speak, he'd been killed resisting arrest. A special coroner had testified that the wound in Bosch's head was consistent with a .303 rifle bullet and that the damaged bullet, with traces of blood on it, found by Colonel Anderson, had been fired by the sniper's weapon. Only Clay Anderson and a CIA agent in Ottawa knew who had recommended the "highly qualified forensic medical expert".

"They weren't happy," Scott warned with a slight slur. "The report should have read that after a short and occasionally fair trial the guilty bastard was taken out and . . . hanged."

Sloerill roused himself slightly. "Will they send another Bosch?"

"Doubt it, ol' buddy. Not safe. I think the message got through." He peered at his friend over the rim of the glass. "At the risk of sounding motherly, why not take some leave? Get away. Get laid. Do both. Chantilly can handle this mare's nest for a week."

"Soon," Sloerill promised. "Too much to do now."

"Screw that, George. Look, come back with me tomorrow. There are females in Ottawa you wouldn't believe. I guarantee you height, weight and tit size, in bed one hour from touchdown. Deal?"

"With your morals you should have been a pilot. Besides, I don't think I'd feel safe in Ottawa. Especially now."

Scott sat up slowly. "What are you up to, you silly bastard?"

"The new officer rotation policy. Three months' active service up front, then off to something safe. I've been exempted because they no doubt hope the ALQ will get me."

"No, they're scared of you. Come on. Your people need a rest, and speaking of scared, that raid shook up our Ottawa heroes. Troops are everywhere. They're sending an extra battalion for your HQ protection."

"Answer the question, Fred. Is this policy official?"

"Sure. The war won't last forever, you know. Look, this has nothing to do with the screw-Sloerill gang. We're short of people with combat experience, so we're gonna shoot as many officers through the dirty end of things as possible."

George's eyes were now fully focussed. "And the men? The officers get rotated. What about the men?"

"Oh, we pull them out too, say in a year, probably less."

"Pulled out to what, a staff job? Zuke will love that."

"Don't be bitter. They get a rest,. Some get posted as instructors, the rest get slotted into battalions guarding places like Come-By-Chance in Newfoundland. Safe, George—unless they drink too much Newfie screech. Let somebody else pull the can a while."

"Somebody may be pulling two cans when my resignation hits the Minister's desk next week."

"Not funny, George!" Scott growled, his face serious, the once friendly eyes glinting. "We didn't ask for this damn war, but now we've got it, we're going to use it for the long-term good of the military."

"I'm too tired to argue, Fred, but our 'miracle' is the fact that most of my people are bilingual. A lot of the time we speak nothing but French. We talk to the locals and we listen to them. Break this gang up and you're in deep doo doo. Imagine a corporal from BC going up to a unilingual French-Canadian and saying 'Hi, Frenchie, seen any froggie patrols today?' We'd be up to our ass in ALQ in a week.

"We don't want to go to Newfoundland, Fred. We want to go home, and we can end this war faster than anybody. Talk to Clay. Ask him what rotation did to the Americans in Nam. I'd hoped we were smarter than that."

"What makes you think you can pick up your marbles and go home, old buddy? This is a war. No rebates. No money-back guarantee."

George got up unsteadily. "I've created p-precedents before. Cancel the policy or cancel the war or start watching the news. This isn't a game. This stupidity will kill people—p-prolong the war. I do not ac-accept ro-rotation," he enunciated carefully. "What I want is *unit* leave, ten days R&R and four days training. Better sell that, B-Gen Frederick Scott, b-because if you can't, I won't be around to see what ha-happens." George walked out, stepping as if between eggs.

When the door closed Fred investigated his glass with great care and decided that it was empty. So, he found a few minutes later, was the bottle. He cradled it in his arms, slowly leaned forward and fell asleep.

They had no chance to talk until Scott left for Ottawa the next day. As they shook hands at the airport, Fred squinted a very bloodshot eye. "I seem to recall a long awful rambling discussion last night. Please tell me it didn't happen."

"I may not have been overly coherent but I meant what I said. Every slurred word."

"Retire?"

"Quit. Press conferences. Publicity. Blood of our soldiers sacrificed, et cetera. CBC and CNN are here on-base. I can be very noisy, Fred."

"Threats aren't very popular up there now, George, and you need more enemies like I need another aching head."

George stared impassively at him. Fred sighed. "Once more, old buddy, I'll see what I can do, but if you want this to fly, it will take money, lots of it. So better get the Minister on-side fast because a hell of a lot of people will be telling him we can't afford it."

"What we can't afford, Fred, is the war stretching out an extra month or six."

"Yeah, but try and prove it will. Shit, George. If you'd joined the Israeli army you'd be ten thousand clicks away and out of my hair. Take care, sport." He went up the steps into the small jet, walking carefully. Minutes later, George watched the plane take off.

The old general was back at the barn where the war had started. He and his aide stood at the sagging doors. The roof had not survived the winter. The hay inside was tumbled and black, the sandbags scattered as they'd been the day they'd moved to Quebec City.

"It was a mistake to come, Jacques. This is a sad place, but we might have left it in better condition."

"It will be a shrine!" the younger man exclaimed. "I will order it restored. Our freedom began here, and we must preserve it so that our descendants will never forget."

The general climbed into the waiting staff car wearily. "A shrine? We will be lucky if it does not become a landfill site."

"Ah, no, General. This barn was the first stone in our temple of independence."

"Tcha, Jacques. The men who knew this place are dead. The new men do not care where the orders come from that kill them. No. Let it go. Think what fun people will have trying to find it in a hundred years. Experts will argue the merits of this field over another. Never try to make history too easy, mon ami. Leave challenges for historians."

They rode in silence for a few kilometres. "Is the war nearly over?" Jacques asked. "We are stronger, but so are they. Will they leave us alone?"

The general let out a long, slow breath. "You are not so confident then as you were?" he teased gently. "Where is my fire-eating aide that would march to Vancouver?" He patted the young man's knee. "Never mind. It is an old man's joke. I am pleased that you have learned war is not the game that films show."

Jacques nodded. "I have learned, but will it end soon?"

"I doubt if even the Canadians know. Sloerill will be reinforced. Our peace overtures make us look weak and encourage Canada to demand more. We have offered over half of the South Shore as a corridor, yet they hesitate. We must rely on help from the Americans."

"Why would they help us?"

"They want things from both Canada and Quebec. I believe Canada wants all of Quebec and the Americans want them to have only a corridor. I will bet on the Americans. If I am wrong we are doomed, Jacques. As I said at the beginning, we cannot win a real war against Canada. The fools in Quebec City hear some dictator of a fourth-rank African nation say he *may* recognize us and they have an orgasm. If the war goes on much longer this will be a desert. Remember three years ago, Jacques? There were twenty farms within two kilometres of our barn. Now there are none."

After seeing off Fred Scott, Sloerill returned to the bunker, pacing back and forth behind the operational maps and displays until Chantilly pointedly asked if there was a particular operation he was interested in.

George's mood soured even more at the reminder of Sergeant-Major Grigson. He growled a reply and went out to inspect the base, seeing only places that not been repaired or reconstruction going too slowly. From the bunker roof he stared at the blackened circle that had been the Kerner home. Silently he wheeled and went to his quarters.

From a bureau drawer he pulled a bottle of rye from under a pile of shirts. The level was across the middle of the label. He set it down on his desk and poured a four-ounce shot into a tumbler.

Glass in hand he stared at the framed picture Betty had sent at Christmas. It was a pinup. She lay on a sloping sand bar in a bikini, dark hair spread in a fan on the white beach towel under her.

George moved the picture to the left of his desk as he sat. He took a pad of writing paper from a drawer and stared at it for several minutes before picking up his pen.

"Dearest Betty," he wrote carefully and slowly. "I'm looking at your picture and wondering if you can send me a trick one. You know the kind. You tilt them and the bikini disappears. What I really want is a picture that when I tilt it, you'll appear." The thought brought a faint smile to his grim mouth and he began to write faster.

In Cowansville a jeep pulled into Etienne Messier's tree-lined drive at dusk and stopped to let out Peter Forbes. After a word to his driver he went to the door and rang. The butler opened it and ushered him into Etienne's living room.

"Peter. It is so pleasant to see you. I have not had an opportunity to salute your promotion properly. Come. This calls for a very special reserve port."

The butler brought a decanter. Messier poured two glasses and they sat in wing chairs. A light wind brought a scent of long-ago burned wood into the room from the dark fireplace.

"I must say since you called this afternoon, I have wondered as to your purpose. I am told that your Guardsmen are no longer a problem. You have obviously taken hold effectively. A nice change from . . . before."

"It wasn't much," Peter shrugged. "I have some very good men. All I do is turn their natural talents towards winning the war. No, the reason I called is that I'm worried about our mutual friend."

"I was afraid that would be it. You have noticed, of course, that he has again withdrawn into himself, into fortress Sloerill?"

"Where he keeps a good supply of booze."

"That is less important. What concerns me is that he is again the silent armoured man he was before the war. He began to withdraw when Bosch arrived. Now he hides behind his walls. He is afraid of himself again, and he was deeply wounded by the lying that was done to cover up the way Bosch died. He believes it violated the principles that have guided him throughout this terrible war and when principles fail, what is left? Cover up the death of Bosch—I would have proclaimed it!"

"We all had a hand in that," Peter said, uncomfortably. "I'm not happy about my part in it, even though it was done, like most coverups, in order to preserve the perceived greater good."

"For me, I have no doubts at all," Messier said firmly. "When Clay came to me I did whatever he asked, and I would have done more had it been required. George is too important for one such as Bosch to harm."

"I agree, Etienne, though at times I do wonder why an American spook is willing to expend so much energy on protecting George."

"And I but give thanks that he does. However, I do not think that you came to discuss Bosch or Colonel Anderson."

"True. How much do you know about this woman of his in London? Betty Marsh."

"Officially, only what George tells me. John has also spoken about her to me. I understand they write frequently. I would say that it seems to be almost . . . serious?"

"Could you amplify that almost a bit?"

"For George to commit himself to a woman now is, I believe, impossible. It would mean coming out of his shell. Before l'affaire Bosch he could have done it. Not now. What do you know about her?"

"Sir Barney Sandford in my London office had her unofficially vetted. She seems sound. Good family. Father teaches economics at Oxford. Mother ran for Parliament, got elected but broke with Maggie over Europe after one term. Mrs Marsh married a soldier who was killed in Northern Ireland.

"Guts seem to run in the family. Several years ago she was on a flight that was highjacked. She put herself between the terrorist and the man he intended to shoot, persuaded him not to be rash, and once they were safe on the ground played up to the chap until the co-pilot could lay him out with a fire extinguisher."

"Pardon me, but I cannot see a problem here. She sounds admirable in every way. George has often said that being a soldier's wife was harder than being a soldier. On the other hand, broaching the subject to him now would take a man braver than I. If I may ask, why do you now become involved?"

"Because she wrote and asked. I might mention that she wrapped Sir Barney around her finger, which says a great deal. She knows that Bosch was killed and that George was somehow involved. She wants to visit him."

"It sounds like a good idea to me. He must be distracted from his present mood or he will destroy himself."

"I'm afraid she'll distract him too much. After all, he has a war to run." Peter looked at his watch. "Must be off. Thanks for the port and advice." He stood up. "I think I may take a hand—but in his present mood, he may not thank me."

"He will eventually, Peter." Messier walked him to the door. "I can only think it will help him . . . pull out of this depression. We need George—ah—how do you English say—firing on all cylinders again."

From long practice, Etienne turned off the hall lights before opening the door so as not to outline his departing guest. "Think about this, Peter. George is a strong-willed man. In personal matters he tends to withdraw from challenge because of his temper. He needs a woman to complement his strength and also to challenge it. Her courage seems clear, so does her will. I believe that she would be good for him."

Peter gave a cheerful wave as he started down the steps. "I hope you're right, Etienne. See you on the road." It was the standard farewell in the brigade.

Sloerill finished his letter on the eighth page. The paper covered with his aggressive scrawl. He signed his name and lay down on the bed to re-read what he had written, shaking his head. Once more he'd failed to express what he wanted to tell her, what he wanted her to know. Before he finished, the letter sagged in his hand and he began to snore gently, his face turned to the picture on the desk. The bottle still stood by the bed, the level reduced for once by just one drink, most of which remained in the glass.

CHAPTER NINETEEN

Leave

In Messier's living room, George and Etienne were talking over a bottle of ten-year-old Lafontan Armagnac. The general, sprawled in his chair, feet almost in the fireplace, was describing his fight with Fred Scott two weeks before. Messier looked puzzled.

"George, I do not understand your concern. You have fought many times to protect your men. Now you will resign over giving them a vacation or . . . leave? I also think that if this matter is as important to those in Ottawa as you say, then General Scott needs more time. Wait a month, to the middle of June. It is quiet here now."

"Quiet overall," Sloerill corrected. "It isn't quiet for patrols that get shot at. I'm not against leave, only rotation."

"What is the difference between going together and going a few at a time?"

"Under rotation men don't come back," George said wearily. "In six months you wouldn't recognize anyone in uniform around here. They haven't enough French-speaking soldiers to replace our men, so we'd lose contact with the people we're trying to protect."

"Ah. That I understand."

"In addition, it would probably prolong the war by a year. Think of the cost in extra deaths to Canada and Quebec."

"Can you prove it will extend the war?"

"Look, in Viet Nam, under rotation, men did a full year of fighting. That set them against the officers who were only in action for six months. Units never got fully operational. A third of the men were new and didn't know the drill, a third were effective, and a third were watching over their shoulder, because they were on down time."

"Down time, George? Remember, I am a civilian."

"The last few months before a man goes home. He wants to live, so he doesn't take chances. Canada's never used that system in a war—so far. It will destroy the man-officer relationship. Ah well."

He swirled the dark liquid in the snifter, staring at the oily patterns and drank. "I'll give Fred another two weeks. Why don't you work the political side? Rotation would make your job bloody difficult, if not impossible."

"I will, George, now that I understand it."

"Good. By the way, isn't the population mix changing out here?"

"Yes, we're about fifty-fifty English to French now. A few months ago it was almost seventy-thirty. English refugees move on to relatives out west or in Ontario. Our population is growing, but the late-blooming federalists are almost all French-Canadian. Things are not well over there. The benefits of Canada are more clearly seen than in the first heady days of independence. The balance is good, but those who leave . . ."

"Why the hesitation? I thought we were a bit overpopulated."

"We were—we are, but the English who left were Montréalais. Even with the corridor, they could not go back home. They go west and spread anti-Quebec feelings like sour seeds that will raise a crop that may yet choke us all to death."

"The first crop was planted over thirty years ago when the FLQ began planting bombs."

"True, George, but do we not agree that with so much blame on both sides it is fruitless to point to one and say 'you started this'?"

"I suppose, but the separatists always said Quebec could do whatever it wanted. Anyone who said separation would hurt, even a bit, was called a traitor. Now who was right? Who got shafted by the rhetoric?"

Messier sat up straighter. "Is this George Sloerill speaking? Do you remember Canadians booing 'O Canada' sung in French? Racists spitting on the Quebec flag in Ontario? Prentice?—Nationalists, and I am one, saw that for all the talk of bilingualism, the French language would only be allowed so long as it did not threaten the English."

"I think you're wrong, Etienne. Some things don't make headlines but last long after the racists are history. Provincial courts are going bilingual. Thousands of kids are in French immersion. It was working until a few people in Quebec City got greedy and asked for more than Canada could give. When they didn't get it they decided—what was that wonderful phrase—'to hold a knife to English Canada's throat to make them negotiate seriously'. Remember the union that tried that in one of your plants? You broke them."

"I know, George, but progress was too slow, and the young are impatient. Also, there was another force pressing for independence, the force of demographics."

"Come on, Etienne. The English were bailing out, and never in history have so many Québecois claimed French as their mother tongue as today."

"But we have the lowest birth rate in North America. Without immigration, our population will decline in real numbers within thirty years. On the other hand, *with* immigration Quebec will cease to be French almost as soon, and the Quebec you and I love, George, will be no more."

"With people like Prentice, it may be no more anyway. Your scenario is only a possibility. Quebec is losing a war, and in losing, may lose everything. Ottawa will turn the corridor into an economic marvel as an example to the separatists—the way West Germany subsidized West Berlin—and with the economy in ruins and their farms abandoned, Quebecers will vote with their feet and rejoin Canada, a family at a time."

"I believe," Messier said quietly, "that rather than do that, Quebec will join the United States."

"Who's going to follow a politician who says 'OK, plan two is to learn English and join the USA?' Even if they do, the Americans won't allow French as an official language. In a generation we'll be unilingual English except for the folklore crowd doing traditional dances and songs on St Jean Baptiste Day. Ask the Cajuns in Louisiana."

"Perhaps, but I know some of those in power, and they would rather lose everything quickly to the Americans than crawl back to beg Canada for forgiveness."

"Why would the Yanks want them? Yesterday we took Quebec's northern hydro dams. Canada has agreed to build an undersea power line from Newfoundland to Nova Scotia that will bring power from Churchill Falls to the Maritimes. Quebec has lost those resources."

"Do you think Canada will take all of Quebec back?"

"I hope not, Etienne. I hope the war ends before Canadians put too big a price on peace. It may be too late, but there's a chance. I believe that after a few years of independence, Quebecers will vote to come back. I still hope Canada will offer generous terms—but I'm pessimistic, Etienne. I'm not even sure why I'm fighting now."

Messier replenished Sloerill's glass. "You are fighting, my friend, for that hope just expressed. What I hear is the voice of a tired man. Your ideas are still valid, mon cher ami. Now, let us turn from this subject. Permit me to intrude on your private life. Your friend the war prevented me from meeting, Betty Marsh. Tell me about her."

Six days later, on June fifth, the new airport on the flatland north of the Abercorn base was bustling with troops in expectation of a visit from the Prime Minister. Peter Forbes's Guardsmen were scattered through the hills as security. They also formed the honour guard drawn up in two ranks in front of the half-finished hangar, divided into two fifty-man guards with the Regimental and Queen's Colours between them. On their right stood the massed bands of the Guards and FMR. A bus pulled into the parking area and stopped. The Toronto Scottish and Black Watch pipes had arrived.

In full dress uniform, the Drum-Major (Black Watch) stepped out, followed by the pipe-major (Toronto Scottish). "Where'll you tune up, Art?" he asked, giving his mace an experimental twirl.

"I'll take the boys into the hangar, Angus. Back in ten."

"Plenty of time, Pipey. He'll be late. Politicians are always bloody well late."

Twenty-eight kilted pipers followed the pipe-major into the hangar, scattering along the walls, and began to tune, listening critically to the eerie sounds bouncing back at them from the metal walls, adjusting the drones, fingering their chanters. Pipey fussed around them, never satisfied, clucking and hissing at every discordant note.

"Art! Plane coming in," the drum major called. Reluctantly the pipers assembled in front of the drums, preening themselves in their full-dress finery. The hodden grey uniforms of the Tor Scots had been flown in. The new Black Watch uniforms had been partly paid for by the government and partly by a subscription among "their" civilians. The other bands, in khaki uniforms with regimental caps, made enviously disparaging remarks.

As the government plane taxied forward, the official welcoming party moved up to the ramp. It consisted of Armand Chantilly, John Ashworth and the four battalion commanders, with George Sloerill and Etienne Messier in the lead.

When the plane stopped, Sloerill and Messier went inside to greet the Prime Minister. A few minutes later, as the cameras rolled, the man himself emerged on the platform and stood to attention as the guard presented arms. The band played the general salute.

Fred Scott jogged George on the arm as they stood to attention, hands up to their caps. "You owe me a double, George. So does the guard commander if he's still able to walk after Pittman finishes jumping on his balls."

Like his friend, George could talk on parade without moving his lips. "Screw off, Fred. It's a perfect parade."

"Guard commander forgot to dip colours to the PM," Fred hissed. "Too late, old buddy. Not good. I can hear Pittman grinning."

The music stopped and their hands came down. "Guards only dip to royalty and Guards generals," Sloerill muttered as he stepped forward to escort the PM on his inspection. The Prime Minister shook hands with the CO's and stepped into a gleaming jeep driven by an impeccably dressed Sergeant Zukrowski to be driven on a cursory tour of inspection as the pipes played "Green Hills of Tyrol".

After the inspection the official party drove to Base Abercorn. Sloerill took them to the briefing centre. It accommodated up to sixty people, and in the middle, below floor level, was a six-metre-long scale model of the operations area from the Richelieu River in the west to Lake Massawippi in the east and from the U.S. border to a point twenty kilometres north of the autoroute. Sloerill went to the dais at one end and pressed a button. At once, the model lit up in coloured lights showing regimental headquarters and supporting units.

"What you see here is the part of the proposed corridor that we control or dominate," George began. "The situation at present is, the ALQ have effectively ceded all territory south of the autoroute. They have virtually abandoned the city of St Jean, except the recruit training base and military college. We have not occupied the territory because we don't have the men. We hold a hundred-and-fifty-kilometre line only because we have the advantage of interior lines and superior Intelligence. Our other advantage is that the ALQ are reluctant to lose men fighting for an area they know they'll have to give up.

"Later M Messier will brief you on the civilian side of things. At the moment it's relatively quiet, and that's the way I want to keep it. We get a few cross-border raids and some bombs. However, my Intelligence Section, run by Colonel Anderson, tells me that these are not militarily significant. This maquette is used by units to learn or relearn an area before moving into it. Men may spend up to two hours a week here."

"Can't you do the same thing with a helicopter ride?" Pittman asked.

"Not really, sir. I can't airlift whole companies, and avgas costs more than plaster of Paris.

"Now, you can see troop locations on the model. Moving from west to east, you can see the FMR, Guards, Black Watch and Tor Scots. Red lights indicate battalion headquarters; blue lights, company HQ's; and pinpoint lights are platoons. Support weapons are in orange, artillery in green and armour in white. If you wish to ask a question, press the button on the arm of your chair."

The visitors watched the flickering display without stopping it. Sloerill stepped off the dais. "Next, gentlemen, comes the underground command post or CP, the nerve centre of the operation. It can only accommodate five visitors at a time. A word of warning: the bunker mascot is a cat named Burlap. She has no fear of human feet whatever and frequently comes to stand on them. Please be careful where you step."

Sloerill won his laugh and led them away with General Pittman bringing up the rear. He had not smiled, and he wondered who had tipped off Sloerill that the Prime Minister liked cats.

Before the formal mess dinner that night, George returned to the CP. To his surprise, the Prime Minister, General Pittman and Fred Scott came with him. They entered the dark ops room and took chairs behind the duty officer, Armand Chantilly. He waved to the Prime Minister, whom he knew well, but paid no further attention to the visitors.

As reports came in, the radio operators called out locations to the men and women who kept the map displays up to date.

"Patrol of six Sugar Delta Tango's moving towards ARK," one signaller reported, and a flag was placed on the map near Bromont.

"Ark?" the PM whispered to George.

"A codeword, sir. It's a small farm with two horses, two cows, some goats, chickens, a bunch of dogs, cats and two geese."

"Don't you ever use map references?" Pittman asked dryly.

"As little as possible, sir. Most locations are couched in local references to confuse the other side who have the same maps but who lack English cultural background."

Pittman was about to reply when George held up his hand. "Excuse me, sir." He tapped Armand on the shoulder. "What about Whisky Bravo?"

Chantilly checked his watch. "We'll try to contact them now."

"Perhaps I can explain, sir." Fred Scott moved closer to the PM. General Pittman leaned over to hear, keeping an eye on Sloerill.

"I wish you would," said the Prime Minister. "I can see people are looking concerned. Is this a big operation?"

"Not really, sir." Fred spoke quietly. "The new ALQ commander in Granby began to act dedicated from day one, sending out fighting patrols and ordering harassing fire from his artillery. General Sloerill tries to discourage that sort of activity."

"What do we do, send a note asking him to cease and desist?" Pittman's voice stayed carefully neutral.

"That comes later," Scott replied. "The first step is to mount a small raid by a commando team which destroys a power line, ammo dump, bridge or on occasion, if the ALQ doesn't get the message, a headquarters. The teams are evacuated by helicopter.

"Etienne Messier then sends a message to remind the ALQ that this territory is Canadian and that their attacks hurt civilians. He points out how vulnerable they are to counter-measures and suggests that they stop."

"And that works?" the PM demanded. "A small raid and a note?"

"The last two *small* raids cost the ALQ seventy-three casualties and took out their main power line to Sherbrooke for two weeks. Tonight's score should be equally impressive. The orders were to hit hard."

"Whisky Bravo, this is Tango Charlie. Any pigeons? Over." The operator had been repeating the call for almost two minutes.

"Why don't they answer?"

Sloerill turned to General Pittman. "They may not hear us. It may be too dangerous even to listen. They may be dead." His voice was sharp.

"Whisky Bravo, this is Tango Charlie, any pigeons? Over."

"Tango Charlie, this is Whisky Bravo. The last supper is prepared. Two guests may refuse your invitation. Over."

Chantilly consulted his code book. "Tell them dinner is at 0400."

The Prime Minister was leaning forward with interest. He was actually listening to the voice of a soldier behind enemy lines. It brought the war close. "Can you translate that, General Scott?"

"Yes, sir. 'Pigeons' asks for a report . . . carrier pigeons—messages. The reply stated that they were ready for evacuation but two patrol members are wounded."

"Why wait until 0400 to evacuate them?" Pittman demanded.

"The patrol operates on a five-hour time advance, sir. They will rendezvous with the wokkas at 2300."

"And the reference to the last supper?"

"More misdirection, sir. It sounds like a meeting with an agent or some kind of betrayal. We play every angle so the ALQ can't rely on anything they overhear nor trust their interpretation of what we say." Sloerill looked at his watch.

"I apologize, gentlemen, I was concerned about that patrol. Dinner is waiting." He had invited several civil council members and five officers from each unit to meet the Prime Minister. Afterwards he would thankfully hand the visitors over to Messier.

As the group left the Ops Room, Fred Scott moved closer to Arm-and Chantilly and they began to talk in low tones.

The party was a rouser. General Pittman and General Vinet stayed after the civilians left, and some time after midnight Pittman introduced the mess to an old RCAF game called "Bombing Run".

When that began to pall, General Vinet got everyone going on a game named "Grease the Gun". On the command "load" a man lay on a blanket on a long, tipped-up table, a match in one hand, the striker in the other. Piled cushions provided a landing pad and the human cannonball, once launched by sliding the blanket up the table, had to strike the match in mid air. Only Peter Forbes and Clay Anderson had succeeded by the time the party ran out of steam at four in the morning.

Arriving at work a few hours later, Sloerill looked in on John Ashworth who was sitting very erect behind his desk, wearing his forage cap. "I hope you have mess damage forms ready," Sloerill said, ignoring the cap's "I am not here" signal. "Last night may have set a new record."

Ashworth groaned. "I know. What broke up the furniture? I went to sleep in a dignified sort of way and when I woke up the mess looked as if it had been bombed."

"It had. In 'Bombing Run' a lot of folding chairs are dropped from a great height and senior officers get pelted with lettuce."

"Glad I missed it. How do you want your coffee, and have you seen Clay?"

George groaned. "One question at a time, no hard choices. You didn't 'miss it', you were draped over a fireplace fender. I want black coffee, and I don't care about Clay."

"I may have led him astray with the second port decanter." John poured a steaming mug. "On the other hand, he did down three Wawa's with some mad Highlanders."

The Wawa or Wahwahron (Rifle regiments called it "Green Death") consisted of an ounce of vodka and two of creme de menthe. Sloerill shuddered. "If he hasn't surfaced by 0830, send a search party."

The office door banged open and Fred Scott breezed in, the missing American in tow. "Morning all!" he boomed. "Is this yours? I caught him trying to climb a radio mast after the party and took him home."

Clay seized a mug of coffee gratefully while Fred continued, relentlessly loud. "I've a feeling that any spy caught today will have to walk in, confession typed, and sit patiently until someone figures out how handcuffs work." He looked at the malevolent eyes glaring at him. "I'll be back when you're feeling better—say next month?"

Clay winced as the door closed noisily. "Champagne," he grunted, opening the file cabinet nearest to John's desk.

"You're mad." Ashworth shuddered. "But . . . oh no!" Clay fished a bottle from the drawer. "My God! You're not going to drink it, are you?"

Clay opened the champagne and reached for a glass. "We all are, Junior. Ah. Here's the Bromo, now hand me the salt."

George and John watched in horror as the CIA man dumped two capsful of Bromo Seltzer into a tall glass, added a pinch of salt and gingerly poured in about a cup of champagne. Before the explosive mixture could erupt from the glass, he drank it down.

He sat there for a long moment, then smiled. "Ahhhh! I got that from a very Guardee major in London. Coldstream Guards to be exact." He got to his feet. "Thanks for the hospitality, gents. See you on the road." With barely a stagger he left the room.

"I couldn't," Ashworth mumbled, but Sloerill was already reaching for the Bromo.

By the time they saw the Prime Minister off that afternoon, their hangovers were long gone. The staff car stopped beside the one finished hangar on the field. Sloerill got out and went inside to an area that had been curtained off for a VIP lounge. The Prime Minister was there. General Pittman wasn't.

"Before we meet the press, General Sloerill," the PM beckoned him closer, "I want your opinion on something. M Messier and I went over it this morning—I can see what a help he's been here—but now I want the military view of a man who knows the area. As you know, we're committed to an Ontario–New Brunswick corridor. Is there a military reason why the corridor shouldn't take in the entire South Shore?"

"No sir," George replied crisply. "The problem is to administer it afterwards."

"Why? You haven't had much trouble here."

"This area was always federalist. When the fighting began most of the local separatists left and were replaced, more than replaced, by federalist refugees. The civil organization was in our hands anyway. Once we expand, it won't be that easy. There aren't many federalists there now, and the ones who are left aren't mayors of towns."

"Surely that isn't a military problem, general."

"It can be without civilian–military teamwork. Soldiers can't unify Canada. We can only make make Quebec willing to talk peace. The stronger our military position, the better you can negotiate. But the military position depends as much on how peaceful it is in our rear areas as how many tanks we have up at the sharp end."

"Of course all of this is theoretical, general. No decisions have been made. Still, you agree that we can take the area if necessary?"

Sloerill nodded slowly, although he felt he should have made more of the point that it wouldn't be as easy as the PM seemed to think.

"Fine. I want to thank you for this chance to see what's going on here. It's been highly instructive. Now, you're going to hear this later, but I want you to get it from me first. Most of the medals you put in for are approved, and I'm handing out some today. Secondly, I ordered General Pittman to send you more men—a lot more. You deserve our support, general. Frankly, it was your good news that kept us going in those early grim days. Canada will not forget what you—and your men—have done."

Having turned on the force of his personality, the PM was about to launch into a speech when he saw one of his aides signal from the door.

"Well. Come out and hear it all over again." The Prime Minister took Sloerill's arm as they stepped out into the TV lights. That night the country saw on the news a smiling PM standing between two sentries, arm in arm with the war's only real hero. They were chatting comfortably and the PM laughed at something the general said to him.

The next day George was surprised to see Fred Scott walk into the Ops Room. "Morning, Fred. Didn't you leave with the political horde yesterday?"

Scott found a seat. "Not me, old buddy. I'm your shadow till tomorrow noon."

"What happens then?" George asked suspiciously.

"A parting that's such sweet sorrow. Also, congrats on your new-found if belated ability to win friends and influence Prime Ministers. General Pittman will be walking on eggs until his staff figures out a counterploy. By the way, never mind thanking me for the note on the PM's fondness for cats. All in a day's work—"

With a perfunctory rap on the door, Clay Anderson looked in. "If you're busy, sir, this can wait."

"Come in. It seems General Scott's becoming a fixture and worse, one that expects gratitude. You told me the PM liked cats at least two hours before he did. How's the spy hunt coming?"

"As they say, sir, search parameters are narrowing. The technical boys at Langley are going crazy trying to decode messages which *may* be encrypted, filtered to destroy the voice print, then sent as a burst—backwards. I'm pinning my hopes on the information I'm leaking selectively. Unfortunately, nothing's showing up on the other side."

John Ashworth looked in. "Sorry to break up the Mafia meeting, godfather, but the new troops start arriving in twenty minutes. The control tower just called it in."

George reached for his beret. "Doesn't anything happen on time around here? They're at least an hour early."

"One hour, twenty-three minutes, to be exact. Will you give the new units your patented limited war lecture together or one at a time?"

Sloerill hesitated. "Armand can do it. I'm meeting Etienne at eleven and that just gives me time to meet the CO's."

The two new units were the Royal Winnipeg Rifles and the Governor General's Foot Guards from Ottawa, sister regiment to the Grenadiers, who usually called them the Footpads or Googly Fooglies. Both had been converted to the unique four-square configuration of Sloerill's force.

The CO's were waiting in the airport VIP lounge, accompanied by old hands Peter Forbes, Terry Gascoigne, Pierre St Pierre and Jan Berkowitz. John Ashworth made the introductions.

"General, may I present Lieutenant Colonels Thomas Barkley of the Foot Guards and Gene Frechette of the Winnipeg Rifles."

"Nice to hear a gallic name from out west," George commented in French as he shook hands with the lanky, fair-haired Rifleman.

"Sir, I'm the first in my family to speak French in fifty years," Frechette replied in the same language. "However, about half my men are from St Boniface and other French towns. I practice what I learned on my army language courses on them."

"And how about the Footpads?" Sloerill turned to Col Barkley, a smaller, intense man who reminded him of Leo Markos.

"Not bad, sir," Barkley replied in strongly accented Ottawa Valley French. "We're sixty percent bilingual. I recruited from Ottawa to Cornwall. It was slow at first, but we got the French population on side. I think my boys are ready for your limited war."

"You only think?" Sloerill asked a bit sharply. "They'd better be."

"They'll be all right, sir," Barkley insisted. "The thing is, when we first opened for recruiting as a full battalion, we got quite a few lads turning up wearing lapel buttons that read 'Save the environment, kill a frog'. We deselected those fast, but there's some hard feeling. That's why I concentrated on French-Canadian recruits."

"Glad to hear that. I'm sure you'll cope. Now, gentlemen, I haven't a great deal of time, so bear with me until tonight when we go over everything in detail. Essentially, this is what I want you to think about.

"The Footpads relieve the Black Watch tomorrow and in forty-eight hours the Highlanders will be in the air to the Maritimes. Can do, Jan?"

Berkowitz nodded quickly, as Sloerill had known he would. "The FMR will go into reserve, replaced by the Winnipeg Rifles. A week after Jan's boys leave, the FMR head to New Brunswick for their bilingual R and R. A week later when Jan comes back, the Grenadiers go, and after them the Tor Scots.

"Troops get ten days' solid leave and four days of tactics. When they get back, Guards, Watch and FMR will take two weeks of the battalion training they haven't had before. Finally, we start brigade exercises. We've been acting like independent units. It's time to start being an army."

On the way back to the command post Scott, George and Ashworth had squeezed into the back of a staff car. The air conditioning wasn't working, and the windows were open. Fred Scott wrinkled his nose.

"Shut the window, John. Something large and noisome died out there. Whew!"

Sloerill had been half dozing but roused quickly. He pointed to a line of sheet-metal roof tops belonging to a mink farm. "That's where your smell is coming from. A new factory just moved in."

"Let me tell you, I won't apply for a job. What kind of a factory smells like that?"

"An ol-factory!" George crowed. It had been years since he'd caught Fred so neatly.

"God! Open that window at once, major," Scott ordered. "OK, George, that's it. I was supposed to wait until noon, but not now. Babe Trinker's getting One Div in Ontario and as of next month I am *Major-General* Fred Scott, Officer Commanding Two Div in the Gaspé. The only reason I am not already so exalted is that I lack operational command above battalion level. Therefore, starting in two days, I take over your huge army while you, on the written order of the Minister, take three weeks' leave."

There was a tense silence in the car. "And what happens after that?" Sloerill's voice was dangerously quiet.

"Why, you come back and I go to my just reward." Fred touched his friend's arm. "Relax, old buddy. I'll run things your way. The Ottawa Mafia aren't ready to move, and when the axe falls my hand will not be on the handle. OK?"

Two days later Ashworth accompanied Sloerill to the airport. For the first time in nine months George felt superfluous. Etienne refused to speak about anything except how to care for a case of twenty-year-old claret he had sent over. Fred Scott had settled in, and much to everyone's surprise the war was still running efficiently.

A Challenger jet was waiting, gleaming silver in the late afternoon sun. Etienne, Armand and Toupée had split the leasing cost. Zuke carried on the luggage as George stood at the ramp feeling out of place. He was tanned, but his colour was sallow and uneven. He knew he needed rest, but he couldn't just sleep for three weeks, and apart from that he had no idea what to do. A suite had been reserved for him at the Park Plaza in Toronto. For two days he'd tried to call Betty, but her phone had rung unanswered.

"Still here?" George turned to find Peter Forbes behind him. "Hoped you'd be. I've a bundle of mail for my home office and since a number of the men now have relatives in Ontario, I volunteered you as postman."

Sloerill took the package. "At least Etienne sent some plonk," he grumbled. "All I get from you are errands."

"Not at all." Peter and John pushed him towards the ramp. "Wine has its uses in the proper setting, but I fancy the Guards have done you rather better than that."

George was about to ask what that meant when Zuke returned, a sly look in his normally watchful eyes. "Well, sir, have a good time and don't do nothin' I wouldn't." He saluted for the first time since the Prime Minister's departure and sauntered off to the staff car.

"There you go, George. Officially cleared for everything." Peter smiled and gave George a shove. "Now get on the bloody plane before we have to carry you."

Wordlessly George shook hands and climbed into the aircraft. Moments later the slender jet shot down the runway and swept into the air on a sharp climbing turn to the west to avoid overflying ALQ territory.

On the ground Peter checked his watch as the plane climbed into the setting sun. "In about thirty seconds I should think—unless the poor bastard fell asleep in the aisle."

"He'd better not," John Ashworth said with a grin. "He has to stay awake long enough to appreciate our hard work."

Far from asleep, George was slumped in one of the wide executive seats. His head was turned towards the window but he didn't see the ground or the clouds. Each part of his body felt like lead, so heavy that the idea of standing to remove his tunic seemed impossible. At the same time he felt as if he were floating, relieved of the weight of responsibility—the weight of lives lost because of his decisions—the mutilated—the blind. He'd sent his wounded back to a score of towns as broken memorials of the war. People no longer talked of the "frogs" rolling over or taking to the woods at the sight of a gun, but against that there was a growing tide of hate whipped up by racists like Prentice, a tide that if not stemmed would drown every politician who advocated anything less than destroying Quebec. How many of his men had died to prevent such bitterness? Given what was happening, had he been right to wage a limited war?

From the galley, Betty Marsh watched him through a gap in the curtain separating the main cabin from the bar-kitchen. Peter Forbes had called her in London three weeks ago, told her about George's leave and made it clear that he needed her. She'd agreed to come, and Peter's efficient Sir Barney Sandford had smoothed a path as if for royalty. Not the slightest hitch had occurred—or if it had, she had not been permitted to see it.

What had sustained her hope until now was the effect of George's letters and phone calls superimposed on the image of him she had from their three weeks of tentative dates and growing mutual attraction in London before the flight back to Montreal that had brought him to a war.

Watching him sit unmoving, she wondered if the man she had known and more than half fallen in love with was still there. From his letters and calls she knew that the death of Bosch was eating away his soul; that his enemies were growing stronger and more determined; and that he was questioning the reasons for the war he was so skillfully fighting—but under all the self-doubt and anxiety she had felt his determination to go on.

Was this exhausted man still determined? Could she approach him? What words—if there were any—would break through to the man she remembered? During the skyjacking she hadn't known what words to use as she'd stepped between the gunman and his intended victim, only sensed that he wanted to be saved from himself. The words had come. This time she'd have to wait until those coal-black eyes met hers to see if the man she'd come three thousand kilometres to meet was still behind them. Soundlessly she moved past the curtains and into the lounge, stopping by his chair.

"Hello?" she said tentatively, sinking to her knees on the plush rug, careful not to touch him. She had to be close, yet not so close as to make his escape (if he wanted to escape) awkward for them both, and the nearest chair was an impersonal distance away.

His eyes opened slowly, focussed, widened as he recognized her. "Betty?"

She saw a brief flicker in those dark eyes and shut her mind to the pain and fatigue in them, concentrating on the fierce spark that had flared at the moment of recognition. Now she could risk getting closer and touched his arm. "It's me, George."

He seized her arm in a crushing grip. his fingers sinking deep into her flesh. He didn't know he was hurting her, he only knew that he had to prevent this recurring dream from escaping like all the others. "Say you're here!" he demanded fiercely, his eyes locked with hers. "Say it!"

"I'm here, George," Betty said. Ignoring the pain in her arm she moved closer, turning so that her side was against his thigh, she looked up and saw the savagely tight line of his mouth soften slightly as he took in her words.

His powerful hands pulled her onto the chair with him. With one arm, Betty drew his head onto her shoulder and began to stroke the short black hair, seeing the streaks of grey that hadn't been there before. Slowly, as if fighting a set of invisible chains, George's arms went around her body and held on.

Forty minutes from takeoff, the pilot switched on the Fasten Seat Belts sign. Neither passenger noticed. Betty had felt the gradual slackening of George's tension with every minute of flight, the slow relaxation in neck muscles that had been like steel cables. She stroked his head and whispered meaningless words of comfort until as the plane began to let down, he took her face in his hands and kissed her.

"Where in hell have you been?" he growled as their lips came apart briefly. "And why wasn't I with you?"

Up front, the pilot was being told by Pearson International Air Traffic Control that he was being vectored in on a priority landing schedule. He nudged his co-pilot.

"Hey, Lee. Warn our passengers we're wheels down in ten minutes. Tell the general that for two bucks I'll park this thing a kilometre from the civic reception they laid on. If he objects to the price, I'll do it for free—but you'd better cough on the PA before you go into the lounge. It's been too quiet for a reunion someone can walk in on."

CHAPTER TWENTY

Win Some, Lose Some

George returned early in July, and his men knew at once that the ebullient, swaggering figure that strode off the plane was not a new man, it was the old one. The commander who had driven them from victory to victory and led them through a short but deadly terrorist campaign was back.

"Don't bother to get up," he announced, bursting in on Fred Scott and John Ashworth. "I just want to ask what's happening." He slapped the sandbag wall affectionately. "Kept the old wallpaper, eh? Come on, somebody. Ask me how I feel."

"How do you feel, sir?" Ashworth asked dutifully.

"Like the transmission of a racing car, fully engaged!" Sloerill bellowed. People in the hall were smiling. They hadn't heard that full-throated sound in months.

"God!" an old hand muttered. "I haven't seen him like this since the Tor Scots arrived. Now you new sods'll find out what *real* work is like."

It took George four days to get a grip on things, four days of prowling and personally inspecting every corner of his private army, testing it for strains or weaknesses. The Winnipeg Rifles and the Foot Guards were adjusting to the demands being placed on them, and every man who could was studying French. Grudgingly he admitted that *perhaps* Fred Scott hadn't done too bad a job, and called a meeting.

After listening to the reports, he leaned back. "From what you say things are going well, so let's get our ass in the grass again. You did some battalion training after your leave. Now we're going to work up brigade ops—actually, two brigades."

"Thank God," Terry Gascoigne exclaimed. "I was beginning to wonder if the largest unit that was recognized down here was the platoon."

St Pierre was more restrained. "We will need that," he agreed, "if we plan to attack someone, that is."

"We may," Sloerill said seriously. "We don't have a complete corridor yet, remember. Beyond that, who knows?"

"That 'who knows' sounds interesting." Gene Frechette looked eager. His bilingual Winnipeg men were working well with local civilians, even better with the pretty ones, and were happy warriors.

"Well, I don't want it to go beyond this room," George began, "but leave was quite an experience . . . I didn't mean that!" he bellowed as the room erupted in coarse laughter.

"I lost a small fortune when you came back tanned," Chantilly said. "I had bet you wouldn't see the sun at all."

"I think we might wait until we have met the lady before making such judgements," St Pierre gently chided them.

"What I'm trying to say," George continued with a grateful smile, "is that the civilian attitudes I found scared me silly. Betty and I did some sightseeing. Everywhere we went, I was the man who'd shafted Quebec and fought the damned frogs to a standstill."

"Did you mention my name?" Chantilly asked easily, but his eyes glittered a bit.

"I mentioned everyone's name, but they're stirred up. In one interview the reporter spent half an hour trying for an anti-French statement, tossing out gems like 'Isn't it true, general, that French terrorists are killing English refugees?' Dear God! I damned near punched his teeth out, but Betty had coached me, so to stop him, I only noted his excellent physical condition and wondered why he hadn't joined up. Fast end to interview.

"We can do something about it. Ask your men when they write home to mention how well they get along with Quebecers, talk about their loyalty. That's it, gentlemen. Oh, Toupée, Gene? Stick around. I'm planning a little land grab out east, and I want you to handle it."

The next day Sloerill briefed Clay Anderson on the Canadian anti-French climate in case there was something he could do.

"That's out of my department, sir. By the way, I wish to congratulate you and the future Mrs Sloerill on your engagement."

"Thanks, Clay. It's like one of those old war romances. She'll be coming back in August, just before the wedding. Etienne's best man—and I want you to watch him."

"Etienne?"

"Damn right. He and Ashworth want to invite the entire cabinet, half of NDHQ, all local officers down to lieutenant, plus most of the local councils. If Montreal weren't in ALQ hands he'd probably book the Forum for our reception."

"OK, sir, I'll watch, but I'm not sure I'll squeal on him."

"Not you too!" George groaned. "Just a *quiet* wedding, Clay."

"Seriously, sir, you should reconsider that. Remember, your scalp is still up for grabs, and what have you done for them lately? The ALQ won't give you a fight, so let the wedding do some PR. War hero weds on field of battle. As long as the public's on your side they can't touch you."

Sloerill shook his head. "No, and I order you not to 'take steps' as you might put it. With that line you could persuade Betty to hold the wedding on Parliament Hill in the nude. New topic. Your spy?"

"Still there, sir. I just can't get a handle on him or her. I have quite a few bits and pieces, but they don't fit together into a picture."

"Well, as you say, he or she isn't really hurting us so far as we can tell. Anything else?" He noticed that Clay was less forthcoming than usual.

"Well, sir. I understand that there's a certain curiosity about why the CIA is so involved in protecting one Canadian B/Gen."

"The subject has been mentioned."

"My government's primary interest is a corridor to keep Canada intact no matter what else goes down. Langley thinks that keeping you in one piece is the best way to get the corridor. Nobody told me that watching your non-unified back would be this much work. Even so, sir, it's been fun and a pleasure."

"Why thank you, Clay. I guess I haven't made your job easier."

"Amen, sir. Amen. You see, you think they're just after you. I figured it had to be more than that, and had Langley look into it. Now, when

Hellyer became Minister of National Defence in the sixties, he paid the usual visit to Washington, where, according to rumour, he may have gotten the unified bug. The idea was General MacArthur's. He faded away, but after his ideas got shot down in Congress, disciples like General Haig might have influenced Hellyer to try an all-marching-all-singing-all-dancing unified system. If it worked in Canada, it might be sold to Congress.

"In any event, you proved that unification doesn't work. The hundred and forty-two nations that studied unification agreed. The Israelis were downright pointed. They said *they* needed an army that could fight. Your top brass were in deep shit and decided to be stubborn. In my experience people trying to defend bad ideas tend to be nastier than most. *That's* why you—and this brigade—are enemy number one."

"So what can they do—if I keep winning?"

"Not much, but they have to discredit you and what you've done. As the war winds down desperation may set in. They might try to get me yanked—or get my job specs changed."

"Should I be reading between the lines here?"

"Nossir. I'll spell it out. If my role changes that's between me and Langley, but unless I'm specifically forbidden to continue with SAPS, you get that as a freebie."

"SAPS?"

"The Sloerill Ass Protection System." Clay's face was serious. "The initials are on a sign in my office. If it disappears, and I'm saying this under my current orders, the rules have changed and you're on your own."

Le Ministre de la Guerre was wet and unhappy. For two hours he had walked in the rain behind a cortège from the Assemblée Nationale up past the Citadel and out onto the historic plain where the State of Quebec had buried its most famous general.

It had been his dying wish to have his aide buried beside him. Bouget had considered that two coffins would detract from the impressive ceremony. The aide had been quietly buried the day before.

Now the old general's replacement stood across the desk in the baking office. There was no air conditioning; power was rationed for Quebecers so that Americans in New York could remain cool. July had been hot and dry. August promised to be hotter and wet.

Already the Minister missed the old general. He had understood politics. This new firebrand did not.

"And I tell you, general, the cabinet will tell you—President *Bouget* will tell you, the corridor must be abandoned. We cannot defend it!"

"But we can make them pay for it!" General Legrand insisted. "They can pay in blood for every kilometre they steal from us."

"And we will pay double," the Minister said wearily. His legs ached from the long walk and he sat down. "What are you doing about anti-aircraft defence?" The old general had died when his jet had flown into a mountain trying to evade a Canadian CF-18.

"As my paper said, Minister, the best anti-aircraft defence is a fighter plane. We must have more."

"We can't afford them. What we can afford are ground-to-air missiles. We really don't have the money for them either, we pay double for military supplies now, but at least they're cheaper than new planes. What is the current military situation?"

"Sherbrooke and Granby are strong. Sloerill is back from leave and our Intelligence people say he is getting married. Perhaps that will make him less ambitious."

The minister knew from experience that the effect of marriage was usually the opposite. He said nothing. Legrand was brave, but war required more than courage. He sneezed and rang for his secretary. Perhaps she would know of a store that still had a supply of antihistamines.

Under Fred Scott the corridor had been extended to the Maine–Quebec border. Now Sloerill intended to start isolating the city of Sherbrooke. He had two big infantry brigades. Armand Chantilly's "1st Guards Brigade" (Grenadier Guards, Foot Guards and Tor Scots) guarded the originally held territory. The "1st Rifle Brigade" (Black Watch, FMR and Winnipeg Rifles) in the east, under the command of Acting Brigadier Gene Frechette, began to expand north towards Sawyerville and Island Brook.

Unwilling to command from a desk (although more and more he had to), Sloerill had flown to the site of the coming battle. When he got there, the Rifles had taken Sawyerville, and the FMR, near the Maine border, were about to attack St Mathias. Colonel St Pierre gave his orders and came across the stony slope to sit beside George on a pine-covered knoll.

"It will be half an hour before we engage. The brush is so thick here that only a snake can move quickly." He sat down and stretched luxuriously on the thick bed of fallen needles. "I indicated that I would be pleased if an attack could be made by 1400."

"You indicated, did you," George grumbled. "The FMR must be the only parliamentary regiment in Canada. Cromwell would have loved you."

"I doubt it," St Pierre said tartly. "He was un anglais. You order. I explain, ask questions and encourage debate. It takes longer, but I have not heard complaints about our success. As you know, for my Fusiliers the way is not so clear-cut as with the others."

"The men I've spoken to seem keen enough."

"Oh, they are keen, but to answer the question you did not quite ask, we are well but not happy."

"Does this move bother them? Do they feel another regiment should be doing it?"

"Ah, non. We are proud to be selected." St Pierre smiled. "The Guards are fine for airport security and pretty ceremonies. When you need men in the bush, you choose les Fusiliers."

"Then why aren't they happy? You and I haven't had a chance for a good talk in some time, Toupée."

"It is the war. There is no firm aim. The men analyze every speech, every phrase for hidden meaning. They decide what the speech said, then ask me if they are right. I do not know how to answer. Too often they suspect that Canada really wants all of Quebec back."

"And they wouldn't support that?"

"I do not know that either," St Pierre admitted. "The men trust me. If I tell them 'we will never be asked to cross the St Lawrence,' and I am wrong—" He shrugged. "You see," he looked directly at Sloerill, "under this Canadian uniform beats a very small separatist heart that acknowledges the right of Quebec to exist as a nation."

"You never said this before. Can't you come to me with problems as you did?"

St Pierre gave a half-shrug. "Before your leave, I did not dare. You were too hard. I made the excuse that you were tired but I was afraid of what you might tell me."

"It was a bad time," George admitted. "John's been letting me know by asking me to confirm some of the bloody-minded orders I issued. Peter and Armand tried to put me right a few times. Why not you?"

"I am more nationalist than Armand. I was afraid to sound defeatist. I had actually planned to see you—"

"Why didn't you, for God's sake?"

"I made an appointment. Then came the raid on your headquarters. Then came l'affaire Bosch. After that you put up a wall. I did an Appreciation, decided I could not storm the wall and called off my attack."

"You weren't the only one to see the wall, Toupée. It's down now."

"For which your fiancée is to be thanked, I think. Did she also convince you that the death of Bosch was necessary?"

"It wasn't. I could have handled him some other way. I killed him in a fit of blind rage that he triggered by threatening to destroy everything we'd done. Betty showed me that my temper was a greater menace than Bosch ever was. I don't know how she did it, but I haven't felt so free in twenty years."

"Saved by the love of a good woman," St Pierre teased affectionately. "Etienne tells me that you are again like the boy he knew in school. I do not wish to reopen the subject, but you only advanced the death of Bosch a little. Plots had been laid. You killed a dead man."

"Thanks for telling me, but I'm glad nobody else has that on his conscience. Now, tell me a bit more about that tiny separatist heart. Can it still beat for Canada as well as for Quebec?"

"Ah, yes. Cyr had no mandate to destroy Canada, but the coup did not surprise me. Sentiment for independence had gone too far to stop. Passions were too high and so it had to happen, no matter what the cost. The separatists were preaching an unending sermon about 'humiliation', 'rejection' and Quebec's divine right to do what she wanted, no matter what Canada said or did.

"No one in Ottawa had the guts to deny it. Instead, they promised us a bilingual nation sea to sea. Such nonsense angered Quebecers, but the federal government needed the threat of the 'wicked' separatists to get re-elected. Vote right or Canada dies! The old expression should be changed to read, 'Whom the gods would destroy they first make politicians.' No one tried to integrate the new power of Quebec with the old establishment.

Nobody mentioned that our 'distinct society' is based on culture and geography, not language. I like Gene Frechette—but you, an English Quebecer, are deeper in my heart than any Manitoban French-Canadian can be.

"The foolish rhetoric of both sides was like a series of small slaps, never quite enough to provoke a fight, but always enough to create resentment, and so the final step was taken without considering how such resentment would affect that step. Now we are trying to glue something back together that is badly broken—less badly than had you stayed an extra week in London, my friend—but broken. The question is this: what comes after the fighting?"

George sifted pine needles through his stubby fingers, shaking his head. "I don't know, Toupée. Even on day one—well, day three, I no longer believed Canada could take Quebec back. You're telling me, indirectly, I was right. Unfortunately, the great Canadian public may not agree. Too many have died. Too many 'last ditch' conferences have failed. I'm afraid people—on both sides, but mainly in English Canada—will say, 'Now fix it for good.' " George sighed. "I told the Prime Minister that soldiers couldn't solve his problems. I don't think he believed me, but—" He was interrupted by a long burst of rifle fire from deep in the trees.

St Pierre sprang to his feet. "It is starting. I had better tend to my children."

"I have to go as well. If you need help, holler. No restrictions on gunships or artillery this deep in the boonies."

"I try to do without them. It has become a matter of pride that we can kill or not kill more selectively than these modern aids. Will you think about what I have said? I suspect there may be a small separatist heart beating under your tunic as well."

"Possibly, but my soldier's heart beats best when it's in tune with yours and Armand's and others. Bonne chance today, and when it's over come back for a talk. We have some new brandy in the mess you'll like."

St Pierre returned to the shallow depression where his signallers were working, not seeming to move quickly but covering the ground with long easy strides. Sloerill watched him go and started down the hill to the track where his humvee was parked. Zuke moved out from behind a rail fence and began to follow, his eyes as usual searching the ground and trees ahead for any sign of an ambush.

"You didn't hear anything we said," Sloerill flung over his shoulder as he jumped down from a rocky ledge.

"I never do," Zuke retorted as he followed. "That stuff only confuses us poor toe caps—slugs too . . ." He pushed into the trees, shaking his head.

The first peace meeting took place in the basement of an unused Anglican church in Drummondville. Those attending had spent a lot of thought on a place where they could assemble safely. The new government, while still democratic, was growing intolerant of anything that looked like dissent, and their definition of dissent was widening. Fourteen people were identified and admitted.

When all were present, Adhémar Justin, the man who had called the meeting, put down his coffee and stood up.

"I open," he began, "by welcoming M McGuire and M Young, two anglophones who did not flee, because like ourselves they are good québecois. We welcome them and we want to hear their views tonight.

"Our government is lying to us. Tonight on CBC I saw our delegation rebuffed at the United Nations. I switched to Radio-Québec to hear that recognition is but days away. I have seen supply ships being boarded by the Canadian navy. Bouget says all ships are getting through. CNN shows the Canadians capturing territory near Sherbrooke, using the French-Canadian soldiers that Bouget still claims do not fight for Canada. I believe CNN. The man they interviewed, a Colonel St Pierre, *was* québecois. One of the ships I saw being boarded was the one my uncle in Montreal said they were waiting for."

Justin paused to gather himself for a special effort. "As you know, I worked for Bouget. I fought for the 'Oui' side in the 1980 referendum. I supported the necessity of a coup, even by that secret federalist Cyr. Now I say this. Our people will disappear if we lose the war. At least in Canada we survived two hundred years. There. I have said the unsayable. How do you feel? What do you say?"

One by one the men agreed. Only one man, J.F.X. Benoit, questioned the situation. "I am not such a fool as to believe the government, to detect their lies we only need open our eyes, but why believe CNN? Are they not the same Americans who supported Canada from the beginning?"

"You only *watch* CNN, Jean François. You do not understand enough English. If they wished to lie to us, they would do so in French. What I have seen and heard is real. Montreal is a shell. Our countryside is barren. Every day the Canadians move down the Gaspé closer to Quebec City. In what the English call the Eastern Townships this Sloerill advances. Do you believe we can win?"

"No, Adhémar. And in three weeks it will be September. It must end before winter. What I cannot see is how we can stop them."

"That, is why we are here, Jean-François. M McGuire—Artur— what have you heard from your relatives and friends in Canada?"

"That they are very angry and that Quebec must pay—"

"How much must we pay, Artur?"

"They don't know. The Acadians and the French out west and in Ontario joined the war with enthusiasm because they felt they were at risk. They are still at risk, despite the many who have died for Canada. What Quebec must pay, I don't know."

"Then we must find out, and we must do something. I suggest we start making a list of all those we know—*know*—will support us."

On General Pittman's order, Sloerill and John Ashworth had been secretly flown to Ottawa on the night of August first, driven next morning to NDHQ in a closed staff car and escorted to Pittman's suite on the twelfth floor. Sloerill went in alone.

They sat chatting for a few minutes while an aide served coffee; then the CDS, responding to the tension he could feel, made a mild complaint. "I must say, George, you don't look like a happily engaged man about to win both a bride and a double promotion."

Sloerill put his cup down carefully. He'd been holding it at chest level as if to ward off an incoming rocket. Finally he smiled, stood up and took the hand Pittman was holding out to him. "Thank you, sir. To be honest, I had no idea as to why I was—double promotion?"

"A bit slow there, George," Pittman said genially, sitting down again. "Sorry about the secrecy. Security, you know. First of all, let me say that while it isn't official yet, last night at dinner the PM told me we're going for the whole South Shore except for suburban bits around Brossard and St Lambert. They still need a debate over there," his hand waved towards the distant parliament buildings, "but we have our marching orders. Cabinet is on side and since the government's a coalition, the talk is for show only."

Thinking of St Pierre, Sloerill asked a question. "Why do they need so much?"

"The corridor is to be a province and it has to be viable. I don't play politics, but they picked Sherbrooke as the new capital, and communications, roads, et cetera, dictated the rest. I wouldn't worry about it, George."

"Who'll be doing all of this?"

"You, mostly. Fred Scott's division in the Gaspé is cleaning out the last ALQ there. Once that's done, he'll meet you opposite Quebec City. I believe the boundary we picked was Route 173. You'll get the details tomorrow."

"And Babe Trinker?"

"His job is to threaten Montreal, then on Labour Day swing into the Chateauguay–Valleyfield–St Jean bit you missed last year. His east boundary is the Richelieu. You two can work out where his responsibility ends and yours starts."

Sloerill had noticed the implied criticism and sat forward. "General, I know that some people dislike my methods. I'd like to explain them and ask a question or two."

"I'd enjoy an explanation of your methods, George. You don't give us much of that, which I suspect is part of our problem."

"Sir, when this started, it was chaos. I took what I could and put it together in a way I hoped would work. My method wasn't designed. Like Topsy it just grew, and it worked, so we kept going. The unified system didn't respond to my needs fast enough."

"Hmmm. I can see that. Of course, the system was on a peacetime schedule too. That will slow up anything, and from up here your actions often looked sinister. Now, you have a question?" Pittman was smiling.

"Must I ask, sir? I'm a B/Gen. Jumping up two ranks makes me a lieutenant-general—with a corps?" His voice grew wary as the thought struck him that he'd be commanding a desk, not men.

"Nothing else can do the job we've given you. I bought this all the way, George. I may be an airman, but my philosophy is always to go with what works. It has to do with the reality that in the air if something doesn't work, it's a long way down.

"Bartholomew got us the resources. Talk to Charlie Vinet. He put together most of the elements you'll need. We're light on expensive toys, but so are the ALQ. Most of the high-tech stuff is yours. The ALQ have some new missile systems and artillery. You'll get the tools to take them out—at the last minute for security reasons. We bought a system field-tested in the Gulf. Impressive. Fire a shell and before it lands, a computer-aimed shot is on the way back. They call it 'Fire and Die'."

"This is a two-division corps? Infantry?"

"Yes, with two attached armoured brigades. There's also a lot of artillery. Have you anyone in mind to command the guns?"

"Chantilly," Sloerill said without hesitation. "I know he has only a militia background, but he's better than most regulars I know."

"Fred Scott agrees. Matter of fact, he tried to steal him. I'll approve Chantilly with pleasure. We're short of senior Gunners. We lost most of the best ones at Mobile Command. Do you have any strong preferences for your divisional commanders?"

"Not really. There was a lecturer at Staff College who impressed me. A Brigadier-General Finch. Eddy Finch. Is he still in?"

"Yes. He sorted out our militia problems. Did a fine job. Excellent choice. Will he command the semi-division you have at present?"

"I want him to. I'm also concerned about naming two brigadiers in it. I don't want to limit Finch, but—"

"Try some names out on me, George. It's my final call, anyway."

"I want Pierre St Pierre to command the Rifle Brigade."

Pittman hesitated. The brigadiers had been selected, but St Pierre was influential in the Prime Minister's party and had used his direct line into the PMO[1] at least once on Sloerill's behalf. He had to be handled gently.

"I think that'll fly, but he lacks command experience. Why don't we send him to General Scott? You'll have him back in time. Who else?"

"For the Guards Brigade, Peter Forbes."

"No way. You're high-profile, and we can't have a Brit in a senior job. To be honest, it's bad enough he has a battalion. You aren't running a private war now. I recommend Brigadier-General Fortin for your Guards Brigade. He's an ex-Van Doo colonel who stayed loyal." Sloerill nodded

---

[1] Prime Minister's Office

and Pittman went on. "Now, about your personal staff?"

"Ashworth as a colonel, and I can work the rest out with Vinet. All I want are officers who are flexible. That brings up another point, sir."

"What's that, George? I have a meeting in an hour."

"The ALQ are dug in, and they'll be tough. I'd like it understood that if the war drags on, my corps gets my unit rotation programme. Relief by units, not individually."

Pittman's face hardened. "Have you any idea what that will cost?"

"Has anyone calculated what prolonging the war costs per month?"

The two men stared at one another for a long twenty seconds. "I'm told you're prepared to resign on the issue?" Pittman asked quietly. Sloerill nodded, knowing that he was about to lose his most effective weapon.

"Very well," Pittman said tightly, "but you aren't going to change a system that has worked well for twenty-five years. If you could prove our system was wrong, that would be different. All you've done is prove that yours works too."

Pittman pushed his coffee away to signal the end of the meeting. "Let me tell you something, George. You've been fighting the system. Now you're part of it. You may think you can use the war to kill unification. I suspect you can, if you try hard—but to do that you'll have to *lose us the war*. I don't think you'll go that far.

"Secondly, you mentioned a long war in terms of rotation. Think of it in another context. A long war, even a medium long war, will force Canada to go the whole nine yards. The country wants peace—after Quebec is punished. Unless you wrap it up fast, George, you'll be doing street fighting in Montreal next summer."

Pittman stood up. Sloerill mustn't know until the last minute that Canada intended to take back all of Quebec anyway. He wanted to end on a friendly note. "You've done some interesting things, George. Staff College will debate them for years. But remember, war's an aberration for Canada. After it's over we go back to square one again, unified and dull—and you and I will be gone. Remember that. Writing's a risky profession, and a man with your reputation can land a pretty impressive job if he makes his move while people remember what we soldiers did for them."

Sloerill put on the blue Guards beret he still wore. "That means I have a week," he said wryly. "I'll stick to writing. The war's given me lots of material." His face was impassive as he reminded Pittman that peace might not mean security for unification. "Will I see you tonight?" he asked in a neutral-friendly tone. "The Minister sent round a note this morning. I'm commanded to have dinner with him."

"I was going too," Pittman lied genially, "but things are too hectic here. Our land forces are now over eighty percent militia, and it's a madhouse—an expensive madhouse, as I keep telling the PM. Anyway, see Vinet and pop by tomorrow. We'll have lunch here, the three of us. This operation has to be fast, George. Fast, fast, fast."

Sloerill saluted and went out, his mind churning. As a corps commander, his hands-on style would be curbed, but in return he had a chance to infect a lot more people with his radical ideas, young officers who would come to power later.

Ashworth looked up from a *Maclean's* magazine with Sloerill's face on the cover as George came into the outer office. He started to rise.

Sloerill put his hands on his hips. "I'd think that even a temporary, acting colonel would get up faster when a lieutenant-general walks in." He didn't give Ashworth time to digest the two pieces of information before going on. "Come on. Float lightly behind me over to General Vinet's office. We have a corps to organize."

John Melling slipped into the Oval Office, wondering what had happened in the hour the President had been closeted with the French Ambassador to the UN. Jules de Repentigny had asked for a special one-on-one meeting, no aides present. He'd even unbent enough to leave his official translator in New York.

The President stood with his back to the big window behind the desk, outlined in the Washington summer sun. It was his "I've made up my mind, now let's do it" pose and it almost always spelled trouble.

"Sit down, John. We've a lot to do." Melling was relieved when the President sat too. At least the meeting would be an exchange, not the stone-tablet pronouncement kind.

"Have a nice chat with the Ambassador?" Melling asked to remind his boss of how overtime the meeting had gone.

"It was frank, cordial and will disrupt life for a month," the President said with a grin. "We're looking at the policy-shift thing."

"Canada?" Melling knew the French policy on Quebec was putting immense strains on the new European Union. The British and Dutch were unshakably on Canada's side. The Germans and Italians leaned Canada's way. Spain and France supported Quebec. The impasse had to be solved.

"What are we looking at, sir—in general terms?"

"Recognition of Quebec in October. The French buy a corridor that won't kill Quebec and we let France supply them. But I told de Repentigny we'd never accept foreign troops in North America. We'll wink at advisers, but if I find real French soldiers in the stew, we'll back Canada forever."

"And what's France paying for all this?"

"We divide the arms sale pie and cut down on competition. They'll also back off on farm subsidies and not oppose our changes to the GATT."

Melling thought for a moment. It was a policy shift of considerable size, but not beyond the bounds of credibility.

"How do we handle the UN thing? Chester is very pro-Canada."

"The French think Chester needs a vacation. At the end of September, France'll call a snap vote, and with Chester away we won't be able to organize a defence."

"Can we keep the lid on for a while? Our Canadian policy is generating good polls that will help push three delicate bills through Congress."

The president waved his hand in dismissal. "Handle it any way you want, but make sure Canada understands they settle for a corridor or life gets rough. Start working through their Ambassador down here. Perhaps I should meet her.

"Make sure the CIA gets the word. The corridor is policy. We handle Canada. Watch the French. Their role is to make Quebec strong enough to avoid defeat. They send equipment and a few advisers, period."

After four hectic days, Lieutenant-General Sloerill and Colonel Ashworth flew home. John brushed an imaginary fleck of dust from his sleeve, admiring the four wide gold bands of a full colonel as he did so. "You know," he said, turning the sleeve to catch a gleam of sunlight on the gold, "for all your pessimism, we actually *do* have a corps."

Sloerill nodded. "We do, John. Vinet and Pittman did a great job, despite the fact they still want my ass."

"Isn't a double promotion a funny way to achieve said trophy?"

"I win," George said simply. "But in a year I've gone from civilian to lieutenant-general. The chances of making a mistake are five to the tenth power greater than before. They also want me to attack by September twentieth—less than a month away. On the other hand," Sloerill grinned boyishly, "the Minister promised to scrap unification after the war. He's been bitten by the political bug and may go for the top job when it's vacant."

"You could run for parliament with him. I like that one."

"An esteemed trait of a staff officer is that he never gives his commander wild ideas. I'm having enough problems with my own."

"What? You want the job of CDS?"

Sloerill shuddered. "Not on a platter. No. It's the lopsided military balance. Fred Scott has the right size force for the Gaspé. Babe Trinker has a bit too much to grab a small area the ALQ won't defend seriously, and we're way over-strength for our job.

"With what we have, once we roll someone may say, 'Don't stop. Head for Montreal.' I wish Toupée were here, he has a feel for these things."

"Would crossing the St Lawrence be a problem?"

"For the French Canadians among us, yes. I'm not talking just FMR either. Half the original gang are French Canadian. Given an order to take it all back, I'm not sure what the reaction would be—" He stopped as an idea hit him. "In fact, I'm not sure about my reaction to such an order. Mutiny would take the gloss off what has been a brilliant war career."

He shook his head. "Too paranoid. Anyway, once we get home, set up a liaison team of bright captains and majors. Montgomery used them to keep track of an army group back in '45. I want that system myself."

Ashworth made a note, then pointed to the lit No Smoking sign. "Time to buckle up as well as buckle down, sir. Hey, do you think that now I've reached the rank you started out with, Zuke will salute me on a regular basis?" Sloerill gave him a derisive look. "No, you're right. Staff officers must not indulge in fantasy."

Prentice's third Toronto rally almost filled Maple Leaf Gardens. Attacks on him in the media had kept some people away, but the crowd was with him. He was keeping pressure on the government, while shifting the focus of his speech so that the windup stressed the need to make Quebec pay and defined the humble role the province would play in a new Canada.

He was a big man, six foot four and just over two hundred muscular pounds with the shoulders of a boxer and the hips of a cowboy, both of which he'd been. He stood on a starkly empty stage under the now familiar "One Canada" banner, his big-boned face and dark hair making him look like the Marlboro man. He paced the empty stage like a TV evangelist, a microphone in one hand, feeling the audience, playing to their fears and needs until at the end they would flock down to donate to The Cause.

A new, expensive sound system sent his words booming around the hall or let it whisper among the steel beams until people had to strain to hear. Now, near the finale, he stopped pacing and came center stage. "Remember the needless deaths! Remember the billions of dollars we Canadians have paid and are still paying because of greedy Quebec! Had those billions been spent properly, Canada could be a paradise with jobs for all and a medicare system treating all Canadians as equals. Will we let Quebec say 'Sorry' and walk away from the misery and debt they've caused?"

A ragged "No" came back to him, but not strong enough.

"Are they going to get away with it? Are they?"

"No!" The shout was stronger and more together.

"Are they?"

A roaring "No!" began to fill the hall.

"Are they?"

"NO! NO! NO!" the crowd howled back.

Ready to launch into his closing, Prentice hesitated as his timing was upset by sounds from off-stage. The security men should handle interruptions. As he returned to his audience, trying to regain the rhythm, an ordinary-looking man burst out from the wings.

"Goddamn bigot!" he screamed. Few in the audience could hear the words but they saw the man advance on Prentice, apparently intending to attack.

"Get out," Prentice yelled and took a menacing step forward, his temper rising at this insignificant person who was ruining his pitch.

The audience saw the small, poorly dressed intruder throw a punch that somehow evaded the defending arm and struck Prentice on the nose. He bellowed in anger and lashed out. His blow caught the man squarely and flung him five feet to land on his head. Ten thousand angry people waited for him to get up and scuttle away in defeat. The man did not move.

A first aid crew rushed onto the stage. One felt the man's pulse in the wrist, then at the neck. He shook his head and the other two ran for a stretcher. As the security staff made a path, the man was carried away. Prentice knew that he'd lost his audience. As blood streamed from his nose, he made a final muffled plea for funds.

Outside on College Street, an ambulance received the patient and went wailing its way to a hospital. A TV camera caught the man's face, deathly pale, a narrow line of blood coming from the corner of his mouth.

For five days the man lay in a coma. His picture and dramatized accounts of the unequal exchange sold thousands of papers. The looming Prentice, his handsome face made ugly by fury, filled magazine covers and tabloids, a fist casually smashing aside the defensive arm thrown up by his victim or his hate-filled face staring down at the still figure at his feet.

On the fifth day the man died, still unidentified. The Attorney General of Ontario charged Prentice with assault, manslaughter and incitement to violence. The news conference Prentice called at the jail to defend himself was marred by demonstrators demanding his scalp. Well-informed stories about his financial manipulations began to circulate, and every paper ran pictures of the victim's funeral and his tombstone (paid for by an anonymous donor) that read "To an unknown Canadian murdered by hatred".

No cameras recorded the arrival of an unmarked hearse at the hospital the night of the man's death. No one saw a look-alike body wheeled into the temporarily unguarded room, the muffled figure that left it moments later, or the closed van that drove him to Pearson International Airport. Once his beard had regrown, no one connected the Canadian navy's former lightweight boxing champion with the face that still occasionally appeared on TV, often under the heading "Do you know this man?"

CHAPTER TWENTY-ONE

The Sabine Women

The Quebec inner cabinet that met in Montreal on the fourth of
September was a dispirited assembly. President Bouget had circulated a list
of every Quebec army success of the last three months, copies of secret cor-
respondence between Paris and Quebec City, and data on the size of the
military depot France was building for them on the island of Miquelon in
the Gulf of St Lawrence. Nothing dispelled the gloom.

"I tell you, we have but to defend ourselves a little longer and international recognition is ours," he insisted. "On October first France will
petition the Security Council, seconded by the Chinese, to admit Quebec to
the UN. The Americans will not veto, nor will Russia. The British are
wavering as the Americans press them to abstain."

"And what will be left of our Quebec?" Adèle Chantilly asked
sadly. "We agree to a corridor, but will Canada return our hydro sites? What
will this General Trinker do who is menacing Montreal? And day after day
our people abandon us. Who will be left?"

"They will return once there is peace." Bouget tried to sound confident. "I want to hear Canada's real intentions. They are debating the idea
of making Montreal an international zone. We can agree to that if it's under
our control, but if they ask more we will hurt them. Now to the business of
protecting our land. General Trinker is advancing towards Sloerill. We will
not resist—much. In Gaspé, we have stopped General Scott. When Sloerill

attacks, we will bloody his nose. The Minister of War has a plan. Minister Beauchemin?"

"Our planes have been shot down," Adèle scornfully interjected. "Our soldiers will die like the Iraqis in Kuwait. Armand used to tell me of the stupidity of moving soldiers when the enemy controls the air."

"This is not Iraq," Réjean Beauchemin snapped. "We have missiles. Sloerill does not bomb civilians. We need only delay him to give France time to save us."

The second peace meeting in Drummondville was going badly. Forty people wanted to end the war, but no one had a plan they all could accept. The most popular ideas were a petition and a strike. Few believed that Bouget would pay attention to a petition; and as for strikes, with unemployment at thirty-five percent, who would notice one?

Adhémar Justin rose from his place at the head table and pounded a gavel for silence. "Let us take a break to let tempers cool. We are agreed that the war must end. Surely we can agree on a way to reach our so-called leaders. We can talk again once we—"

"You're a fool, Adhémar!" a woman shouted from the audience. "Like your father before you and your grandfather the député with Duplessis, you think talk is the answer. Talk will not end the war!"

"Who are you, madame?" Justin peered in the direction of the voice. "If you wish to speak, please stand up and be recognized."

"I *am* standing," the tiny woman cried. "You know me. Cécile Demers. I had a business until men started talking about what a fine thing independence would be. I agree the war must end. Why did you not talk against it starting? All night I have listened to men talk, talk, talk. Enough!" She moved to the aisle. "Enough talk from men. Follow me, ladies. We can meet in my empty store."

"And you will end the war from there?" a man yelled scornfully.

"Perhaps, but we will be spared your inflated opinions, Louis. Women have ended wars before. I would say 'remember the Sabines', but with your education, you would think only of rape." Her bird-like eyes flicked around the room, selecting supporters. "Alice, Geneviève, Léonie, Denise, Shirley, Marie-Claire. Come. You too, Anne-Lise. All of you come if you want something done."

To good-natured laughter and catcalls, sixteen women followed the tiny firebrand. Justin shook his head. "As if they can stop the general who took Valleyfield yesterday. At least they left the coffee and sandwiches. Recess for twenty minutes."

As new units poured in, Sloerill felt more and more uneasy as the feeling grew that he had too much muscle for his job. Behind his desk a map, covered in pins and flags, denoted the location of every unit. He stared a moment longer, spun in his chair and pressed a buzzer.

"Sir?" a sergeant asked from the door.

"Tell Colonels Ashworth and Anderson that I can see them now, and if Brigadier St Pierre arrives I want to see him too."

As his visitors came in Major Burlap, now promoted to corps mascot, slipped through, jumped on Sloerill's desk, sat down on a pile of papers and began to purr.

"Let me put this stuff away, and I'll be right with you." Sloerill went to the safe with a pile of folders. As the heavy door opened Burlap scrabbled across the desk in fright and bolted from the room.

Ashworth watched her go. "I've tried to train her not to panic when a safe opens." He threw an accusing look at Anderson. "Since it's your fault, I think you should take on the task."

"Someone has to." Sloerill laughed. "Yesterday I opened up and Burlap ran right over Betty's picture and broke the glass. OK, enough catastrophe. Are the last units in place?"

Ashworth nodded and Clay Anderson looked serious. "I have the latest intelligence reports. The ALQ are planning to make a real fight for Sherbrooke and Granby."

"Good. I don't intend to fight there. Both will be encircled and left alone. Anything else?"

"General Trinker should finish up today. As we forecast, almost no resistance, but a British Columbia regiment got chewed up near Chateauguay when they got too pushy. They took almost two hundred casualties, seventy-six dead. BC will be in mourning tomorrow."

George shook his head. "I warned him. The ALQ are seasoned troops. Sixty percent of his men have never been shot at. Yes?" he called, hearing a rap at the door.

St Pierre walked in. "I am glad to see that one thing does not change. One can always find you three in an office telling dirty stories." After the welcomes, St Pierre pulled up a chair. "I am back. I have inspected my brigade, and all is ready for the twentieth—apart from the fact that we will all be exhausted. No change in plan?"

"No," Sloerill confirmed. "I talked to General Finch this morning. Your Rifle Brigade will push almost to Drummondville. Guards Brigade takes over to Levis. 4 Div seals off Sherbrooke and Granby."

"Ah, the beauty of a large-scale map," St Pierre said softly. "Between one place and another it is but a step. I bring greetings from Fred Scott, who says that he may be a day late in arriving at Levis. He was receiving new orders as I left him."

He looked at the map. "So many men, so little land. We still do not cross the river?"

"My orders are to retake the corridor, Toupée. I just hope we can do it before casualties make our political masters want more."

"Then careful speed is of the essence?"

"Yes." George looked at his friend sympathetically. "It isn't what we think is fair, it's what Canadians feel is fair. The faster we win, the better it will be for everyone."

"Merde!" It was the first time anyone had heard St Pierre swear. "I will drive hard, but as you say, we cannot afford too many dead soldiers. It is good that we lead the breakthrough. At least the casualties will be among us québecois. I will be more at ease when the Guards reach Fred Scott at Levis and we stop. I am not sure my Fusiliers would obey an order to go further." He turned to Clay appealingly.

"Cannot your agents convince Bouget that if he fights hard he will be destroyed?"

Anderson looked pained. "Not many people ask janitors and electricians how to run a war, Toupée, and Bouget doesn't trust our diplomats any more."

There was a strained silence. "Eh bien." St Pierre got to his feet. "I must report to General Finch, and I want to see Armand about his fire plan. A bientôt." He went out.

Ashworth also got to his feet. "I'd better check with Armand too. He doesn't even say 'hello' any more, he just shouts 'ammunition!' as he goes by even though he has so much now that Brome County's been declared a no-smoking area."

The door closed leaving Clay Anderson seated, with no apparent intention of leaving. "Something on your mind, Clay?"

Anderson nodded. "Did I ever explain that a bit of intelligence is called a piece?"

"I don't think so. Do I need to know?"

"Perhaps. We build intelligence like a jig-saw. Once you fit all the pieces together, you get a usable picture. Take our spy now."

"I thought you were going to take him?"

"In time, sir. Here's what we do. My people find out what the Quebec government knows. John and I evaluate who had access to each piece and when. That gives the picture frame, the edge pieces. Then we start to fill in. The person is clearly well placed."

"Does he—or she—know what we're planning now?"

"My reports indicate that he expects to. It's a he, by the way. I suspect that by the end of today he'll have your attack plan."

"Are you saying he's in this headquarters?"

"Not exactly, sir."

"Would it spoil your fun if I ordered you to name your suspect?"

"Believe me, sir, this is no fun. When we got down to six names, I bugged every vehicle they might use and installed radio locators. They aren't accurate in the hills despite what they do on TV, but they'll get you close. After three messages we'd narrowed the choice down to two men. We began tailing them and hit the jackpot last night down near the border. The radio's in his car and he uses a fake fishing rod as an antenna."

Sloerill's mouth was dry. He knew a man who always carried a fishing rod. "Etienne?" he whispered.

Anderson nodded, his expresion unhappy. "I'm really sorry, sir. I like him . . . but . . ." He tossed three pictures onto the desk.

Sloerill stared unseeing at the fuzzy infra-red photos of his friend bent over a radio. "What have you done about this?"

"Nothing, sir. He hasn't been anywhere important all day. He's made no phone calls apart from the usual civil affairs things. We can wait—a few hours."

Sloerill rubbed his hands hard against his forehead. "I can't think now, Clay. Give me an hour—" His head rose quickly as an idea struck. "Now that I know, we can deny him any further information . . ."

Clay was shaking his head. "We still can't be sure he won't get it. He's on a first-name basis with every officer over the rank of major. If it's any consolation, sir, he's protected you at some risk. He saved you from the bunker raid. He had to know about it. He's probably not even a real spy. My guess is he got trapped out here and decided to do what he could."

"Why haven't you arrested him? Will he lead you to more spies?"

"I doubt it, and I didn't arrest him because if I did he'd be shot."

"What in hell are you talking about? We don't shoot people in Canada!"

"You do now. I think you call them 'Special Orders-in-Council'. Death to spies. They've already shot a colonel and four civil servants."

"In secret? They can't do things like that!"

"Get real, sir. Those guys set up the Dorion fiasco. They were found guilty at a secret trial one day and shot the next. If they have Etienne and anything goes wrong with your attack, he'll be the next to die."

"Nothing will go wrong. The ALQ can't stop me."

"No, but they can make you bleed." Anderson took a deep breath. "I'll tell you something I probably shouldn't, but it's under my 'protect Sloerill' mandate. You can't tell anyone else."

Sloerill nodded dumbly. "OK. Despite what you've been told, Canada intends to get it all. My government's policy is now a corridor, period. That's why Ottawa's pushing. They have to win before Washington exerts enough pressure to stop them—say by September thirtieth."

"Why are you telling me this?" Sloerill shook his head in anguish. "I don't believe an independent Quebec can survive, but they need to learn that for themselves. Whose side are you on?"

Anderson's eyes were pained. "I could have gone all week without you asking that. Look, sir. Your government will soon present ceasefire conditions to Quebec that they can't accept. General Trinker will head for Dorion. Now comes the sticky bit. When Quebec refuses the conditions, he goes for Montreal. Same plan as before, no doctored gas. At Levis you're ordered to cross the St Lawrence, grab Quebec City and head west."

"How do you *know*, Clay? How many spies does your government have in Ottawa?"

"I didn't need spies. We've got over two hundred LO's [1] buying drinks and listening. The betting is you'll refuse to cross. Suddenly the Canadian hero George Sloerill is charged with refusing a legitimate order. There's also this: once Messier's revealed as a spy, they might claim you were in cahoots and shoot you both."

"I don't see how we can avoid that," Sloerill said dully. "I have to arrest him to protect my men."

"There's another way, sir. Let me handle it. If you do it, you'll screw it up like you did with Bosch. I can help you out. Believe me, an executive action like your Intelligence people pulled on Prentice is preferable to a firing squad. My solution isn't even close to perfect, but it's the best I can see, and I've been looking for workable alternatives ever since I saw those pictures."

Anderson went to the door. "You're meeting your divisional commanders in an hour, and you're getting married in a week. Think about it. My suggestion's the best one you're going to get."

When the door closed, Sloerill's face sank into his hands. He had often told soldiers to put civilian lives before their own. Could he put Canada before Etienne—no—that wasn't the choice. He had to choose between having him murdered by Clay or shot by Canada. There was no way he could decide that and nobody he could turn to for advice. Dimly he became aware of voices in the hall and looked up.

"Dreaming of the wedding?" Messier asked lightly as he slid into the room, the protesting face of a sergeant behind him. "Or mourning the loss of your freedom? Marriage is not so bad. I recommend it."

Sloerill waved the sergeant away and sat silently as Etienne outlined fresh changes to the wedding plans. A few more people *had* to be invited. As George listened, he saw Etienne's eyes stray to the situation map marked with attack routes, report lines, timings, objectives: the meat and potatoes of any battle.

Etienne was sitting where St Pierre had been, his face turned exactly as Toupée's had been as he appealed to Clay to persuade Bouget not to fight too hard. He heard an echo of Clay's answer, "Bouget doesn't listen to janitors and electricians."

---

[1] Liaison Officers

"George! You must pay attention. Believe me, you will need this on the fifteenth," Messier protested.

"That's it," Sloerill said softly. A plan had sprung into his head, complete as it had when he'd devised the Longue Pointe raid. Bouget would listen to Etienne.

"I'm sorry." He smiled for the first time, the tight lines of his mouth relaxing. "I can't concentrate with the big battle coming up, not even to cut back your guest list again."

"Ah, that," Messier sighed. "I can see that your map is more than usually filled with small pins and flags."

"Have a look," Sloerill invited. They stood by the map while he explained the points of attack, how flail tanks and rockets would open ALQ minefields, how the new artillery system would obliterate ALQ guns, how bridging equipment would bypass blown bridges.

"Enough, enough!" Etienne protested. "Pity me. I am a civilian and you lost me ten minutes ago. I have but one question. Where in all of this are the FMR and my son?"

Sloerill's finger pointed. "Here. The FMR lead the initial assault." Messier paled and his smile faded.

Striking quickly, George continued. "There's something more. I want you to believe this, Etienne, for your sake, for mine and for Robert's."

"Of course I will believe you. I always do. Why should this be different?" Messier looked puzzled.

"This war has finally united Canadians. They feel they bent over backwards to accommodate Quebec and were cheated. We know it isn't that simple, but that's how they feel." George couldn't use the information Clay had given him but he could come close.

"If the war looks like dragging on all winter and if the ALQ put up too good a fight and too many Canadians die, the government will demand that we reclaim all of Quebec."

"I know, George. You have said all this before. My Ontario friends confirm what you say, but what can I do? I cannot talk to Bouget."

"Not even on your car radio?" Sloerill asked quietly. There was a long silence.

"You know then—and Clay Anderson." Messier accepted the discovery quietly.

"And Clay says if you're caught you'll be shot."

"Because I love Quebec? No, George. You did not hesitate to use Clay's information to kill my québecois. The ALQ used my information to the same purpose against Canada. It is not pleasant to be a spy, but I am not ashamed of what I have done. I believe in a free Quebec and shall say so at my trial. My government will exchange me."

"They don't have anyone of your stature to exchange. I don't want you to die before a firing squad."

"I have no choice. Suicide is impossible for me. It would be best for you, I suppose, but there are some things a friend cannot ask."

"I'm asking you to live!" Sloerill almost shouted. "Do you think I can hand you over to some kangaroo court to be shot?"

"George, please." Messier said softly. "I will not betray my country. You must not betray yours."

"The South Shore," Sloerill said harshly. "Can your Quebec survive losing it?"

Messier nodded. "Yes, if we can still sell electricity to the Americans to buy the food and things that even québecois need to live." A spark of anger glowed in his dark eyes. "Why do you torment me by rehashing these old points? Do whatever you must. I only ask that it be quick."

"It'll be quick all right," Sloerill said grimly. "Quick out of here." He lifted a hand to cut off any protest. "I know you don't give a damn for Canada, but you love Quebec. If I give you a chance to help Quebec—and I believe, help Canada too—will you take it?"

Messier didn't reply for a moment. "I don't know, George. I would do anything for Quebec and almost anything for you. What is this chance that you offer?"

"The chance to let Quebec survive—a smaller Quebec than you planned on, but independent. You'll also save a lot of Quebec lives."

"And what do I do for Canada?" Messier asked bitterly.

"Save some Canadian lives, lives of men you've known for a year. I believe you'll save Canada too. I don't believe in a Canada without Quebec or a Quebec without Canada. If independence doesn't work, we can come back together after the anger's gone. It isn't a sure thing, but it's a chance for both our countries. Will you take it?" George was leaning across the desk, pleading with his friend. Etienne suddenly smiled.

"I have often said that when you become emotional, you forget essentials. Bon. It is a wonderful idea, but it is a dream and I do not see how your dream can be realized."

Sloerill shook his head. "My brains must be addled." He too smiled. "What I want you to do, old friend, is to go to Bouget with my plan and tell him that resistance is hopeless and that he must surrender the South Shore—but not too quickly. I attack on the twentieth. He must hold me up so that I do not reach Levis before the end of the month—but without heavy casualties. I can't tell you why that date is important, but it is."

"If I could get to Bouget I could persuade him. The Cabinet is half-prepared anyway," Messier said almost to himself, "but I cannot do it from prison—or from my car."

"No prison. Will you try, Etienne?"

"And our north? What about that?

"I can't promise, but I believe that by October you'll be able to negotiate a treaty that will at least let you buy cheap power from the Cree. After all, Quebec built the dams."

Messier gave an expressive shrug and his shoulders slumped. "I seem to be out of choices. It is a pity the old general is dead. His replacement Legrand is a fire-eater. Will Ottawa let you advance so slowly?"

"I'll be afraid of another Dorion and be very careful. We and the ALQ will do a dance. There'll be people killed, but fewer—on both sides."

"But how can I get away? Clay is watching me. My chauffeur said we were followed coming over here. I did not believe him."

"You were. Listen, the Guards are in Bromont. Peter's away but Pierre Coté's senior major. He'll pass you through the lines if I tell him to. I'll call him now."

The operator connected him quickly with the Guards CP. "Hello, Pierre. Sloerill here . . . fine. Look, I need a job done and done right. I'm sending Etienne over. Set up a truce with the ALQ on the road we use to exchange wounded prisoners. Do it yourself. Hand him a white flag and see him across the line."

He listened for a minute. "That's right, it is odd, but it's essential. He has a message for the Quebec government that must be delivered. I'll bring an order to confirm this once my meeting with the divisional staffs is over. OK?"

Pierre agreed and Sloerill continued. "Expect him in about half an hour. You meet him at the Bromont airport." A sudden thought struck him. God alone knew what precautions Clay had taken or was taking right now.

"Pierre? This supersedes any order, past, present, or future from anyone. Etienne has to be across the border within the hour." He hung up.

"Go. Don't stop for anyone. Just get across the line." He scribbled a note. "Zuke's outside. Give him this and take off."

Etienne made up his mind. "I would not believe this from any other man, George. It will work, my friend. I will make Bouget listen. Perhaps, after a few years have passed, we can have a drink together in Montreal—ahh."

"Andrée?" Messier nodded. "Don't worry. Nobody is after her. I'll see she's safe and send her across the river next month."

"Ah, well. I did look after you, George. My people were very angry with me for getting you out of the headquarters that night."

He paused again. "Well," they said together. "We will not do that again for a long time, cher ami." Etienne shook George's hand, then turned and left quickly.

Sloerill sat down to think. His plan was based on the trust built over thirty years. Etienne would not reveal the detailed plans unless Bouget agreed. He hoped Clay would understand that he'd done the right thing.

"Sorry to break in, sir," Ashworth put his head in at the door. "Your meeting begins in ten minutes. Everyone present and accounted for."

Clay Anderson was walking, turning the problem over in his mind, looking for a way to save Messier and failing. As he turned back towards the headquarters bunker, he saw the Bentley pull out of the parking lot, heading for the main gate.

He looked for the men assigned to follow it. One car was wallowing across the field, both front tires flat. His head snapped around at the sound of a crash. A truck had blindsided a second vehicle leaving its parking slot. He saw Zuke climb down from the truck and cursed. That idiot Sloerill was acting alone again, sacrificing himself to let his friend escape.

Clay sprinted for the building that housed his Intelligence section. "Pete!" he yelled, smashing the door open. Everyone in the room jumped. "My office. Now!"

The duty officer came at the run and shut the door. "Listen, up, Lieutenant." Anderson spoke formally. "For all unit IO's.[2] Message. Etienne Messier is ALQ agent. Apprehend at all costs. Kill to prevent escape. Report all contact to me. Message ends. Security classification, Secret." He took a deep breath.

"Now, if the General helps Messier in the mistaken belief that he's doing the right thing, the Guards will be involved. Get two good men up there with sniper scopes. Do you have a question, lieutenant?"

The duty officer had a million, but one look into Clay's ice-cold eyes drove them from his mind. "None, sir, but can I have this in writing?"

Clay scribbled out the order, signed it and slammed out. On the steps he paused. Had he forgotten anything? No. Messier would die and it would look as if he'd been shot by the ALQ when he got too close to the border. Sloerill? He'd be antsy for a while, but he'd see that it was best for everyone eventually. The man was what might be called a romantic realist.

What about himself? Clay knew that his orders to protect Sloerill didn't cover this. So his career was on the line—again—along with the general officer's star he'd been conditionally promised.

He shook his head. He'd never operated that way and wasn't about to start. Besides, he was following American policy overall. Sloerill had to take the corridor before the President could tell Canada to be satisfied with the South Shore. He was confident that Sloerill, with the information he now had, would arrive at Quebec City about the time American and international pressure combined to make Canada accept a cease-fire.

He half-turned back to see if his orders had gone out, then stopped. He'd done his job. If Messier escaped it was fate. Besides, he *liked* him. "What the hell," he thought. "If he can get past all that shit, he deserves to make it."

"Excuse me, sir." A sergeant was saluting him. "General Sloerill's compliments and I'm to remind you that your intelligence briefing starts in three minutes. I looked all over for you, sir," he half-complained.

Clay returned the salute and followed the sergeant, reaching for his notes, his mind switching smoothly from intercepting spies to briefing commanders on the capabilities of the ALQ.

---

[2] Intelligence Officers

*

The Prime Minister had called his key people into his office for an announcement. His jaw was set and they knew the boss was angry. Nobody sat down. Joe Gates stood beside Richard Bartholomew at the coffee table, External Affairs and Defence united. Karen Ormsby, like the Justice she represented, held aloof by a window. Allan Brewster leaned against the PM's desk, a sign of his power.

"You know our plans," the PM growled as he paced, "but those damned opportunists in what's called the 'world community' are trying to pick our bones. Community, hell. Scavengers! We've been a nation sea to sea for over a hundred years, and we're going to stay one." Allan's fingernail rapped warningly against the desk and he fought down his anger.

"The President used his support of Canada to win his election. Now he's turning separatist. Joe says The Man himself read our Ambassador a lecture about greed and letting new nations live in the new world order. Well, shit. It so happens that in his new world order France is turning its last North American colony on St Pierre and Miquelon into a military base designed to help Quebec defeat us.

"Now think about this and get back to me by tonight. Tomorrow is the sixth. General Trinker is starting to re-deploy to the Dorion area. Sloerill is set to roll on the twentieth. He has to go faster. Can he kick off by the fifteenth?"

Bartholomew shook his head. "No, sir, but possibly he can do it by the eighteenth."

"Do it. On the twentieth, then, with the attack going full bore, I'll announce cease-fire terms. They'll be tough and there's no way Bouget can accept. I'll give him twenty-four hours to reply. By then Sloerill will be close to Levis. When Bouget turns me down, Sloerill takes Quebec City to cut off the head of this so-called 'nation', General Trinker attacks Montreal, and by the time the Yanks wake up we'll have our country together again."

"If I may, sir," Bartholomew spoke up. "General Scott's a better choice to cross the river. Sloerill's men will be tired and will have taken casualties, possibly heavy casualties." He was thinking of Sloerill's potential problems with his French-Canadian soldiers.

"No," the PM said abruptly. "General Pittman has given Scott new orders. His third brigade and the Canadian Airborne will assault the island of Miquelon. If France doesn't like it, tough. They've no business there, and when I show the UN pictures of the troops, tanks and guns they put in—against a NATO ally—there goes France. No, Richard. I discussed it with Pittman. He agrees with your assessment, but Sloerill has to do the job because Scott can't.

"All right." The PM's eyes swept the group. "Karen, work up something on the Monroe Doctrine. France was allowed to keep St Pierre and Miquelon in 1759, but those islands are in *our* waters and I won't allow them to be used against us. You and Joe work up a statement expressing shock and dismay at being stabbed in the back by an ally. Write it so people can interpret 'ally' as being France *or* the US. Also, start a rumour that a cease-fire is almost ready to go and any pressure could blow it. That may shut the United States up for a day or two.

"Finally, I'm still working on words with Allan here, but in general, my terms to Bouget consist of five points. One. Quebec to cede all territory now held by Canada and reaffirm the agreement that we keep the South Shore. Two. Quebec to return all prisoners and pay for or replace equipment illegally seized at the onset of fighting. Three. Quebec to agree to reparations set by UN tribunal. Four. Quebec to subsidize the cost of some French language services outside Quebec. Five. Quebec to accept in a peace treaty a clause that if their nation goes belly-up, they return to the Canadian federation on the same terms as when they joined."

The Prime Minister smiled. "By the time that's stroked, it will look reasonable to the UN and satisfy the thirst for revenge in English Canada. We've got ten days to get the cabinet on side. Joe, get cracking on the statement you'll make to the UN after we take St Pierre and Miquelon."

As he sped towards Bromont, Messier's thoughts raced over what he'd been told. George's appeal to influence Bouget was genuine; but what if the rest was a mere trick to save Canadian lives? What if he'd been fed false information about Canadian intentions? What if Anderson had known of his spying for weeks, even months, and had waited till now to guarantee the success of one huge deception?

Another possibility: Anderson's determination to protect George was proven. Having a spy as a best friend would hurt George. Was there a sniper at Bromont? One shot would remove a major military and political embarrassment. He began to perspire. In the undercover world nothing could be taken at face value, and especially not friendship.

When they reached the Cowansville–Knowlton turnoff, Messier tapped the glass behind the driver and the car pulled over.

"A change of plan, Yvon," Messier said. On Sloerill's map, the FMR had been moving into a position along the autoroute between Bromont and Foster and would be busy settling in. Besides, he knew their officers well, and they would accept his story.

"Take the road that parallels the autoroute near Fulford," he told his chauffeur. "Three roads lead up to the border fence, and we can use one of the tracks if the roads are blocked or guarded. I will radio the ALQ that we will cross there."

The FMR had taken over from the Black Watch of the Highland Brigade, who were being withdrawn in preparation for their move on Sherbrooke. They had traded friendly insults with the Highlanders, assuring them that there were no women or beer where they were going because the FMR had made the former too happy to go out with mere anglais and had drunk up all of the latter that was available.

The B Company commander in Fulford sent a platoon of men along the dirt road paralleling the autoroute that was the unofficial boundary between Quebec and Canada. As they started out, their radio operator received a message from the battalion intelligence officer that an ALQ agent might be in their area.

When the patrol reached highway 215 the officer waved them to a stop and called Robert Messier over. "There is a message for us at company headquarters about the spy, Fusilier Messier. They will not send it by radio. Go back and pick it up."

Robert turned his jeep around and headed back, automatically checking the side roads leading to the autoroute as he went. Sand had been spread for a hundred yards at each entrance and kept brushed smooth to show the tracks of infiltrators. At the second entrance, he saw tire tracks that had not been there fifteen minutes before. He swung the jeep onto the narrow road and began to drive forward, going up a gentle hill.

Thick woods grew on both sides, but after two hundred metres he came to a clearing. He stopped at the edge and looked around. To his right was a Bentley, the doors open, smoke pouring from the back seat. A hundred metres ahead of the car two figures he knew, the family chauffeur and his father, were walking briskly towards the chain-link fence along the overgrown four-lane highway. Even as he watched, Yvon threw his coat over the barbed-wire top and began to climb as his father waited. Robert felt as if he'd been turned to ice. His father was a spy. That was why the message had not been sent by radio. Etienne Messier, head of the civil council and George Sloerill's friend, was a spy who was now trying to escape.

Across the highway half a dozen ALQ soldiers watched the fugitives. Robert set his rifle on automatic and took aim, bracing the weapon on the jeep. It was a long shot, but as a qualified marksman he had successfully made longer ones.

He controlled his breathing as the tall post of his foresight covered the dark figure on the fence. One squeeze and both would die, his father and Yvon, the man he'd known all his life. His father's coat caught in the wire and as he struggled to get free, his image blurred in the sights.

"I cannot," Robert whispered and lowered the rifle, furious at his weakness. This was not his father, it was a spy, a man responsible for hundreds of deaths—and he could not pull the trigger. Yet it was impossible to let a spy escape.

He put the rifle down and picked up the radio. "Adieu, papa," he said softly, then pressed the switch. "Hello Seven Six Alpha, this is One Two Bravo. Quick shoot target. Two men on road at figures niner two three, two zero niner. Moving south to north." He looked up. Messier and Yvon had dropped to the ground on the other side of the fence and were now walking towards the waiting ALQ, waving their handkerchiefs in the air.

Three thousand metres away six Vickers machine-guns swung onto the invisible target, the officer calling the coordinates from his plotting board.

"Number one gun—on!"

"Two gun—on!'

"Five gun—on!"

The remaining gun commanders raised their hands one after another. "On!"

"Two belts. Rapid . . . fire!"

Six guns began to hammer in long four- and five-second bursts, sending a stream of bullets arching over the trees to plunge in long belts of fire ten metres wide by forty metres long, interlocked to cover a twenty by one-hundred-metre oblong that swung back and forth as the gunners tapped right and left between bursts.

Robert heard the distant cough of the guns and reversed his jeep back through the trees. He would not watch or call fire corrections. Either the bullets would do the job he could not or the spy would get away. It was out of his hands.

A squadron of Canadian CF-18's intercepted six French transport aircraft full of men and equipment five hundred miles east of Newfoundland and forced them to divert to Gander. When five Canadian planes appeared on the radar screen at Miquelon airport, the uncertainty whether they were French or not delayed the alarm until it was too late. At 5:00 AM on September fifteenth, five hundred Canadian paratroopers and a six-man CNN crew took the airfield and prepared to defend it against the 2500-man French garrison that had been quietly building up over the past six months.

At 7:00 AM, as leading elements of the French army deployed to attack the airfield, four Canadian destroyers slipped out of the patchy fog and began to shell Miquelon harbour. By noon General Scott's third brigade had landed with twenty tanks. Leaving their British amphibious landing craft on the beach, they pushed inland. After rockets from CF-18's had destroyed twelve tanks and having lost nearly a hundred men in a failed attack on the airport, the French general surrendered. Sitting in Fred Scott's caravan and drinking Scotch, General Bussières complained about Canada's failure to declare war before the attack. General Scott refilled his glass and produced copies of six protest notes sent to France in which the Canadian government had implicitly threatened invasion unless the French army left the islands. Both men smiled tightly at the CNN cameras covering the surrender of France's last North American possessions.

Sloerill had left Abercorn to move into the command post he would use in the coming battle. He had learned about Messier's death on the day after it had happened. His last chance to save lives on both sides was gone, and he grimly set about the task of keeping those on his side as light as possible.

Clay Anderson kept a low profile. He'd admitted that there had been a fifty-fifty chance Sloerill's plan might have worked. Sloerill had acknowledged that had Messier failed, what he had known could have seriously blunted the attack, and that Anderson had been right to issue the orders to apprehend and if necessary kill him. Sloerill had not spoken to Robert. Colonel Gendron and General St Pierre both insisted that the young man should be left alone, watched over by his friends in the regiment.

The attack on the eighteenth went almost as planned. Sloerill's opening artillery barrage forced the ALQ to reply, and the new Canadian counter-bombardment system destroyed eighty percent of the ALQ guns within hours. ALQ radar systems were smashed by Shrike missiles as soon as they became active. When the FMR advanced, supported by seventy Challenger tanks, the opposition melted away. At the end of the first day they were at Acton Vale, thirty kilometres southeast of Drummondville. Granby and Sherbrooke were isolated. The Prime Minister smiled and invited the press to a breakfast next morning on the grounds of 24 Sussex Drive, at which time he would make a statement.

That evening a dozen women gathered in the big farmhouse kitchen of Cécile Demers. A long table held piles of doughnuts and thirty four-gallon jugs of cariboo, the potent Quebec drink made from pure alcohol and red wine and spiced according to regional or family taste.

Cécile was standing at the huge refrigerator, its door covered in the clear plastic normally used for grocery lists or family reminders. Tonight her blue marker pen had recorded the names of over fifty towns and cities, and she was writing more as they were called to her.

"Dosquet and Neuville," a woman called, reading from her list. "That's across the river. Also Roxton Pond and Roxton Sud. I have an English friend in Roxton Sud. She will do well for us. She says the Fusiliers Mont-Royal passed through this morning."

"Good," Cécile muttered, writing the names down. "Are we all right in Levis and St Foy? Anne-Lise?"

"Fine in Levis," a plump middle-aged woman replied. "My friend there was a separatist organizer, but she too is fed up with war. Her best helper worked for Cyr. St Foy? It's full of fonctionnaires. I talked to one or two I know. They're hopeless, so I gave up."

"I was surprised," another one chimed in, "to get such good support from the area this Sloerill controls. The TV said they were all English." "And you believed it?" another scoffed. "I called an English friend in Cowansville. We were delegates at the convention that elected Cyr. I promised we would do our part, and she promised to do hers. She has ten women helping her and all but two are French!"

"The English are québecois too," Cécile said. "Too many of us have forgotten that these last years—le temps de folie. Language is no way to judge friends. We québecoises, English and French, want this war to end." She copied a few more town names on the board from a list, then straightened up to her full four-foot eight. "That should do it. Every town we need is here. Tomorrow we go to work. Do you all know the signal?"

"When the church bells ring," half a dozen women chorused.

"Then let's test the cariboo," Cécile stated firmly. "Not only men enjoy it." Quickly she passed out cups of the potent brew, then turned to the woman whose family had been neighbours to her family for sixty years.

"You, Alice Brown. Your people came here first. They stayed when we French became the majority. After Cyr declared the independence I had worked for, I did not speak to you for a month, but when my son was killed in the Gaspé, you were the first to bring food and hold my hand and cry with me. Give us a toast. Do it in English."

Alice lifted her cup. "That is not right. To my friends n'importe la langue. A toutes mes amies, I give you peace—un pays tranquille—an end to war, la fin de la guerre!" A dozen cups rose and came down empty.

"Ahh, that puts fire in the belly!" Cécile cried. "No more," she admonished as some reached for seconds. "Save it for the soldiers tomorrow."

"What if you are wrong, Cécile?" one woman asked nervously. "We do not know soldiers well here. What if they shoot?"

"They do not shoot women. You sound like the men, who are probably still talking."

"The English might," the woman persisted.

"They have not, and they will not now. Their army is led by québecois. Now, put your fears aside and go home. Our army likes to move at night, to hide from the American satellites. Be up early tomorrow. Go! Be determined, and if the soldiers give you a hard time, scold them like the men-children they are."

*

Overnight each side assessed what had been gained or lost and what must be done next. Fred Scott had left the Airborne regiment as a garrison on Miquelon and had pushed west almost to Montmagny.

The FMR and Winnipeg Rifles spent the night cleaning up around Acton Vale and Melbourne so that the Guards Brigade could advance on Drummondville the next day.

The ALQ command, caught between converging forces, had wanted to fight General Scott. They'd been overruled by Bouget, who ordered an attack on Sloerill. The conflict meant that reinforcements for their army in the southeast did not begin to move until almost dawn. As they started, the streets of every village and town filled with tables, chairs and people. However frightened, nobody would let the columns of tanks, guns and swearing soldiers pass.

In the Gaspé, General Scott's push stopped at Montmagny. The coastal road was jammed with people; the four-lane autoroute with cars, tractors and farmer's families. By the time the ALQ could find enough men to send against him, the bridge across the St Lawrence from Quebec City to Levis was blocked by a huge picnic.

The advance of the Guards Brigade stopped in Roxton Pond, where crowds stalled the Grenadiers on the outskirts of town; the Foot Guards were trapped in Windsor. Commanders demanded advice from the next higher level of command.

At 9:00 AM, Andrew Bryce flew General Sloerill to Roxton Pond. Passing over towns full of waving people, they landed in a field beside Colonel Forbes's helicopter. Peter came to meet them, followed by his brigade commander, General Fortin.

"It would appear, sir," Peter said with a smile, "that the populace is tired of our war. Two tanks that got into town are covered with children. My armoured personnel carriers are mobile graffiti exhibits, and an inordinate number of Guardsmen are at serious risk of lipstick poisoning. The rest are ingesting dangerous amounts of a drink called cariboo. The Sabine women strike again. All in all, sir, I suggest we call off the war and go home."

As Sloerill studied the map, listening to reports of blockages all over Quebec on Laurin's radio, General St Pierre arrived by helicopter and joined them, smiling broadly.

"I am happy to say that the units of my brigade still ahead of Peter's men are hemmed in. Colonel Gendron sent a patrol to the ALQ under a flag of truce. They report that the Delta Tangos are as confused as we are."

"Have you talked with the civilians doing this?" Sloerill demanded.

"A few. They insist they are blocking everyone, ALQ and Canadian Forces—who is this?" A fourth helicopter was settling dustily down in the corn field.

Before the skids touched down Clay Anderson was running towards them. "He may have an answer," Forbes said hopefully.

Anderson did. "Sir, there's hardly a town in Quebec that doesn't have a demonstration going. Pictures at eleven, as the press boys say, but let me tell you, this dawg's huntin' real good."

"Which in English or French means?" St Pierre asked.

"Back home, when we hear a half-baked idea we say 'That dawg won't hunt.' Well, the idea to stop the war is far from half-baked. We're also running down a rumour that President Bouget's on his way to Mirabel airport with half his cabinet."

"So who's in charge over there, Clay?" Sloerill pointed in the general direction of the front lines. "Perhaps we can arrange a cease-fire."

Clay checked his notebook. "Brigadier-General Roy."

"Initials J.P.?" General Fortin demanded.

"Yes, sir. Jean Philippe. Ex-regular Canadian Army."

"We shared a room at Staff College. With your permission, sir," he asked formally, unused to the easy ways of Sloerill's HQ, "I can set up a meeting. If as Colonel Anderson says this is happening all over, the fighting may end, but we must determine a cease-fire line. Are we still speaking of a corridor only? If Bouget has indeed run away, who can we deal with?"

"Let Ottawa handle that," Sloerill said, his eyes on Anderson who was listening to a report on his radio. "I want to formally shut down the fighting so nobody else gets hurt." He turned to Laurin.

"Tell Colonel Ashworth to report this situation to Ottawa, then tell General Scott what we're trying to do. Yes, Clay?"

"It's official, sir. Bouget's gone. He took the senior ALQ commander with him, and if my notes are right, Roy is next in line for the job. As far as who's in civilian control," his blue eyes gleamed, "he left one Adèle Chantilly holding the bag."

Sloerill gave a great whoop of laughter and flung his beret high into the air. "It's just so damn perfect!" he yelled and grabbed St Pierre by the shoulders. "Nobody wins and nobody loses!"

He turned to General Fortin. "I want to meet Roy. I think we met on an exercise in Germany once. Toupée, the FMR can join the party, but hold one company on stand-to. Do the same with your Grenadiers, Peter. It's over! It's damn well over!"

The Prime Minister stepped out of the back door at 24 Sussex Drive precisely at 9:00 AM to greet the fifty or so press people he'd invited. General Pittman had offered to brief the newsmen but had been told to stay home. This was the Prime Minister's day.

He mingled with the crowd, jokingly refused comment even on the weather (warm, with a hint of rain to come). He worked his way towards a small dais and lectern topped with at least twenty microphones. Occasionally he spoke to a favoured reporter, as he got closer to the place where he'd reveal the peace offer to Bouget. The magnificent Ottawa River and distant Gatineau Hills of Quebec would be his backdrop.

A waiter whispered in his ear. The Prime Minister frowned and beckoned to Bartholomew, the senior cabinet minister present. Joe Gates and Karen Ormsby were at the UN doing damage control over the invasion of St Pierre and Miquelon.

"Richard. Pittman's on the line, trying to horn in on the show. Get rid of him, will you? We have to be in the House in twenty minutes. If it's really important, I'll see him after lunch." A premonition struck him. "If it's a military disaster, wave at me from the back porch and I'll stop whatever I'm saying. Go."

As Bartholomew left, he heard the whuckering sound of a helicopter and looked up. A familiar white Huey was overhead, the letters CNN clear on its belly. The Prime Minister waved, stepped to the podium and began to read his conditions for a cease-fire.

Lieutenant Blackwell, commander of the security platoon posted to 24 Sussex Drive, hated newsmen. They complained about equipment searches; they complained about having to stick to certain paths to avoid anti-intrusion devices and about everything to do with security. Blackwell turned to his sergeant.

"Aim two Stingers at that chopper. Make the bastards nervous. They know even C bloody NN isn't allowed to overfly this place."

In the house Bartholomew excitedly took details of the fantastic story Pittman was telling: the defection of Bouget, the people blocking the roads to both armies, the broadcast by Madame Chantilly asking for peace with honour, not demanding that any part of Quebec be independent because, in her words, "the people have decided the question today."

In the helicopter, the cameraman in the open door turned to the man behind him. "They have missiles pointed at us."

"Can't be helped. Shut up while I listen to this." The man, wearing an earphone, frowned as he heard the PM's five conditions for a cease-fire. As he began to elaborate on the points, he took the phones off. "That's it. Canada wants blood." He turned to the pilot. "Make a final pass behind him so we can get a reaction shot from the press, then get out fast."

"Just in time too," the pilot said, turning the machine. "Ottawa tower is telling me that if we don't leave we'll be shot down."

As the helicopter made its final pass, a third crew member swung a gatling gun over the cameraman's head, centered his sights on the Prime Minister and opened fire, yelling as the man who had betrayed Quebec by declaring war was torn apart by a torrent of bullets, his body thrown forward into the splintered wreckage of the podium.

Almost at once the Stinger missiles fired at point-blank range. Two seconds later the helicopter exploded. As the gunner died his heavy weapon jerked to send a stream of bullets through the crowd of reporters. The last hundred bullets smashed into the official residence as the helicopter, now a blazing ball of wreckage, somersaulted over the lawn to crash in front of Government House across the road.

One bullet smashed Bartholomew's left hand braced on the desk. Dazed, he reeled back. Then he heard the screaming. Forgetting his wound, he ran out into the carnage. Fifteen wounded, dead or dying reporters lay on the lawn. The Prime Minister's body, an unrecognizable heap of bloody rags, lay in the wreckage of the dais, a forest of headless microphones swaying above it.

Bartholomew remembered that the news conference was being carried live across the nation. He ran up to a CBC cameraman.

"Is that thing working?" he demanded. "Can you broadcast?"

"Wh-what?" the man responded, dazed and shocked. "Yeah . . .
sure . . . but there's nothing . . . my reporter's over there . . . dead . . .
oh shit . . . they're all dead!"

"Point that thing at me," Bartholomew ordered sharply and the
cameraman obeyed.

"Where's the mike?"

"Up there." He pointed to the smashed dais. "No . . . wait, there's
one built in." The cameraman unplugged the mike cord, the habit of having
to put out a picture, whatever disaster was happening around him, over-
coming his shock for the moment. "Just look at me and talk."

Bartholomew moved to turn the camera away from the swathe of
bloody bodies. "This is Richard Bartholomew speaking," he began, "Minister of National Defence, and until Karen Ormsby returns from New York,
acting Prime Minister. These murders were the act of madmen, not of the
Quebec government. There is no Quebec government. President Bouget
and his cabinet have fled. The war is over. A cease-fire is in place. The
people of Quebec are blocking roads to all military traffic, ours and theirs.
The fighting has stopped. There was no need for this slaughter. The war
is over. The terrorists are dead, and I assure you that we will find out who
sent them."

Bartholomew wanted to reassure the viewers but he felt dizzy and
knew that he was rambling. The scene in front of him began to blur. People
at home saw him raise a hand to his cheek and try to speak. The cameraman
zoomed in on the now bloody face.

"Terrorists . . . responsible . . . war's over . . . please? Send help.
There are so many wounded here." The face disappeared and when the
camera pulled back, Bartholomew lay on the ground, semi-conscious but
trying to get up while a soldier began to bandage his bloody hand. Back at
the CBC studio, the producer recovered enough to kill the keening sound of
screaming. Leaving the grim picture up on the monitor, he cued the studio
panel to start analyzing what they'd seen. The audience wasn't listening to
the experts: the image that held them was Bartholomew's blood-smeared
face and his controlled and steady courage in the face of calamity.

EPILOGUE

Victory?

Two weeks after Adèle Chantilly's surrender, Quebec airports, bridges and roads opened without fanfare. Refugees began to return. The ALQ piled or destroyed their arms and went home. Three days later, the only official Quebec flag flying was at the Citadel in Quebec City. The war was over.

Sloerill had been given the job of organizing the one Canadian victory parade in the former Republic of Quebec that Mme Chantilly had agreed to. It was to be in Quebec City, but like Richard the First he was denied the right to enter the city he had fought to reach. In Ottawa, Acting Prime Minister Gilles Leroux had expressly forbidden his presence as being too dangerous and provocative. Leroux was government leader because as a Quebecer he had no chance of replacing the dead Prime Minister, and those who did have a chance trusted him not to influence delegates to the leadership convention that would be held in November.

Brigadier-General Fortin had told Sloerill about the promise that the Van Doos' Colonel had exacted: the Citadel would surrender only to a French-language regiment. Sloerill laid his plans accordingly.

On a sunny mid-week morning, nearly a thousand troops were lined up at the entrance to the bridge into Quebec City As they waited they stared across the river at the stone walls above the cliffs and at the lone blue and white flag defiantly flying there. General Fortin had worked out the formalities of surrender with the ALQ garrison commander, a former Van Doo lieutenant who had been on the last regimental parade. Now they waited for the last actors in the drama to arrive.

The FMR sat by the road. In the parade their weapons, unloaded, would be carried slung. After an almost unanimous secret ballot on the question, they had insisted that the ceremony must include men from the "English" regiments of Quebec. They had earned the right, and the FMR refused to march unless that right was granted. Guardsmen, Highlanders, Dragoons and Gunners had changed cap badges and replaced one hundred and seventeen new Fusiliers who had seen no action and were not yet full members of the family.

A bilingual chorus of catcalls greeted two busses as they stopped. Down stepped one hundred Van Doos in full dress, released from NATO. Two scarlet-clad officers led the mascot Baptiste to the head of the column, and General Fortin gave the order to advance.

In the Citadel, seventy members of the ALQ Brigade Royale waited, all that remained of the original four hundred-odd. They watched the parade cross the bridge and disappear under the cliffs into the labyrinthine streets of the lower town. The garrison commander looked at the flagpole where an ALQ officer stood ready to lower the Quebec flag. Beside him, indistinguishable in similar combat uniform, a Canadian officer held the Maple Leaf ensign that had come down a year ago. Around the ramparts, TV cameras were poised to record the event for history.

Company Sergeant-Major Weitz (an FMR corporal for the day) slipped on the cobblestones and banged his knee. "If I'd 'a' remembered this fuckin' hill, I'd 'a' left you bastards to climb it alone," he growled.

Beside him, Fusilier Godin was red-faced and panting. "What's the matter, Weitz? Forget your French? That's the trouble with Guardsmen. If the ground isn't flat enough for a parade square you panic and want to go home."

"Fuck you, frenchie," Colour-Sergeant (and corporal for the day) Zukrowski said cheerfully. "Button up or when we come back down, I'll ride you like a toboggan."

"Silence, là!" an officer snapped, and the men continued to climb. Far ahead Baptiste bleated a protest as his hoofs scrabbled against the rough stones.

While the Van Doos and FMR climbed, Sloerill flew Air Bryce to the military camp north of the city where the ALQ had held their POW's. John Ashworth, Clay Anderson and Pierre St Pierre had agreed to come once Major Bryce had been impressed with the desirability of his passengers' surviving long enough to enjoy peace. The Winnipeg Rifles had flown in that morning and were sorting through the prisoners.

After a relatively sedate flight, the helicopter settled down in a cloud of dust. Trucks were starting to carry the former prisoners away and a dozen helicopters waited at one side ready to ferry seriously wounded or ill men to hospital.

Sloerill went to a row of stretchers and was talking to a wounded Fusilier when John Ashworth touched his arm. "Sir?"

"What is it, John?"

"You may not believe this, but look at the man they're carrying out of the hospital now."

George looked and his heart pounded. On a stretcher two Riflemen had put down, sickly-white skin pulled taut over protruding cheekbones, lay Etienne Messier. George was halfway across the field before he saw that Etienne's legs were gone at the knees. His rush slowed.

Messier turned and saw him. The dark eyes flashed but his expression did not change. "I might have known you would come," he said quietly.

"Why are you with the prisoners?" George demanded as he knelt beside the stretcher.

"It is simple. Bouget did not believe my story, and when I then refused to expose your detailed plan, he had me arrested. Later he wanted to shoot me, but I was hidden by my fellow prisoners and a few guards. I have names for you, George. This time, names of men and women who remained civilized amid this foolish war. You must protect them."

George shook his head. "No need. There's a general amnesty. We aren't even asking France to extradite Bouget. But give me the names anyway. I want to thank them. Dammit, Etienne, I heard you were dead!"

"I almost was. Yvon and I were struck down by your old machine guns. By the time the ALQ soldiers got us to hospital I had lost much blood, then there was infection. Medical supplies were short, so they had to amputate. They say I may walk again in a year."

"You'll be walking sooner than that," George insisted. "Betty and I had to delay our wedding and you're still my best—what do you mean, no?" Messier was shaking his head.

"Do not ask this, George. We were friends, and I hope we will be again—but not now. The war . . . the killing . . . the defeat. It is too much. It overwhelms even our friendship. My heart must mend as well as my legs before we can be true friends again.—Robert? How is he? How is Andrée?"

"Both well. I'll find out what hospital you're going to and have her there an hour later. Robert made corporal. He's at the citadel now, in the final parade."

"And still so bitter? Still determined to leave Quebec?"

"I don't know, Etienne. Toupée said he'd become more reasonable. That's why he got his stripes. What can I get you?"

Messier shook his head. "Solitude. Let me bury my anger and frustration decently. I was betrayed by both sides, George. Leave me alone now. I will write when my struggle is over. Hello, John," he said as Ashworth came closer. "I am glad you too survived. Please take George away now." Messier's eyes closed resolutely.

As after every Canadian war, once the shooting stopped there was a rush to get rid of the soldiers who had won it. NDHQ announced its demobilization plan. No matter what regiment men had served in, they were to be posted to regiments from their home city or province to be sent home. General Pittman began a PR blitz designed to win public support, stressing the savings that had been factored into every military consideration.

Backed by Bartholomew, Sloerill had insisted that regiments be demobilized with the men that had fought in them, no matter where they had come from. The Toronto Scottish, that had come to Quebec as an awkward amalgam of men from the Algonquin Regiment, the Grey & Simcoe Foresters, the Brockville Rifles and the Highland Fusiliers took them all back to Toronto for the final parade. After that, the men who had come from other places to become temporary Tor Scots were sent home. In Montreal, regiments slipped almost surreptitiously into the city to reoccupy their looted armouries and to say goodbye to the men from across Canada who had become part of their families.

Armand Chantilly talked to Adèle on the phone daily as she tried to make Ottawa understand the few innovative ideas that had blossomed under independence which she wanted to save. She was not under arrest and could have gone home, but she chose to remain in Quebec City. Like Messier she needed time for wounds to heal. Armand knew that she would be back. Among his officers and men, few were so lucky. Most families split by the war remained divided, too bitter for reconciliation.

Sloerill signed his release papers (a second and third time for the TV cameras) at the Guards armoury on Esplanade Avenue and briefly joined the mess party before slipping away to his home in Cowansville, where Betty was waiting.

Their reunion was almost at once interrupted by a call from Richard Bartholomew, inviting him to join his leadership campaign team. Sloerill was trying to refuse when Betty took the phone out of his hand.

"Thank you so much, Mr Bartholomew. George needs a few days at home, he's really exhausted. Then he'll be glad to help you win the leadership. If you don't mind, I may tag along as an extra hand—and keep an eye on my intended until I can get him to the altar." She listened briefly, fending off George with one arm. "Wonderful, Richard," she said warmly. "We'll see you in Ottawa at the beginning of the week then. Bye."

She hung up and turned to George, shaking her head sadly. "You spend a whole war fighting something called unification, barely putting a dent in it. Then you almost refuse to help the one man who could do the job properly. Really, George. It's a good thing the great Canadian public don't know their hero's tactical ability is limited to war—when you're tired," she added quickly. "But do think about it, darling. With you beside him, Bartholomew's a shoo-in. When he's PM unification will go, and guess who'll be asked to design the new system? . . . Wait . . . George? . . . I thought you were exhausted." Betty wrapped her arms around his neck as he carried her upstairs. "I should have said we'd arrive on Tuesday. Oh well." She kissed him and pushed the bedroom door open with her foot.

Four days before the leadership convention began on November nonth, Bartholomew was holding a last strategy meeting in Ottawa before moving to Toronto. Allan Brewster had joined the team as soon as Richard declared his candidacy. Grace Dunbar, Minister of Intergovernmental Affairs, had fought the two hundred ninety-five delegate riding battles.

Normand Descelles, Treasury Board, was running the financial campaign. George Sloerill (with two days off to get married) organized the candidate's travels, made sure he arrived at the right place at the right time and got the advance work done. Betty Sloerill ran the campaign office, kept each element of the many-tentacled organization in touch and on track, and unofficially took charge of settling the inevitable turf and ego wars that erupted almost daily as people grew more tired and more irritable.

Bartholomew, after a punishing race and running on Scotch, coffee and desire, rapped a pencil against a glass to open the meeting. "Let's start with Allan's delegate count. Good news can't be repeated too often."

"It can if it makes you complacent," Brewster said with a smile. "However, the news isn't *that* good. Thanks to Grace's tremendous grassroots organization, we have eleven hundred and seventy-five committed delegates. Normally, that many first-ballot votes create a bandwagon effect that's hard to stop. The magic number is fifteen hundred and ninety-six. Karen Ormsby has three hundred and twenty-six and will be third on the first ballot. Joe Gates only has a hundred and fifty, mostly from his home province, but he's just in for show. Some of our people are worried about him, but he wants to be a king-maker not a king. Remember, though, he has more clout than his numbers indicate. His people will go where he tells them to, and a lot of delegates will follow them.

"The man we're toe to toe with is Bill O'Hagan. He will clock in at between nine hundred and sixty-two and nine hundred and seventy-one votes. When Ormsby drops out, most of her votes go to Bill, but she won't quit until the rules force her to.

"The key people are the roughly six hundred delegates committed to fringe candidates or elected on neutral slates. We need at least a hundred of them on the second ballot. If we don't grow then, we're in trouble, and if we don't win by the third we lose. Front runners either wrap it up quickly or become historical footnotes.

"George, you're the key here, front and centre for the delegates. You're a hero. We polled the loose delegates, and they'd almost all vote for you if you were running. That's all from me." Brewster sat back.

"A lot of Karen's votes will come to us," Bartholomew confidently insisted. "She's nowhere near as anti-Quebec as Bill is, and she'll be influenced by what Joe does."

"What worries me is the possibility of violence in Quebec." Grace spoke up firmly, knowing that this view was unpopular, "Every delegate saw that assassination, and let's face it, despite the official line, it was done by an extreme wing of the ALQ. Richard handled it right when he blamed terrorists, but they were *Quebec* terrorists. My people at the riding level had to face that in almost every fight."

"I know, Grace," Bartholomew said tiredly. "But in the first place, we can't do anything about it. Second, O'Hagan's anti-Quebec stand is so extreme that nobody with an ounce of moderation can support him on a second ballot. My message of generosity to Quebec won eleven hundred delegates with more to come. O'Hagan's 'grind the bastards into the dirt' line got him nine hundred rednecks. We'll take the convention on the second ballot and we'll have over two thousand votes. Count on it."

Brewster shook his head. "I hate to admit it, but there's a lot of truth in what Grace says. The anger's just under the surface. Madame Chantilly damped it a little by being reasonable, and our best card is that it was Quebec women who stopped the war. That plays well among women delegates, even O'Hagan's, but we'd better not forget that it's there. I believe that if there's violence, even up to the day before we vote, O'Hagan will have time to work it up, and if the anger comes out he can win."

"We'll rely on George to keep it in check," Bartholomew said firmly. "Are you up to that one, George?"

"I hope so," Sloerill said slowly. "A lot of my ex-soldiers are delegates. But I think it's a mistake to ignore the anger." He and Betty had discussed the problem the night before. "Let's go with the fact that Quebecers—Quebec women stopped the war."

"Believe me, George," Brewster insisted, "the sentiment's too volatile to touch. Quebec women stopped it but Quebec men started it, a lot of the delegates are saying."

"Enough doom and gloom." Bartholomew got the meeting back on track. "Betty? Is your organization set up?"

"I'm working with Grace's people who know the delegates, but we're going to need money to pay the observer registration for some key people who didn't get official delegate status. We'll meet every train, plane or bus. No hard sell, just the message that you want to bring the country together, not tear it apart. No mention of O'Hagan. John Ashworth is running the delegate tracking system. Tony Manieri's in charge of floor communications, and I've got a secure link between provincial delegate leaders and our headquarters at the hotel."

"Sounds good. Organized but not an intimidating steamroller that turns delegates off. OK, my speech. I'll attack the idea of reparations on the grounds that we need the Quebec economy, not their dollars. I'll tell them what reparations did to Germany in 1918. I'll remind them that if we smash Quebec flat we'll have to spend billions to rebuild the province or pay more billions to a permanently unemployed population." He looked at Sloerill. "I'll blame our early military failure on unification and promise to root it out if we win the election in March. It's six months later than the constitution mandates, but not bad, considering. The leader of the opposition agreed to the date because if the winner of our convention decided to ride the PR wave and call a snap vote, he's dead. Now, what's our financial picture, Norm?"

On the night the convention opened, bombs exploded at the armouries of every militia regiment that had sent men to the war and at government buildings in Ottawa and Montreal. A group calling themselves "Les Patriotes Nouveaux" announced that Canada would become another Northern Ireland unless Quebec was released from its chains.

THE END